GYM JUNKIE

MEN OF MARX SERIES

T L SWAN

ALSO BY T L SWAN

My Temptation (Kingston Lane #1)

The Stopover (The Miles High Club #1)

The Takeover (The Miles High Club #2)

The Casanova (The Miles High Club #3)

The Do-over (The Miles High Club #4)

Miles Ever After (The Miles High Club – Extended Epilogue)

Mr. Masters (The Mr. Series #1)

Mr. Spencer (The Mr. Series #2)

Mr. Garcia (The Mr. Series #3)

Our Way (Standalone Book)

Play Along (Standalone Book)

The Italian (The Italians #1)

Ferrara (The Italians #2)

Stanton Adore (Stanton Series #1)

Stanton Unconditional (Stanton Series #2)

Stanton Completely (Stanton Series #3)

Stanton Bliss (Stanton Series #4)

Marx Girl (Stanton Series – set 5 years later)

Gym Junkie (Stanton Series – set 7 years later)

Dr. Stanton (Dr. Stanton – set 10 years later)

Dr. Stantons – The Epilogue (Dr. Stanton – epilogue)

ACKNOWLEDGMENTS

It takes an army to write one of my books and I have the best army in the world.

To my writing team, my mum, Vicki, Am, Rachel, Lisa K, Nicole, Lisa D, Nadia, Charlotte, Jane, and Jodie: thank you. You don't know how much I appreciate the hours and hours of work you put in reading every draft of my books. I rewrite everything so many times, and I know I'm exhausting, and being drip fed chapters every couple of days must drive you all insane.

To my editing team, Victoria and Virginia, thank you for coming on this ride with me. I'm so lucky to have you both.

To Linda and my PR team at Foreword: thank you for everything you do for me.

I've made a new friend this last year and she is pushing me forward in my dreams of becoming a screenwriter. Thank you, Rena. You are my angel.

To Hang Lee, the cover goddess of the world. You nail it every time. I just give you the images now and you know what to do. Your talent makes my life so much easier. Thank you.

To my girls in the Swan Squad, you rock and make me laugh every day. Your support is what keeps me going on lonely author days.

To every single person who has ever downloaded one of my books, you are so appreciated and are making my dreams come true.

To my beautiful husband who this year retired to care for our three teenage kids so that I can write more.

Without you, I wouldn't have my beautiful kids. I wouldn't be living this amazing life, and I definitely wouldn't be able to write love stories... because I wouldn't know if true love really existed.

You are my reason.

I love you.

xoxox

GRATITUDE

The quality of being thankful: readiness to show appreciation for and to return kindness.

DEDICATION

I would like to dedicate this book to the alphabet.
For those twenty-six letters have changed my life.
Within those twenty-six letters, I found myself
and live my dream.
Next time you say the alphabet remember its power.
I do every day.

STANTON TIMELINE

Stanton Adore
Stanton Unconditional
Stanton Completely
Stanton Bliss: The Epilogue

Five years later - **Marx Girl**
Seven years later - **Gym Junkie**
Ten years later - **Dr Stanton**
Dr Stantons The Epilogue

PROLOGUE

Tully

THE OLD WOMAN walks in front of me and I watch the sway of her hips, as well as the flick of her stylish, silver hair, and I can't help but smile. I hope I have sass like that when I'm her age. I'm always fascinated when I see an elderly person who appears to be in the prime of their life.

What makes them so happy?

Why are some people dancing through life with joy, while others spend their limited time doing nothing more than preparing to die?

Lately, my mind has been clouded with these thoughts, to the point where they keep me awake at night. I sip my coffee as I stare into space and contemplate life's questions.

What is the meaning of life?

You hear the question thrown around carelessly so often but recently it's resonated with me on a deeper level. I get it now. I get why so many people ask the same question because I, too, am curious of the answer. I wonder at what age I'm supposed to work this out.

Happiness is what, exactly?

The shopping centre is crowded today, and I'm suddenly brought to a halt by my hand. I turn back to see what Simon is looking at.

"Do you like this one?" he asks as he stares through the glass at the diamonds on display.

Frustration fills me. Not this again. "Simon." I frown, not knowing how to put this nicely. "I don't want an engagement ring."

He smiles, distracted by the bling in front of him. "Of course you do. All women want to get married one day."

I exhale heavily. Why doesn't he ever take the not-so-subtle hints? "I'm too young."

Simon takes me into his arms and smiles down at me. He looks so mischievous and handsome, and I'm unable to help but smile back.

"I love you," he whispers.

I wrap my arms around his shoulders. "I love you, too."

"Well..." He raises his brows. "Don't you want to make me happy?"

"You know I do." I smirk

"So, marry me."

I frown again. This time seems different than all the other times he's spoken about it. "You're serious?" I ask.

"Deadly."

My chest tightens, and just like that, panic rises from deep in my stomach. I love Simon. More than anything, I love Simon, but we've been together since we were fifteen years old. I always just assumed we would break up along the way like normal teenagers do when they grow up. I never, ever intended to stay with my childhood sweetheart forever. I've always had plans for when we eventually broke up.

A break up plan, if you will.

Climb the Himalayas.

Explore Antarctica.

Fight Dragons with swords.

Do anything other than be *normal.*

Alas, maybe that's not how my life's going to go.

I stare up at Simon and force a smile to my face. He's hopeful and his eyes are filled with so much love that I get a deep sinking feeling in my stomach.

Guilt.

This beautiful man has been nothing but good to me and loves me so much, and all I think about all night, every night, are the places I want to travel to without him.

No friends, no boyfriends, no expectations. Just me.

The vile taste of guilt runs through me. Why do I feel this way? I hate it.

I kiss him softly on the lips as my eyes search his. "Let's talk about it tonight, babe."

"I can't wait any longer. I need you as my wife... now."

I fake a smile.

Please, don't make me choose.

I can't lose him. He's a good man. The best. I know I'll regret it for the rest of my life if I let him go.

"Let's go inside the store and try some on you now. You can pick whatever one you want." He takes my hand and tries to pull me into the jewellery shop, but I freeze on the spot and pull back.

"No."

He turns back to face me, his eyebrows rising in surprise. "What do you mean, *no*?"

"I mean..." I hesitate for a moment and swallow the lump in my throat. "I mean I don't want to try on rings today."

He frowns. "Why not?"

"Because I don't feel like it." My temper begins to rise. How dare he railroad me like this? We've never even discussed this properly before today. I mean, sure, he's hinted, but a hint is a long way away from actually trying on engagement rings.

"Well, I do," he says, his tone clipped.

My chin rises in defiance. "And I told you that I don't." I turn away from him and march back to the car.

I don't want to leave but I sure as hell don't want to try on engagement rings even more.

It's 3:00 a.m., and I stare at the clock as it ticks over to 3:01.

The sound of Simon's gentle breathing is a constant reminder of what I stand to lose.

The room is dark with a shadow of the large oak tree swaying across the wall. Occasionally the sheer drapes sway as a draft from the open window catches them.

Why did we have to meet so young?

And why do I feel like this? If I understand why, then maybe I can tackle the problem head on.

It's not like I want to be with anyone else, because I don't. I can think of nothing worse than being with another man, so why do I feel like I need to run far, far away?

I just wish I had some time on my own—time to stand on my own two feet, you know? To make my own decisions and choices, travel where I want to, when I want to. I just need twelve months. If I'd had that freedom two years ago I would have been well and truly over it by now.

Would Simon give me twelve months?

Could I ask him to give me twelve months to be alone, and

then meet back up and get engaged, settle down and live a happily ever after life?

No, that's so selfish. I couldn't ask that of him. It wouldn't be fair.

My heart starts to beat faster.

Would he do that for me?

What if he met someone else and fell madly in love? I couldn't handle it. I couldn't go through life watching Simon love someone who wasn't me.

I'm the person he loves; I'm the person he is meant to be with. This is a dumb idea. Of course, he would meet someone else. He's gorgeous and intelligent. A young up-and-coming anaesthetist like him would be snatched up.

I get out of bed in a rush, go to the bathroom, turn the light on, and stare at my reflection in the mirror. My heart is beating fast at the sheer thought of losing him.

"Stop it," I whisper to myself. "Don't fuck this up. He's beautiful. Marry him and forget this stupid nonsense."

Day five of no sleep.

I lie on my side and watch as the clock ticks over to 3:23 a.m. My pillow is wet from my tears. Simon and I have been fighting all week, and now he's not talking to me.

He's forcing me into a corner to marry him or leave.

Make a decision.

I feel like I'm on the precipice of Hell because I know what I need to do, and I feel sick about it. I'm going to ask him for a twelve-month break. I need to be honest and tell him exactly how I feel. I love him desperately, but I need this time to discover myself. In the back of my mind I know I could lose him, and if I do I'll spend the rest of my life with a broken heart regretting the decision I'm about to make.

I could never love anyone else. Simon is my soul mate.

But if I don't leave I'll spend the rest of my life wondering what would have happened if I did.

Twelve months and I'll be back with you my love, and I'll be the best fucking wife you could ever hope for.

You have my word.

CHAPTER 1

Brock

EIGHT MONTHS LATER

"MORNING." I smile as I walk through the large office space. Two rows of five desks sit in one main hall. There's a hive of activity going on, and this is where most of our work is done. Down a corridor, to the right, is my private office, along with the bathrooms and storerooms. Cindy is working in reception, and apart from Jesten and Ben, the other men who work for me haven't arrived for the day yet.

My company is Marx Security, and we're private investigators. Each of the men who work for me have a past in the armed forces or the police force. They all come with baggage, that's a given, but they're also hard as fuck, which is what I need. There are ten of us at the moment, with another three joining us from the United States soon. We take on special cases and are employed by the government or clients that have enough money to be able to afford us. Very few civilians can, but we get the results that others don't and we're worth every penny.

"Hey," Jesten greets me as he studies his phone.

"Hi, Brock," Cindy coos, leaning forward and resting on her elbows as she grins over her computer.

I force a smile and drop my head as I walk past her and into my office. I knew it wasn't a good idea to hire her. I knew it before she even opened her mouth. Gorgeous, young, and as tempting as hell, Cindy is a walking, talking recipe for an X-rated after-hours meeting on my desk. Luckily for her, I take my job very seriously and I've worked too damn hard to fuck it up now with my hungry dick. She wouldn't be able to take what I have to give anyway. She acts like a bad girl, but I know her type. She's way too pure for my tastes. The poor fool is now openly swooning over me every day, and I have to tell you, it's fucking annoying. One of these days I'm going to tell her just how much. I dump my bag onto my desk and look around my office. It's neat, modern, and was decorated by my two sisters, Natasha and Bridget. This is my happy place now. Back when I was a navy seal, the dream of opening this business was what kept me going throughout my lengthier deployments.

There's a large, rustic timber desk in my office, as well as a trendy abstract painting, a leather wingback chair, and an ottoman that sits by the window. We run the business out of a converted warehouse that has high ceilings and rustic floors to give it an industrial yet modern feel. The business is successful, and every day is different. That's what I love about it the most.

Ben pops his head around the door, so he can see into my office. "You ready to go?"

"Yeah, sure thing." I stand and grab my things, and within two minutes, Jesten— who we call Jes—Ben and I are on our way to our first meeting of the day.

We work in threes, that way we can ensure the safety of everyone. Jes and Ben are my partners. Funnily enough I met them both through my sisters. One married one sister, the other had the hots for the other sister, but he wasn't as fortunate. Somehow, through it all, I gained two great friends and employees out of it.

I got lucky.

We drive down the road in my car. "So, where are we going?" I ask.

Jes flicks through the paperwork from his position in the back seat. "To see a Hilary Chancellor."

"What's her deal?" Ben asks.

"Middle aged, very wealthy. Her husband died and it was determined a suicide."

My eyes find Jes in the rearview mirror. "And the wife doesn't think it was?"

"She does, but she thinks he was having an affair before he died, and she wants us to find out who the woman was."

I scrunch up my face. "Fuck off, man, we don't do that kind of shit. I couldn't give a flying fuck who was sucking his dick."

"Same," Ben mutters as he stares out the window, uninterested.

"The thing is..." Jes continues. "I studied his autopsy report and I'm not so sure it actually *was* suicide."

My eyes find Jes again. "What makes you think that?"

"It doesn't add up. The time of death, where he was

found... it would have been near impossible for him to have done it all alone without any help. I also saw that he had past anal trauma."

My eyes flick to Jes in the mirror in question. "Mr. Chancellor liked cock?"

"Seems so, although I'm not sure if his wife would have been aware of that from just reading the autopsy report. It wasn't exactly spelled out in those terms."

I frown as I turn onto their street. "Okay, then let's go find out."

We pull up outside a luxury house that backs onto Sydney Harbour, and I instantly smile when I see the view. "Very nice."

"What stupid prick would kill himself if he lived here?" Jes mutters under his breath.

"Right?" Ben whispers as we approach the front door.

I ring the doorbell, and a male servant answers the huge door. "Yes, hello, we've been expecting you. Please, come through." He shows us through the house and takes us out to the backyard which has spectacular views across the harbour. "Please take a seat." He smiles as we all sit down. "Can I get you a drink or anything?"

"No, thanks." I smile. Mrs. Chancellor approaches from inside, and we all stand immediately.

"Mrs. Chancellor, I'm Brock Marx. My colleagues are Ben Statham and Jesten Miller. It's a pleasure to meet you," I introduce us as we all shake her hand and pass over our business cards.

"Thank you for coming." She's an attractive lady in her late forties who is immaculately dressed and has a killer body. She looks around nervously to see if anyone can hear us before she sits down.

Hmm, interesting. She clearly doesn't trust her staff.

"I'm very sorry about your husband Mr. Chancellor," I say. "Our sincere condolences."

She smiles softly. "It's been six months now and I miss him more every day."

"So, why are we here?" I ask.

She takes a folded piece of paper out of her pocket and slides it across the table.

04123378903

"Phone number?" Ben frowns.

She nods. "Yes. But I have no idea whose." She smiles, as if embarrassed.

"After my husband died, I found this phone number in his cell records. I think it may be one of a secret girlfriend's."

I roll my lips. I hate this fucking shit.

"You think he was having an affair?"

"I'm not sure, but he called this number on the days that I was going out of town, which leads me to believe that it is someone he would meet when I was away."

We all nod and exchange subtle glances. How do you tell someone that you suspect their husband was seeing another man, not a woman? "Mrs. Chancellor, I'm very sorry but I think you have the wrong idea. We don't deal with infidelity cases," I tell her.

"I have reason to believe my husband was being blackmailed."

"Why?" asks Jes.

"He sold a million dollars' worth of shares on the week he disappeared, but the cash has never been recovered."

"It's not in any of his accounts?" I frown.

"No, he withdrew it in cash on the day that he died."

Okay, my interest is officially piqued. "What do you know about this phone number?" I ask.

"Only that it was disconnected on the day of his death."

"Hmm."

"That's where I need you. I know you can find out who that number belongs to."

I nod and take the piece of paper from her. "We will look into it and be in touch. I will need access to bank statements so that we can do a full investigation."

"Brock?" she says.

"Yes."

"My husband was dying of brain cancer and was fighting to survive. I know he didn't kill himself," she tells me with sadness in her eyes.

What the hell? I did not know that...Interesting.

We shake her hand, and she leads us out through the house. I turn to her before we leave.

"Thank you." She smiles.

"We can't make any promises."

"I don't care if he was having an affair. But I want his death ruled as murder, not suicide. It's killing my children to think that their father ended his own life."

I nod and shake her hand. "I fully understand. We'll be in touch."

Once outside and away from Mrs. Chancellor, we climb inside and start the car. "Where to now?" Jes asks.

"We need to brief with the boys."

"Okay, so this is where we are at." The boys are all sitting in a group around me, and Cindy is taking the meeting minutes. I point to the blackboard in front of me as I start to go through the point form cases we are working on. We do this every couple of weeks as a group of twelve.

"Through the week, we were contacted by one of the murdered girl's fathers. He has put out a bounty."

They frown in concentration as they listen to me.

"A million dollars to any person or persons who finds the killer."

"What case is this?" Mason asks.

I blow out a breath because this case is confusing and hard to explain. "This particular story goes back a long way, and one of our very own was, in fact, a suspect for one of the first murders." I gesture to Ben who nods in acknowledgment.

The boys all frown harder, their interest piqued.

"Six years ago, an extremely wealthy friend of ours had sex with a high-end prostitute. Unbeknown to him, she filmed him on three occasions having sex with her. She then went on and threatened to go to the paparazzi with the footage if he didn't pay her millions of dollars."

The boys all listen intently.

"He didn't pay her. Instead, he had his security team try and retrieve the footage tapes. But before they could, the prostitute was found dead at the docklands. She had been hogtied and shot in the back of the head. Her body was severely beaten before they finished her off."

"Did this wealthy friend of yours kill her?" Mason asks.

"No." I shake my head. "He had nothing to do with it, although I will admit that it had run through his security team's mind."

The boys all glance towards Ben as they try to connect the dots.

"What was her name?" Cindy asks as she takes the notes.

"We will call her TC," I reply. "TC." I put a photograph of her up on the noticeboard and pin it in place. "Gorgeous, young, and capable of earning five-thousand dollars for just four hours work."

One of the boys lets out a low whistle.

"TC was bribing many men. At the time, we thought she was working alone." I begin to take photographs of the six other women and pin them up beside TC's. "However, since then, a further six high-end call girls have met the same unfortunate fate as our dear TC."

"You think it's a serial killer?" someone asks.

I shake my head. "No, I don't. I think the girls were all working for the same person."

"What do you mean?" Jes asks.

"I believe they were working for someone who was... maybe still is blackmailing girls to get the footage of them with high profile men and women so that they can then blackmail the clients into paying for their silence."

"You think he kills the girls once they've done their job?" Big John asks.

I shake my head again. "No, I think he kills the girls to keep them in line. Think about it. What high-end prostitute wants to be filmed doing what they do?"

The boys all nod as they process the information. "Girls of this calibre," I point to their images on the board, "do not want to be filmed under any circumstance."

"I think he's either killing women who refuse to do what he demands, or perhaps he's letting the other girls know what's going to happen if they don't fall into line."

The boys fall into hushed conversations on possible theories for a moment.

"Do we have any suspects?" Jes asks.

"We do," I reply. I take out an image of a man and put it onto the board alongside the deceased girls. "We have two, actually." I point to the first image of a middle-aged man Italian man. "This is Eli De Luca."

"Who's he?" one of the guys asks.

"Eli De Luca is second in command of a powerful crime empire run by one family." I pull out three more images and pin them to the board. "His father Lorenzo is the head. A multi-millionaire who, *apparently*," I air quote and gesture to the image, "owns a granite and Caesarstone importing business."

"Apparently?" someone else repeats.

"I say apparently because he also owns six clubs in the Kings Cross district and runs the biggest drug ring in Australia. Importing stone is his front."

I gesture to the images of the other two men. "One brother is a lawyer, but we have no further information on him other than he represents only big-time criminals and mafia. He represented Joshua my brother-in-law once. The other brother..." I gesture to the other image. "He lives in Italy, and we have reason to believe he runs the business over there."

"So, you think it's this De Luca family behind these murders?" Jes asks.

"To be honest, no," I answer. "They are successful criminals already. There's a lot of groundwork to do when blackmailing people, so it makes no sense that they would risk bringing attention to themselves by having all these women as witnesses. It's too messy for them, they are smarter than this."

The boys all nod as they listen. "Who's the second suspect then?" Jim asks.

I pin up another image and the men all gasp. "Yeah, you've all seen him before."

I turn and smile at the guys. "Steven Coleman. Or you may know him as the Senior Sergeant of Police down at the station. They call him Cole."

"Why is he a suspect?" someone pipes up.

"Ben interviewed a girl when he came back twelve-months ago, and she gave an ID to match his image, but she wouldn't say his name out loud. She was edgy about being recorded. She freaked out halfway through the interview and ran. Unfortunately, she was found dead from a drug overdose a week later."

"Was she really murdered?" Jes frowns.

"We don't know, but she *was* pretty heavily into drugs, so it could have just been an overdose. Her autopsy gave no reason for us to think anything else. We don't know if Cole is linked to this case for definite, but we *do* know that the girls are scared of him. I need you boys to work on this in between our other cases. A million dollars will be a nice buffer to have in our bank account."

My phone rings and I wind up my part of the meeting to go take the call. "So, that brings us up to ten cases we're working on at the moment. We also took on another one this morning that Ben is going to brief you on now."

I push once, twice, three times, and I exhale heavily as I finish my set. "You're up," I pant as I stand. I drain my water bottle and Ben lies down on the weight bench before he pushes the heavy dumbbells high in the air. We're in the gym and it's 9:00 p.m. We've just finished work for the day. Ben's wife is at my sister, Natasha's house, and we came here before he picks her up. Ben's my brother-in- law, married to my other sister, Bridget, and he's one of my closest friends. Not family by blood, but most definitely family by choice.

He finishes his set and stands to wipe the perspiration from his brow with his towel. "We got that thing tomorrow night, yeah?" he pants, his hands planted firmly on his hips.

"What thing?" I frown as I sit down on the bench.

The front door opens, and I glance over at the mirror as a woman walks in. The way she walks commands my attention, and I turn towards her instantly. She has a confident air about her. Not many women have it and I can smell it a mile off.

Her big blue eyes and olive skin are an unusual combination with her strawberry-blonde hair. I watch her walk by and put her earphones in, and then head over to the treadmills and bikes. She's wearing black tights, and a black tight singlet with a hot pink sports bra underneath. I can see her every curve. My cock twitches in appreciation. She may just have the most perfect bone structure I've ever seen. She turns, catching me staring at her, and gives me a lopsided smile before she continues on her way.

Ben watches her for a moment and raises his eyebrows before his eyes come back to mine with a knowing smirk.

"Jesus, right?" I murmur under my breath as I lie back down onto the bench. I do my set and stand again, my attention falling back to the mystery woman.

She's riding an exercise bike to warm up. She's definitely athletic. Her body is toned and muscular... but not too muscular. It's just right. She has large, luscious breasts, and I feel my intrigue rise at the perfect specimen before me.

Ben lies down to do his set, but my eyes stay glued on the woman. "You should probably go ride a bike or something," he mutters as he begins to lift the heavy weights above his head.

My eyes stay fixed on her ass. "The bike isn't the only thing I should probably ride," I reply dryly.

Ben nods in agreement.

I take a drink from my water bottle, unable to peel my eyes from her ass.

Seriously, *fucking hot...*

Ben's phone rings and he answers. "Hey, babe." He listens for a moment and frowns. "Yeah, okay, I'm coming now." He sighs.

I smile as I watch him listen to his wife Bridget, and I can tell she's ranting on the other end of the phone.

He listens for a moment and looks to the ceiling, and I chuckle to myself.

"Yeah, okay, babe. We'll pick some up on the way home." He frowns harder. "You'll be all right?" Bridget says something else before he replies. "I'll see you soon. I'm leaving now." He hangs up and gives a subtle shake of his head as he blows out a breath.

"She's going to bust your fucking balls before she has these twins."

"Without a doubt." He sighs as he retrieves his towel.

"What now?" I ask.

"Indigestion," he replies dryly.

I break into a broad grin. "You have to listen to her complaining about indigestion?"

"You'd be surprised what I have to listen to, Marx. Indigestion is the least of my fucking worries. Try picking out a baby name with her." He shakes his head, exasperated. "One name would be bad enough but picking two is near damn impossible."

I laugh. Bridget hates everything about being pregnant. She's making Ben's life a living hell. "Can't wait for these kids to arrive." I smile. My reasons are totally selfish, of course. I want my playful sister back. This hormonal, cranky version is micromanaging me to my death.

Ben winces. "Same here. Four more months to go."

"Ha, that's if she lets you live that long."

Ben drags his hand down his face. "Right?" He picks up is phone and other belongings. "See you tomorrow."

"Yeah ok." I think for a moment. "What did you say we had on tomorrow night?"

"Tash's birthday dinner."

"Oh, yeah, that's right. See you in the morning."

I watch as Ben walks out the door, and then my attention returns to the beauty on the bike.

I've never seen her here before. I wonder who she is. She looks to be in her mid-twenties, tall—about 5ft 8—and she's naturally pretty. She's probably a model.

I continue with my workout, and every now and then my eyes flicker over to her. A few times I catch her looking back at me in the mirror before she snaps her eyes away, as if annoyed that I've caught her ogling.

I should go over and say something. No. What do I say? *Oh, hi, you look fucking edible.*

Creepy guys try to pick up women in the gym all the time, and I am not that creepy guy. I walk over to the pull-up bar and strap the weight to my belt. I slowly pull myself up and begin my set of chin-ups. My knees are bent up behind me and I can see her in the mirror in front of me.

Stop it.

I drop my eyes to the floor and concentrate on the task at hand. Up, down, up, down. I glance up and notice she has completely stopped peddling on the bike as she watches me. I have to drop my head to hide my smirk.

So, you like watching chin-ups, baby, do you? I decide to do an extra twenty for good measure. I wouldn't want to disappoint her now, would I? I do my chin-ups and she begins to peddle slowly as she watches, and then, as if remembering where she is, she looks away in a rush.

Fuck it, I'm going to go and talk to her. I may never see her here again. I'll kick myself if I don't say something.

She gets off the bike and moves over to the sit-up section. It's then that I notice she has left her keys on the tray of the bike.

Bingo! My opening.

I wipe my face with my towel, and with my heart still pumping hard from all that physical exertion, I walk over and pick up her keys. Then I walk over to where she is lying on her back on a mat.

She has her eyes closed and her earphones in, so I stand and wait for her to notice me. My heart is still beating fast as I watch her come up into a sitting position and lie back down. I can see the muscles in her stomach contract as she sits up.

Fuck. She's hot.

She continues to sit up and lie back down, and I get an image of her lying down for me in the same position, naked.

Legs up, stomach contracted, cunt...

Fuck. Stop it.

I shake my head to snap me out of my wayward thoughts.

She finally notices me and quickly pulls her earphones out.

"Sorry, didn't mean to startle you," I say, holding her keys up and jiggling them in the air.

"Oh, thank you." She smiles warmly.

Her voice is husky and sexual, and damn if my balls weren't already paying attention, they are fucking now.

"I'd forget my head if it wasn't screwed on." She breathes, and then frowns as if not knowing what to call me.

Or... you could get your head screwed off. "I'm Brock."

She smiles, and then says something but I don't hear her properly. The only word I did catch was, "Pocket."

I frown. "Your name is Pocket?" I ask in surprise.

She laughs. "No, my name is Tully. I said I need a pocket."

"Oh." I smile, feeling stupid. "I kind of liked the name Pocket."

She smiles up at me. "You wished my name was Pocket?"

"Kind of. Haven't you ever wanted a friend named Pocket?" I tease as I raise my eyebrows. *Cock pocket* to be exact.

She laughs freely, and I clench my fists at my sides. There is definitely something about this girl.

"Thanks, Brock." She reaches up and takes the keys from my hand.

"You're welcome, Tully Pocket."

She smiles warmly up at me for calling her Tully Pocket and she bites her bottom lip, leaving a heavy silence sitting between us.

"I haven't seen you here before," I say.

"I only joined last week. This is my first visit."

"You're here late," I say as I look around the gym, noticing that we are the only two left in the place.

She looks around as if having the same sudden realisation. "Yeah, I guess. I like to come when nobody else is here."

"Me, too."

Our eyes linger on each other's for an extended moment.

I point to the weight bench behind me with my thumb. "I better get back to it."

"Okay." She smiles again. "Thanks again, Brock."

Damn it, I don't want to get back to it at all. I want to stand there and listen to her husky voice and imagine it saying filthy, perverted things to me. I walk back over to the weights and begin a set of arm curls. My workout should be over by now, but fuck it, why not stay here and admire the scenery? Can't hurt, can it?

We both continue to exercise in silence for another half an hour, our eyes intermittently flicking to each other. I can tell she's into me.

Fuck it, I'm just going to ask her out. This is so not my usual form, but she's seriously gorgeous. She's back on the treadmill again now, running before she finishes, no doubt. I'll go and get on the rowing machine next to her and ease into the conversation from there.

I take my position on the rowing machine and begin to move. I can feel her eyes on my back.

My legs straighten as I row harder and harder, and perspiration begins to run down my face. Should I just ask her on a date or should I make it more casual and suggest we go for a drink now? Hmm, it's Tuesday night. She probably has work tomorrow. I can feel her watching me, so I really give it to the rowing machine. Suddenly, the rope of the rowing machine breaks and I fly backwards and hit the wall. A piece of the rope breaks away and it flies onto her treadmill, making her trip and fall spectacularly to the floor.

"H-holy shit," I stammer as I jump up.

"Ouch," she hisses.

"Oh my God, are you all right?" I ask. I grab her two hands and pull her from the floor.

"Not really." She rubs her hands over her thighs in embarrassment.

I look down to see her knee has a deep burn from the treadmill belt and blood is running down her shin. I point to her leg. "You're bleeding."

She looks down at her leg and frowns. "Great." She puts her hands on her hips and glares at me. "This is all your fault."

"My fault?" I say, surprised.

"Yes. Your fault. If you weren't showing off and trying to be Superman, this wouldn't have happened. You broke the rowing machine cord by being stupid."

I put my hands on my hips. "I wasn't showing off," I snap. "It was obviously faulty."

"Oh, that's crap and you know it."

"I'm telling you right now, I wasn't showing off. I train *hard*."

"I train hard," she mimics.

I begin to get ticked off. "Obviously, Tully Pocket, you were always the child who got angry and blamed other children whenever she got hurt."

She rolls her eyes, unimpressed. "Well, obviously you were the child who was always trying too hard to be a superhero."

"Trying too hard?" I interrupt her. "I'm not fucking trying at all."

She raises her eyebrows, annoyed. "Whatever." She storms off towards the bathroom.

Did she just *whatever* me?

Nobody *whatevers* me.

I pace back and forth for a few minutes until I can't take it any longer, and I storm up the hall towards the bathrooms.

There are four doors. All of them are unisex and all fitted with a shower and a toilet. Each door is now closed, and I have no idea which one she is in.

"Tully," I call.

No answer.

"Tully Pocket!" I call.

"What?" she snaps through the farthest door. "Go away. You're annoying."

I take it back, this woman isn't hot, she's fucking obnoxious. I open the door and find her sitting on the floor with a wet tissue, trying to wipe up the blood on her leg. I sink to my knee beside her.

"Are you okay?" I ask.

She shrugs but stays silent.

Empathy wins, and I *do* feel bad. "Here, let me clean you up." I stand and put my hands on her hips, lifting her to sit on top of the basin.

She stays silent as I inspect her knee. "It's deep," I say softly.

She nods.

My eyes rise to meet hers, and I'm suddenly aware that we are alone in a small space. I bite my lip and turn my attention back to her leg. "I'm going to get the first aid box. I'll be right back."

"Okay," she whispers.

I go to the office and retrieve the small, red first aid box, and I return to the hall. I stand outside the door for a moment.

Just fix her leg and go home.

I open the door and find her sitting up on the counter where I left her. She smiles softly as she runs her hand through her hair, her anger clearly now replaced with embarrassment. "Sorry," she whispers. "I'm flustered."

My eyes hold hers for a moment. I put the kit down, open it up, and get the saline out, snapping the little pod open. "This might sting a bit." I begin to pour it on her cut and she hisses, involuntarily grabbing my shoulder. Her touch feels good and I inhale through my nose. *This is not the time for sexual thoughts, you dirty bastard. Keep your mind on the job. Band-Aid application, fool.*

I wipe up the excess blood as she watches on in silence. Her hand is still on my shoulder and I can feel the heat burning me through my shirt from her touch. I slide my hand up her calf to lift her leg, and goose bumps scatter her skin.

I feel my cock twitch in appreciation and I have to grit my teeth. Not fucking now.

The energy in the room begins to swirl between us and my eyes rise to meet hers.

"Does it hurt?" I ask softly.

She nods, and I know she can feel the electricity between us, too.

"I'll put the Band-Aid on and you'll be as good as new," I tell her, distracted.

She smiles softly and nods again. "Thank you."

She watches on as I carefully apply two bandages and I slide my hand down her calf muscle one more time. Goose bumps scatter again, and my eyes rise to meet hers.

"Goose bumps?" I ask.

She swallows the lump in her throat as her eyes hold mine.

The air crackles between us and my eyes drop to her parted lips. Large, pink, and so fucking hot.

"What are you thinking?" she whispers up at me.

My mouth opens to speak but no words come out. My chest rises as I try to contain my arousal. This is ridiculous. Unable to help it, I reach down and put my thumb just under her bottom lip and pull her mouth open so that her lips part. "You want to know what I'm thinking, Pocket?" I whisper.

She nods, her mouth is open with my thumb resting on her bottom lip.

"I'm imagining how you'll look with my cock in your mouth."

CHAPTER 2

Tully

My eyes widen and my heart begins to race.

What the fuck? Did he really just say that out loud? His thumb is resting on my bottom lip.

I pull away from his thumb, and I run my tongue over the burning spot from his touch. "I'm not the type of girl you think I am," I tell him. "In fact, I'm offended by the insinuation that you think I'm a slut."

A trace of a smile crosses his face. "Is that so?" He pulls back from me and turns his attention back to my knee.

"That *is* so," I snap.

"Forgive me." His eyes come back up to meet mine. "I'm not normally like this, but you..." His voice trails off.

But I what? What was he going to say?

His large frame takes over the room. His jaw is square, his eyes are dark, and goddamn it if he isn't the most handsome man I've seen in my life. He looks down at me, electricity buzzing between us.

"I was quite sure you were picturing how my cock would look in your mouth, too?"

I laugh, not because it's funny but because it's such a man thing to say. Is that every man's fantasy? To have a random woman dream of sucking his cock? "Actually, no." I chuckle.

His hand glides up my calf muscle again as his dark eyes hold mine. "If you were to imagine something about me, what would it be?" he asks.

I swallow the lump in my throat. What are you doing, Tully? This little game of imagination you're playing here is stupid. "I may have one question."

"Such as?"

I shrug, feeling braver than I should. "I wondered how you'd kiss."

His eyebrow raises as he moves closer to me and puts a finger underneath my chin to lift my face to his. "Really?"

I nod, unable to speak from his close proximity. Why did I just say that?

Satisfaction flashes across his face. "You want to know how I kiss, Pocket?"

I swallow again.

In slow motion, he moves closer and closer, until he's only a few centimetres away from my lips.

My heart is sprinting in my chest as I watch him.

"I'll tell you what..." He breathes, so close that I feel his breath on my lips.

"What?" I whisper.

"I'll show you how I kiss if you put your arms around my neck."

I frown.

He takes my arms and slowly puts them up over his broad, muscular shoulders.

"Now what?" I whisper. Oh my God, is this really happening?

"Now I'll pull you close." He grabs my hips and jerks me forward on the counter, pulling my legs apart so he can stand between them.

My arousal starts to thump at his close proximity.

"And then..." He grabs a handful of my hair and pulls my head back aggressively. Goose bumps scatter up my arms from his natural domination. His eyes darken as he sees me become powerless to his touch.

My heart is beating so fast that I feel like I'm about to go into cardiac arrest.

He slowly bends and licks my open lips. My stomach clenches in appreciation.

Sweet Jesus.

His lips slowly take mine, and his tongue slides through my open mouth. Unable to help it, my eyes close as I drown in pleasure.

I can feel his dick harden between my legs, and he kisses me again—deeper this time. His tongue takes mine and wakes it from its dormant sleep. We kiss again and again. He grabs my hips and pulls me forward onto his hard erection.

Fuck!

Then, somehow, I lose control, and both my hands are in his hair while his dick rubs back and forth against my sex and he grinds my body onto his.

"Fuck," he murmurs against my lips. We begin to kiss so violently that our teeth clash, and he picks me up and falls onto the bench seat in the corner, arranging me so that I'm straddled over his lap.

With his hand on my hipbone, he begins to rock me back and forth over his hard cock. Our kiss is slow and erotic and the word 'whore' rolls around in my empty head.

I can't stop. He's too good at this. Oh God.

Stop. Get up and leave, I tell myself.

But my body won't let me. It wants what he has.

Brock's hand slides down my tights to grab a handful of my behind, and he really begins to drive me onto his body with force. His open mouth is ravaging my neck.

My legs are open, and I can feel how big he is underneath his thin shorts as he drags my throbbing sex back and forth over him through my tights.

My body quivers and I jerk. Oh no. I stiffen, realising just how close an orgasm is.

"Don't fucking pull back from me," he growls. He slides his other hand into my tights, grabs my ass with two hands, and really begins to ride me. "Let me have it." He bounces me up and down as he kisses me almost violently.

My hands rise from his shoulders, to his jaw, to his hair. I've completely lost control of myself.

God, I haven't made out through clothes since high school. There's a lot to be said for it. This is so hot.

I can feel my orgasm building, back, forth, deeper and deeper. His lips, his smell, his teeth on my neck... the whole combination is fucking lethal.

"Brock," I pant.

He smiles up at me, satisfaction written all over his face.

Talk me out of this. Say something that will make me leave. "Say something," I breath as I rock.

He smirks as he watches me ride his dick like a woman possessed. "No. I'll pretend to be a gentleman."

I frown at him in question, and for a moment my arousal

fog lifts. I need to know what else he might say. "What would you say if you weren't a gentleman?"

His eyes flash with arousal, as if that's the very question he has been waiting for. He slides his right hand out of the back of my tights, and in one quick movement, he puts it down the front and then slides his two thick middle fingers into my dripping wet sex.

Oh God.

Both of our mouths fall open; his in pleasure, mine in shock. Our eyes are locked.

"I would tell you that I want you to contract that beautiful, tight cunt around my fingers." He pumps me hard and I cry out. "Earn it," he growls, pumping me so hard again with his fingers that my legs come up automatically.

It's near painful, but God damn, the burn is good. "B-brock," I pant heavily.

What the actual fuck is happening here? I'm in a gym bathroom, being dirty-talked and finger-fucked by a God.

My face scrunches up as I look down at him. This is too much. I'm too turned on. This is too public.

I don't even fucking know this guy.

As if sensing my fear. "Kiss me," he whispers up at me. My lips take his again, and this time his kiss is soft and tender. He slowly fucks me with his thick fingers, my legs are splayed open over his parted thighs.

"You feel so fucking good," he murmurs against my mouth.

That's it, I can't take it anymore. I spiral out of control and clench hard around his fingers. Brock growls in appreciation as I come in a rush.

My body jerks violently, forcing me to release a throaty moan as he continues his onslaught. His large fingers slowly circle through my dripping flesh. I'm swollen and tender.

We kiss, and it's not a crazy arousal kiss. It's a kiss of appreciation, as if somehow, he already knows that I'm not the type of girl who would normally ever do this sort of thing.

Our lips are locked, and I smile against him. "What... the hell?" I pant. "What just happened?"

He looks up at me as he licks his lips, and I know he's contemplating his next words. His hair is dishevelled and arousal dances in his eyes like fire.

"I'm not having sex in a gym," I whisper.

"Then come home with me." His eyes are fixed on my lips, and I know he's still rock hard under those shorts.

"I don't even know you," I whisper.

"What a perfect way to get to know me."

I smile shyly, and we kiss again. Sense returns at once. *Leave. Now*. I stand, and he stands too, leaving our faces only millimetres apart. My heart is still racing from my orgasm. "I have to go. I had no idea the kind of medical service you were offering for a skinned knee."

"You got the intensive treatment." He lifts my chin with his pointer finger and brings my face up to meet his. "It's nice to meet you, Tully Pocket." He kisses me softly.

I smile as mischief shines through. "The pleasure was all mine... literally."

"Bitch," he whispers with a cheeky grin.

I look to the door. "I have to get going."

He frowns. "Are you really going to leave me in this state?" He points to his crotch.

I smile and kiss him quickly. "Lucky for you, you have a good imagination and can easily imagine my lips around your cock. Finish the job for me when you get home."

"Tully," he groans.

I take off, leaving the bathroom and hearing the door bang behind me.

Jesus, I've got to get out of here before he talks me into going home with him. I power walk to the shelves where my bag is waiting at the front.

Did that really just happen?

I pick up my bag and head for the front door when I hear the bathroom door bang open. "Tully Pocket!" Brock calls.

I close my eyes with my back to him. Damn it, I nearly got out of here. He jogs the length of the gymnasium until he's close to me, and I turn to face him.

"I'll see you here tomorrow night?" he asks hopefully. "Same time?"

I stare at him for a moment and bite my bottom lip.

He cringes suddenly. "Oh, shit. I can't tomorrow night. I have a thing on for my sister's birthday." He thinks for a moment. "I'll see you here Thursday night?"

I stare at him.

"Nine o'clock."

"How many women do you pick up at the gym?" I ask.

He smiles softly. "Only one. You."

I fold my arms over my chest and tilt my head to the side, waiting for him to tell the truth.

"No, seriously." He laughs. "I have never done anything like this before. Not in a gym, anyway."

I roll my eyes and try to act unimpressed, but I soon have to turn to hide my smile. "Goodbye, Brock."

"Where's my goodbye kiss?"

I turn and blow him a kiss. He pretends to catch it and then plants it on his face.

Our eyes linger on each other as the air crackles between

us. He smiles softly as he watches me. My stomach flips as I walk away from him.

There is something about this guy. Could be the white-hot orgasm he just gave me, of course.

Damn. Go home, whore bag.

With renewed determination, I turn towards the door.

"See you Thursday, Tully Pocket!" he calls.

"Why do you call me that? I'm not a pocket," I ask as I walk away.

"I could think of lots of things to put in you."

I bite the inside of my cheek to stop myself from smiling. Dirty bastard.

I leave the gym and walk out and get into my car. After I start the engine, I sit for a moment in the dimly lit parking lot and I smile goofily through the windshield as I grip the steering wheel with both hands.

What the actual fuck just happened?

I place a drop of the solution onto the glass and smear it across the film. I wait for a moment, and then bend to inspect it through the microscope. I smile as the computer in front of me runs its cross checks. It reads as a *99.5% match*... finally!

"Got him."

"You do?" Rourke frowns from his place on the workbench beside me.

"Yep." I bend to see the microscopic molecules bounce around on the glass film in front of me.

"Let me see," he says, barging in front of me.

I move to the side and Rourke looks through the microscope, a slow smile creeping on his face before he turns to me and we high five.

"He did it." I look through the microscope again, with the last results that just came in. We have a match. "I fucking knew he did it."

"Me, too."

Rourke is my partner in crime. Or should I say he's my partner in crime detection.

As a Forensic Scientist with the Federal Police, my days are spent analysing evidence, proving suspects are guilty, or in some instances innocent. A regular day for us may be analysing semen, crime scenes, studying photographs, or working with cold corpses. You name it, we do it. We've just found a positive match to DNA that was retrieved from a dead body found in a lake.

There's a monster out there who has taken five beautiful young women's lives. Ironically, despite his clever scheming and cover-ups, the semen was eventually found on a tissue in the suspect's garbage bin. I pat Rourke on the shoulder as I walk past him. "It doesn't pay to wank in tissues, Rourke."

"Sure doesn't, that's why I flush mine down the toilet."

I smile as I take off my gloves and pick up the phone to dial downstairs. Taz answers on the first ring. "Hit me," he says.

"We got him. It all lines up."

"Are you fucking serious?"

"Yep. A positive match." I smile proudly.

"You beauty. We got the motherfucker!" he yells to the others in the office. The sound of them cheering blares through the phone and I laugh. We thought this guy was guilty for months, but we just couldn't prove it. Undercover police have been going through his garbage in the middle of the night for months, and up until today we've been coming up empty-handed.

"Hey, do you still need a hand moving on Saturday?" Taz asks.

"Is that okay?" I wince. "I hate to impose."

"Anything for our favourite nerd," Taz replies.

I smile. The boys downstairs are like big brothers to me. I've worked here at the Federal Police quarters for three years and I love it. Every day is different, my work colleagues are some of the greatest people I know and solving crimes has become part of my blood. I'm addicted to the thrill of the chase. I never thought I would fall into forensics. Research was my original plan, but my brother Peter is a detective downstairs. He applied for the job on my behalf and, thankfully, I've ended up here and couldn't be happier.

I'm moving at the weekend. My landlord rudely sold my apartment and I had no choice but to find a new home. My friends, Taz, Peter, and the police boys from downstairs are helping me move.

"We'll have you moved in a couple of hours."

"Thanks, I really do appreciate it." I smile. "Now, go and arrest that motherfucker."

"Will do, boss." He hangs up and I turn back to Rourke, my trusty partner. The nerdy scientist with a heart of gold. "I think we deserve sushi for lunch."

"I'm even getting spring rolls today." He widens his eyes, exaggerating his excitement. "Splashing out."

"Oh, you rebel. Living life in the fast lane."

He throws his arm around my shoulder. "You have no idea how wild I can get, Tully Scott."

The elevator doors open and Cole walks out. The two of us stop in our tracks. He's the boss from downstairs, and lately he's made it his mission to be in constant contact with the forensic team. It's never been like that before, but I have to admit, it's nice to have someone from management recognise what we do.

"I was just coming up to congratulate you guys," he says as he shakes both of our hands. "A job well done. Congratulations."

"Thank you." I smile. "Although it's really the guys downstairs who deserve the accolades."

"Not at all." He smiles. "You've been working together for months on this, and I'm extremely happy with the outcome."

Rourke and I exchange looks, and I hunch my shoulders up like an excited child. "Thank you, sir. It means a lot."

"Where are you off to?" he asks.

"Lunch." I frown, not wanting to be rude. "Do you want to come?" I ask.

He smiles. "No, I'm going to go and check in on the others. Are they in the lab?"

"I don't think so." I look to Rourke.

"That's okay, I'll check anyway. You kids have a nice lunch break, hey?" He slaps Rourke on the back. "Congratulations again."

The elevator doors open, and Rourke and I practically float inside. I look over at him.

"Guess I'm getting the spring rolls, too."

The bar is bustling tonight. Music is playing throughout the building, setting the right ambience with the help of the sporadically placed fire lanterns that line the outdoor perimeter. I smile at Callie from across the table. She's my best friend and has been my partner-in-crime since we were the age of twelve.

Callie looks around at our surroundings. "I swear, I'm so horny I could fuck a tree right now." She sighs.

I hold up my margarita in the air and she clinks her glass to mine.

"To not fucking trees," I say, raising my brows as I take a sip. Callie laughs.

My phone beeps with a text. It's from Taz.

We just arrested him.
Well done, Tull.

"Yesssss," I hiss. "They got him."

Callie beams. "Oh wow, that's amazing. Congratulations, babe." She holds her drink up. "Another toast! To kicking ass in the lab."

I giggle and clink our glasses again. My eyes widen as I remember my news. "Oh my God, I forgot to tell you."

She licks the salt from her lips as she looks up and waits for me to continue.

"So..." I pause because this story seems so ridiculous that it couldn't possibly be true. I mean, I hardly believe it myself. "I hooked up with a guy last night."

"What? Where?"

"At the gym."

Her mouth falls open. "At the gym? What do you mean *at the gym*?"

I put my hands over my eyes, letting the embarrassment win for a moment. "It happened in the bathroom."

When I peek through my fingers, I see her eyes practically bulging from their sockets. "What the fuck? You hooked up with a guy in the gym bathroom?"

I laugh. "It's ridiculous, I know."

"How the hell did this come about?"

I shrug. "Well..." I think for a moment. "He was there, and I was there..."

She frowns as she sips her drink, listening intently.

"We started chatting a bit. He was so gorgeous."

"How gorgeous are we talking?"

"Like, fucking gorgeous—stupid hot. He starts showing off in front of me, acting all caveman, and I was pretending I hadn't even noticed him."

"Damn it." She bangs her hand onto the table in front of us. "Why don't hot guys ever show off for me?" She slaps her forehead. "I'm easily impressed. I could do with some showing off, for Christ's sake." She shakes her fist to the sky. "Is that too much to ask for, universe?" Her attention falls back to me. "Sorry. Go on."

"This guy was on the rowing machine, going hell for leather fast, and I was running next to him on the treadmill. I was totally distracted by the muscles in his back."

She frowns as she listens and continues to sip her drink.

"Then he pulled on the machine so hard that the cord broke and a piece flew off, landed in front of me and tripped me over."

She cringes on my behalf. "Is this true or is this like a joke and the punch line is coming up?"

I laugh and cross my finger over my chest. "Cross my heart."

She puffs air into her cheeks. "Okay, go on..."

"I skinned my knee really badly."

"Are you all right?"

"Fine now," I mutter. "I was so flustered, though, that I told him off for being a show off and stormed into the bathroom.

She frowns as she listens.

"That's when he followed me in."

"Where was the gym workers?"

"There was nobody else in the gym, just us. It's a twenty-four-hour, unmanned gym."

"This is the new gym you just joined?"

"Yes." I hesitate as I try to remember all the details. "And it was definitely after 9:30 p.m. by this time."

"Why so late?"

I shrug. "I don't know. I worked late and that's what time I actually got there."

"Okay, so this hot guy follows you into the bathroom and then what happens?" She's sitting forward in her seat now, waiting for the rest of the story.

I shrug. "I don't really know what happened next. He cleaned up my knee and there was all this sexual chemistry between us. I asked him what he was thinking about."

"*And*?" She frowns.

"He said he was imagining what his cock would look like in my mouth."

Her mouth falls open. "He did not."

I raise both eyebrows and nod. "He did."

"Oh my God." She tips her head back and drains her glass. "Then what?"

I shrug. "Next minute we're kissing like animals and he's pulling my hair. Before I know it, I'm on his lap and then he has his hand down my tights."

Her eyes bulge again. "What?"

"I know."

"You got fingered in the gym by a stranger?" She gasps.

"Shh!" I snap as I look around in embarrassment. "Keep your voice down."

She leans in towards the table, remembering where she is. "Let me get this straight: you got fingered in a gym bathroom," she whispers.

I nod.

She snatches my drink from me and drains that glass, too.

I laugh.

"And?"

"Well, I came, and then I got the hell out of there."

She stares at me, horrified. "You *came* and left? Like a guy?"

I nod. "Kind of."

"Who are you and what have you done with my best friend?"

"I know, right?" I shrug. "I don't know what happened. This guy was off-the-hook and somehow I completely forgot who I was."

She rolls her eyes. "Damn it, I need to go to a new gym. This is ridiculous. I'm over here at my shitty gym, horny as hell with not a finger in sight. Why doesn't this shit ever happen to me?" She sighs dejected.

"Do you want another drink?" I ask.

"Yeah, I'll come with you for the walk." We stand and make our way over to the busy bar, taking our place at the back of the line. Callie laughs as she stares at me, clearly still in shock. "Finger fucked in the gym bathroom. Whatever next?" she whispers, her eyes twinkling with mischief.

I feel a hand snake around my waist from behind, and I turn, completely stunned to see Brock behind me.

"O-oh," I stammer, caught off guard.

What's he doing here? Shit, he didn't hear us, did he?

He's wearing a black V-neck T-shirt with blue jeans, and he's towering above me with his hand splayed across my entire stomach.

"Hey," he says smoothly as his eyes drop down my body. I'm wearing tight leather black pants with a burgundy off-the-shoulder top and high, black ankle boots. My hair is down in subtle waves. Suddenly, Brock kisses me quickly on the lips. "You look fucking delicious," he murmurs, his eyes drifting down my body again.

I smile and then look over to Callie who is staring at him, rendered speechless.

"Erm. Callie, this is Brock. Brock, this is Callie."

He smiles sexily. "Hello, Callie." He turns his attention back to me.

"Brock is my friend from the gym," I add, trying to make my point to Callie.

Callie's eyes widen as she connects the dots. "*This* is your friend from the gym?" she whispers.

Brock smiles darkly and winks at me, knowing full well that I've obviously told Callie all about him.

Oh God.

Suddenly, three men walk over, and I nearly swallow my tongue. "Tully and Callie, this is Joshua and Ben, my brothers-in-law. This one here is Adrian." He pauses and then smiles fondly at the blond man. "My adopted brother. My sisters adopted him, so I guess I'm stuck with him."

Adrian narrows his eyes and acts offended.

I've never seen four men, who are all so good looking, in one place together ever in my life. These guys actually hang out? Joshua is tall with a dark chocolate buzz cut. He's ridiculously handsome and wearing a white shirt with blue jeans. Ben is masculine and looks like a total bad ass. Then there's the blond who is quite simply divine.

The blond man smiles. "Hello, Tully." He looks me up and down, assessing every inch of me.

Jeez. All I can do is smile awkwardly.

The men then go back to their conversation and order

drinks, but Brock links his pinky finger with mine and pulls us out of the surrounding conversations.

Suddenly, it's just the two of us in the room.

"I want to see you, but I can't blow my sister off. It's her birthday." He gestures over to a table, and I see two gorgeous brunettes and a blonde woman sitting together drinking cocktails. They are laughing together.

"Oh, I wouldn't expect you to." I smile. "Go and have fun with your friends."

His eyes drop to my lips and he kisses me again, softly and tenderly. "What are you doing later?" he whispers.

My eyes find Callie who is staring, wide-eyed and astonished at this beautiful male specimen whispering sweetly in my ear.

I gesture to Callie. "It's a school night, so we're going home soon."

He turns to Callie only briefly before he looks back at me. "So, I'll see you tomorrow night? Nine o'clock?" he asks as he squeezes my hand in his.

I can't help but smile softly. He really is quite... "Sure. You bet."

"Nice to meet you, Callie." He nods and rolls his lips together, as if thinking to himself, and then he kisses me quickly again, just once, before disappearing back through the crowd.

Callie and I watch him walk away. We can't take our eyes off those large, muscular shoulders, that tight ass, and the best damn arm porn I've ever seen.

"Holy fucking shit," Callie whispers, sounding kind of angry. "*That's* the guy you made out with at the gym?"

I bite my bottom lip to stop myself from smiling goofily. "Uh-huh."

"I have no words." She shakes her head. "Actually, I do. I'd be a fucking gym junkie if I were you."

I break into a broad smile.

"Who the hell are his hot friends, anyway?" She frowns. "Do they go to this fantasy gym, because if they do, that's it! I'm changing gyms."

My eyes seek out Brock and his friends. "I don't know, his brothers I think." I shrug. "I'm pretty sure they are all married to his sisters."

Callie eyes the table of men. "Lucky bitches."

I frown as we shuffle up towards the front of the line. The boys are back at the table by this time. "Do you mind if we go home soon?" I ask. "I don't want to seem like a weird hanger-on."

Callie shrugs and links her arms through mine. "Sure. We'll have one more drink and then leave."

Twenty minutes later, we're walking out of the front doors and are on the way to the cab rank. "You know, I was thinking," Callie says. "If I were you, I would be totally stalking him, serial killer style. He's ridiculous."

I laugh. "He is a bit."

"A bit." She sighs as we hit the kerb. "A lot."

I look up and stop dead in my tracks. Simon is walking along the other side of the street with his arm around a blonde woman. This is the first time I have ever seen him out in the eight months we've been broken up. I watch as he pulls her lips to his mouth, clearly saying something to her that causes her to laugh. They're both having fun.

My heart drops into my stomach and tears instantly fill my eyes. "Oh my God," I whisper to no one in particular.

Callie's eyes widen, and she stops on the spot. "Shit."

I take out my phone and immediately call Simon's number, my heart in my throat as it rings. Pick up, pick up. Pick up, baby.

He fishes his phone out, looks at the screen, and then stuffs it back into his pocket.

He didn't want to speak to me.

He chose her over me.

My bottom lip begins to quiver as I stare at them through blurred vision.

They laugh out loud and disappear around the corner.

Pain lances through my chest.

"Come on, babe," Callie says as she puts her arm around me. "Let's go home."

CHAPTER 3

Brock

"Oh no." Bridget frowns. "Here it comes again." She puts both of her hands over her chest to try and stop the oncoming heartburn. "I can't deal with this pregnancy shit." She looks at Natasha. "How come you didn't get heartburn when you were pregnant?"

"Because she had human children. Your baby's father is an ape," Joshua says dryly as he sips his beer.

Bridget fakes a laugh. "Ha-ha. You're so funny." Her face drops as she sips her Coke. "All I want is a marga-fucking-rita. Is that too much to ask for?"

Joshua chuckles while Ben reaches over to pick his wife's hand up. He kisses the back of it in sympathy. The man's a saint. Bridget's pregnancy has completely stolen her sense of humour and any semblance of my beautiful, easy-going sister. Some women glow while pregnant. Bridget is not one of those women. She's grown horns.

Big, evil fucking horns.

"Just wait 'til those two babies come out and stretch your vagina to oblivion," Abbie says nonchalantly. "It will be huge. Like a giant crevice."

Ben chokes on his drink, coughing and spluttering. Joshua laughs and slaps him on the back.

I wince. God, the things I have to listen to. No man should have to hear this.

"What, like yours?" Adrian snaps, completely outraged that Abbie would say such a thing.

Abbie screws up her face. "Oh, shut up, Adrian. Like you would know anything about vaginas."

"She's got you there," Joshua says smugly.

I tip my head back to the sky in frustration. Seriously? I'm giving up a night of unrivalled pleasure to listen to my sister whine about heartburn and hear about over-stretched vaginas?

"I see you, Brock," Bridget snaps. "Don't roll your eyes at us."

I look at her, deadpan.

Ben smiles sarcastically, happy that someone else is her target tonight.

We are sitting around a table of the crowded restaurant, but my mind is a world away from this lame conversation. I glance over to Tully who I have just seen at the bar as she talks to her friend, and I clench my jaw. I don't want her to think I was blowing her off. She seemed to understand.

My eyes drop to the sway in her hips and her ass.

So... fucking... hot.

I've been hard all day thinking about her.

She's wearing tight black leather pants and a feminine flowy top that shows just enough skin to drive any man out of his damn mind. Funnily enough, she's dressed just how I like my women to dress: understated and casually sexy. I don't like it when women try too hard. It has the opposite effect on my libido. Her hair and her face are pure perfection.

I get an image of those big pouty lips and I feel my cock harden. I catch my bottom lip under my front teeth as I remember what she looked like on top of me last night. *Damn.*

The girls and Adrian—or Murph, as we call him—drop into conversation. I'm sitting in between Joshua and Ben and my eyes go to find Tully again.

"So?" Ben murmurs so that nobody else can hear us. "How did it go from you checking that girl out in the gym last night to you kissing her on the lips at the bar just now?"

Joshua leans in to join in the conversation. He runs his pointer finger back and forth over his lip as he listens.

I scratch my head and shrug. "We kind of got busy."

Bens glances up at the girls to make sure they can't hear us. "Where?"

"In the gym bathroom, after you left," I whisper.

Joshua laughs and pinches the bridge of his nose. "Un-fucking-believable."

"Fuck off," Ben whispers, taking a quick look back at Tully. "How do you get busy in a gym?"

My eyes float back to the girls who are still deep in conversation. "I broke the rowing machine and tripped her over."

The boys both lean in as they listen. "And?" Ben asks.

I hold my hands up in defeat. "I did what any gentleman would do." I pick up a sweet potato wedge from the plate in the middle of the table and throw it into my mouth.

They both frown.

I chew it and swallow. "I took her into the bathroom to clean her up."

Joshua rolls his lips, amused. "The old 'pretend to be a doctor' trick." He shakes his head and sips his beer. "It's been working for Cam for years."

"Right?" Ben mutters, unimpressed. Cameron is Joshua's brother. He's a doctor and does ridiculously well with the ladies.

Joshua picks up a fry and bites it, speaking around it. "Did you close?"

I sip my beer and shake my head. "Nope." I then glance over to see Tully and her friend leave through the front doors. "Although, it's very fucking high on my priorities list."

"What's high on your priorities list?" Bridget interrupts.

"Going to the gym, Bridget," I reply flatly. "Stop eavesdropping."

Natasha and Bridget roll their eyes and go back to their conversation while the boys' attention drifts back to me. "So, what now?" Ben asks.

I sip my beer. "Tomorrow night, I close the deal."

Tully

I roll the pen to me on the desk with my fingertips, and then I roll it away. I've been doing this for an hour now, staring into space at my desk.

"You okay?" Rourke asks from his desk beside me.

"Yeah, I guess."

"You're off today."

I turn my attention his way and give him a sad smile. "I am."

"Anything I can do?"

I exhale heavily and take my hair out of the ponytail it was in, quickly redoing it into the elastic. "You can take me out to lunch, if you want."

"Sure thing. What do you want to eat?"

I shrug, uninterested in the world. "Anything fattening."

He bends and gets his keys from his briefcase. "Anything fattening, here we come."

We leave our office and get into the elevator. I stay silent and, thankfully, he lets me. That's the beauty of Rourke. He's the perfect work colleague, somehow knowing when I need to talk and when I just need the silence. He knows everything about me and yet never asks a single question. Like a healing balm, he slowly draws anything toxic out of me without me realising it.

Simon, my ex, is weighing heavily on my mind. I know that I was the one who gave us a forced break but it still hurt to see him laughing with someone else last night. I get a vision of him with her in a headlock and my stomach clenches. We used to laugh around town like that together.

Are they sleeping together? Of course they are, you idiot.

I taste bile in my mouth and I run my hand through my hair in total dismay. I can't take this. I feel suffocated, unhinged and crazy. At this rate, an unplanned trip to Borneo may be exactly what I need to clear my head.

I take out my phone and click into my travel app. What flights are on sale this week?

I've been on four overseas trips this year, but suddenly, I need to get out of here as quickly as possible again. What's Simon even doing in Sydney, anyway? He's been living in Melbourne since we broke up. I had no idea he was even here.

Rourke glances down at my phone and sees the app I'm scrolling through. He raises an eyebrow and then returns to stare at the back of the double doors, acting as if he doesn't know what I'm doing.

What am I doing? I don't even know anymore.

The elevator doors open and we walk out into the parking lot.

"McDonald's greasy enough for you?" he asks.

I nod. "Yep."

We drive in silence to the parking lot. My phone pings a message, and I glance at the screen. Simon. I narrow my eyes and open the message.

Hey, Tull
Sorry I missed your call last night.
I'm in Sydney for a conference.
I'm busy all day with work but I'll call you tomorrow.
Hope you are well.
xoxo

I click out of the message angrily.

"Hope you are well," I mimic in a snarky voice. "Asshole. Work conference, my ass." I shake my head in disgust and turn to Rourke. "Simon is fucking someone while on a work conference this week."

Rourke frowns as he drives. "How do you know that?"

"Callie and I saw him last night."

He turns to stare at me. "With a girl?"

"Yes, with a girl." I roll my eyes at his stupid questions. I'm so not in the mood for them today. "He wasn't with a man, was he? We went down to the food and wine festival last night and seemed to see everyone we know."

The car stops, and I get out, slamming the door hard behind me.

"What are you going to do?" Rourke asks as he runs to catch up with me.

I open the door to McDonalds with force. "Well, right now, I'm going to eat everything on the damn menu, followed by two hot fudge caramel sundae chasers."

Rourke raises his eyebrows as he walks beside me, half scared to speak. "Okay then." He looks up at the menu board with his hands in his pockets. "Let's get started."

I pull the tape through the dispenser and carefully seal the last box. I look around my living room at all the piled-up boxes. "I think we're nearly done." I smile.

"Thank fuck." Rourke sighs. "There's only one thing worse than moving."

"What's that?" Callie frowns as she licks the hot chocolate from her spoon. She gave up packing at least twenty minutes ago.

"Moving someone else," he answers as he slides another box over to me for it to be taped up.

I smile, grateful for my beautiful friends. "Thanks so much, guys. I couldn't have packed this house up without you."

"Yeah, well..." Rourke pauses for a moment. "After the day you had, I thought we may have been out drinking tonight instead."

Callie frowns, her attention bouncing back and forth between us.

"God, you should have seen her raging around and shit," Rourke says.

Callie's looks my way in question, and I roll my eyes. "I was stressed."

"Because?" she asks.

I shrug but don't answer.

"Hope you're well," Rourke mimics in a baby voice.

I tape the box up, ignoring Callie's questioning stare.

"I think Simon is just..." I shake my head as I search for the right words. "Maybe trying to work out what he really wants. You know, find the difference between a girl he wants to marry and a girl who's nothing more than a good time. There is a big difference between the two," I say.

Callie rolls her eyes and waves her spoon around in the air. "Here we go." She looks at me, deadpan. "Can you hear yourself right now, Tully?"

"No, hear me out. There are two types of people on Earth. The ones you love and want to marry." I pause for a moment. "For me, I want to end up with Simon. But then there are the ones you just want to fuck."

Rourke stops what he's doing and frowns, as if he's hearing this theory for the first time.

"Yeah, I get that. So?" Callie continues.

"What type of person am I?" Rourke asks.

"The kind you marry," Callie and I both answer in unison.

Rourke screws up his face. "I fucking hate that kind of guy. Why am I that kind of guy?"

"You just are." I sit on top of the box. "And, I was thinking about it. I've been on two dates since Simon and I didn't like either of the guys."

"That's because you're a fucking idiot," Callie snaps. "If you really wanted Simon, you would be with Simon."

I try to think of someone I know that I can use as an example between the two different types of guys. "Oh, I know, take the gym junkie, for example."

Callie's eyes light up. "Oh God. Him! If you don't fuck him, I will."

I giggle. "See, perfect example. He's the kind of guy you would have fun with and fuck, but you could never dream of a future with him."

"Why not?" Callie asks.

"Because of the way he is. He's just so *sexual*." I frown as I remember myself being all whoreish in the bathroom with him.

"And this is supposed to be his flaw?" Callie frowns. "You need fucking therapy." She rolls her eyes.

"Even I have to admit this gym junkie sounds hot," Rourke adds.

"Well, you fuck him, Rourke. He's obviously a player who does this sort of thing all the time. He got me all hot for it in the gym bathroom, and you'd have to be an idiot to fall for a guy like that."

Rourke's eyebrows rise, impressed. "You can actually pick up girls in the bathrooms? Where is this gym at, because I need to join as soon as possible?"

"Get in line," Callie snaps. "You should see this fucking guy." She drags her hand down her face. "And his friends, all suave and buff looking. Christ."

I laugh and continue sticking the boxes together.

"Aren't you supposed to be meeting him tonight?" Callie asks.

"Yeah." I shrug. "I'm not going to go."

Her eyes widen. "Why the hell not?"

"I'm tired, I have to finish packing for the move tomorrow, and...."

My voice trails off.

"And what?"

"Simon," Rourke sighs, disgusted. "She's sitting here thinking of fucking Simon and being loyal to him."

"It's not Simon!" I snap.

"Well, Simon's probably balls-deep in his," Callie air quotes, "non-wife material right now, and I can guarantee you that he's not thinking about you, Tully."

I fake a smile. "Funny."

"It's true."

I stare at her for a moment.

"Get your mind off Simon. You need to have fun. You do have to admit that the gym junkie would be fun." She puts her hands over her heart and throws her head back to the sky to feign fainting. "Oh God, so much fucking fun."

I look at Rourke as he holds his hands up in the air. "Don't look at me, I'm trying to work out how to jump the fence here. I need to convert myself from the marrying type of guy to the fucking gym junkie kind of guy... on the double."

"You want to be the marrying type of guy," I tell him.

"No, I don't. I want to be the fucking type of guy. Nobody wants to be the marrying type of guy. Not even guys that are married want to be the marrying type of guy."

I laugh.

Callie stands. "Come on, Rourke, let's go. Tully needs to go to the gym." She blows me a kiss. "Go to the gym, meet your gym junkie, and for the love of God, forget all about Simon."

I swipe my key over the door scanner at 9:35 p.m. I'm late, but after not wanting to come and deliberating the whole thing for over an hour in the shower, I'm finally here.

I'm not really sure why but what the hell. It can't hurt, I suppose.

I walk into the gym and look around. There are a few guys up the back, and one girl on the treadmill.

Brock's not even here. All that overanalysing for nothing

Damn it.

I get onto the treadmill and start walking. I turn up the speed and walk faster. I suppose I'll just work out then. That's an anticlimax.

I took an hour to psyche myself up to be here and he doesn't even show.

Fucking typical.

All men piss me off.

Oh well, his loss. I turn up the speed and begin to jog, but when I look up in the mirror there he is. I see him. He's sitting on the weights bench in the corner, and he gives me a slow sexy smile. He's wearing a white T-shirt and navy sports shorts.

My stomach dances in excitement. I force a smile to my face and then look down, pretending to be uninterested.

God. He's *so*...

He's probably nothing more than a prop.

That's what I would do if I owned a gym. I'd pay gorgeous guys to hang out and just be present. It makes good business sense, for sure.

I run for fifteen minutes, while he does his repetitive weights sets and watches me. To be honest, I wish he would look away because I'm dying over here. I can't run for this long normally. I'm totally showing off and I may go ass over tit at any moment, and skin my other knee down to the bone.

One man finally leaves the gym, and then five minutes later the other one follows. Another group of guys walk out from the back, until there is just one woman left in the gym doing sit ups. Brock's eyes fall over to her, and I wonder is he thinking the same thing as me:

Buzz off, woman. Why are you in the gym so late at night, stupid?

I stop running and bring the treadmill back to a walking

pace. I wipe my face with my towel and watch as the lady finally packs up her things and leaves through the front door.

Brock's eyes find mine in the mirror and a dark smile crosses his face.

Shit, my heart begins to beat so fast. I keep walking, and he stands to make his way over to me.

"Hello," he purrs.

I smile goofily. "Hi." Why does he have to be so damn sexy? I can't even pretend to be cool.

He puts his hand over mine on the handrail and I feel the energy zap between us.

"I've been thinking about you all day," he says.

My eyes hold his as my stomach flips. "Y-you have?" I pant.

He nods slowly, his eyes never leaving mine, not even for a second.

"W-what were you thinking about, exactly?"

"I was thinking that I need to talk to you in private."

I smile, God is he for real? "Is that so?" I look around the empty gym. "Is that why you had to wait for everyone to leave so you could come and talk to me?"

"Well, I didn't want anyone to be suspicious of the two of us *talking* the other night in the bathroom."

"Talking?" I smirk. "Is that what you call it?"

He smiles sexily and my stomach clenches. *Don't smile at me like that.*

"Yes." He pauses and rolls his lips together, as if amused. "It was a very... *stimulating* conversation. For some more than others."

Unable to help it, I laugh. "Yes, it was a *very* stimulating conversation that we had the other night."

His eyes find mine. "Did you enjoy it?"

What's it going to be, Tull? I get a vision of Simon with that girl.

Sink or swim.

"I did." Our eyes are locked. "Very much, actually."

Oh God, this guy makes me want to be a dirty whore.

Satisfaction flashes across his face and he licks his lips. He runs his hand up my forearm and his eyes follow his own touch. "I have something else to tell you."

I act surprised. "You do?"

"Yes" He pauses for a moment. "I do."

"What?" I ask, trying not to fall over on the treadmill from his touch alone.

"I can't tell you here, Pocket." His focus shifts to my lips.

"Why not?" I feel the burn from his gaze.

"It's private."

He takes his hand off my arm and I frown at the loss of his touch. "Where do you want to tell me this private information?" I ask as I play along.

"We should probably talk where we talked last time." He bites his lip to hide his smile.

"Really?" I widen my eyes.

He nods slowly.

I continue to walk on the treadmill.

"So, I'm going to go into the discussion room now," he says smoothly.

"The discussion room?" I raise my brows and laugh again. "You are something else."

"I know." He chuckles, and then gestures up to the ceiling. I look up.

A camera.

Shit.

“I’m going to go into the discussion room. You should follow me in, say, five minutes.”

“But, they’ll see us,” I whisper.

“Not once you’re in the bathroom. You just have to stay in there for five or so minutes. If we don’t enter or leave together, no one will know a thing. The tapes won’t be looked at unless there is an incident and they’re watched back.

“Oh.” I frown, and without another word he disappears up the hall with his gym bag in tow. I walk for another five minutes with my heart beating out of control. This is so naughty, so freaking hot, and I have to say, so out of character for me, it’s not even funny.

I’ll just go and talk to him—see what he has to say. I hope he kisses me again. His kiss was to die for. Who the heck is this guy, anyway?

I would never do this normally. I’m not the kind of girl who meets up with guys in a public bathroom. My eyes drift to the hallway as excitement runs through me.

Am I that kind of girl?

I bring the treadmill to a slow stop, my heart hammering in my chest, and I take my towel, bottle, and I walk up the hall to the bathrooms. I look up and see the camera positioned at the end of the hall so it shows all five of the bathroom doors. I quickly drop my head to hide my face.

As long as I don’t walk back out, he said I’m fine.

God, if anyone ever knew I was doing this, I’d die.

I walk to the end door and take the handle in my hand. I freeze for a moment and close my eyes. My heart is hammering hard as I take one last glance back up the hall. Should I leave? No. Just do it.

I open the door and rush in, quickly closing the door behind me. I flick the lock and turn around.

The room is filled with steam and the shower screen is open. Brock is naked, already in the shower, when he turns to face me.

His large shoulders and chest have soap lathered all over them, and his hair is dripping wet. His stomach is rippled with muscles, and his huge hard cock hangs heavily between his legs.

He smiles sexily. “Took your time, Pocket.”

Holy. Fucking. Shit.

“Brock.” I stare at him. “W-what the hell are you doing?”

I glance back to the door, damn it. I can’t leave for a few minutes.

He looks at me intently and rubs the soap all over his chest. “Taking a shower. What does it look like?”

“You’re incredible.” I shake my head in disgust. “I’m leaving right now.”

“Why?” He gives me a slow sexy smile and holds his hands out to the sides. “Taking a shower is a regular, everyday thing. I just wanted to be clean for our conversation.”

The bastard.

“You want to have a conversation with me with,” I gesture to his groin, “with your dick hanging out.”

He looks down at himself and then back up at me. “Does my dick offend you?”

“Yes.” I gasp. “Your dick offends me.”

I glance down right on cue. That is the most beautiful dick I’ve ever seen. Okay, sure, I haven’t seen that many but I’m sure it’s the most perfect one there is. For fuck’s sake, this guy is so overconfident I don’t even have words to describe him, and why the hell is all this turning me on?

This is un-fucking-believable. How on Earth did I get myself into this situation?

He continues to rub soap over his chest before he moves down and soaps his groin area up. I have to concentrate to stay focused on his face again.

"Why?" he asks.

I frown. "Because... because..." I search for the right choice of words. "Because it's the assumption that I am comfortable with you being naked that offends me, and I'm definitely not... comfortable." I shake my head and throw my hands in the air. "I'm so not comfortable right now."

"If it makes you feel any better, you should know that I'm completely fine with you taking your clothes off, too." He shrugs casually. "For our discussion."

I smirk. "You're an idiot."

He smiles that sexy smile again and I feel my insides begin to melt. "I think I'm just honest."

"How is *this* being honest?"

"Well..." He pauses a moment as he soaps up his groin again.

"Will you stop doing that!" I snap. "It's very distracting." I concentrate hard on keeping my eyes up to his face.

"Big dicks don't lie," he says with a lifted brow.

I stare at him, completely lost for words, and I really want to hoot with laughter. "You did not just say that?"

CHAPTER 4

Tully

His eyes are alight with mischief. "It's true. Big dicks don't lie, and I have a few truths to show you."

Unable to help it, I smirk and my eyes drift back down. "You're distracting me again with…" I put my hands out towards his groin, "that."

He smiles sexily. "When I do this?" He takes his cock in his hand and strokes it.

My eyes widen, and I swallow the lump in my throat.

"Does this distract you?" He breathes.

He strokes again, and his dick hardens even more. Holy mother of fuck. I shake my head and I try to act cool. "M-maybe. Yeah," I mumble shakily.

It's as if he's spurred on. "What about when I do this?" he whispers darkly, putting his leg up onto the shelf before he really begins to pull himself. I frown as I watch him. I've never seen such a sexually confident man before. It's very overwhelming.

Oh God.

His chest has a scattering of dark hair, and he has that trail of hair that goes from his navel down to his neat, short pubic hair. I can see every muscle in his stomach and arm as he strokes himself.

"I should... go," I whisper.

"Do you really want to go?" He strokes slowly. "Or do you think you should go because that's what a good girl would do?"

Sweet Jesus.

Be a bad girl, be a bad girl, be a bad girl.

My mouth goes dry and I press my lips and squeeze my legs together.

"Nobody is here, Pocket." He slowly strokes himself and then closes his eyes in pleasure.

I watch him, entranced. Every cell in my body has begun to pump and I can hear my pulse in my ears as my body goes into overdrive.

"Nobody will ever know what happens between us," he breathes. The room is filled with steam and the water is beading over his face.

My eyes meet his.

"If you want something, Pocket," he licks his lips slowly, "you should take it." He jerks his cock with force and I feel it in my sex. I clench to try and stop my arousal from clouding my judgement.

My eyebrows raise.

Dear father, forgive me, for I am about to sin. I'm going straight to hell on the Slut Bus.

Brock curls his finger. "Come here."

I stand and watch him.

"Come here, my Tully Pocket," he commands.

Like a zombie in a trance, I do just what he says, and I walk to the side of the shower. Extra slowly, he leans down and kisses me. His lips are soft and he sucks them at just the right pressure. He towers over me, and I can feel the heat emitting from his large body. My hands reach up to rest on his large biceps as he kisses me softly. I'm trying hard to ignore the fact that he's completely naked.

My eyes close as pleasure takes over.

He kisses me again and again, and with each kiss I feel more of my resistance fall away.

"You need to give yourself what you want, Pocket." He kisses me again. "Not what you think you should want. What you really want."

He reaches down, picks up my hand, and places it on his dick. Instinctively, I wrap my fingers around him and I close my eyes. He's soft and hard, and it's been too damn long without a man.

"You want this." He cups my jaw and sucks on my lips again. "I know you do."

I've lost control of the situation, or he's gained control. Either way, I'm screwed... literally.

"I have to have you." When I look up again, his dark eyes hold mine, and he slowly pulls my shirt off over my head. Then he turns me, takes off my bra, and his open mouth ravages my neck from behind. His hands are splayed across my stomach. Oh my fucking God.

What's happening here?

Do I tell him to stop? My mind begins to race.... but I don't want him to stop.

Brock bends and takes my shoes off, and then he pulls

down my tights in one quick movement until I'm standing naked before him. His lips take mine aggressively as he pulls me in under the water and pins me against the wall with his body.

Fuck.

Too late...

We stand under the water and he kisses me like his life depends on it.

I've never had this before—never been so hot for it that nothing else in the world matters. This is crazy.

Crazy good.

I can feel his hard cock up against my stomach and my nerves flutter.

Nobody will know.

He's big; bigger than I've ever had before. He lifts me, our lips staying connected, and he wraps my legs around his waist and pins me to the wall. His hand reaches up from underneath and he slides three fingers into my throbbing sex.

"Oh," he inhales sharply. "So. Fucking. Tight."

We kiss aggressively, losing control. *Ah, give me what I need.*

"You're frying my fucking brain, Tully," he whispers as he starts to work me aggressively with his fingers. I grip onto his shoulders for balance. I can feel his muscles contract as he moves. Our eyes are locked, and God, he looks so beautiful right now.

He kisses me softly, his tongue dancing with mine, our cheeks rubbing against each other's, and I know this is stupid, but it somehow feels... right?

"Say the word, baby," he murmurs against my lips.

Oh man. We kiss again and again, and I can't stand it. His fingers are inside of me, his cock hanging just below.

I shouldn't be here wanting this, but screw it. How could I walk away from this experience?

Screw everything!

"Fuck me," I breath. "Fill me up." We kiss violently. "Give me what I need."

He inhales sharply and the last of his control slips away when he slams me up against the wall.

Suddenly I remember. "Condom," I pant. "You need a condom."

He immediately puts me down, exits the shower, and heads straight for his gym bag. I pant and walk out after him. He bends and takes out a condom and my arousal dissipates a little. "You have a condom in your gym bag? Why am I not surprised?"

His eyes rise to mine. "Don't give me that fucking tone, Pocket." He breaks the packet open and rolls the condom on. He pulls me from the edge of the shower and turns me away from him so that I am leaning over the vanity and facing the large mirror in front of us. "This condom was packed in my bag for you," he snaps as if annoyed. He lifts my leg and impales me in one sharp movement, and I cry out. My mouth hangs open as I stare at our reflection in the mirror. His face hangs over my shoulder, his eyes dark and locked with mine in our reflections.

He hisses. "Oh, fuck, yeah." He pulls out slowly and pushes back in. I instantly moan and close my eyes.

"Tight." He groans. "Fucking tight."

"Brock," I whimper. "So... good." I'm stretched out like never before. He's filling every inch of me perfectly.

He pulls out slowly again, and then pushes back in.

His eyes drop to the place where our bodies meet and he bends me over farther so he can really see our connection. He smiles darkly, completely fascinated.

"You're fucking perfect." He slams me hard and I cry out.

Then he's fucking me, Brock style.

Hard and fast.

So, so hard.

I watch us in the mirror, lost somewhere between Heaven and ecstasy. His face is focused, while my face is completely submissive. My eyes are rolling back in my head. Any hope I had of acting like I wasn't enjoying this has gone out the window.

He feels good—too good. This is just insanity.

The sound of our skin slapping together rings out in this steamy, heated room. I begin to convulse.

"I'm going to come," I whisper.

His eyes rise to meet mine, and then he brings his fingertip to his mouth, wets it, and rubs it into my behind.

I convulse harder, and he pulls out, and in one quick movement pushes himself into my ass.

I scream out, and my face pushes up against the mirror.

He stills, realising that this is not something I've ever experienced before. He pulls my ear to his mouth. "Shh, baby," he whispers as he tries to calm me. "I got you."

"Ah," I whimper.

"Shh." He kisses my ear softly. "You can do this, Pocket."

I drop my head as I try to deal with all of him.

"Kiss me," he whispers. He takes my lips with his as his fingers move around to my clit. He circles it with just the right amount of pressure and my body begins to open for him.

I've never been owned like this.

He moans as he slides home again, and the power from his body forces me forward. My body contracts as the strongest orgasm I have ever had rips me apart.

"Yessss," he growls out.

His eyes are hooded, his mouth hangs slack, and his smile is dark as he rides me hard. "That's it, baby," he chants. "That's it."

I continue to convulse from the orgasm as he rides me, the two of us covered in perspiration.

I'm in shock.

He grabs my face and brings it closer to his to kiss me deeply. I feel his cock jerk deep inside of me as he cries out against my lips.

He stills, and our faces rest up against each other's as we pant.

What the fuck was that?

He's still deep inside my behind when he tenderly cups my breast and kisses me softly over my shoulder.

Why does this feel intimate?

We kiss for an extended time until he whispers, "I'm going to pull out, baby."

I frown, unsure why he's telling me, but when he does I whimper. "Ouch." That hurts.

He turns me towards him and pulls me under the shower to hold me close under the hot water while peppering me with kisses.

"That was insane," he whispers against my skin.

If I could speak, I would but I'm completely overwhelmed, my body is still tremoring from the deep orgasm he's just given me. My behind is burning. My sex is still on fire.

My morals... *they're completely shredded.*

He lifts my face to his with his finger under my chin and my eyes meet his. "You ever done that before, Pock?" he asks softly.

I shake my head, filled with shame.

He smiles softly and kisses me again. "Feels good, huh?" He pulls me to his chest and holds me close. I nod against his skin.

What's happening here?

I feel needy and attached. Am I that pathetic that amazing dirty sex is all it takes?

As if sensing my fragility, he carefully washes me as I stay tucked against his chest.

"You're coming back to my house to sleep, Pocket. I want you next to me tonight." He kisses my temple softly and I smile against him, feeling a little of my strength return.

"I don't even have a towel," I murmur. "I'm very unprepared for all this. What kind of gym junkie are you, anyway?"

He chuckles. "You get out first and use my towel. Just wait outside for me. I'll stay here for a few moments and be right out."

I get out of the shower and wrap the towel around me. Brock smiles as he watches me intently. I look down at myself and the water all over the bathroom floor.

I think there's only one thing worse than ripping off your gym gear during a heated bathroom sex romp, and that's doing the walk of shame while trying to put tights and a sports bra back on when you're still half wet and the guy who just fucked you is watching. Tights are hard to get on when I'm dry and alone in my bedroom. This is just appalling.

Kill me now.

I smile in embarrassment. "Will you turn around?"

He frowns. "What for?"

"Because..." I wobble my head around to try and articulate myself. "I would like some privacy, please."

He raises his eyebrow sarcastically. "After what we just did, you want privacy to put tights on?"

I widen my eyes as if he's stupid. "Yes."

He shakes his head and turns his back to me, continuing to wash himself instead.

I dry myself quickly and then peel my panties out of my

tights. I have to hop around to get them on. Of course, they fall into the water and get soaking wet. *Damn it.*

I try to distract him. "Look at me, just the poor, unsuspecting gym attendee who happened to get accosted in the bathroom."

"Yeah right." I can hear the smirk in his voice. "You weren't involved in any of that at all."

"I wasn't actually," I tease as I continue to dress.

"Stop talking shit or I'm going to bend you over and do it again." He leans out of the shower and slaps my behind. I yelp and swat him away. "I seem to remember hearing the words: fuck me, Brock. Fill me up. Give me what I need." He widens his eyes. "Sound familiar?"

"Nope, you've been watching too much porn and are obviously delusional," I say as I shake my top out and throw it over my shoulders.

He laughs, leans out, and grabs my T-shirt, dragging me to him. He kisses me tenderly. "I never saw any porn that good," he mumbles against my lips.

I smile softly and run my hands through his hair as I stare at him. "Never?" I whisper.

He shakes his head. "Nope."

Is this his way of saying that was the best sex he ever had?

He kisses me again. "What about you?"

Our faces are only millimetres apart. "I think, Brock…" I frown. "Wait. What's your surname?"

He laughs. "Marx."

I giggle because this is just insane. How did we just have sex and I don't even know his surname? I shake off the thought and continue. "Well, I think, Brock Marx, that *you* fuck like a god."

The air crackles between us as we stare into each other's eyes.

"And, I can't wait to do it again," I add.

He smiles and licks his bottom lip, and then leans in to kiss me. The kiss is slow and tender. He does it again and again, and soon he's out of the shower holding me close against his wet body. "I need more of you," he breathes.

The sexual chemistry between us is ridiculous. "I'll wait outside for you."

I walk out into the bathroom and keep my head down as I make my way up the corridor. My behind is smarting, and my legs feel like jelly from the super strength orgasm I just had. I catch sight of myself in the mirror and my stomach drops.

My hair is in a loose bun on top of my head and I have a rosy glow to my face.

The just fucked look.

I drag my hand down my face and close my eyes, letting a little bit of shame creep in. I can still feel the tingles in my body from where he's been. Still feel his stubble on my face, his tongue in my mouth...

He casually strides out of the bathroom, and my eyes rise to meet his. He smiles sexily and winks.

I smile gratefully, he makes this seem natural. It probably is for him.

God.

"Have you eaten, Tull?" he asks as he approaches me.

"Erm." I hesitate because my mind is literally jumbled. Have I eaten? "I'm not hungry."

"Okay, your place or mine?"

I frown. "I'm moving tomorrow. My place is filled with boxes."

"Oh, where are you moving to?" He gestures to the front doors and we walk out into the parking lot.

"Just a few blocks away. My apartment was sold."

"Do you need help moving?" he asks. "Is this you?" He points to my car. It's a white hatchback.

"Yeah." I open the door to my car and stand in between the car and the door.

"No, my stepbrother and friends have got it." I peer up at him. "Thanks, anyway."

He smiles and tucks a piece of my hair behind my ear. "My place, then?"

I know I should go home, but I'm not quite ready to let him go yet, so I nod. "Okay." I glance over at the fancy black Range Rover in the parking lot. "Is that your car?"

He smiles down at me, nods, and then leans in to kiss me softly.

"Do you have any idea how beautiful you are?" he whispers.

I smile against his lips and put my arms around his neck.

"Hang on a second, my phone is ringing." He shuffles around in his pocket and digs out his phone. It must have been on silent. He narrows his eyes. "Jesten."

"Jesten?" I frown.

"He works for me." He answers the phone. "Someone had better be dying, Miller," he snaps.

I watch him.

He frowns as he listens, closing his eyes, as if annoyed. "Seriously?"

He listens again.

"Fuck's sake, fine. I'll be there in half an hour." He listens again. "No, I'm in the middle of something here. I'll be half an hour." He hangs up and his eyes come back to me.

I force a smile. "Everything okay?"

"The alarm at my office has been tripped and the security company won't shut it off until I get down there." He leans down and kisses me softly. I wrap my arms around his neck once more.

"You have an office?" I ask.

"I own a security company." His hand roam down to my behind and he squeezes.

I giggle. "And your alarm is going off."

He smiles as he tucks the hair behind my ears again. "Ironic, huh? We're not security as such. Private investigators."

"We?"

"I employ ex special forces soldiers. Ten men work for me."

I frown. "Are you….?"

"Navy Seal."

I swallow the lump in my throat. "You're a Navy Seal?"

"Ex." He smiles. "I'll take you back to my house, then I'll quickly dart out and sort it. I won't be long."

I cringe as I imagine waiting at his house alone for him to come back. "Oh, that's okay. I'll just see you later."

His face falls. "No, I want you there when I get home." He kisses me again.

"Honestly, I've got to move tomorrow, anyway. I have to be up at the crack of dawn."

"Fucking alarm," he mutters under his breath. "Give me your phone."

I dig around in my bag and fish it out. He takes it from my hand and dials his number, the two of us watching as his phone vibrates. "Got it," he says. He licks his lips as he stares down at me. "I'm not ready to say goodbye to you yet."

I smile up at him and I feel my heart flutter.

"Why don't you come to my office with me now and we can leave your car here?"

"No. Call me tomorrow." I frown. "Actually, with the move tomorrow, perhaps you could call me Sunday instead."

He kisses me slowly and I smile against his lips. "I'll see you Sunday, my little Tully Pocket."

I laugh. "Can you think of a better nickname for me than Tully Pocket? I sound like a toy."

He smiles cheekily. "You can be my toy."

I roll my eyes and get into my car. He closes the door for me. I wind down the window to see him better, and he leans down to kiss me through it. "You drive carefully," he says.

"Yes, Dad."

He taps on the roof of the car, and I drive out of the parking lot, giving him a shy wave as I go.

My eyes rise to watch him in the rearview mirror as he climbs into his expensive car, and the farther away I drive from him, the more I feel the disgust in myself begin to rise.

I wake to the sound of my alarm blaring. I wince and quickly slap my hands over my face. I can't handle today. I've cried all night. I've never been so disgusted in myself in my entire life. I let a guy who I didn't even know, fuck me up the ass in a public bathroom. I'm a lowlife—a lower than low whore bag. My eyes fill with tears as I think of Simon. My beautiful, gentle Simon. The man who would never take me anally. The man who only ever made me feel good about myself.

What have I done?

I've forced him into the arms of another woman, that's what.

God, what would he think of me if he ever knew what I did. I drag myself into the bathroom and stare at my reflection in the mirror.

An ugly version of myself stares back at me. A dirty version.

My apartment is quiet and sombre. So lonely.

I get into the shower and pour the soap onto my hands. I

begin to wash myself as more tears form. I scrub my skin until it is red and raw.

How do I get this feeling of disgust off me?

Make it stop. I slide down the tiles until I'm sitting on the floor, crying the shame away.

CHAPTER 5

Tully

"THAT'S THE LAST ONE." Peter smiles as he puts the heavy box down on the floor.

"Thank you so much, Pete." I sigh as I reach up and give him a kiss on the cheek.

"Anything for my sister." His eyes hold mine and he keeps me in his arms. Feeling uncomfortable, I pull from his grip.

Peter is my stepbrother. He's also a detective downstairs. Along with the boys from work, he's spent all day moving me in. The others finished about half an hour ago. It's just turned 7:00 p.m.

Peter produces a bottle of champagne from a box, and I smile. "I thought we should celebrate," he says as he pops the cork. I rustle around in a box and find two coffee cups for us to use. He fills our cups slowly.

I take a sip and my eyes hold his.

Here's the thing, and I've never told a soul this, but Peter is attracted to me. I know he is. When I was twelve and he was fourteen and our parents had just met, he expressed his undying love for me. I told him then and there it was never going to happen, but over the years I've felt his eyes on me when he thinks I'm not looking.

I always thought I'd imagined it, but lately, and especially since his wife left him, and I broke up with Simon, he's been lingering around after our conversations, as if he wants to say something else.

I don't like him that way. I see him as a brother, and to be honest, I'm kind of beginning to feel uncomfortable being alone with him. And I hate that because we do get along really well. I just wish I didn't have this feeling lurking over me; like he is going to put it on me at any moment, every time we speak.

"You might be scared tonight," he says.

I smile and begin to unpack a box of cups into the kitchen cupboard as a distraction.

"I might stay the night," he says casually.

I look up from my unpacking duties.

"No, it's fine. You don't have anywhere to sleep."

"I could sleep with you." His eyes hold mine. "We could spoon like old times."

I press my lips together. Do I address this now? Honestly, I'm just too fucking tired and emotionally worn out from Brock to even think about this shit today.

"Callie will be here soon. She's sleeping with me in my bed tonight." I fake a smile.

"Cancel on her."

"No, I would never do that. Thanks, anyway. You should get going, I don't want to hold you up any longer," I say, knowing I need to get rid of him.

His eyes hold mine and I know that he wants me to ask him to stay.

He's my stepbrother. Yuck.

"You going to be okay?" he asks.

"Yes." I smile as I look around my new apartment. "Perfect. I'll just potter around now and get the boring things done."

He looks around at the piles of boxes everywhere. "Damn, moving is a bitch, huh?"

"Don't I know it." I sigh. I'm going straight to bed after he leaves, but I'm not telling him that. I'll at least pretend that I'm motivated and going to put shit away with Callie. After my escapades at the gym last night I hardly slept a wink, I'm absolutely exhausted.

Callie had a wedding on tonight, and Rourke got called into work, so it's just me here in my new apartment. Something Peter doesn't need to know.

I walk to the door to give him the hint. "See you later." I smile as I open it.

"Bye." He sighs.

"Thanks so much." I kiss him quickly, nearly pushing him out the door before I close it behind him and sigh in relief.

I look around my new apartment and smile. It has a really good, homey feel about it. It's a little old, but it has polished timber floors, big windows, and lots of natural light. There are two bedrooms, a big kitchen, and a brand new bathroom for me to swoon over.

I love it. It really feels like a new beginning for me.

My phone rings. I glance over, see the name, and I scramble to answer it.

"Hello."

"Hey, Tull," Simon says, sounding happy. I close my eyes at the sound of his voice. "How are you?" he asks.

"Good," I reply in a clipped tone. "I called you the other night."

"Yeah, sorry. I was at work and missed your call."

I narrow my eyes. "When did we start lying to each other?" I reply flatly.

He stays silent.

"I saw you, Simon." I pause for a moment, wondering if it is a good idea to talk about this over the phone. "Who is she?"

Silence....

I close my eyes, the hurt rising in my chest.

"She's nobody, Tull."

I look up at the ceiling. "She sure looked like a somebody."

"You wanted this break."

"To travel," I hit back. God, if only he knew what I'd been doing. Oh, that's right, I don't want to fucking know it myself.

"So, I'm supposed to just sit here and wait for you to decide if you're coming back," he asks, annoyed.

"I am coming back." I pause. "*Was* coming back," I add.

"You are fucking coming back, Tully. Don't give me your shit and say you *were* coming back now."

I stay silent.

"Tull." Simon pauses on the phone. "I love you. Being with other people just makes me appreciate what we have so much more."

I feel the lump rise in my throat again. Other people? How many have there been?

"Do you know how much it hurt last night when I saw you look at your phone and put it back in your pocket, and then put your arm around her?" I whisper, holding back my tears.

"Tully," he whispers. "Baby, don't."

"Don't what, Simon? Don't be upset that you're fucking other women?"

I screw my face shut as pain lances through my heart. He's slept with someone else. I've turned into a dirty whore. What have we become?

The innocence between us will never be the same again.

This is my worst fucking nightmare.

"You wanted a break." He hesitates for a moment. "I hope you're experiencing new things, too. It was just one night. I'll never see her again."

"N-new things," I stammer. "Having sex with other people is new things?"

"Stop it. Stop with the fucking mind games, Tully. You wanted a break. You got it. In four months, you come back to me with this fucking shit out of your system, okay?"

I stay silent.

"Because I love you and I still want to marry you."

I listen, waiting, unable to speak.

"Okay?" he whispers.

I feel a little mollified, but I can't help myself. I have to ask. "Do you care about her?"

"No. Not like that, anyway."

"Are you sure?" I whisper as I look around my apartment.

"You're the girl I love. You're the girl I'm going to marry, I already know that. There isn't a doubt in my mind."

I smile softly, my hope returning.

"Get it out of your system, Tull." He sighs.

Trust me, it is well and truly out of my system. In fact, the system is completely fucked up. I frown. "Is that what you're doing?" I ask.

"Yes."

I listen, unsure if I want to hear this, but who am I to judge after what I've just done?

"So that when you come back to me, I can be the best damn husband you ever dreamt of."

My eyes cloud over and relief fills me. I really needed to hear that. "I miss you," I whisper.

"I miss you, too. Do you love me?" he asks.

I nod and wipe a stray tear away. "Yes, I love you. Don't ignore my fucking calls again or I'll lose my shit."

He chuckles. "I promise, I won't, but I mean it, Tull. My time in Melbourne finishes in three months and then I'll be back. Don't make this break we've had be in vain."

Fear fills me. "What if we don't find our way back to each other, Simon?"

"We will." He pauses for a moment. "I promise, we will. A love like ours will never die and you know that."

"Why do you have to be so reasonable all the damn time?" I sigh.

"I don't know." He pauses, and I can tell he's smiling. "This wise woman I'm in love with gave me this pep talk eight months ago. I think she may have been onto something."

"That woman was an idiot to ever let you go." I smile softly.

"She didn't let me go. She still has me."

My eyes fill with even more tears. "Let's just get back together now, Si."

"No. We have to do what we said we would. I'm going now," he says.

"Why?" Should I tell him what I've done? No, I can't. I can't ever tell him about Brock.

"Because, Tully. You wanted this break and I'm giving it to you."

"D-don't go," I stammer, suddenly panicked. I want to hold onto him for a bit longer.

"Tully." He sighs. "Go and have fun."

I frown. "Do you ever think about me?" I ask hopefully.

"All the fucking time."

"I love you."

"I love you, too. Goodbye." The phone clicks and he's gone.

It's 9:00 p.m. and I'm lying in my bed in my new bedroom. I can't find my sheets but I don't give a fuck. I'm too tired for this shit. I'm in my sleeping bag.

My mind keeps going over and over my conversation with Simon, as well as the woman he was with.

He said he doesn't have feelings for her and I can honestly say that I can relate to that detachment.

I get a vision of Brock. I hate that he affects me so much. Every time I think of him— which was every time I moved today and felt where he had been—I feel sad.

Sad that we met the way we did. Sad that he's wired the way he is.

And really sad that I had so little respect for myself that I just handed myself over to him.

I never thought a man who I didn't know and who didn't care about me could talk me into something so easily.

I'm weak.

Forever tainted.

My phone beeps with a text and I frown when I see the number come up. Who's that?

Hope the move went well.

See you tomorrow.

XOXO

My eyes widen. Oh my God.

Brock! What does he want?

I throw my phone onto the floor as if it's a bomb, and angry tears burn my eyes.

"Leave me alone," I cry. "Don't call me again. I hate you for making me feel like this."

I cocoon myself in my sleeping bag and roll into a ball. My misery takes over and I cry tears of shame.

Brock

I dial the phone number and stare out the window, looking over at the horizon as I wait for the call to go through.

It's dusk, and the lights from the city are twinkling down below.

I've been counting the hours until I could call Tully. Weirdly, I've never been so keen to meet up with a chick in my life.

"I'll take her for dinner, and then for drinks. After that..." I stop and listen as it starts to ring.

It rings and rings until it rings out. I hang up before leaving a message.

I frown. Hmm, maybe she's in the shower.

Annoyed, I open a beer. Patience isn't my strong point.

I pick up the remote for the television and flick through the channels, waiting an hour for her to call back. It's 7:00 p.m. now and I'm getting antsy.

Ring, ring, ring, ring, ring, ring.

***"Pick up!"* I snap. I wait for her voicemail, and then I hear her cheerful, husky voice.**

. . .

Hi, this is Tully.
Leave a message.

I pause for a moment. "Tully, this is Brock. Call me." I hang up, sip my beer and turn my attention back to the television, unimpressed.

I don't wait for chicks to call me back. They always fucking answer my calls. This is annoying.

I had plans for us tonight.

10:00 p.m. now, and I glare at my phone on the coffee table. So, she's not fucking calling me back, hey? What's her problem?

This is a first.

I walk into the bathroom and tear off my clothes to get into the shower.

I let the hot water run over my head and down my face as I stare at the tiles.

An uncomfortable feeling comes over me as I scrub my body aggressively.

Fuck her, then. I don't need this shit.

I do my last chin up and pant as I fall back to the floor, taking a quick glance at the front door of the gym.

With my towel, I wipe the perspiration from my face and neck. I check the time on my phone and stare at it for a moment.

It's 9:30 p.m. on Monday night. Tully's not here like she

was all last week. She hasn't called me back and I'm getting majorly pissed off.

What is her fucking problem?

I put my earphones in and lie back on the weight bench to do some flies.

I push the weights into the air as replay the last time I was with her here.

She was happy to see me, and then she met me in the bathroom. I was naked.

Then we…

I frown.

Maybe I was too much for her?

An uneasy feeling sweeps over me again. It's the same one I've had since yesterday, and I don't like it one little bit.

I push the weights into the air angrily. The sex isn't her issue. It can't be. She loved it. She loved every damn minute of it.

She came like a fucking freight train.

Then, why?

Maybe she's got a boyfriend. I sit up and drink my water from my bottle as I contemplate that for a second.

I narrow my eyes and stare into space. No. If she had a boyfriend she wouldn't have let me kiss her in the public bar the other night.

Fuck me. Fill me up. Her words come back to me. Oh, she wanted it, all right. I didn't imagine that.

I sit up and stare at my phone again, clicking through to find her name. My finger hovers over her number.

Do I call again? Fuck it.

I dial her number and I sit, waiting as it rings out again. I clench my jaw. I dial again, and this time I wait for her voicemail.

Hi, this is Tully.
Leave a message.

"Tully, it's Brock. Stop playing your stupid fucking games and call me back," I snap. I hang up, stand, and grab my bag, heading straight for the door.

When she does call me back she's getting a fucking mouthful.

I'm not putting up with her shit. I storm out of the door and throw my bag into my car. My phone rings and I scramble to pick it up. But the name Ben lights up the screen instead of hers. Fuck's sake. I answer in a rush. "What?" I bark.

"Jesus, what's up your fucking ass?"

"Nothing. What the fuck do you want?"

"I'm calling to see if we're training in the morning, you fucking moody bitch."

I roll my eyes. "Yep. See you at 5:30." I hang up, annoyed, and scroll through my phone until I get to her name. My finger hovers over her name again.

No. Don't call again.

I bite my thumbnail as I stare through the front windshield of my car, my leg bouncing as I think. I don't know her surname. I don't know where she works. I don't know where she lives. I have absolutely no way of finding her unless I look her up on my work computers, which I have warned my staff against ever doing. It's instant dismissal to trace someone and invade their privacy that way. I narrow my eyes, clench my jaw, and start my car in a temper.

I should have dragged her back to my house that night. What was I thinking, letting her leave? My fury begins to boil.

I can't pursue this any further unless she calls me back or comes to the gym.

The ball is completely in her court.

And it fucking pisses me off.

I push the heavy weights up with my legs. It's 6:00 a.m. now, and I'm in the gym with Ben, my closest friend. He's not my closest friend because he's been my friend the longest, because he hasn't. But Ben was in love with my sister Bridget for five years from afar. He called me every week to check in on her and put her wellbeing in my hands. During that time, and with all those late-night phone calls, our guards were completely let down with each other.

We talked about shit that we don't talk about with anyone else.

I suppose, because he had to share his weakness with me, I have shown him mine in return, it has grown into a deep understanding of each other.

He thinks like me, he feels like me. We just get each other.

He probably knows me better than anyone, and at a time like this, when I've got something on my mind, it's impossible for him not to notice.

"Spill," he says.

I push the weight in the air.

"Spill what?"

He gives me a sarcastic glare. "You've been a cranky bastard for two days. What's your problem?"

"I don't have a problem." I huff as I stand.

He takes his place on the bench. "Bullshit." He does his set.

I lie back down to do mine. "I've got the shits with that chick, that's all."

He frowns. "Who? Miranda?"

I roll my eyes. Miranda is a girl I see sometimes. She's trying to make friends with my sisters to get to me and it annoys the hell out of me. "No, not fucking Miranda. I'm off her."

Ben frowns.

"That chick from here. Tully, the hot redhead."

A smile crosses his face. "Oh, her." He sips the water from his bottle.

I clench my jaw. It annoys me that she's so hot.

He lies down to do his set. "So, what's the problem?"

I shrug. "You tell me. We hooked up. It was smoking hot and now she's not returning my calls."

"This is the time we talked about the other night when you didn't close?" he asks.

"No. I saw her again."

He smirks and raises a brow. "And?"

I shrug.

He smiles. "Where?"

"Here."

"Did you close?"

"Slammed the door shut."

He chuckles and does another set. "And now she's not answering your calls?"

"Nope. And I don't fucking get it."

He thinks for a moment and we move to another weight bench. "Well... what happened?"

I shake my head. "We hooked up, it was white hot, she fried my fucking balls, and now she's disappeared."

He frowns. "Why?"

"I don't know." I think for a moment and I push the idea out of my head.

"What?"

I shrug. "I lost my head a bit."

"You were rough with her?" He frowns.

"Rougher than I meant to be." I run my hands through my hair. "She was just blowing my fucking mind, you know?"

He watches me carefully. "Did you hurt her?"

"What?" I shake my head. "No, I didn't hurt her. She was fucking loving it."

My face falls. "It was her..." My voice trails off.

"Her what?"

I wince. "I popped her cherry."

His eyes widen in surprise. "She was a virgin?"

"No. God no." I exhale heavily. "Anal."

His face falls and he stares at me, deadpan, and then, as if unable to believe what he's hearing, he bursts out laughing.

"What?" I snap.

"You met a good girl in the gym, you fucked her up the ass in a public toilet, and you have to ask why she wants nothing to do with you?" He laughs out loud. "You are so fucking stupid."

"She... she loved every minute of it," I stammer.

He shakes his head in disbelief. "You can't just take whatever you want from good girls like her."

I frown.

"How long has it been since you were with a nice girl?" He stops what he's doing. "A really good girl who doesn't fuck around?"

I stare at him. I haven't been with a good girl for years. I've forgotten the last one. I like my girls bad to the bone. "What relevance does that have with anything?"

"Everything."

"Why?"

"Because you can't take a good girl the way you want to. Not the first time, anyway. Not the first twenty times, actually."

"What do you mean? That's ridiculous, I'll take them how I want them, and they'll fucking love it." What a ridiculous notion. I've never had a woman not want to come back for more.

"You have to train them up, they aren't wired like us. You have to train their body and mind to take us how we want to take them," Ben says.

"That's bullshit. She loved it, came like a fucking freight train."

"If she loved it, she'd be back for more."

I stare at him, my mind a clusterfuck of emotions.

"Man." He shakes his head. "If I tried that shit on Didge straight up I would have been dumped in a second flat."

"You had to wait? I can't believe that. Why would you wait for something you both want?" Wait. Didge is my sister. Disgust fills me. "I can't believe we are having this conversation."

He rolls his eyes, frustrated with my stupidity. "That's the thing. Good girls aren't wired to know that they want it. You have to show them how much they actually do. *Slowly*."

I shake my head. "That's not it. I know that's not it. You don't know what you're talking about. I'm telling you, she loved every minute of it."

He raises his eyebrows. "Maybe? But, I married a good girl. Stan married a good girl—your sisters—and we both had to wait to do what we wanted in the bedroom."

I curl my nose, crease my brows and groan out loud. "I do

not want to know what you and Stan do to my sisters, and I don't fucking wait for anyone. I do what I want in the bedroom, when I want." I walk towards the bathroom.

"Brock!" Ben calls. I turn back to him.

"You fuck bad girls how you want because they only want your cock."

I stare at him for a moment. "And what do good girls want?"

His eyes hold mine. "Your respect."

"Got a minute?" Miller ask as he knocks on the door of my office. It's later in the day, and my conversation with Ben has been at the front and centre of my thoughts all day.

"Yeah, what's up?" I look up from my computer. "Take a seat."

"I just got the records in," he says as he falls into his chair.

"Ah, okay. Hang a sec." I pick up my phone and dial the extension. Ben picks up. "Ben, do you want to come in here for a second? Miller has something."

"Sure thing."

Moments later, Ben walks in and takes a seat. "What did you find?"

"Okay," Jes says as he opens a manila folder with the records inside. "So, I did a trace, and according to bank records, Mr. Chancellor withdrew money from an ATM on George Street on the days he made the calls to that number."

"Same ATM machine?" I ask.

"Yep, every time, which indicates he went somewhere close to this autoteller."

"Did you run the checks?" Ben asks.

"Yes. We hacked the hotels within a five-mile radius to see if we could get any idea on where he was going?"

"Any luck?"

"Not under his name, but on each day that he made a phone call and withdrew cash, a hotel room was booked at the Star Casino in the name of Webber."

"Every time?" Ben frowns.

"Yep."

"Bingo." I smirk. "Dumb fuck used the same name." I shake my head. "Honestly, some people are so thick. We need to get security footage from inside the hotel and find out who he was meeting."

"Do you want to go down there now?" Jes asks.

I turn back to my computer. "Yeah, give me ten to finish this report."

Jes stands. "Okay, meet you downstairs."

It's Thursday and I'm sitting in the car as I wait for Ben and Jesten to come out. I call Tully's phone number for the fiftieth time this week.

My anger is at an all-time high.

How dare she not answer my calls? Who the fuck does she think she is?

The phone drops out without the call going through, and I narrow my eyes.

I dial again, and it does the same thing. She's blocked my number.

She wouldn't.

The boys come out and get into the car. I put my hand out to Ben who is now sitting in the passenger seat. "Give me your phone."

He opens it and hands it over. I type Tully's number into his phone and listen and it rings first go.

"Hello," she answers.

My fury explodes. "Are you fucking serious?" I growl.

The phone clicks as she hangs up, and I punch the steering wheel with force.

"Jesus fucking Christ," Jes cries from the backseat. "What the fuck, man?"

I rip the car into gear and take off out of the parking lot. I'm so angry right now, I can't even see straight.

Ben's clearly trying hard to stop himself from smiling as he stares through the windscreen, but I glare at him anyway.

"Who was that?" Jes asks from the backseat.

"Boss man got dumped." Ben smiles sarcastically.

"Fuck off," I snap as I take the corner with speed. "I do not get fucking dumped."

Ben chuckles. "Oh, really?"

My furious eyes turn to him in the passenger seat again. "Don't fucking bait me today, Statham. I'm in the mood to kick some serious ass."

Ben and Jes chuckle, thinking this is a great joke.

We drive downtown towards the police station. The traffic is everywhere. "Fucking move!" I yell out the window.

"Jesus. Calm down," Ben mutters under his breath.

Some idiot is pulled over to the side and is letting someone out. I put my hand on the horn. "These fucking idiots have no idea how to drive!" I yell out the window.

"Take a fucking chill pill," Jes urges from the backseat.

I glance over to the sidewalk. There's a restaurant there with tables and chairs out in the sun with parasols shading them. It's packed with people.

I put my hand back on the horn. "Hurry the fuck up!" I yell out the window.

I glance back over to the restaurant and catch sight of something, and then I narrow my eyes. You have got to be kidding me?

Tully is sitting at a table with a man, eating lunch.

My anger explodes, and I yank the handbrake on. "Circle the block." I get out of the car.

"What the fuck?" Ben snaps. "What are you doing?"

I leave the car in the middle of the road and I storm towards the restaurant. I barge through the door and up to Tully's table.

Her eyes widen when she sees me. "B-brock?" she stammers.

I look down to the man she's with. I've never been so angry. I grab him by the scruff of his neck.

"Leave. Before I fucking kill you."

CHAPTER 6

Tully

HOLY FUCKING SHIT, no.

"Brock!" I cry. "What are you doing here?"

"Move, fucker!" He growls at Rourke as he tears him from his seat and throws him to the side. Rourke falls onto the floor before he quickly scrambles to his feet.

My eyes widen in horror. "Brock, what the hell do you think you're doing?"

"I don't."

Rourke goes to say something and stand up for himself, but Brock turns towards him like the devil, daring him to try. Rourke frowns, and then shrivels in fear. His eyes flick between the Brock and I. "I'll wait outside for you, Tully."

I glare at him. *Wimp.*

Brock falls into the seat opposite me and sits back in the chair. He lifts his chin and glares at me. My heart begins to race, and perspiration heats my armpits. He's radiating thermonuclear energy. I don't think I've ever seen anyone so angry.

"What do you think you're doing?" I fold my arms in front of me. "Don't you dare treat my friend like that."

He leans forward and puts his elbows onto the table. "Shouldn't the question be: what the fuck are you doing?" he growls in a whisper.

"I'm having lunch, what does it look like?"

Brock clenches his jaw. "Who's that fucking guy?"

"None of your business," I snap.

He slams his hand onto the table and I jump. "Do not fucking infuriate me, Tully." He growls again. "And why the fuck aren't you taking my calls?"

I narrow my eyes at him. Of all the nerve. He's obviously never been rejected before and he's seriously shocked. Well, I'm not playing his game.

"Because, I'm not interested."

His eyes blaze with anger. "Now tell me the real reason."

"What?" I whisper angrily. People are starting to look over at us now. I lower my voice. "You are so fucking conceited. I didn't enjoy it, okay?"

He glares at me. "Bullshit."

I shrug, as if unimpressed. I just need to rip the Band-Aid off and be mean to get rid of him once and for all.

"It was incredible. I was there, Tully. I know how it felt."

My eyes hold his. *It really was.* I force myself to shake my head.

"You're delusional. It wasn't that great, Brock."

"Cut the bullshit and tell me the truth."

Of all the nerve, this guy is seriously out of line here. "Fine. It was okay. Very average, I guess."

He leans into the table. "Are you trying to piss me off? Because it's fucking working," he growls.

"Brock," I whisper. "I don't like you. I don't want to see you again. Stop calling me."

"Bullshit. Tell me the fucking truth and I'll leave you alone."

My eyes fill with tears because I don't want to say it out loud.

The truth hurts.

"Tully." His voice falls softer as he sees my tears. "What is it?"

"You make me feel dirty," I whisper.

His face falls.

"I don't sleep around."

He clenches his jaw angrily, his eyes holding mine. I can hardly see him through my now-blurred vision. "You're only the second person I've ever slept with and you fucked me up the ass in a public bathroom," I whisper angrily. "And I hate myself for it."

He takes my hand tenderly in his. "Tully," he whispers softly. I stare down at our entwined hands and I just want to sob. I hate that I like his touch. I hate that he makes this all seem normal and okay.

"Don't, okay," I cry as pull out of his grip. I stand so quickly that my chair falls back onto the floor. "Leave me alone, Brock. I don't like the way you make me feel." I leave the restaurant and rush through the front doors but, of course, he comes after me.

"Tully, wait, we need to talk."

I turn towards him, furious that he has, once again, made me weak at the knees. "No." I push him hard in the chest. "You said if I told you the truth you would leave me alone."

He tries to wrap his arms around me. I push him away. "Don't fucking touch me!" I cry, completely losing control.

His eyes hold mine, and I know he's trying to work out how to handle this situation. He's completely out of his depth here.

I crease my eyes together to try control the tears. "I hate you for making me feel like this."

His face falls. "Stop it," he whispers.

"Go back to your whores, Brock." I angrily swipe my tears away. "Leave me the fuck alone." I turn and storm towards my work building.

"Tully!" he calls out to me. "Tully, you get back here!"

I put my head down and power walk away from him.

I feel relieved as I said it, but I have a sinking feeling about never seeing him again.

To be honest, I'm just glad it's over and I don't have to think about it anymore.

I blow out a breath and angrily swipe the tears away as I power back to my office. I walk into the building, take the elevator to my office, and find Rourke sitting at his desk.

"Thanks a lot," I shoot at him as I throw my bag onto my desk. "Where did you go?"

Rourke looks at me, deadpan. "Excuse me. In case you didn't notice, your Hulk of a gym junkie boyfriend was going to punch my lights out."

I roll my eyes and drop into my chair.

"He's fucking crazy, Tully," he mutters. "He must be on steroids."

I pick up a pile of files, drop them onto my desk, and they land with a thud. "Well, you won't have to worry about him anymore."

"Why?"

"Because it's over. I ended it."

He looks at me flatly. "Does he know that?"

"He does now."

He frowns and gets this stupid look on his face.

"What?" I snap.

"Does he fuck as crazy as he acts?"

I twist my lips and nod.

His eyes hold mine.

"And, your point is?" I ask.

He shrugs and goes back to his work.

"What?" I snap.

"It's been a long time since I saw a man get that passionate about anything." He begins writing something down on his file.

"What's that supposed to mean?" I frown.

He shrugs. "I don't know what it means, but I know that I never saw Simon get the slightest bit jealous of you. We could go out all weekend and have sleepovers and everything."

I stare at him. "So?"

"Well, that dude nearly ripped my head off just because I was sitting with you."

I stare at Rourke for a moment as my mind tries to catch up with his thought process. "I don't understand what you're trying to say."

"I'm saying I would give anything for someone to be that passionate about me." He looks at me flatly.

I screw up my face in disgust. "Then go to the gym and hang in the toilets, if you're lucky,

someone might come and fuck you up the ass." I shake my head. "It would not surprise me one little bit."

He rolls his eyes. "Why are you so dramatic?"

"Because I'm getting back with Simon and I don't need this shit."

Rourke gets out of his chair. "Whatever." He takes his files and disappears downstairs to the other lab. I turn on my computer and stare at the screen.

Why the fuck did I change gyms?

I walk out of the elevator in my building and up the hallway towards my apartment when a door opens. A girl with black hair comes out into the corridor. She's wearing old fashioned, un-matching clothes. I saw her the other night when she was talking to a girl downstairs in the foyer. She's quite pretty underneath her horrible styling.

"Hello," she says to me.

"Hi." I smile and walk past her.

"I'm Meredith."

I turn to face her. "Hi, Meredith. I'm Tully."

"You just moved in this weekend?"

"I did. Do you live in that apartment?" I ask to make conversation.

"Uh-huh. My mother pays my rent because she doesn't want me to listen to her having intercourse with her boyfriend anymore."

I blanch. What the hell? Okay, that's just way too much information. She would be my age or close to it; at least twenty-four. Why the hell does her mother pay her rent? And why would she want to hear her mother having intercourse?

Sick.

I force a smile. "Really nice to meet you, Meredith. I have a lot to do, so I'll see you later." I turn and begin to walk down the hallway towards my apartment.

"Tully?" she calls.

I turn back. "Yes."

"Do you want to be my best friend?" she asks hopefully.

"Erm." I pause for a moment. *What the hell?* "You want me to be your best friend?"

She nods eagerly. "I've never had one before. I ask everybody, but nobody wants me."

"Oh." She must have problems. She looks so hopeful, smiling goofily at me.

Empathy wins. "I already have a best friend. Her name is Callie, but you can be my friend too, if you want?" I shrug. "We can all be friends together."

Her eyes widen with excitement. "Really?"

I smile, feeling like I've done my good deed for the day. "Yes, really."

She nods as she pretends to play it cool. "Okay, I'll see you around."

I smile. "Okay." I turn away.

"I'll see you around because now we are in a gang together."

I hesitate for a moment as I crease my face up. "Not really a gang, though, is it?"

"More like a wolf pack?" she asks excitedly.

"Sure." Jesus, what the hell? "See you later then." I turn... again.

"Ah-wooooo!" she calls out.

I turn to see she has her head back and is howling like a wild dog.

"We could have a wolf call," she says. "For our wolf pack."

I stare at her.

"You know," she adds seriously. "In case someone gets into trouble, we have a wolf pack call."

What the hell have I gotten myself into here? Does she think this is *The Hangover* movie? "See you later, Meredith," I say.

She howls again in response.

Fuck me.

I rush to my door, quickly dart in, flick the lock, and lean on the closed door behind me.

What next?

At 7:00 p.m. there's a knock at the door. I get up to open it in a rush.

"I have pizza and beer ready and I am at your service." Callie smiles as she holds the pizza box in the air.

I hold my hand out for her and kiss her cheek as she walks past me. "Come in."

She throws the beer and pizza onto my coffee table, looking around with her hands on her hips. "Wow, Tull, the place looks amazing."

I smile as I look around my new apartment. "I love it here, Cal. It's closer to everything, and the apartment just feels so homey, you know?"

She walks to the kitchen and takes out some plates before she comes back to the living room and begins to serve us our pizza. "Sorry I couldn't talk today when you called. My boss is a huge asshole," she says as she hands my plate over to me. "I'm going to knock him out one of these days."

I giggle. "That's okay. I was just calling to have a meltdown, anyway. You dodged a bullet." I take a bite of my pizza and frown. "Hmm, so good."

"Tell me what happened. Gym junkie had a 'roid rage?" she says around a mouthful of pizza.

I nod as I chew. "Completely. Grabbed Rourke, threw him out of the chair, and totally lost his shit."

"What did he say?"

I crack open my Corona beer and take a sip. "He was

carrying on because I wouldn't answer his calls all week. I told him it was over, and then..." I shake my head in disgust.

"What?" She frowns, falling serious.

"I told him how he made me feel but now I feel kind of stupid about it."

"No, it's a good thing. He needed to know the truth," she assures me. "What did he say once you told him?"

Knock, knock, knock.

"Who's that?" I mutter.

"It might be him," Callie teases.

"I fucking hope not." I answer the door to see Meredith standing in the hallway.

"Hello," she says, as if annoyed.

"Hi."

"You didn't tell me we were meeting up tonight?" She walks past me into my apartment.

Callie frowns at me in question. "Oh my God," I mouth behind Meredith's back to Callie as she walks past me.

"Hi, wolfy," Meredith says to Callie.

Callie stares at Meredith, and then her eyes rise to me in question.

"Callie, this is Meredith."

Meredith smiles happily and shakes hands with Callie.

"Meredith asked me to be her best friend today," I say. *Get the hint, Callie.*

Callie's eyes flicker between the two of us as she clearly tries to work out the dynamics of what's going on.

"So, I told her we could all be best friends," I explain.

Callie fakes a smile. "You did? Fancy that." She sips her beer.

"Yes." I stare at Callie as I try to maintain a straight face. "And Meredith thinks we should make a wolf pack now."

Callie chokes on her beer. "Excuse me," she whispers through a raspy throat. "A wolf pack?"

I nod and, unable to help it, I giggle. Meredith bounces onto the sofa and smiles happily, crossing her legs in front of her.

If only I could read Callie's mind. I can't imagine what she's thinking, but I know it'd be fucking funny. I need to explain myself a little more.

"Meredith has never had a best friend," I continue.

Callie's face falls. "Oh, really?"

"And Meredith's mum pays her rent for her so she doesn't listen to her having intercourse anymore."

Callie's face falls farther, and I can see her connecting the dots. "Your mum listens to you having sex?" She frowns.

"No." Meredith shakes her head. "I listen to her having sex."

We both stare at her as the horrific thought rolls around in our heads.

"She's good at it, too, because her boyfriend moans loudly," Meredith adds.

Callie's eyes are the size of saucers as she tries to make sense of this weird person in front of us.

Manners eventually get the better of her. "Would you like a beer, Meredith?" she asks.

"No, thanks," Meredith says flatly. "I can't drink beer. It makes my vagina smell."

Callie's eyes widen in horror.

"Yeah, you know sometimes you just think, fuck, this pussy smells," Meredith says casually.

Callie stares at her, deadpan. "Can't say that I do."

I can't help it; I get the uncontrollable giggles. *Who the hell says this shit?*

Meredith looks to me. "It's not funny, Tully. It's a real hot mess down there. No beer for me. Ask my mum how bad it smells."

Callie's face pales, and I can see that she's getting a really bad visual in her head as she holds her pizza up, mid-air.

I burst out laughing.

Meredith folds her feet up in front of her and smiles broadly as she looks between us. "So, what do my friends want talk about?"

"Anything but your reaction to beer." Callie sighs as she sips her drink. "Or your mother sniffing it."

I'm still laughing. "I agree. Anything but that."

It's Friday afternoon. 2:00 p.m. to be precise, and I'm downstairs at the police station going through some evidence with one of the detectives, Martin. We're sitting at his desk, each with a coffee in hand. I like Martin. We have an easy friendship. He doesn't try too hard to be cool or funny, he's just who he is. I've had a good week, I'm settled into my new apartment, and I have plans for the weekend with Callie and Rourke. It's been seven days since I had my bathroom fling with Brock. I think I'm finally beginning to forgive myself a little.

I guess it's just one of those things. No matter how much I regret it, I can't go back and change anything so, as Callie says, why beat myself up about it?

Nobody else cares. Why should I?

He wore a condom, I told him how I felt after it, and he obviously got the message because he hasn't called me again since.

Whatever the reason, I feel better about it, anyway. Maybe that's just because I got a chance to say my piece to him.

"There's always a chance with the investigation that prior events will be brought up," Martin says.

"No, that won't do. I need to see someone about it now," I hear a familiar voice demand from the front reception desk.

I know that voice. What the...?

I turn and see Brock and his friend from the gym talking to the receptionist. Brock is asking to see someone.

Shit.

I turn in my seat so that my back is to the reception area, hoping he can't see me.

I stare at the computer screen in front of me as I eavesdrop on the conversation he's having with the police officer at reception.

"I want to know who was driving the police car with the number plate **NGH 167** last night," Brock states.

"I'm sorry, sir, we can't give that information out to the public."

"I'm not the public, I'm investigating a crime and have reason to believe that one of your officers may be involved."

My eyes widen as I listen in. Shit.

"That's completely out of line, and I can assure you that false accusations can and will get you prosecuted in a court of law. Now, please leave."

"Nope. I'm not going anywhere until I know who was driving that police car last night."

"Sir." The policeman sighs. "I don't even have access to that information."

"Who does?"

"The person who does isn't in again until Monday."

"Piss off." Brock sneers. "Do you really expect me to believe that you don't know who's driving the fucking cars around?"

I frown to myself, knowing that the officer is telling a

complete lie. The vehicle information is in the back room for all to see. Everyone has access to it.

"Do you feel comfortable about doing that?" Martin asks, interrupting my thoughts.

I glance over at him. Huh? I have absolutely no idea what he's talking about.

"It's in the printer now," he says.

I frown and glance over at the printer. What the hell is he talking about? Martin's phone rings. He answers it and nods. "Can you grab that from the printer for me, Tully, please?"

"Sure." I stand and try not to face the front reception. I walk over to grab the paper from the printer and stare at it for a moment. Hopefully Brock's gone by now.

I drop my head, walk back, and slink into the seat.

"Tully?" Brock's voice calls out.

I scrunch my eyes shut. Damn it. I turn and see Brock watching me. I offer him a smile. "Hi." Shit, I can't be rude, so I walk over to the counter.

Brock frowns, clearly confused. "You're a cop?"

"Erm." My eyes flicker to the policeman standing nearby us. "No, I'm forensics."

His face falls. "You're a scientist?"

I nod nervously. "Uh-huh."

He's wearing a white T-shirt, blue jeans, and damn it, he looks so handsome I could cry. He's the epitome of tall, dark, and handsome.

"You work here?" He points to the floor.

I nod, unable to stop myself from smiling at the shocked look on his face. I wonder what he thought I did for a living.

"Yeah, for a long time now. A couple of years, actually."

He and his friend exchange looks.

"I've got to get back to work." I smile at his friend. I think his name is Ben, if I remember correctly. "Nice to see you both," I say casually.

Brock frowns as he watches me. "Yeah. See you later."

I turn and go back to the desk Martin is sitting at. "I have to go upstairs. Can we finish this later?" I whisper.

"Sure thing."

I walk over to the elevator and push the button so that the doors close. I exhale heavily once they do.

What are the chances?

It's 6:00 p.m. when I walk out of work. I make my way over to cross the road, and I'm on the edge of the curb when I look up and I see him, my steps faltering.

Brock is standing under a tree, his right shoulder resting against the trunk.

I freeze on the spot and he gives me a lopsided smile before he comes towards me.

"Hi," he says lightly.

I twist my hands in front of me nervously. "Hi."

"You didn't tell me you were a science geek."

I smile awkwardly. "Trying to hide it." I grip the strap of my handbag with white knuckle force.

Brock smiles flatly and scratches his head. "Can I talk to you for a minute?"

My eyes hold his. "What about?"

He steps back onto his back foot as if frustrated. "Tully, I just want to talk to you for two minutes. Can we get a drink or something?"

"No." I glance over to the road. "I have to catch my bus."

"I can drive you home, if you want."

I swallow the lump in my throat. I don't want him to know where I live. "No, that's okay. Thanks, anyway."

He drops his head, defeated. "You're not going to get over this, are you?"

"Brock," I whisper.

"I'm sorry, okay, I didn't know."

I stare at him.

"I hate that I made you feel dirty," he says sadly.

I watch him, unsure of what to say.

"I can't stop thinking about it. It's fucking with my head."

I exhale heavily. "It wasn't you."

"It was, you said so yourself."

"No, Brock. I said I am disgusted with myself."

His eyes search mine.

"I don't blame you at all. I asked for it, begged for it, actually." I shrug. "I just don't like the way it made me feel after, that's all."

He picks up my hand and holds it in his. "You're the first girl I've dug in forever."

"But I know I'm not the first girl you've fucked in forever." I pull my hand from his grip.

He frowns.

"Brock, we're just wired differently." I smile sadly. "And that's okay. That's what makes you, you, and what makes me, me."

He stares at me as if trying to understand. "Why haven't you been back to the gym?"

"I cancelled my membership."

His face falls. "What? You hate me that much?"

"I don't hate you." I shake my head. "I just don't trust myself with you."

"Why not?"

"Because you are stupid hot."

He smiles, almost shyly. "You know..." He glances up, pausing and drawing in a breath before he finally decides to say whatever's on his mind. "That vanilla sex you think you need... it's never going to do it for you."

I raise my eyebrow. "You're giving me sex advice now?"

"Tully." He sighs and scowls slightly. "I know it's not going to happen for us now. I've fucked that up. I've been thinking about what you said, and you were right: we are wired too different."

"Why do *you* think we're so different?" I ask.

He shrugs. "I want to have fun, and you want to be serious and good."

I clench my jaw in annoyance. That's not true. I want fun, too.

"But I want to tell you something, and please, don't take it the wrong way."

For fuck's sake. What's he talking about now?

"I know women's bodies."

I roll my eyes in disgust. Isn't that the filthy truth.

"No, hear me out. You need to know... you're naturally submissive during sex."

My eyes meet his.

"Vanilla, passive sex will never do it for you." He shrugs. "It just won't."

"You don't know what you're talking about. I love normal sex, Brock, in a bed with someone I love."

"Maybe, but you also need to be taken and loved *hard*. You enjoyed it, Tully. I know you did. You came so hard you nearly snapped my dick off. Why don't you just admit the truth to yourself?" His eyes hold mine.

I smile sympathetically. He just doesn't get it. He never will.

"Is it all about the sex for you?" I sigh. "Is that really all that matters?"

"No." He frowns, reaching for my hand. "I'm just telling the truth."

"Your truth and my truth are two different things. We will never see eye to eye on this subject. We can only ever be friends and I'm okay with that." I pull away from him.

"I don't want you to hate me."

"I don't, this is about me, not you." I smirk. "You're way too hot to hate."

He gives me a slow, sexy smile.

"See you later." I turn and walk towards the bus stop.

"Tully Pocket!" he calls. "It was fun, hey?"

I turn and smile at him, walking backwards towards the bus top. "Have a nice life, Brock Marx." I blow him a kiss and he smiles, catching it and slapping it against his cheek.

I laugh and turn back away from him one last time, walking away with renewed vigour. It's a bittersweet moment in my life.

Mainly because it was the last time I saw Brock Marx.

CHAPTER 7

SIX WEEKS LATER

Tully

I LIE BACK and direct my face to the sun, feeling the warmth of the vitamin D sinking into my skin.

This is the life. I'm carefree and having the summer of my life.

"I need to get some laser," Callie grumbles to herself as she inspects her bikini line around the edges of her pink bikini. She glances over at me. "When are you due again? We should go together."

I frown as I think. "I just had it. I'm not going back for ages."

"I wish I had the money to get my vagina zapped by an electric current that would paralyse the hair follicles," Meredith says, her voice monotone as she lies on her towel next to me.

"You should get a job," Callie tells her, lying back on her towel and closing her eyes.

"I've been thinking about becoming a prostitute," Meredith says seriously.

"What? Why?" Callie frowns, horror etching her features.

"Well, duh." Meredith widens her eyes, calling Callie stupid without actually saying the words aloud. "You get paid to have sex with men."

I smile with my eyes closed. Somehow, and I honestly, really don't know how, Callie and I have adopted Meredith. Our twosome has now become a group of three. Meredith is actually kooky, funny, and gives us hours of entertainment.

We don't know her diagnosis, but we know she is somewhere on the spectrum. We have gotten used to her lack of brain-to-mouth filter, and underneath all of those highly inappropriate comments, there's a young woman who is just doing the best she can. She's a good person, and both Callie and I feel protective over her because we know how hard she has been done to over the years. We both feel that we are all Meredith has in her life now. There is a reason she met us.

Her mother is somewhere on the spectrum, too, which hasn't helped the situation. Meredith had no guidance at all on what is appropriate to say out loud to people.

The three of us are currently at Bondi Beach. It's 3:00 p.m. on a perfectly sunny Saturday. The beach is packed, and music is playing from the bar across the road.

"Are you a virgin, Meredith?" I ask, curious as to why she's always wanting so much sex.

"No," she answers casually.

Callie and I both sit up, resting on our elbows as we watch her. "Who did you have sex with?" I ask, surprised.

"Frank."

"Who's Frank?" Callie asks.

"He's the cleaner of our building."

My mouth falls open. "What the heck, Meredith?"

"But it's a secret."

"Why?"

"Because Frank has sort of got a girlfriend."

Callie and I look at each other, shocked. "So, you slept with him when you knew he had a sort-of girlfriend?"

"Yep. In the broom closet, in the basement."

"Meredith," Callie groans. "You can't sleep with someone when you know they have a girlfriend."

"But his girlfriend is Peachy Sue. She doesn't care."

I curl my nose up. "Peachy Sue? Who is Peachy Sue?"

"She lives on level one." Meredith smiles up at the sun, completely relaxed. "She sleeps with men for money."

Callie and I look at each other again, our eyes getting wider and wider. "A prostitute lives downstairs?" I dare myself to ask Meredith.

"Yeah, and they call her Peachy Sue because her vagina is as soft as a peach. Frank says it's juicy like a peach, too."

I fall back on the sand, exasperated. "So, Frank fucked you because his girlfriend fucks other men."

"That's right."

"Do you still fuck him?" Callie asks, fascinated.

"No." She lies still for a moment. "I used to, a lot, but I'm not doing that anymore."

"Why not?"

"Because he keeps ejaculating in my mouth and I don't like the taste of it."

A giggle bubbles up in my chest.

"I think I want to do what Peachy Sue does," Meredith says.

"Why?"

"Because I'm horny all the time."

"God, me, too." I sit up and dust the sand from my legs and I put my hair up into a bun on the top of my head. "That damn gym junkie has ruined me. What I wouldn't give to be..." My voice trails off. "I'm a sex-starved nympho." I look out over the people swimming in the water. "My phone vibrating in my pocket nearly gives me an orgasm these days."

"What's a nympho?" Meredith asks.

"Someone who wants to have sex a lot," I reply.

"Then I'm a sex-starved nympho, too," she says seriously.

"Why don't you just get a boyfriend, Meredith?" I ask.

She shrugs. "I don't know anyone who wants to be my boyfriend."

Callie looks at me quizzically, and I shrug back at her. We've been debating on whether or not to take her on a night out with us. We have no idea how she is going to handle social situations. The crazy thing is that you get used to her weirdness. It's actually endearing.

"Maybe you should come out clubbing with us sometime," Callie suggests casually.

Meredith's eyes widen. "Could I?"

I smile. "Of course you can." I think for a moment. "You can wear my clothes, and we will do your hair and stuff." Because God knows, we can't take her out in her own clothes.

"Will I find a boyfriend?" she asks.

I giggle. "Hopefully."

Callie sits up with renewed vigour. "Come on, girls, let's go. I've got an idea."

"What?" I frown up at her.

"We're going to the sex shop to buy some big, hardcore dildos." She stands and flicks out her towel. "I've had enough with this being horny business. Let's take this into our own hands... literally."

Meredith's eyes find mine. "What's a hardcore dildo?"

Callie smiles mischievously. "Come on and I'll show you."

One hour later

Meredith frowns as she studies the huge dildo circling around and vibrating in her hand. "Are you sure that's what you do with it?" she asks innocently.

"Oh, yes." Callie smirks. "Completely sure."

"You just stick it up there?" Meredith pushes it up in the air and frowns.

"Yes." I smile. This is hilarious. "But you have to use lube, too."

"Lube?"

"It's a cream that you put on your vagina to make you wet. It means it doesn't hurt and just slides right in."

Meredith is completely fascinated as she watches the huge black dildo swirling in her hands. "I wish I knew about this before we went to the beach."

"Why?" I ask.

"Because this would have been great to do on my towel."

I put my hands over my face and laugh.

"God's sake," Callie snaps as she snatches it out of Meredith's hands. "You don't take it everywhere with you. It's not a book." She looks at me in disgust. "It's for at home when you're in bed."

Meredith nods. "Okay. I get it." She thinks for a moment. "Or for the broom closet."

"Yes," Callie says. "Private times only."

We all get one and head to the counter where the cashier

rings up our purchases. “Do you need batteries?” the cashier asks.

Meredith glances at Callie and me in question.

“Yes, please,” Callie answers.

I look at the packets of batteries on the counter. Screw it, I don’t want to run out in the middle of something. I pick up four packets for myself, and I hand the other two a packet each.

Meredith reads the instructions on the vibrator’s packaging, frowning when she then looks down at my four packets of batteries. “If you’re going to masturbate for three whole weeks, you need to take time off work,” she tells me loudly.

“Shh.” I look around the shop. I snatch my paper bag from the cashier and nearly run out of the shop doors.

I hear Callie laughing behind me. Buying this shit is always appalling, but buying dildos with Meredith is horrifying.

It’s midnight and I’m alone in the quiet of my bedroom. It’s this time of night that my mind plays tricks on me. I begin to over-analyse and think about things I shouldn’t be thinking about. Reaching over, I take my vibrator and lubricant out of my drawer. I turn the light off and I get comfortable in my bed.

I don’t let myself think about him in the daylight hours, but at night, in circumstances like this, I have no choice.

Brock.

Beautiful Brock.

It’s ironic really, the man who made me feel dirty is the very same man that I fantasise about when I’m alone.

His words have repeated over and over in my head a thousand times in the last six weeks.

“I know women’s bodies... You’re naturally submissive...”

I can see his face so clearly when he said it. I really don’t think he was trying to upset me, but why did he have to plant those thoughts in my mind at all?

Was he warning me?

Was he giving me a message that he thought I needed to know?

"Vanilla, passive sex will never do it for you. It just won't."

I frown as I remember our conversation. I wish it hadn't happened. I really do, because it's planted a seed—an evil seed—that is growing and festering inside of me.

"You need to be taken and loved hard. You loved it, Tully? I know you did. You came so hard that you nearly snapped my dick off. Why don't you just admit the truth to yourself?"

Was he right? For ten minutes, I lie in the silence and ponder his words. I've thought about them a lot. I wish I hadn't been annoyed with him at the time for saying it. I could have asked him more questions. I could have got him to explain things to me.

Why did he feel the need to warn me about my own body? Am I that inexperienced that I don't even know what I need? It's all so confusing. I pick up the vibrator, put it under the blankets, and I open my legs.

I close my eyes and think of him.

My heart races, my legs quiver, and for just a moment, I let myself believe that he's here with me.

Brock

I fall to the mattress with Tara giggling as she lies down beside me, while Kylie falls from her hands and knees to be by my other side. My heart races out of control from the orgasm I've just had. With a girl under each arm, I close my sleepy eyes. I'm exhausted. We've been at it for hours. Our

legs are a tangled mess, each of us covered in a sheen of perspiration.

I always have fun here. These are two of the most beautiful girls I've ever met. They're wired like me. The three of us have been hooking up casually for months.

The last few times, though, something's been off.

Kylie kisses my chest and closes her eyes. Tara runs her hand through my hair and mumbles something sleepily right before she falls asleep, too.

I bite my bottom lip and stare up at the ceiling above me.

What?

What is it?

Why do I have this off feeling every time I have sex?

I've been getting around a bit—more than I normally do, actually.

One girl, two girls, twins... Hell, I even did three at once the other night.

It seems like I'm searching for the reason; trying to gain some kind of perspective as to why I'm feeling unhinged lately.

I used to go out, have fun, pick up on the way home, fuck hard, and then wake up feeling like a million dollars.

But not lately.

My mind goes to Tully at once, and her sharp words come back to the forefront of my mind.

You make me feel dirty.

I get a vision of her and my stomach tightens.

I wonder what she's doing right now?

Tara snuggles against my chest. It makes me frown. I don't want to be here.

I slowly peel the girls off of me, and I climb out of the

bed. Normally, I would stay the night and have more of both of them for breakfast before I leave in the morning.

I walk into the bathroom, flick the light on, and I stare at my reflection in the mirror. My hair is wild, my face flushed, and my cock's still semi-hard.

I just blew five times. I should be relaxed to a near comatosed state.

So, why aren't I?

You make me feel dirty.

Five words have never stung so much.

I scratch my head in frustration and go outside to the spa bath to retrieve my clothes. I get a vision of myself sitting on the side of the spa as the girls took turns sucking my cock.

Jesus.

I walk inside and pull my jeans up as I look at the two beautiful women asleep, naked on the bed.

What the fuck's going on with me?

I throw on my shirt and shoes, grab my keys, and quietly leave.

Once in my car, I pull out into the night, winding the window down to let the wind run through my hair.

There are no cars on the road at 3:00 a.m. but I don't want to go home just yet.

I drive to the beach, park my car, get out and walk down to the sand. I sit for a while with my hands over my knees, and then I finally lie back to rest on my elbows, just watching the waves roll in. The sea breeze blows across my face, and I run my hand through the sand as I stare into the night.

What is it?

What's wrong?

. . .

"Okay, so we have cross-checked all hotels where the name Chancellor has been used and there's only this one we can find," Ben says. "If he *was* seeing a man on the side, I'm not sure when he did it. His wife says he didn't go out at night or on weekends, and he never seemed to have a day off work. The only times we can see that he had the opportunity is where we caught him on the security tapes."

"What's your point?" I ask.

"Either one more of the girls in the footage is a transvestite or…" He pauses.

"Or what?" I frown.

"Or he was seeing someone at work and they were fucking in the bathroom."

I nod as I process the information. "Have you put the feelers out to see if anyone thinks he was that way inclined?"

Ben shakes his head. "Yeah, but we came up empty-handed. Not one person, suspects anything."

"Hmm." I look at the images of the girls as they arrive and leave his hotel room. "They don't look like trannies." I frown.

"You'd like to think that you would be able to tell, hey?" He smirks.

"Right?" I chuckle. "Fuck, imagine getting a chick home and she flops out a cock."

Ben laughs and pinches the bridge of his nose.

"Anyway, I've got to go down to the police station," Ben says. "I'll be back in half an hour."

I stand in my chair. "I'll come for a ride."

Ben smirks as he walks out the front door.

"What?" I eye him as I follow him.

"How come you always want to come for a ride to the police station now? You fucking hate that place."

I look at him, deadpan, and then get into the driver's seat

and start the car. "No reason," I mutter. "It gets me out of the office."

He smiles and throws me a cheeky wink.

We drive to the police station in silence. Eventually, I park the car and switch off the engine. "I'll wait here."

He frowns over at me. "You're not coming in?"

I run my pointer finger along the bottom of the steering wheel. "Nah."

"She might be there today."

My eyes rise to meet his. "Who might be there?"

Ben huffs out a laugh. "Don't give me your fucking bullshit, man. Who do you think you're talking to?"

I stare at him blankly. "What are you talking about?"

"The girl."

"What girl?"

He rolls his eyes. "Whatever. You're a fucking idiot." He gets out of the car.

I watch him walk across the parking lot and disappear into the police station. I take the opportunity to call Bridget, my sister. I know she's at Mum's with my other sister, Natasha.

"Hey." She sounds excited to hear from me.

"Hello, fat guts." I smirk.

"Brock."

"Yes, Bridget." I grin.

"You can say that shit when you're joking about it. Not when it's actually true."

I chuckle and stare through the windshield.

"I'm growing two humans inside of my stomach. The name *fat guts* is a damn compliment. My name should be fat everything."

"What are you guys doing?" I ask.

"Just about to go shopping. Can you sneak away and come with us?"

It is a quiet day and I don't have much on. "How long are you going to be?"

"Ages." She sighs. "Come and sit on the benches outside the shops with me... *please*?"

"Didge." I frown. "You know I hate shopping."

"We can have lunch. Come on, I haven't seen you alone in weeks, and soon, you won't be able to go anywhere with me."

"Why not?"

"Because I'm going to have two screaming kids in a pram."

I wince. This is true. I exhale heavily. "Yeah, okay, call me in two hours." I hang up.

Ben walks back to the car and jumps in, smiling over at me like the Cheshire Cat.

"What?"

He passes me a small piece of paper.

"What's this?" I ask.

Tully Scott

Ben raises his eyebrows and smirks. "I got a name."

I look over at him flatly. "Why?"

"Cause I'm the man." He hits the dashboard. "Drive," he commands.

I shake my head in disgust. "If I wanted to call her, I would have called her."

"Except for..." Ben points at me, "that small matter of her blocking your number, as well as her hating you and shit."

I fake a smile, screw up the piece of paper, and throw it into the backseat. "Keep your nose out of my business,

Statham. You're like a big fucking girl." I start the car and pull out into the traffic. "You want coffee or what?"

I sit on the bench outside of the clothing boutique, sipping my water.

Bridget is sitting next to me with her legs up on the chair. Tash and Mum are inside the shop with Natasha's bodyguards loitering around. It's funny how I don't really notice them much anymore. Her husband, Joshua Stanton, is loaded, and due to their history, Natasha has to have protection with her at all times.

I glance over at my sister. A question has been burning in my brain and I know she's the only one who can answer it truthfully. She's a good girl who fell in love with a man like me.

"Didge, when you first met Ben, how did you get together?"

She smiles softly, her face becoming nostalgic. "Well, the chemistry was instant. We really liked each other, that much was obvious."

I watch her as I listen.

"But of course, we couldn't do anything about it."

Ben was Natasha's husband's bodyguard, and the boss's sister-in-law was strictly forbidden.

"So, you snuck around?"

"Why are you suddenly so interested?"

I shrug. "I don't know. I just know you and Ben were very different so..." My voice trails off.

"We didn't sleep together for a long time. Months, probably."

"Months?" What the fuck?

"No, we were just friends at first. I think Ben was scared he was going to fuck it up. He would sneak me out and I would go over to his house. We would watch movies and just hang out, you know, talk and stuff."

I stare at her. "Talk?"

"Yeah."

"What on earth is there to talk about for months?"

She shrugs. "I don't know, but it's how I fell in love with him."

I smirk.

"What?"

"Talking to that dopy bastard made you fall in love with him? God, Bridget, don't tell anyone that story."

She giggles and nods. "Unbelievable, I know."

We sit in silence for a moment.

"Sometimes it's nice to make friends with someone first. It's how women, you know, become comfortable with a man who would normally..." Her voice trails off this time.

I stare across the park in front of us. "Normally what?"

"Normally just want to fuck me. If he had wanted that and only that, we would never have gotten together. It gave us time to, I don't know, transition to each other's lives and personalities. Really get to know each other."

I stare at her again, my mind a clusterfuck of emotions.

"But what happened if you were friends and then nothing else happened?"

She shrugs. "Then I had a really cool new friend, and that would have been okay, too. You can't just fuck random women forever, Brock." She smiles. "One of these days, you might actually meet a woman who you want be friends with."

"I highly doubt that." I smile.

She punches me in the arm. "It happens to the best of us, buddy."

It's 1:00 a.m., and I'm in my bed, staring at the ceiling.

My conversation with Bridget is weighing heavily on my mind. I *have* been feeling off lately, and maybe...

No, that can't be it.

Can it?

I know I'm not comfortable with the fact I made Tully feel dirty. In fact, it makes me sick to my stomach to think about it. I don't know why. It's not like she means anything to me.

I roll over and toss and turn for another two hours until I can't stand it any longer.

"Fuck's sake!" I snap in frustration.

I go downstairs to my garage wearing only my boxer shorts, and I scramble around in the backseat of my car. I feel across the upholstery on the floor, and then up over the seat. I get my phone and put the torch on, searching the entire backseat.

Damn it, it must have blown out of the window or something. It was a week ago when Ben gave it to me.

I exhale heavily and am just about to close the door when I see the scrunched-up piece of paper tucked inside the pocket of the door.

I smile, pick it up, and read the name:

Tully Scott

I take the stairs two at a time and open my laptop.

"Okay, Tully Scott. Who are you?"

CHAPTER 8

Tully

"Wow." I smile at Meredith, my eyes wide in disbelief. "Check you out."

She twirls proudly and puts her hands on her hips. "Pretty hot, huh?"

Callie giggles as she picks up her bag and keys. "You sure are. Let's get going."

Callie and I have spent the afternoon giving Meredith a makeover. We're just about to take her to her first club. She looks amazing, and not at all like the daggy girl we first met. She's wearing a tight black dress of Callie's, and her hair has been set into big Hollywood curls to compliment her smoky eyes and big red lips. Callie and I are very proud of our handy work.

"Selfie!"

We lean in together, and Callie takes a photo of us all. This is a big moment in Meredith's life and I can feel her excitement. We take the photo of the three of us laughing, and I smile as I stare down at it on my phone. Meredith looks so happy. We take the elevator, and when the doors open on the ground floor, a group of five girls are just coming out of an apartment. They catch my eye because every one of them is stunning. It's unusual to have so many gorgeous women together at once.

"Hi, Meredith." One of them smiles, and then, as they approach us, they all begin to circle Meredith as if she's some kind of exhibition.

"Damn girl," one says. "Look at you, being all hot."

Meredith smiles proudly "We're going clubbing. These are my new friends, Callie and Tully," she announces.

"Hello." They all smile.

Callie and I smile, and my heart flips a little. Meredith really does have a good heart. I hate that she's so misunderstood.

"Have fun," the girls call as they disappear out the front doors before hitting the street and climbing into a parked, black SUV.

"Who are they?" I ask Meredith.

"That was Peachy Sue and her friends."

"Oh." I watch their car disappear around the corner. "Her friends?"

"Yes. Her work friends. The ones who sleep with rich men."

Callie's eyes meet mine. "Wow, I'm impressed by how gorgeous they all are," I whisper. They're not at all what I imagined prostitutes to look like. "Who knew?"

"How do you know them again?" Callie asks.

"I have drinks with them sometimes while they get ready for work." She shrugs. "Well, I have drinks and they have blow."

"Blow?" I ask.

"Cocaine," Callie mutters as she quickly reapplies her lipstick.

"Oh." I frown. "But, didn't you say you slept with Peachy Sue's boyfriend? I'm confused."

"No, he wants to be her boyfriend, but she doesn't like him. That's why he didn't want her to find out about us so that it wouldn't ruin his chances."

I cringe in disgust. "This guy sounds like a real sleazebag, Meredith. Stay away from him."

She nods. "That's what Peachy Sue said." She thinks for a moment. "Her and Wendy Woo said I was too good for him."

"Who's Wendy Woo?"

"The girl with the dark hair who was with them."

"The Asian girl?"

"She's Thai," she tells me.

"She was gorgeous," I say as I turn and watch their car disappear into the distance.

"She has a dick. It's big. She fucks rich, married men up the ass."

Callie's and my eyes widen. "Really?" I whisper. "She's a lady boy?"

"Yeah. Rich, straight men like to be fucked by a man who looks like a woman. She makes the most money out of all of the girls." Meredith shrugs. "Creepy, huh?" She fakes a shiver. "It gives me the heebie jeebies."

"God," I mutter as our cab pulls up.

"Where to?" The cab driver asks over his shoulder.

"The Ivy."

Meredith bites her bottom lip and giggles like a little kid. Callie holds her hand out to me and I slap it. Seeing Meredith this excited has already made the night for both of us. Anything else from this moment is a bonus.

. . .

The club is packed to the rafters. There are beautiful people everywhere, and we're drinking cocktails in the bar. I'm wearing my white trousers with a white, strapless top, gold, strappy stilettos, and a matching clutch. My long, strawberry hair is down and pinned back on one side. I have my favourite gold Grecian makeup on. I always feel good when I wear this outfit. I get a lot of compliments. The white seems to compliment my olive skin.

"Can you believe how much fun she's having?" Callie asks as she watches Meredith. I look over and smile. Meredith is dancing and laughing with a group of guys and girls, looking like she really is having the best time of her life. "She's danced with just about everyone in this place." I shake my head. "I honestly didn't know how she would handle this, but she's in her element."

"I know. Let's get another drink." We put our empty glasses down, make our way to the bar in the next room, and stand in line.

"I'm a bit hungry, actually," I say as I look around. "How did we forget to eat?"

"I don't know," Callie mutters. "I'm starving, too."

A piece of ice hits me in the chest, and I look around in confusion. Who the hell is throwing ice?

I push my fingers through my hair, which now has ice in it. That's annoying.

"Do you girls come here often?" a unknown voice asks from behind us. We turn to see a cute but young guy. He could only just be eighteen if he's lucky.

"We do. You?" Callie asks.

Another piece of ice hits me, and I look around again. Who the hell keeps doing that?

"I'm Tom," the boy answers.

"Hi, Tom," I say, distracted as I look around.

Another piece of ice hits me. "Who the heck is doing that?" I search all around the club, craning my neck to look everywhere I can.

The young boy behind us sees someone he knows, and he begins to talk to them, leaving us to turn back and face forwards again.

Then, across the crowded room, our eyes meet, and he gives me that slow, sexy smile of his.

My stomach flips and, unable to help it, I smile goofily.

Brock is standing against the wall with three other men beside him.

Holy fuck.

He curls his finger and wiggles it, signalling for me to go to him. I shake my head and smile shyly. Oh my God.

I point to my feet. "You come here," I mouth.

He instantly pushes off the wall and my heart races. Shit. Within a second, he's standing next to me. "Well, if it isn't my favourite nerd." He looks me up and down slowly. "Looking all... angelic."

I try to bite back my ridiculous smile. "Well, if it isn't my favourite crazy person."

He chuckles and leans forward to kiss me on the cheek. "Hello, Tully Pocket," he breathes down at me. He's so tall, towering above everyone around him. Tonight, he's wearing a maroon T-shirt with black jeans. His dark hair and broad shoulders make me weak at the knees.

Why the hell is he so damn gorgeous?

Over the last six weeks I've wondered if my mind had somehow exaggerated his gorgeousness, but nope; I can confirm that he is, in fact, the perfect specimen.

"Hi." My eyes linger on his beautiful face before they flicker to Callie. I quickly remember my manners. "Callie, this is Brock. You remember him, don't you?"

Callie smiles broadly, rising up on her toes and bouncing in excitement. "I do. Hello."

He smiles that sexy smile again, and I know that he knows, that Callie knows. Oh jeez, why does everybody know?

"It's been a while," he says smoothly.

I nod, an intelligent reply escaping me. Not as long as you may think. Unbeknown to you, in my mind you make a nightly visit to my bedroom. Oh, man, I'm such a loser. He probably hasn't thought of me again since we last walked away from each other.

Callie drifts away to the front of the line to order our drinks.

"It has been a while," I push out. "How have you been?"

His sexy eyes hold mine, and I feel the heat in his gaze. "Good, you?"

I nod stupidly again. Woman, get a hold of yourself. "Terrorise any more girls at the gym lately?"

His face falls.

"I didn't mean terrorise like *that,*" I correct myself quickly.

Oh, just shut the fuck up, right now.

"What did you mean then?" he asks, unimpressed.

"I meant… you know," I ramble nervously. "I meant, call someone fifty times until you get blocked, and then tear their friend from their chair at lunch?" I blurt out.

"In that case, no." He licks his lips slowly. "I save my special crazy just for you."

I smile goofily. "That's good then," I whisper.

He raises a brow. "Is it?"

I bite my bottom lip as our eyes lock. Jesus. I probably shouldn't drink anymore.

His eyes drop slowly down to my feet and back up to my face. "You look gorgeous."

"Thanks." I smile nervously.

The three men he was standing with approach us, and Brock smiles their way. "Tully, this is Jesten, Mason, and Scott."

"Hello." The three men all shake my hand and smile back at me. Every one of them is buff and gorgeous. I swallow nervously. There are four gods in the world, and they are all in the same place at the same time, here with me.

Callie turns around with our two drinks, and her eyes instantly widen when she sees who I'm standing with.

"Callie, these are my friends, Jesten, Mason, and Scott," Brock introduces.

"Hey, Callie." They smile.

Callie hands me my drink and gives me a look that definitely says *holy fucking shit, Tull.* I take my drink, thank her, and take a sip.

"Margarita?" Brock asks.

I nod.

He chuckles. "You would get along with my sisters well."

"Why?"

"They have a slight margarita addiction going on."

"Me, too." I smile nervously.

One of his friends goes to the bar.

"So, what have you been doing?" he asks, making conversation.

Fantasising about you. "Nothing really." I shrug. "Working, keeping busy. What about you?"

"Same. Working, nothing much." His eyes linger on mine, and it feels like he has something he wants to say. We fall into an awkward silence, and I glance around the club for something to do. Callie is now deep in conversation with Brock's friend.

God, this is uncomfortable.

I sip my drink, remaining silent.

"I just wanted to..." His voice trails off.

I frown and wait for him to carry on, but he doesn't. "You wanted to what?"

"I just want you to know that I regret being so..."

I wait.

He shrugs, his words failing him.

"Crazy?" I whisper.

He bites his bottom lip to stifle his smile and nods once.

I smile back.

His eyes rise to meet mine. "I know you don't like crazy."

My heart is beating so fast. "I sort of do, but maybe just a little less crazy would have been a good idea."

"Perhaps."

"Are you always so crazy with your girlfriends?" He blinks. "Oh, I didn't mean that I think I was your girlfriend." I put my hand on my chest. Why did I just say that? "That's not what I meant." I widen my eyes. "That came out all wrong."

He breaks into a beautiful smile. "I know what you meant, and no, I haven't done that before."

For some stupid reason, I want to know what he hasn't done before. The sex or the stalking? "What do you mean, you haven't done *that*?"

He shrugs, and just for a moment his macho mask slips and he seems embarrassed. "Called someone a hundred times and become jealous to the point of insanity."

"Then why with me?"

"If I knew why, I wouldn't be talking to you right now. It's been on my mind for six weeks."

The air between us crackles. "You know, you are quite likeable when you act sane, Brock Marx."

He smiles mischievously. "Yeah?"

"Yeah." I sip my drink.

"Likeable enough for you to forget how we met?" he asks.

"Maybe."

He clinks his beer bottle against my glass. "Let's start again. Truce?"

I can't help but grin. "Truce."

He holds his hand out to shake mine, and I frown, confused when I let him take my hand in his.

"Hello," he says, as if he's never met me before.

I smirk. Why does he have to be so cute? "Hello."

"What's your name?"

"Tully." I giggle. "What's your name?"

"Oh, I'm Brock."

"Nice to meet you, Brock."

He bows. "The pleasure is all mine, Tully Pocket."

Our eyes are locked and electricity is sparking between us.

His friend comes back from the bar with a huge tray of shots, and he passes us all two each.

"What the hell?" I whisper, mortified, and his friends all laugh right on cue.

Brock sinks two of the shots from the tray instantly, his eyes coming back to me.

"I'm going to regret this," I warn them all.

"Some things are worth regretting." His eyes hold mine and he gives me the best *come fuck me* look I've ever seen.

I know what he's talking about, and it isn't these stupid shots.

"I have no doubt," I whisper. I pick up the first shot glass and he moves closer. He puts his hand on my hip bone as he stands over me. Oh jeez, what is it about this guy?

There it is. The power that his body has over mine. I swear, his touch, his presence, it's unlike anything I've ever encountered.

I'm completely powerless to it. The moment he touches me, all I want to do is please him. Our eyes lock, and I hold the shot glass as I consider backing out of this drinking challenge. "Do it," he mouths.

I tip my head back and feel the heat of the Tequila slide down my throat.

I lick my lips as I stare at him, and I am instantly taken back to the night in the bathroom when he was daring me to take his body. This man is the peer pressure king.

"Again," he mouths.

I lick my lips, and he squeezes my hipbone with his fingers. I tip my head back and drink it again.

"Good girl," he whispers in my ear.

I close my eyes as the heat rolls down my throat. I'm dizzy, and it's not because of the drinks. It's because of his electric touch.

What I would give to have a do over with him? In a bed, alone, with no interruptions. I mean, it wouldn't *technically* be any worse than what I've already done, because it's the same guy. Would it?

I go over the scenario in my head to try and justify it to myself.

Callie and Brock's friends seem to hit it off instantly. After a few moments, they move to the dance floor to dance.

Brock's hand slides down to my behind, and he leans down to whisper in my ear. "I have a confession to make."

"What?" I whisper as I concentrate on not reaching up and putting my arms around his neck. How is it that I feel instantly connected to this guy? We don't even know each other, but somehow, I feel like I do.

"I came here tonight looking for you."

I smile, pressed against his face as excitement runs through me. "You did?"

He nods, and his hand squeezes my behind.

"What are you going to do now that you've found me?" I stare up at his lips.

"Show you a few things."

I smile darkly. God, I like the sound of that. "Like what?" I breathe. I get a vision of him flashing himself to me and I can't help but grin. "Are you going to flash me?"

He chuckles in surprise. "Possibly." His hand squeezes my behind again and I feel my arousal start to thump. "Although I must admit, I'm a bit wary of where to start."

I look up at him.

"I don't want to scare you off. You do seem to have impossibly high expectations."

"Maybe you should try being a gentleman," I whisper in his ear.

He grabs me aggressively on the behind. "I'm no gentleman, Tully."

My heart hammers as I stare into the depths of his eyes.

This is it, the moment where I have to set him straight. If I put up with him saying he will never be a gentleman, then I can't complain when he isn't one.

"You'll need to learn how to be a gentleman with me, Brock, because I'm not a slut. And I'm most definitely not easy."

Our eyes are locked and he clenches his jaw. It's as if there is nobody else in the club, just us. "What are you saying?" he whispers, and I feel his warm breath dust my ear.

"I'm saying that I would like you to dance with me."

"I don't dance."

"Learn."

"I don't learn things that don't interest me."

My eyes search his, and I lift my chin in annoyance. "Okay, there's my answer." I try to walk away, but he grabs my hand.

"What are you doing?" he asks.

"I'm going to dance, and for the record, if you don't want to learn things that interest me than I have no interest in learning yours."

"I'm not ready to dance yet."

"I am." I turn and walk to the dance floor just as a song comes on that I love. I meet Callie and Brock's friends and I begin to dance with them.

I glance over to see Brock standing where I left him with an annoyed look on his face.

Oh well, tough shit. I asked him to dance and he knocked me back.

He doesn't dance... pftt. So, does he think I should stand next to him like a little puppet all night?

For the next two hours, I drink way too many cocktails and shots, and I dance with Callie, as well as a few different people. I bounce between Meredith and her new friends, Brock's friends and Callie, and I have no intention of going back to talk to Brock who is standing in the exact same place near the bar. Every time I look his way, there's a different girl trying to pick him up.

Ugh. It really is annoying that he is so good looking.

"Isn't this the best time ever?" Meredith cries as she bounces up to me. We've hardly seen her all night.

"It is. Who is that guy you're talking to?" I ask.

"He used to live in our building. He moved out a year ago. His name is Rick."

I feel large hands slink around my waist from behind, and I

turn to see Brock standing there.

"Hello," I say, slightly taken aback. He's been glaring at me all night.

He nods, distracted. "Hey."

"This is Meredith," I introduce them. "This is Brock."

"Hello." She smiles over my shoulder at him.

"We're going," he says.

My face falls. "Oh, okay, I'll see you later then."

"No. I mean, you and I are going. Together"

I stare at him, stunned. "But, I'm not ready to go yet."

"Tough shit. I am."

I raise my brows in question. "Excuse me?"

"I said, we're going."

My anger begins to simmer. "And I said I'm not."

"Don't be a fucking pain in my ass. We're leaving."

"What?" I snap.

"I'm not standing here watching you dance with every fucker in the club for one second longer."

My mouth drops open and my eyes flicker to Meredith. She's watching Brock intently.

"Do you want to take her home to have sex?" she asks innocently.

"That's not happening," I hit back.

Brock narrows his eyes at me, and a guy walks past towards the dance floor. "Hey, do you want to dance with me?" I ask the stranger.

He smiles as if he's won the jackpot. "Sure."

Brock grabs my hand. "What the fuck are you doing?" he growls.

"Dancing." I fake a smile. "Remember, that thing you have no interest in learning."

"Don't you dare dance with him."

I smirk and tilt my head.

"I fucking mean it, Tully. Don't fucking push me."

"Goodbye, Brock. Go fuck one of your girls who you don't have to put any effort into."

He glares at me.

"I don't need a man," I tell him confidently.

"That's right," Meredith interrupts. "She has a huge vibrator."

"What?" he growls as his eyes blaze. "You think a fucking vibrator can replace me?"

"I do, actually, because unlike you, my vibrator isn't an entitled ass who thinks that he's God's gift to women. He does his job and keeps his mouth shut."

"Get in the fucking car before I drag you outside."

"Go fuck yourself." I turn and walk to the dance floor. I'm so angry, I feel like I can hear my thudding heartbeat in my ears. Who the hell does he think he is?

That man is a complete asshole.

The cab pulls up at my house at 4:00 a.m., and I stumble out onto the road.

Meredith and Callie went onto another club with everyone else, but honestly, I just couldn't. I'm so tired. I pay the driver and stumble up the pathway, stepping back when I see Brock leaning against a tree.

It's dark, I'm alone, and he's glaring at me.

"Took your fucking time," he growls. "Where have you been?"

CHAPTER 9

Tully

"DANCING," I reply flatly.

The sensible girl inside of me should be outraged that he's here. However, the masochist in me is thrilled.

Good girl versus bad girl. There's a whole lot of wrong in that sentence.

It should be no contest.

"How do you know where I live?" I ask as I open the foyer door with my key.

"I'm a private investigator. I know a lot of things about you."

"Ha," I huff as I push the door open. "You must be crap at your job then otherwise you'd know I like to dance."

He fakes a smile. "Witty."

Should I ask him in? He's not drunk or anything, and he is a private investigator. I guess he must be trustworthy. I hold the door open. "Are you coming?"

His eyes hold mine for a moment, as if he's surprised that

I've actually invited him in so easily. The truth is, I do want to talk to him, but I'm not doing it outside in the cold.

I get into the elevator and he stands beside me silently. His large frame overtakes the space, the power radiating from his body.

God, this is unbelievable. What the heck am I doing right now? Three hours ago, I swore to loathe him for all of eternity. How does this work? He's a hot guy who I've been fantasising about for weeks. He goes caveman, loses his shit at me, leaves the club, and then he turns up at my house at 4am... and I just go right ahead and invite him in like he's an old family friend.

You idiot.

I bite the inside of my cheek to stop myself from smiling as I stare at the floor.

The doors open and I walk out like a woman on a mission, and a woman who knows exactly what she's doing and why she's doing it.

To be honest, I have no frigging idea what I'm doing, but the fake-it-til-you-make-it strategy seems like a good starting point. I open my apartment door and walk inside in a rush, throwing my keys onto the sideboard and flicking my shoes off without grace.

"Oh, man," I sigh. "What a relief. Those shoes are the devil."

Brock puts his hands on his hips angrily, and my eyes rise up to him and his hostile stance. It makes me smile. He is such an open book. He has absolutely no control over his emotions. If he thinks it, he says it, and damn the consequences. To be honest, it's an admirable quality that he holds, and I wish I could do it more often. I guard most of my thoughts and would never say them out loud.

The funny thing is, even with all of this hostility, he doesn't scare me one bit. I bet he's a big pussycat under all this alpha-hole wrapping.

"What's that look for?" I ask.

"You piss me off."

"Me?" I point to my chest. "What did I do?"

"You danced with every other bastard in that club and completely ignored me."

"And?"

"And, I didn't fucking like it."

I smile. "Is that so?"

His anger is escalating at my lack of interest in fighting with him. "Yes. That's so."

I shrug and walk into the kitchen and pour myself a glass of water. "Do you want one?"

He follows me in, frowning at me like I'm stupid. "No, I don't want one."

I drink the whole large glass of water as he watches. Then I fill my glass again and repeat the process. I hear him sigh when I go to fill my third glass.

"Oh, come on. You can't be that fucking thirsty."

I smirk and walk back into my bedroom. He follows me.

"I'm not going to stand around for hours while you dance with other people, you know," he says with petulance in his tone.

I take my pyjamas out of my drawer, and close it with a slam. "Okay."

"What does okay mean?"

"It means okay, don't stand around. Go home. No skin off my nose."

He narrows his eyes at me and I can see his fury bubbling just beneath the surface. "It's like that is it? You just don't give a fuck?"

I walk into the bathroom and he follows me there, too.

"You don't even give a fuck if I leave right now?" he asks angrily.

I shrug. "You're a big boy. You do you."

"Stop being a fucking smartass, Pocket," he growls.

My eyes snap to him and I shake my head. "No. You don't get to call me that tonight."

He tilts his chin to the ceiling. "And why not?"

"Because, Pocket is your pet name for me, and when you're acting like this and pissing me off, you don't have a right to make me sound so familiar."

"So, you *are* pissed off with me?"

He seems to like the idea that I'm pissed with him. God, he really does want a good fight. Well, he's not getting one from me.

Is fighting the way he communicates? Hmm. Interesting.

"I never said I wasn't angry with you." I squeeze my toothpaste onto my toothbrush and begin to brush my teeth.

"Stop brushing your fucking teeth. I'm in the middle of talking to you."

I spit my toothpaste in the sink, and I have to stop myself from smiling at his impatience. "Yes. You pissed me off, and maybe next time—if there is a next time— you will dance with me when I ask you to before you lose the chance altogether."

Our eyes meet in the mirror. "Is that a threat?"

"That's a promise." I smile sweetly.

"You think you can actually make me dance with you by threatening me?"

"Do you think you can actually stop me dancing with an ill-timed tantrum?"

"You were dancing with other men. I had every right to get annoyed."

I screw up my face and spit the water back into the sink before rinsing and putting my toothbrush away. "Shut up, Brock." I shake my head as I walk back into my bathroom. "We're not together, and it's too late for this shit. I'm going to bed."

He stands and watches me for a moment, clearly confused.

"Turn around," I tell him.

"What for?"

"Because I'm putting my pyjamas on." I huff.

"I've seen you naked."

"Not when you're in time out, you haven't."

His face falls for just a second until a small smirk creeps into place. "You're putting me in time out?"

I nod. "Uh-huh. Turn around."

He turns his back to me, and I smile and throw my pyjamas over my head.

"For the record," he says with his back to me. "I decide who is in time out around here."

"No, you don't. I'm the boss of us," I reply calmly.

"What?" His head snaps around, and he looks over his shoulder.

"Turn around."

"You are not the fucking boss of us, Tully. I'm the boss of us."

"Nope." I go to the linen press and take out two blankets. "You are the boss when it comes to the sex between us. You're the..." I narrow my eyes as I think of the right terminology. "You're the operations manager. Physical contact is the operations."

He screws up his face. "And what the hell are you?"

"I'm the general manager." I smile sweetly. "So, basically, I'm the boss around here, and if you don't like it, I don't care."

I shove the two blankets into his hands.

"What's this?" He frowns as he looks down at them in his hands.

"Your blankets. You're on the sofa."

"What?" He's outraged that I would even suggest such a thing. "I'm not sleeping on the fucking lounge."

"Okay. Don't. Go home."

He glares at me.

My eyes hold his. "Sleep on the sofa, take your time out like an adult, and tomorrow morning you can take me out for breakfast where, just maybe, we can have a civilised conversation without arguing."

He narrows his eyes. "I'm not sleeping on the fucking lounge, Tully."

"Okay." I smile. It really is fun being a bitch to him. This could be my new hobby. "I'm going to bed. Lock up when you leave."

"What?" He laughs without humour. "You're not fucking going to bed."

I climb into bed and turn the light off.

"As the operation's manager, I have not signed you off your shift yet. You still have work to do. Hours and hours of hard labour."

I smile into my pillow at him playing along with me.

"You don't have any managerial powers today. Time out overrules any operation management. Get on the sofa."

"You're fucking unbelievable, "he mutters under his breath as he walks back into the living room.

I smile into my pillow again.

"Never once, in my entire life, have I been told to sleep on the lounge," he mutters in disgust. I can hear him pacing back and forth as he decides what to do. "I'm going home."

"That's a pity," I call. "I'll miss you at breakfast. I wanted to go to the beach, too."

"The carrot your dangling isn't that tempting. I can get eggs and sunshine anywhere," he calls, but I can tell he's spreading out the blankets on the lounge.

"Okay." I smile. "I might need my sunscreen rubbed in, that's all, but it's okay. I'll get someone else to do it."

"Fuck, Tully!" he snaps. "I swear to God, you are pissing me off big time. Stop threatening me."

I giggle into my pillow. B*ig dope.*

"Good night, Captain Cranky Pants," I call.

There's silence for a while. I hear the lock on the front door click and then the creak of the lounge as he lies down. I smile again. *Did I just win that fight?*

"Goodnight, wench," he finally tuts.

I giggle and pull my blankets up to snuggle in.

I hear him groan. "This lounge is harder than the fucking floor."

"Sleep on the floor then," I call back. "I'm glad it will be softer for you." I giggle as I imagine him on the cold, hard floor. "I like how you're thinking outside the box with your problem solving." I put my hand over my mouth to stop myself from laughing out loud. "Keep this up and you might be in for a promotion."

"Fuck off," he mutters into his pillow, and I hear him punch it three times.

I smile broadly and close my eyes.

Disciplining Brock Marx could be fun.

I wake to the sunshine streaming through my bedroom windows. I must have forgotten to close my drapes last night. I inhale deeply, roll over, and I begin to doze back off.

Hang on. My eyes snap open. Is Brock here?

I sit up in a rush and listen. I can't hear anything.

I quietly climb out of bed and sneak into the living room. My eyes widen at the sight in front of me.

Holy mother of fuck.

Brock is lying on his back wearing only his little black boxer briefs. His blankets are thrown on the floor along with his clothes. One hand is up behind his head, the other down his pants as he holds his dick. His legs are spread wide and he is sleeping like a baby. My eyes roam over the perfect specimen. What the hell? I didn't know men who looked like this actually existed.

He's huge, buff, and looks like some kind of stripper that you would pay anything to see. His stomach is a mass of ripples, and he has a scattering of dark hair on his chest as well as a small trail that runs from his navel, disappearing into his briefs. His dark eyelashes flutter, and his big pouty lips make me want to bend down and kiss them.

I watch him for a moment, how do I handle this?

The horn bag in me wants to straddle him and ride him 'til dusk. The prude in me wants to sit down and talk sensibly with him about his appalling behaviour.

The bitch in me wants to fight him.

But it's all of me who wants to spend time with him today. Like a puzzle I need to complete, I just want to know what makes him tick.

As I watch him, my mind goes to Simon. I frown to myself, wondering what he's doing now and who he's doing it with.

I used to always think we were soul mates, but maybe we were just young and naïve. It makes me sad to think that we may have lost what we had. He's due back in a couple of months, and the last time I spoke to him he said he was moving in with me. To be honest, I don't even know what I want anymore. I don't think he does, either. But we have to try; we said we would.

Is it fair to Brock to start something when I know it already has an expiry date?

His dark hair hangs over his face, and he licks his lips and strokes his dick in his sleep. I smile. Brock is not the kind of guy that I would ever end up with, anyway, and he'll probably be on his bike searching for his next plaything before the week is out. I'm worrying for nothing.

Why do I always have to overthink everything? Just take it for what it is: a bit of fun.

A bit of fun with a really hot guy who is the polar opposite of Simon.

I would be an idiot not to have some fun with him while I still can.

I go to the bathroom and use the toilet, contemplating the choices in front of me. I can either:

1. Ask Brock to leave and regret it for all of eternity.
2. Fuck his brains out and feel like a dirty slut again.
3. Spend some time with him, lay out a few ground rules, and see how he handles it.

He may not want to take the time to get to know me, but I suppose all I can do is ask.

I wash my hands and brush my teeth.

If I fuck him, he *will* leave, and I will probably never see him again.

But isn't that what you want?

If I ask him to leave before I fuck him, I will be kicking

myself tonight. And he was right, my vibrator could never replace what he could give me.

I really only have one choice. Spend the day with him, set out some ground rules, and perhaps build a friendship so that we can have a week of casual sex without me feeling like a wayward nun.

Then we part our ways as friends. Voila! Problem solved.

I get my bad boy fix, and then I go back to Simon and live happily ever after. I smile at my reflection in the mirror as I fix my hair.

Girl, you're a genius.

I walk out into the living room to see Brock stirring. He stretches as he opens his eyes and sees me, his smile slow and lazy. "Good morning, Pocket." His voice is husky and sexy.

Damn. Maybe we could skip the getting to know each other part and get straight down to business.

No! Play it cool.

"Good morning." I smile.

He sits up, resting on his elbows, and my eyes drift to his bare chest and strong shoulders. His olive skin has a golden tan to it.

"Sleep well?" I ask.

He frowns and lies back down. "No."

I smile. "I slept like a baby."

"I bet you did," he mutters dryly. I sit down on the bottom of his lounge, and he lifts his legs to put them onto my lap.

"Where are you taking me for breakfast, Tully Pocket?" He yawns.

I rest my hands on his bare feet. "I know just the place."

"Or we could just skip breakfast and go straight to the sunscreen part." He raises his eyebrow in question.

I giggle. "You would like that, wouldn't you?"

"I would, actually."

"Nope. I'm going to take a shower, and then I'll take you to my favourite café. The coffee is so good."

He rolls his eyes, draping his forearm over his eyes. "Is this like a date?" he mutters flatly.

"Yes, so I expect you to be witty and charming," I tell him as I stand. "Maybe even romantic."

"It's too early for that shit. And I don't do romantic. You're barking up the wrong tree."

"I don't bark. I'm going to have a shower now." I make my way to the linen press to grab a towel. "You are not welcome to come in."

"I can't, anyway. My back is fucked. I'll be lucky to walk again today."

I giggle, make my way into the bathroom, and step into the shower. My eyes stay trained on the door. I don't have a lock. What would I do if he walked in right now? Would he? I wouldn't put it past him.

Stop it.

I quickly wash myself and get out in a rush. After drying myself, I walk into my bedroom in a towel to find him lying in the same position with his eyes closed. Poor bastard. He really did sleep poorly. He's exhausted.

Now, what should I wear?

I put on my black crochet bikini. Lucky for me, I bought this baby as a *just in case I need to be sexy* incident. I throw on a short summer dress that's flowy and white, pulling it over the top of my bikini. I pull my long hair into a high ponytail. When I finally walk out of my room, Brock is gone, and I walk up the hall to investigate.

He's urinating, the bathroom door is wide open. He looks up casually.

I gasp. "Close the door will you."

"Why? It's just pissing. Everyone pisses."

"You're an animal," I say with a shake of my head as I turn and walk back into the living room.

Simon never went to the bathroom in front of me in nine years. These two men are like chalk and cheese.

"You can come in and hold it for me if you want?" Brock calls out.

"No. I'm good thanks." I smirk.

Idiot.

I hear the tap turn on as he washes his hands, and then he reappears, wearing only his black briefs. I have to concentrate not to stare.

"We have to call in at my place to get some clothes," he says as he rubs his eyes.

He really is a beautiful looking man.

"Okay."

I sit on the sofa and watch as he grabs his jeans and steps into them. He slowly slides the zipper up. It's hard not to jump up and drag his jeans back off with my teeth.

He then throws his T-shirt over his head, picks up the blankets, and carefully places the cushions back onto the sofa.

"I wish I could say I had a hard night in a good way," he says dryly.

I smirk.

"But I had a hard night in the worst possible way." He pretends to kick my sofa. "You piece of shit," he says to it.

I laugh.

"You ready?" he asks.

I throw my towel and sunscreen into my beach bag. "Yep. I'll just grab my book."

"You won't be needing that. I'm very entertaining. Let's go."

We walk out into the hall and he takes my hand in his. I look up at him in question.

"I did my time out." He eyes me as he strides forward confidently.

I smile and squeeze his hand in mine. "Like a good boy."

"Don't push it." He squeezes my hand back. "Or I'll show you how good of a boy I'm actually not."

We get downstairs and walk out across the road. "Where's your car?" I ask.

"Around the corner."

We turn the corner and I see his large black Range Rover. Lights flash as he opens it.

"Nice car." I smile as I get in.

"Yeah, it's just a car." He starts the engine. "Where are we going for breakfast?"

"There's a little café a few blocks from here. Where is your house?" I ask.

"Surry Hills."

"Oh, that's close. Just a few blocks away."

"Yeah, I know. I moved here when I found out where you lived so I could watch you round the clock."

I frown at him, and he smiles cheekily, flashing me a wink.

"See, the creepy thing is, I have no idea if you are joking or not."

He picks up my hand and kisses the back of it. "I've lived here for two years."

"Oh." I feel embarrassed that I just said that out loud.

He casually puts my hand back down to rest on his thigh. I can feel his tight thigh muscle through his jeans, and my arousal awakens. I blow out a breath as I concentrate on not trailing my hand up to his crotch and back over his heavenly, thick thighs.

Cut it out, you sex-craved animal.

We drive for a few minutes and then pull up out the front of a row of swanky terrace houses. "You live here?" I ask.

"Uh-huh." He parks the car and gets out.

I frown as I stare at the terrace house in front of me. It's painted a dark charcoal colour with contrasting white shutters. There's a beautifully kept garden with brass numbers on the gate, 39.

It looks like something out of a home magazine. It's not where I would expect a bad tempered stripper to live.

Wow. I didn't expect this.

He opens the large, timber door, and my mouth drops open. Holy shit, it's gorgeous. "This is really your house?" I whisper, suddenly feeling embarrassed about the shitty sofa I made him sleep on last night.

"Yeah, I bought it about two years ago. I've been renovating ever since."

He holds his hand out for me to take, and I do. The living room is large, the floors all dark timber and polished. There is a stone fireplace with a big antique rug in front of it, running against the wall. We walk through the living room to a bright, sunny, all-glass style kitchen and dining room.

"Holy shit, Brock, this is amazing."

"Come upstairs, I'll show you the rest."

I smile as I see his pride shine through.

We walk up to the second level and it opens to a large living room with another blue stone open fireplace. Big cushions decorate the floor, with a big leather comfy-looking sofa sitting in the middle. There's a huge television, too, and I get the feeling this is where he spends a lot of time. He takes me up another set of stairs where the whole top floor is his bedroom.

The walls look like recycled brickwork that have bits of

white paint on them. The bed is a king-size, with black velvet coverings. The carpet and furnishings up here are luxurious.

"I just put a bathroom in." He opens the door to show me a beautiful beige marble tile bathroom with a huge stone bath sitting in the centre.

"J-Jesus," I stammer. "What are you, like, a decorator or something?"

He smiles proudly. "Look at this." He pulls back a curtain at the side of his bedroom, and I see the whole wall has been removed into the terrace next door.

"I just bought the terrace next door. I'm going to join the two together."

My eyes widen.

"Bottom level will be kitchen and living area, and then the two top levels next door will be bedrooms."

He takes my hand and leads me through to the other terrace. I smile to myself, watching him get all animated as he shows me through the dingy apartment.

"Was yours in this state when you bought it?" I ask.

"Mine was worse. I had to basically gut it."

"You did all this yourself?"

"Yeah, my sisters helped with the styling and furnishings."

This is the third time he has mentioned his sisters. "You're close with your sisters?" I ask.

He smiles softly, and I know they get the best of him. "Yeah, they're pretty cool chicks."

I narrow my eyes as I try to remember their story. "Did you say they were married?" All I remember about them was that they were very attractive and married to holy hot men.

"Yeah, Natasha, my older sister, is married to a super-rich dude. His name is Joshua Stanton, and they live between here and L.A. Bridget, my younger sister, is married to one of my best friends. He works for me. You met him. Ben, the guy from the gym."

"I remember. How did it feel when your younger sister hooked up with one of your best friends?"

"I met him through her." He shrugs. "Well, not really, He was Natasha's husband's bodyguard."

I frown. "Joshua has bodyguards?"

"Yeah. They are, like, mega rich. Millionaires. He's an app developer."

"Wow," I whisper.

Brock takes me down to the ground floor of the second terrace. It's so daggy compared to his apartment.

"I'm going to put the large kitchen across here." He shows me. "And then upstairs I'm adding another four bedrooms. It will join with the other terrace on every level."

"Why do you need five bedrooms?"

"Well, I don't right now, but hopefully, one day, I will."

I stare at him and my stomach churns with a wave of nervousness. He means for one day when he has kids.

Please don't get sensible on me. You're my bad boy quick fuck. You don't need to be anything else.

Please just be the meathead I need you to be.

We walk back upstairs, through the opening into his room.

"I'm just going to take a quick shower, okay?"

"Sure."

"You're welcome to come in, by the way." His mischievous eyes hold mine.

I giggle, he's throwing my request to him from earlier back in his face. "I'm good."

"Okay." He shrugs. "Suit yourself."

I hear the shower turn on, and I sit on the bed and look

around. God, this place is beautiful. I lean down and smell his pillow. It smells good—just like him.

I lie down on his bed and imagine what it must be like to live in such a beautiful house. The shower eventually turns off, and Brock comes in with a towel wrapped around him. He stops when he sees me, and he smiles that slow, sexy smile of his.

"What?" I ask him.

"You have no fucking idea how good you look spread out on my bed."

My heart begins to beat faster as we stare at each other.

You have no idea how good you look half naked, I want to tell him, but my mouth begins to go dry.

He drops the towel, drying himself off, and my breath catches.

Damn him for being so comfortable in his own skin.

Holy... shit. That body. I guess if I had it, I would be taking my clothes off all the time, too.

Without another word, he disappears into his walk-in wardrobe, and I close my eyes to revel in the way it feels to have such tingling in my toes. Shit, hold it together, woman.

Moments later, Brock comes back into the room fully dressed, and I find myself feeling a little disappointed.

What's going on with me today? I tell him I want him to be a gentleman, and then I'm secretly disappointed when he is.

I need to get over myself.

"You ready?" he asks.

"Uh-huh."

Again, he takes my hand, and I smile as he leads me down the stairs. I wonder if this is normal for him or whether this is him trying to be on his best behaviour.

Ten minutes later, we arrive at the café and take a seat.

Callie and I come here often. The guy making coffees looks over, his eyes dancing with delight when he sees me walk in.

Shit. He likes me. He's made it well known on many occasions. Brock and I sit at the table outside on the sidewalk, looking over the menus.

"What's good?" he asks.

"Everything," I say as I try to decide what to have. "I'm having the Eggs Benedict."

"Okay." He keeps looking. "I'll get the super foods." He closes the menu and looks up at me, breaking out into a beautiful, broad smile.

"What?" I smile back at him.

"You."

"What about me?"

"Thinking you're the boss of us and shit."

I giggle. "I am the boss of us, Brock."

His eyes dance with mischief. "But I'm the boss of all the physical activity."

"And you seem very happy about that."

"I am, actually." He stretches and inhales deeply. "I feel like I was born for this role."

I laugh. "You're an idiot."

The coffee guy comes over with his pen and notepad. "Hey, guys. How are you today?" His attention is focused solely on me.

"Good, thanks." I open the menu, but I can feel the waiter's eyes lingering on my legs, and then roaming up my body.

"Going swimming?" he asks.

My eyes flicker over to Brock who glances up from his menu and frowns. I giggle nervously. "Yes, I am. I'll have the Eggs Benedict and a skim cappuccino, please," I say. I look up and the waiter is staring at me, smiling with a dreamy look on his face.

"Do you always wear a bikini when you swim, or do you ever wear a one-piece?" he asks openly.

Oh God.

"Erm. Bikini, I guess." Just take the order and go away, I don't want to talk to you today. He's so flirty all the time.

"I'll bet you look good in it." He smiles. He then remembers where he is, and he turns to Brock. "And what will you have, sir?"

"I'll have your balls on a fucking platter if you don't stop looking at her," he growls.

My eyes widen. "B-Brock!" I stammer.

The poor boy stares at Brock, the colour draining from his face.

Brock glares at him. "I'll have the super foods breakfast, and if you flirt with my girl again, I will choke you." He taps the table in front of us. "Right here."

The guy pales.

"Do I make myself clear?"

He swallows the lump in his throat. "Crystal."

Brock hands him the menus. "My coffee had better be good, fucker."

CHAPTER 10

Tully

"BROCK," I whisper as the guy scurries back to the kitchen to hand the order in. "What the hell was that?"

He shrugs, and I can see that temper simmering just below the surface again.

"You can't threaten people like that," I tell him.

"It wasn't a threat. I'm more than happy to follow it through."

"Are you kidding me?" I gasp.

"I won't have you disrespected by a skinny punk in a coffee shop who thinks he can check out my girl right in front of me. He was asking for it."

"I'm not your girl."

"You're here with me so that makes you my girl."

I roll my eyes. "This is supposed to be a romantic date and..." I shake my head, words failing me.

"And what?"

"And so far, this morning, you have urinated in front of me, stripped naked without a care in the world, and now you've told someone you are going to strangle them on the table if they pay me any attention."

"And?" he says dryly. "Your point is?"

"You don't see a problem with that?"

"No." He looks at me as if I'm stupid. "I see a problem if I pretend to be something other than what I am."

I stare at him.

"I bet your other boyfriend used to be all puppy dog eyes and shitting over you."

I smirk. "He was, actually." I would say jump and Simon would say how high.

He rolls his eyes, unimpressed. "Pathetic," he mouths.

"What about your past girlfriends?" I ask. "Surely they wouldn't have put up with your temper."

"I wouldn't know." He purses his lips and looks around the café at the other people, as if he's completely uninterested in this conversation.

"What does that mean?"

"The last girlfriend I had was when I was seventeen."

I frown. "How old are you?"

"Twenty-eight."

"You haven't had a girlfriend for eleven years?" I gasp.

"No."

"So, what? You just sleep with girls and then... leave?"

"Pretty much." He shrugs. "We usually have a mutual understanding."

Our coffees arrive from a female waitress this time, and her eyes linger on Brock a little too long. What is it about this place?

"Thank you," I mutter, distracted. I think on this for a

moment. "Why don't you have girlfriends?" I ask. "I don't understand."

"It's just not something I've ever been interested in. I was in the Navy, away for a lot of the time, and since I got back I've just been having fun."

I stare at him as I try to read between the lines. "When you said that you knew a lot about me, what exactly did you mean?"

His eyes hold mine. "It was no accident we met in the club. I followed you there."

I raise both brows and stare at him.

"I called my friends up and we staged the whole accidental meet up." He shrugs as if it's no big deal.

I try to act unimpressed, but I fail miserably, and I smirk as I imagine him setting up the staging. "Why would you do that?"

"I told you. If I knew the answer to that, I wouldn't be here right now."

For some reason, a thrill of excitement runs through me. *He searched for me*. I take his hand over the table. "I like that you came looking for me."

He sips his coffee, and I can tell he's uncomfortable with this conversation.

"But I have to ask.... why did you? Why me?"

"Because I couldn't get you out of my head," he says softly, a look of uncertainty crossing his face.

I smile as I watch him. If he hasn't ever had a girlfriend, I doubt he's ever had these types of conversations.

Am I the first one to try and break through?

My heart flips in my chest at the prospect, and our breakfast arrives. Brock begins to eat in silence, and I feel like I need to put him at ease.

"Well, Mr. Marx. I probably should inform you that I couldn't get you out of my head, either." I sip my coffee. "You have had a regular position in my thoughts. Even though you're batshit crazy," I add.

He gives me a slow, sexy smile, and his dark eyes drop to my lips. "Have you ever been fucked on Bondi Beach before, Pock?"

I snort the coffee up my nose. "No." I gasp for air, pounding my chest. "Absolutely not."

What the hell? Does he think we are having sex on the beach?

What next?

"Do you have to wreck it?" I cough. "That was supposed to be a romantic moment."

He smiles at me choking while he casually cuts into his toast.

"What are you smiling at?" I ask. God knows what's going through that devious mind of his.

"Nothing."

"What *is* that look?"

"Popping all your cherries is very high priority on my agenda, that's all."

I stare at him. "Well, you certainly popped the main one in a spectacular fashion."

He smiles as he bites the food from his fork. "I haven't even started yet, Pock."

I stare at him, my mind a clusterfuck of emotions.

Popping cherries is Brock Marx's language of love.

What the hell have I gotten myself into here?

"Here?" I ask as I point to the sand beneath us and look around Bondi Beach.

"Yeah, here's good," Brock says.

We spread our things out, and then he falls onto his towel.

"Time to take that dress off, Tully Pocket." He taps my towel laid out next to him, and he throws me a cheeky smile.

I smirk. "Have you been waiting all morning just to see me in a bikini?"

"You bet I have," he replies without hesitation.

My stomach dances with nerves. God, no pressure. I exhale heavily and lift my dress over my shoulders, and he lies back and puts his hands behind his head to appreciate the show.

I feel like a circus act, and I'm quite sure he thinks he is getting more to look at than he actually is. Does he even remember what I look like? I glance down at him nervously, just as his hungry eyes decide to drink in every inch of my near-naked body. Time seems to stand still as I wait for him to say something.

"You're more beautiful than I remember, Pock," he says softly. He pats the sand next to him, and I slowly sit down, and then lie on my back. He leans up on his elbow over me, turning onto his side.

His hand goes to my hip bone, and he pulls my body to fit snug up against his. "Why were you nervous doing that?" he asks quietly.

"You make me nervous."

"Why?"

I shrug. "You're so much more experienced than I am."

He frowns down at me and tucks a piece of hair behind my ear. "Does it bother you?"

"A little," I whisper.

"Why?"

My eyes hold his. How the hell did we get onto this conversation already?

"I've only ever slept with one person, and then...." My voice trails off.

"And then what?"

"And then you."

His face falls slightly. "I hate that I did that to you in the gym."

Shocked that he acknowledged it, my stupid eyes fill with tears, and I blink them away in hope that he doesn't see.

"Hey," he whispers as he pulls me closer. "Was it really that bad?"

I smile and shake my head. "No, it was... it was just out of character for me, and I know that you do that kind of thing all the time."

He watches me for a moment but doesn't say anything, because he knows it's true. What is there to say?

He puts his head down onto his towel for a moment, his thoughts loud but undecipherable. "Where do you see this going, Tull?" He frowns up at the sky, deep in thought. "I don't want you to ever feel like that again."

"What? You mean us?" I ask.

He nods as he turns his head to look at my face again.

"Well, as the boss of us..." He rolls his eyes with a smirk. "I would like us to be... friends."

He smiles softly.

"With a mutual respect for one another," I add.

"Who fuck?" he adds, pushing his luck.

I giggle. "You really need to work on your romantic date material."

He chuckles. "Without a doubt."

"I don't know about the fucking."

His face falls serious. "Why not?"

I frown as I look out over the water. "I don't like the idea of being one of many."

He frowns.

"But then, I don't want to be your girlfriend or anything." I shrug. "It's hard to explain."

"Try," he says as watches me intently, his large hand splaying over my stomach.

"Well, I know we have an expiration date, and it's not like I'm planning a future with you or anything. You're not the kind of guy that will settle down and I'm not the kind of girl who would force you to."

"I like that about you." He kisses my cheek softly. "But...?"

My stomach clenches at the feel of his big, beautiful lips against my skin. "But, I'm really, really attracted to you."

"And I'm really attracted to you," he whispers against my face.

"And you confuse me," I admit.

His hand goes to my jaw and he brings my face to his. "Why?"

Suddenly, we are the only two people on the beach. Nobody else exists again.

"Because you're the kind of man who doesn't hang out with girls like me. I have to wonder what I could offer you that nobody else can. I'm inexperienced, and I don't know how to do any of the things you probably like to do."

He smiles softly as his lips drop to mine, he kisses me, and my breath catches.

He rubs my stomach with his open hand. "The only woman on my mind is you. Have been for a few weeks."

I smile softly up at him.

"And I want you to be comfortable with this." He frowns as he turns and glances across the beach. "When you told me that I made you feel dirty..." He clenches his jaw, clearly remembering that dreaded day, and his eyes come back to mine. "I didn't like it."

I wrap my arms around his big shoulders.

"So... how about we kiss and do things that make you feel..." he tilts his head to the side, "clean."

"I feel like I'm negotiating a cleaning contract."

He rolls on top of me and pins my hands over my head. "You are. And as the operations manager, it is my duty to inform you that you need to undertake an intensive training regime. Starting today. You need to learn the cleaning protocol."

I giggle up at him. "I'm the boss, remember? I set the protocol."

His eyes dance with mischief as he looks down at me. "The boss of us, not the boss of operations. Physical contact is my domain."

I smile goofily.

"You ready to start your training, Pock?"

I kiss him softly on the lips and he releases me from his grip, allowing me to wrap my arms around him. He buries his head into the curve of my neck. "You know we are on a public beach, right?" I whisper.

"Tully. The first lesson you need to learn is that I don't give a fuck where we are. I'll touch you when I want, wherever I want." He kisses on the lips again and grips my jaw. "Got that?"

I smile shyly. What the hell did I just agree to?

It's 5:00 p.m. and we are in a cocktail bar at the beach. We're still in our beach clothes, the two of us relaxed and very touchy with one another. I feel better after our little talk this morning. He knows how I feel now, and he seemed okay with it.

"Do you want to dance?" he asks suddenly.

My eyes widen in excitement. "Really?"

He smiles sexily and takes my hand to lead me to the dance

floor where he puts his large arms around me and pulls me close. The song "Girl Like You" by Maroon 5 is playing. I love this song, and it seems funny that this is the song we should have our first dance to.

I'm beaming up at him. "You *can* dance?"

"Maybe it's time to try new things." He smirks down at me.

"Such as?"

It doesn't seem real being here with such a gorgeous man. All day I've felt women's eyes lingering on him. He doesn't seem to notice, though, and I know he's had this kind of female attention all of his life.

We kiss again and again, and he holds me tight. "I'll make a deal with you, Tully Pocket," he whispers.

"What?" I breathe.

His dark hair is hanging over his eyes as he looks down at me.

"While we see each other, whether that be for a week or for a month, I promise not to see anybody else."

My eyes search his and I immediately stop dancing. "Why would you do that when we both know it's going to end anyway?"

"Because I want to spend time with you in every way."

"You mean sexually?"

"Yes."

I frown, and he begins to sway to the music again. "You said that you didn't want to sleep with me because you didn't want to be one of many," he tells me casually, as if he's making complete sense. Has he been cooking this up in his head all day?

"That's true, but—"

"But what? If you're the only woman I'm sleeping with then there isn't a problem."

"But if we are sleeping together, it complicates everything. How will we end it when the time comes?"

"We'll have an adult conversation."

"Just like that?" I remember how heart wrenching my breakup conversation with Simon was. I never want to go through that again.

"We both know what this is. There are no expectations on either side. We are too different for it to be anything other than a short-term fling."

I bite my bottom lip as I look at him. Could this really work?

He kisses me softly and I smile against his lips. "So, are you dancing with me right now so you can talk me into casually fucking you?" I ask.

"That's right." He chuckles. "How am I doing?"

I giggle. "You're an idiot." He spins me around and his lips meet mine again.

"Don't tell me that you don't want me. I know you do. Wouldn't you rather have this conversation now than later?"

"Yes, I guess."

"We're both consenting adults." He kisses me. "We want each other." He kisses me again. "What's the problem?"

I smile against his lips. "My morals."

He kisses me and grabs my behind. "As the operations manager, I am giving Miss Morals two weeks' notice."

I giggle again.

"She doesn't belong here working in our company. She's too opinionated and lazy."

I laugh as he spins me around again.

"Brock," I whisper as I run my hand up his thick neck and through his hair.

"Yes, Pocket?" He smiles down at me, and somehow this feels special between us.

"I should probably tell you that this song is now our song." My eyes linger on his as we sway to the music.

He gives me a slow, sexy smile, raising his eyebrow in question. "Is this more of the romantic bullshit you keep going on about?"

I smile goofily and nod. "Yep. So, when I ask you what our song is, what will you say?"

"'You Shook Me All Night Long' by ACDC," he offers seriously.

"Yeah, we need to work on that."

He chuckles and spins me around. "Ready to shake you any time you want, baby."

I lick the salt off the rim of my glass, my eyes holding his.

It's 11:00 p.m. now, and Brock and I still haven't been home yet. It's been a good day. The best.

We've been making out like teenagers for hours. He's been kissing me like his life depends on it, and after our talk earlier on the dance floor about him not seeing anyone else, I'm so fucking turned on it's a wonder I'm not sliding off my chair.

In the water, on the towel, right here at the bar—he's all over me.

He doesn't give a damn who's around or what they will think, and it's so hot.

I've never been with a man like Brock. He honestly just does what he wants, when he wants.

His dark eyes hold mine. "You keep licking that salt like that and I'll put you under the table to suck my cock."

God.

With every drink he has, he loses another inhibition, to the point where he has no filter on at all anymore. And it's holy hot.

"A man can only watch you lap something up for so long without reaching his breaking point."

I smile as my arousal begins to hum.

I'd planned on being a good girl, on not sleeping with him again. But his promise of fidelity and sexual training has opened up an opportunity I know I want to take...

In my mouth.

I sip my drink, and then I lean in and kiss him, my tongue rimming his mouth. He grabs my hand and presses it down on his crotch. His erect cock has been throbbing all day.

"We need to go home now," I mumble against his lips.

His eyes are alight with arousal, and he stands immediately. "Skull your drink."

I smile, drain my glass, and before I know it, he is pulling me by the hand towards the cab rank.

Half an hour later, his lips are on mine, his hands are up my dress, and we are bursting through my apartment door like a pair of crazy people.

"Fucking hell," he pants against my lips. "I've never been so fucking turned on in my whole life."

I giggle as a thrill runs through me. I know I'm probably the most inexperienced girl he has ever slept with, but damn it, I'm going to make sure I'm the best.

He drags me into my bedroom and then falls still as he stares at me. He looks like he's trying to calm himself down, rein himself in. My heart begins to flutter.

The mood has instantly gone from crazy arousal to something else that I just can't put my finger on.

"You tell me when to stop, Pock," he whispers as he kisses me softly.

I nod nervously.

He lifts my dress over my head, and then slowly undoes my bikini top, throwing it to the side. His dark eyes roam over my bare breasts and I swallow my fear.

My heart begins to pulse at a frantic pace.

I can feel the heat from his gaze as I stand silent, awaiting instruction.

There's no mistaking who's in control when he touches me.

We both know I'll do anything he wants. His thumb dusts back and forth over my erect nipple, his smile growing as he watches himself touching me.

His eyes rise to meet mine, and then he slowly bends and takes my nipple in his mouth.

My eyes close. *Fuck.*

He moves to the other side and repeats the process, only he bites me this time. Enough that I jump, but not enough to hurt me.

My head tips back to the ceiling and I put my hands in his hair as he works my breasts. He stands and takes my jaw in his hand, his eyes searching mine. "Here's how it's going to go, Pock," he whispers. "I'm going to spread you out."

I swallow the lump in my throat. I feel like I can't breathe.

"And I'm going to lick you up." His voice has dropped to a deep, husky tone—one that calls to me on another level.

He grabs my hair at the nape of my neck and brings my face to his.

"And I'm going to fill you up so fucking good."

He kisses me aggressively, and God, I could come just from this. He bites my bottom lip as he pulls away, and I whimper from the loss of him.

Brock slowly slides my bikini bottoms down my legs and

pushes me back until I fall onto the bed. He then arranges me exactly how he wants me.

He spreads my legs wide.

My breath quivers with nerves and I close my eyes to try and calm myself down.

Just relax, just relax, I chant in my head.

With his eyes locked on mine, he slowly takes his T-shirt off over his head and throws it to the side. His broad chest has a sunkissed tan from today. I can see every muscle in his arms and shoulders.

Good God.

He slides his shorts down his legs until all he's wearing is his grey boxers. He leaves those on, and I know it's so that he doesn't scare me.

I watch him circle me around the bed. It's as if he's trying to work out where to start.

His dark eyes flicker with arousal. "You look so fucking beautiful right now, I can hardly stand it."

I smile softly, and he picks up my hand and kisses the back of it. "Calm down, Pocket," he whispers. "I won't hurt you."

I nod. "Okay," I whisper.

He bends and picks up my foot, kissing the bottom of it while he looks up at me. His open mouth trails up my leg slowly, and I hitch in a breath.

When he gets to my upper thigh, he looks me straight in the eyes and inhales deeply.

Oh God, I have to close my eyes to block him out. This is too much. I can't deal with watching him do this.

What the hell have I gotten myself into? He's sniffing my vagina.

Fuck's sake.

He spreads the lips of my sex open and stares at me for an extended moment. "Perfect pink," he whispers.

My heart is hammering in my chest.

"Come up here," I whimper, holding my arms out for him. This is too intimate.

I can't do it.

"Shh," he whispers before bending down and kissing my open sex.

My head falls back and I nearly buck off the bed.

Holy fucking shit.

"Calm. I need you calm, Pocket," he mumbles against me. His tongue slides through my wet flesh, and he closes his eyes in pleasure while I shiver with a sensation overload.

He starts to lick me, deeper and deeper, my back arching off the bed.

"Fuck, you taste so good," he growls.

I start to tremble. I can't hold it. Oh no.

How embarrassing. He's hardly touched me but I convulse as an orgasm rips through me.

My hand goes to the top of his head. "Brock," I whimper.

He smiles as he continues to lick me up and down, his hands pulling me apart. "Brock, I can't," I pant as I try to close my legs. "We need to warm up to this," I beg. "It's too much. Just get on me."

He sits up, his lips glistening with my arousal, and he slowly licks them as he considers my request.

"Baby, I've hardly touched you," he whispers.

I hold my hand out for him. "Kiss me. Just kiss me," I plead. "Just... can we work up to this, please?"

He stares at me for a moment, as if confused. "You want me to kiss you?"

I nod. My heart is beating so hard that I can hear my pulse in my ears. He starts to crawl up my body.

"Briefs off," I whisper at him.

He stands, and with his eyes fixed firmly on mine, he slides them down his legs.

My eyes drop to between his legs and I feel a flutter of fear. He's fucking huge. "Condom?"

He smiles and licks his lips again.

I find myself smiling back at him. "What?"

"This is not how I roll. I'm the one who gives directions around here."

"Humour me," I whisper. "Just the first time. Please?"

He bends and kisses me softly. "For the record, this is our second time."

I giggle and run my hands over his broad shoulders. "Just for the second time," I correct myself.

He finds his wallet and takes out three condoms, throwing them onto the bedside table.

"Put one on."

"Stop fucking rushing me, woman."

"I'm sorry, I'm just nervous."

He stills and his shoulders slump. I know he's going to honour my requests from here on out. He slowly rolls the condom on and lays down beside me. "Now what?" He breathes against my lips.

I smile as we kiss, and I roam my hands up and down his arm. I can feel every muscle. "Now you kiss me until our bodies come together naturally."

He chuckles and shakes his head. "Is this some kind of voodoo fucking that I am unaware of? Cocks don't enter pussies naturally. You need to push."

I huff out a laugh. "Shut up and do it."

He lifts my leg and wraps it around his hip, kissing me deeply. He slides the side of his dick through my lubricated flesh and my body rises to meet him. "Like this?" he whispers.

I smile against his lips. "Just like that," I whisper.

Our bodies begin to move by themselves as they grind against each other. Our kiss turns deep and passionate, and I know he's as hot for it as I am. His breath is quivering as he fights for control.

His open mouth ravages my neck. "Oh God," I whimper.

He pushes forward at once and his hard cock slides home.

Our eyes lock and I see the arousal dance like fire in his eyes. "Is this okay?" he whispers.

I nod, unable to speak.

He slowly slides out and pushes in again.

I'm stretched to my limit.

Ouch.

"Open your legs farther for me," he pushes out.

I force my legs back to the mattress, and he slowly pulls out, and then slowly slides in, releasing a guttural moan.

"Oh God," I whimper. This is so fucking good that I can't even speak.

He pulls out once more, taking his time before he drives home hard.

He knocks the air from my lungs and I cry out.

"You okay?" he whispers in a panic.

"Great," I pant with a smile. "Fuck me," I beg.

He pulls out and pushes back in, again and again, until my body stops fighting and accepts him.

In, out, in out, around and around. So hard and so good. He lifts himself onto his straightened arms, holding his own weight above me, and then he really begins to let me have it. Hard hits force my whole body to contract around his.

The bed is banging against the wall. I look up at him, looking down at me, and I have this perfect moment of clarity.

He frowns as if he has it too, and he bends to slowly take my mouth with his. We kiss slowly and his body moves gently inside mine. I scrunch my face up against his.

God, this is perfect.

He is perfect.

He lifts one of my legs and I feel it building again. "I'm going to come," I whimper. He starts to ride me hard and fast again, and I swear, I'm going to break. The sound of our skin slapping together echoes throughout my apartment.

I cry out as an orgasm rips through me, and with three hard, long pumps, I feel his cock quiver. He buries his head into my shoulder and shudders as he silently comes deep inside my body.

We kiss tenderly, and his hand cups my face as he stares lovingly down at me. "Voodoo fucking. I like it."

I pant with a smile.

So do I.

It's just gone 3:00 a.m. when I roll away from Brock. He's on his back and fast asleep, looking so hot. Not hot as in gorgeous—although he's that too—I mean hot as in he's an inferno. I feel like I'm burning up on fire. Of course, that could be the hundred margaritas I had tonight. I'm not used to sleeping with anyone anymore.

God, what a night. He had me for a second time in the bed, and then again in the shower. I'm sure we'd be still going if he wasn't out of condoms.

I lick my dry lips. I need a glass of water, so I slowly get out of bed and wince. "Ouch."

Fuck, I'm sore. He's an animal.

I may have gotten my gentle turn the first time, but damn, did he make up for it later.

I go to the kitchen and pour myself a glass of water when, in the darkness, my phone lights up with a text on the kitchen counter.

I frown and pick it up.

The name Simon lights up the screen.

CHAPTER 11

Tully

I SIT at my desk and stare out of the window, unable to wipe the stupid smile from my face. What a weekend, and holy hell, what a man. It's been a long time since I came to work on a Monday this happy. To be honest, it's been a long time since I've been this happy, and it's all because of one man.

The one man I swore to hate for all of eternity.

Brock Marx, sex god extraordinaire, and the real-life devil himself.

I pick up my pen and stare at the file in front of me as I try to focus on my task. I get a vision of Brock crawling up between my legs with his mischievous smile, and I feel myself blush. I press my lips together to hide my smile, taking a quick look around at my co-workers as they work beside me, minding their own business. God, if only they knew the things I gotten up to this weekend.

"What is with you today?" Rourke asks with suspicion. "Why do you keep smiling at nothing?"

I shrug, but my face contorts as I try to control my smile. "No reason."

He gives me a knowing wink. "You going to lunch?"

"Is that okay?"

"Sure." He turns back to his computer, and I quickly pack up my desk and leave the building. I sit in the park on a bench seat, and then I take out my packed sandwich.

I stare at the phone in my hand and wince, knowing I have to call Simon.

I don't even want to speak to him right now. I just want to stay in this naughty bubble of badness. I want to stay where I don't have to think about anything other than how many orgasms I'm going to have. I exhale heavily.

Just get it over with; dial his number.

He answers first ring. "Hey, Tull."

Hearing his voice hits me like a tonne of bricks and the ugly taste of guilt fills my mouth. "Hey, Si." I smile sadly. "Are you okay?"

"Yeah." I can tell he's smiling. "Missing you, though."

My throat closes up at hearing him say that, and I smile through tears. I look out over the park in front of me. God, this is a fucking mess.

"You will never guess what?" he says suddenly.

"What?" I smile.

"I got offered to join the Edward Academy."

My eyes widen. "You did?" My mouth falls open. This is a big deal. "Oh my God, Si, that's amazing."

"I can't believe it." He laughs, and I can tell he's really excited.

"I can. You're the smartest there."

He exhales heavily. “It’s all working out, Tull. I’ll do this transfer to London for a month.”

I frown. “The academy is in London?”

“Yeah. It was either there or the States.”

“Oh, okay.” I frown as I listen, and a strange feeling comes over me. I’m not sad he’s going overseas, just really happy that he is getting this opportunity.

Maybe we are we just friends now? Have my feelings for him changed?

“I’ll do this transfer, and then when I get back, I’ll only have another three weeks in Melbourne before I’ll come home to Sydney for good.”

My face falls. “Oh, that’s great,” I whisper as my mind begins to race.

“So, is your apartment going to be big enough for all of my things or should I sell them before I come home? Did you say it had a single or double garage?”

I stare at the ground underneath my feet as I try to focus on what he’s saying.

He continues, despite my silence. “Maybe you can send me a list of everything you have now so that we don’t double up on any appliances. If I run some ads to sell things on the classifieds, can you monitor them while I’m away?”

Fuck. This is really happening.

“Erm.” I frown. “Sure.” I collect air in my cheeks as I stare out over the park.

Shit, shit, shit.

“Anyway, I’m at work, babe, so I can’t really speak.”

“When do you leave?” I ask.

“Three days.”

I frown. “How long have you known you were going?”

"I found out a few days ago, but I wasn't sure if I was going to take it."

"Why not?"

"I was going to come home and surprise you."

My eyes widen imagining him finding Brock at my apartment *Fuck.*

"See you later, Tull."

"Si?" I hesitate for a moment.

"Yeah?"

I rub the toe of my shoe into the ground beneath my feet. "Are you still seeing that girl?"

"Ah, nah, she's nothing, Tull."

I bite my bottom lip. "That's not what I asked."

"I've seen her a few times casually over the last few weeks." He pauses for a moment. "It's nothing like what you and I have, though, Tully."

I smile, mollified that he didn't lie to me. "I've been on a few dates, too," I whisper.

"You have?"

I nod, even though he can't see me.

"Nobody special, I hope."

I fake a smile, and I scrunch my eyes shut tight. *Oh, he's all kinds of special.*

"You'll be back soon, and then we won't have to worry about other people, will we?" I whisper.

"No, we won't." He stays silent, and I know he's hurt about me seeing someone else, or maybe he's just shocked that I actually admitted it. Why did I tell him? Perhaps I should've just kept my mouth shut.

"I love you, Tully." He pauses for a moment. "Don't ever forget that, will you?"

My eyes fill with tears, and I know he means that I shouldn't forget him while I'm with someone else.

"I won't, Si."

"Are you going to say it back?"

My eyes overflow with guilty tears, and I swipe one away as it escapes onto my cheek. "I love you," I whisper.

"You do want me to come back, don't you, Tull?"

"Of course, I do," I whisper. I run my hand through my hair in frustration with myself. "Go to England and get this over with so we can start again."

"Okay." I can tell he's smiling again now. "I will."

"Goodbye."

"Seven weeks and I'm all yours."

I laugh. "I said goodbye."

He hangs up and I stare at the phone in my hand for a while.

He's still seeing that girl casually, but unlike before when I was hurt, I'm actually relieved now. It means I'm not the only one who is seeing someone else, and at least I was brave and honest enough to tell him the truth. Surprisingly, he seemed okay about it. He's seeing someone else, he knows I'm seeing someone else. Both of us are committed to getting back together, so now that it's all out on the table, nobody is going to get hurt.

My thoughts turn to Brock.

I'm going to ask to see him tonight so that I can tell him about Simon. That way he knows everything, too.

I'll have one last night with Brock and then we can go our separate ways.

I smile sadly. It was so fun while it lasted. But gym junkies aren't the kind of guys you fall in love with.

Brock

We're sitting in the car at the top of the cliff, watching the police go through their investigations down below. They have their gloves and protective suits on, and they also have absolutely no fucking idea what they're doing. We're tuned into the police channel as we listen to their conversations through our radio.

"Do they have any idea who it is?" Jes asks from the backseat.

"Caucasian woman in her twenties. Suspected working girl. Suspected overdoser." Ben sighs.

"Yeah." I roll my eyes. "Because everyone who has a drug overdose throws themselves off a fucking cliff seconds before they OD," I mutter sarcastically.

"Idiots," Ben whispers.

I shake my head and start the car. "That's the seventh girl this year."

"They'll probably not even investigate it because she's a hooker." Jes sighs.

"They won't, but we will," I assure them as I reverse the car from the parking lot. "Who's hungry?"

"Yeah, let's eat."

Half an hour later, we're sitting in the coffee shop, waiting for our lunch.

"So, how did the weekend go with that chick, anyway?" Ben asks.

I sip my coffee. "It was okay, I guess. I don't think I'll be seeing her again, though."

"Why not?" Jesten frowns.

I shrug. "I can think of a thousand reasons."

"Such as?"

"She's too high maintenance."

"Why?"

"Where do I start?" I exhale heavily. "I sat out the front of her apartment on Friday night hoping to catch her, and she didn't go out. So then I went back on Saturday night and waited another two hours, and fortunately for me that time, she did go out. I followed her and called the guys, staged a whole 'accidental meet up' in the club."

Ben frowns, confused. "Why didn't you just *call* her?"

I look at him, deadpan. "I'm blocked, remember?"

"Oh, that's right. You are." The boys chuckle as they recall her blocking me, clearly finding it hilarious.

"Anyway, the boys and I go out and then I do the whole *oh what a coincidence to see you here* skit." I roll my eyes, realising how lame this story sounds. "Things are going great until she asks me to dance. I say I don't dance. Then she gets the shits, fucks off, and dances with other dudes for two hours."

Ben smiles around his coffee, loving this story.

"I lost my shit and left, only to go home and pace for another three hours and find myself back outside her apartment again waiting for her to come home."

"Jesus fucking Christ. Your stalking is next level." Jesten shakes his head.

"Right?" Ben chuckles.

"She doesn't get home until four-o-fucking-clock in the morning, and then she has this whole sexy, passive aggressive thing going on."

"What do you mean?"

"She doesn't want to fight but then she doesn't want to talk to me." I shake my head as I think back. "She puts me in time out and tells me to go sleep on the couch."

"What?" Ben frowns. "Time out?"

I nod. "Uh-huh. I had to sleep on the fucking couch."

The boys burst out laughing. "Why did you stay?"

"Because she's sneaky and she promised me a trip to the beach the next day where I could rub sunscreen all over her." I widen my eyes as I remember something. "This is after she announces that she's the boss of us, by the way." I shake my head. "No shit, like she would be the boss of us."

The boys throw their heads back and hoot with laughter. "She sounds like the fucking boss to me." Ben laughs.

He and Jesten high five each other.

"Whatever. Stupid guy here stays on a fucking bed of concrete, doing as he's told, and then he goes to the beach for the day, following her around like a little puppy dog. My back is fucked by this stage. The two of us end up making out for what feels like eighteen hours straight until my balls are blue and take over my pea sized brain. Some voodoo shit happened and next thing I know, I promising to be monogamous while with her just so that we can have sex."

The boys' faces both drop in shock.

"Basically, I put in seventy-two hours of work to be tied to one chick who makes me sleep on the goddamn sofa. And then, when we did have sex, I couldn't even last long because *I* kept blowing too fucking quick because *she's* that ridiculously hot." I shake my head. "I could go out, pick up, and fuck two different girls and be back home and done in two hours. This chick's way too much fucking effort."

They both chuckle again.

My phone rings and the name Tully Pocket lights up the screen. "Speak of the devil." I answer it. "Hey, Tully Pocket."

"Hey, you." I can hear the smile in her voice.

The sound of her sexy, husky voice brings a smile to my face. "I thought you blocked me."

"That's over now. You're clear."

Ben writes something on a serviette and slides it across the table to me.

Show her who's boss

I stick my finger up at him, and the two of them laugh like they're funny.

"What are you doing?" I ask her, concentrating instead on my call.

"Walking around with a goofy smile on my face."

I roll my lips to hide my smile. "Oh, yeah?"

"Yeah. I met this really hot guy at the weekend and he blew my damn mind."

I smile broadly this time, unable to help it.

Ben slides another note over the table.

Ask her if you can sleep on her sofa again.

I hold my fist up to him. "Fuck off," I mouth, focusing on Tully instead. "Hot guy, hey?" I smile.

"God, I can't stop thinking about how amazing you were this morning. I've been walking around tingling."

I smile, knowing I gave it to her good in the shower this morning. Truth be known, I've had the tingles ever since, too.

"What are you doing tonight?" she asks suggestively.

My cock twitches. "You."

She giggles. "What time will you be here?"

"About eight." I glance up at my two friends who now have their hands up like puppy dogs pretending to beg.

"Fuck off," I mouth. I need to end this call. "See you tonight, Pock."

"Bye, Brock." She hangs up, and Ben scrunches up his serviette and throws it at me.

"What the fuck is wrong with you?" Jes laughs. "She's wearing your fucking balls for earrings already."

"She fucking isn't. I'm giving it to her good tonight, then tomorrow I'm out of there." I cut into my lunch. "End of story."

Tully

I throw my white bathrobe around my shoulders, taking one last look in the mirror to fix my hair. I'm freshly showered and dolled to the nines. I'm completely naked underneath this robe, ready to break free.

Brock will be here any minute and I'm like a little kid at Christmas. Who am I kidding? Spending time with him is better than any Christmas I ever had. I get the tingles deep inside my body every time I think of him, which is all the damn time. He makes me laugh, he's intelligent, and I can't even rate his hotness level because it's just ridiculous. I've never been so physically attracted to another human being in all of my life. I know that Simon and I met when I was fifteen, but I don't think that's it. I think there's more to this. I have no idea exactly what that is, but I intend to find out.

The buzzer sounds from the security panel, and I smile and push the button. "Hello."

"Hi," his sexy voice says, making me smile broadly.

I push the entry button. "Come up."

I go to the door and stand behind it with a huge goofy grin on my face, bouncing on the spot in excitement. I can hardly wait for him.

Knock, knock.

I open the door in a rush, and there he stands. 6ft 3inches tall, wearing a grey T-shirt, a black cap, and black running shorts. His eyes are dark and hungry and my stomach clenches with need.

Stepping forward, he takes me in his arms aggressively and plants his lips on mine. I giggle as he walks us farther into my apartment.

He holds my jaw just as he wants me and kisses me deeply, the two of us standing still for a moment.

Oh God.

His tongue swipes through my open lips, and just like that, in five seconds flat I'm reduced to a puddle. His strong hands slide down my robe until he's cupping my behind and smiles against my lips.

For a long time, we just stand and kiss. I don't really need anything else from him, this is enough.

"Anyone would think that you missed me today, Marx." I giggle.

He raises his eyebrow sarcastically, pulling the cord of my robe until it falls open. His hungry eyes drop down my body. "I missed this beautiful pussy." He grips it in his one hand and jerks me towards him.

"Well, I missed you," I whisper. "All of you." Our eyes lock, and something shifts between us. I kiss him tenderly and his eyes close in reverence.

He peels my robe over my shoulders, throwing it aside. Then he picks me up and throws me over his shoulder. I laugh in excitement.

"Brock, put me down."

He takes off towards the bedroom, slapping me hard on the bare behind.

"Ouch," I cry as I put my hands on his lower back to try and hold myself up. Oh God, what must I look like? I'm naked and bent over his damn shoulder. He throws me onto the bed and I bounce, another giggle escaping me.

"Open," he mouths as he looks down at me.

I slide my legs open.

"Touch yourself."

My eyes widen. What the hell? So much for foreplay. Brock pulls his T-shirt up from the nape of his neck, quickly peeling it off over his head.

"Touch yourself," he commands as he slides his shorts down his legs. His hungry eyes are fixed on my sex.

My heart races, and I know he can't deal with the intimacy between us. This is so new to him, so I decide to do it his way. I slowly slide my hand down over my breast, then over my stomach and through my short pubic hair.

"That's it," he whispers, his eyes are alight with desire. "Show me."

I frown, not understanding what he means.

"Show yourself to me."

I bite my bottom lip. Oh my God. Is this really happening? Ten minutes ago he wasn't even here and now I'm contemplating doing this already? I can't believe the things this man can get me to do. I pull myself apart, and he smiles and licks his lips.

"That's it," he whispers. "Put your finger in, show me how wet you are for me."

My heart is beating so hard.

I slowly slide my finger into my sex, and Brock lifts his chin in approval. "Another," he rasps, his eyes fixed to my sex.

I open my legs wider and slide in a second finger, throwing my head back in arousal. This is too much. Doing this with him watching... directing.

"Work yourself."

I slide my fingers in slowly and then out again, repeating it until he smiles and begins to roll a condom onto his erection. Once in place, he crawls over me.

With his eyes locked on mine, he takes my two fingers and sucks them, making a hissing sound when he inhales. "You taste too fucking good, Pocket. I may be addicted."

He lines himself up and slams into me quickly, making me cry out at once. Slowly, he rolls his hips to stretch me out.

He kisses me softly as he stills inside me. "Hello."

I giggle. "Hello." I kiss him softly. "Now we can talk?"

He smirks as he thrusts into me hard. "*Now* we can talk."

I rub my hands over his broad back, through his hair as he lies over me, his body taking what he wants from mine. His eyes are hooded, and it's like he was about to die if he didn't get inside of me quickly.

"How was your day?" He smirks.

"Good now." I smile up at him.

He lifts my leg and puts it over his shoulder. The change in position hits us both hard and we moan.

"God." He hits me. "You feel so good." He pumps me again, our eyes never drifting from each other's.

I can already feel the orgasm building.

Damn, he's one hell of a lover. He brings both of my legs up over his shoulders as he stares down at me, his body picking up pace.

I can do nothing but watch on and ride the wave of pleasure.

He closes his eyes and tips his head back, the sound of our skin slapping echoing around us.

"Fuck." He grimaces. "Every fucking time." He slams in.

"What?" I pant as I run my hands up and over his shoulders.

He drives home hard and holds himself deep, and my body convulses around his. I feel his orgasm through his cock shuddering deep inside of me.

He falls to me and our lips crash together. I glance over at the clock and burst out laughing.

"What?" he pants.

"You've been here for twelve minutes."

He chuckles, drops his head to my shoulder, and he kisses it softly. "You shouldn't be so fucking hot. You're cooking my balls, they're exploding on impact."

I giggle. "How am I cooking them?"

He smiles against my lips. "Hard boiled."

We lay in a state of bliss on the sofa. Brock is behind me with his arms around my body as we watch television together. All we have is a blanket over us. It's 11:00 p.m. and we have made love five times since he arrived. I just can't get enough of him. It feels different tonight. I feel close to him. But then...

Is that just because I've orgasmed so many times that my body is releasing that stupid clingy hormone? I don't even know anymore.

He kisses me on the side of my face. I close my eyes and smile. I can't remember the last time I was this relaxed.

"Brock," I whisper.

"Hmm," he mumbles against my face. His hand cups my breast, and then he trails his finger down to my sex and circles it through my swollen flesh.

"Why don't you have girlfriends?" I ask.

"I don't know." He continues to circle his finger, and it's not in a sexual way. It's more of an ownership thing. He's doing it because he can. My body is completely open for him and he knows it. "I guess I never met anyone that I wanted to go down that route with," he eventually replies.

I frown. "You know how we said that this between us was a short-term thing?" I say quietly.

He turns my head and kisses me softly, and sliding his finger into my sex, my legs instinctively opening for him.

"Hmm," he murmurs, distracted by my sex. His tongue slides through my open mouth as my body releases another rush of cream.

He moans as he feels it with his finger.

"The thing is..." I whisper.

He pumps me with two fingers and my eyes close. He begins to rock his fingers deeply, and my mouth falls open.

"The thing is, what?" he whispers into my mouth.

"The thing is..."

He pumps me again and my head falls back. I can feel his erection up against my behind again.

"We have a time limit on how long we can do this." I'm totally distracted by how good he feels.

"Why?"

My eyes hold his over my shoulder, his fingers still deep inside my sex.

"I'm getting back with my ex."

He stills. "What?"

"Him and I are on a break at the moment."

"What?" he snaps, tearing his hand out of me and sitting up in a rush.

"No. No, it's okay, because you and I said this was just a short-term thing all along, didn't we?" I stammer. Oh God, I didn't expect this reaction.

He stands in a rush. "You have a fucking boyfriend?" he growls.

"Ex, technically," I whisper.

"If he's an ex, why are you getting back with him?"

"Because we made a deal."

His face creases in confusion. "A deal?"

"Yeah. We were together since we were fifteen and we wanted to try other things."

"Other things? As in *me*?" he growls.

My face falls. "I didn't think you'd care."

"Don't worry. I don't." He storms into the bedroom.

I run after him. "What are you doing?"

"Leaving."

"Why?" I try to grab his arm but he pushes me away.

"Don't fucking touch me."

"What's wrong?" I frown.

"Nothing." He pulls up his shorts and throws his T-shirt over his head.

"Where are you going? Don't leave." I try to grab him again. "Why are you angry with me?"

He glares at me and clenches his jaw, as if stopping himself from speaking.

"This doesn't change anything between us," I say, clinging on to that last bit of hope, but I already know it's changed everything.

"Whatever." He grabs his overnight bag.

"Brock, stay and talk to me." I try to grab his hand. "What is it? What's wrong."

He turns on me like he's the devil himself. "You made me feel like fucking shit for six weeks because I made you feel dirty." He fakes a smile and shakes his head in disgust.

"Brock," I cry.

"Don't *fucking* Brock me!" he yells.

My face falls.

He curls his lip in disgust. "Say hi to your boyfriend for me."

He turns and storms from the apartment, slamming the door behind him.

I stare at it for a long time. I'm hurt that he left but also weirdly relieved that he left, too.

Brock Marx isn't the kind of man you can do just to pass the time.

He is all consuming, and damn it, I wanted another full night with him already.

CHAPTER 12

Tully

All is fair in love and war. But, is it really? Because it sure doesn't feel that way at the moment. I thought I was doing the right thing by being honest with Brock. And by being honest with Simon. So why did everything turn to hell?

Brock's the one who said we had no future. He's the one who said we were too different to spend any amount of extended time together, and I thought he really meant it. Why *wouldn't* I think that? He never once indicated that this was something more to him—that I meant more.

But after his reaction last night, I have this sinking feeling that he was just saying that to protect himself. He doesn't even know how to feel for a woman. This is all so new to him. He's saying one thing but feeling another. I close my eyes in disgust at myself. Last night, before I told him, things were so good between us.

Perfect.

And then he has to go and ruin it by being all demanding. I put my head into my hands and stare at the computer screen in front of me.

I can't read the words. I couldn't care less about the stupid report I'm meant to be working on. I want to run to Brock and make everything better. I hate that he's angry with me. I want to tell him that it was just a bad joke and that I didn't mean any of it, because I can't stand the thought of not seeing him again tonight.

And that in itself is a big fucking problem. What does that mean for my future with Simon? Why am I sitting here sad and depressed over a man I apparently had no future with, anyway? Fuck!

This is my worst fucking nightmare. Who was I kidding thinking that I could sleep with him and not get stupidly attached?

And Brock...

What was his problem? He set the rules here. The terms of our relationship. He never once asked me in the gym if I had a boyfriend. He wouldn't have cared if I did anyway. He was focused on one thing and one thing only.

Sex.

Hard, beautiful, carnal sex. The kind that curls your toes and makes you thank God you're a woman.

I get an image of Brock last night when I opened my front door to him, looking all naughty and mischievous with his black cap on. I smile as I remember the way he walked me backward into my apartment with his lips locked on mine.

I exhale heavily, and I know I'm not going to be able to relax until I speak to him. I just can't stand it for one moment longer. I have to call him.

"I'm going to go to the bathroom, back in a moment," I announce suddenly.

"Yeah, sure," Rourke replies as he stares at the computer analysis in front of him.

I slip my phone into my pocket and go out into the corridor, looking around guiltily. Nobody is around, the coast is clear. I dial Brock's number and I wait.

Ring, ring... ring, ring... ring, ring. It goes to voicemail.

This is Brock Marx.
Leave a message.

I close my eyes. Damn it. I dial again. I know he has his phone in his pocket at all times. He's not answering on purpose. Stubborn prick.

This is Brock Marx
Leave a message.

I wait for the tone. "I know you're ignoring my calls. I'm going to keep calling until you pick up." I hang up, wait five minutes and call back again.

Ring, ring, ring, ring, ring, ring.

"What?" he answers angrily.

A stupid smile crosses my face. "Hi."

"What the fuck do you want, Tully?"

I swallow the lump in my throat. "I just wanted to talk."

"Yeah, I got nothing to say."

"I have."

"I don't care."

"Brock." My shoulders drop. "Can't we be adults and talk about this?" I plead.

"We did that last night. You're going back to your boyfriend. I got the gist of that conversation loud and clear."

"There is more of a conversation to be had." I sigh.

"Not from me."

"Can I see you tonight?" I ask.

"No."

My face falls. "Why not?"

"Because I have a date."

I frown and glance up the corridor. "What?" I whisper. "You're going on a date with someone else? But you promised you wouldn't do that while we were seeing each other."

He stays silent.

"Please, don't," I whisper. "I can't stand the thought of it. We can work this out." I'm in a panic now and not afraid to show it. What if he sees someone else?

Silence again.

"Brock," I whisper.

"Go back to your boyfriend, Pocket." He sighs sadly.

Confusion takes me over and I grab a handful of my hair in frustration. "What if I don't want to?" I whisper.

"Do you?"

I drop my head and stare at the floor. I don't even fucking know. "Can I see you tonight, please?" I shake my head. "Please."

He stays silent for a moment, and I know he's waiting for me to answer his last question.

"Please, Brock. Will you come over?"

"If you can't answer that question then I don't want to see you."

I close my eyes. "What time will you be here?"

"I told you I'm not coming."

I look up and stare up the corridor. "So, I'll see you at eight?" I ask hopefully.

"Bye, Tully." The line goes dead.

I drop my head and close my eyes. A lump forms in my throat as I try to hold back my tears.

He's done with me.

I walk up one side of the living room and back down the other, glancing at the clock over and over again. 8:05 p.m.

He'll come, I know he'll come.

I clutch my phone in my hand. I've been pacing for an hour and I think I've worn a hole in the carpet.

"Please come," I whisper.

My phone rings and I scramble to answer it. When I see the name Simon lighting up the screen, I instantly push reject in disgust.

I don't want to speak to you. I want to speak to Brock.

I begin to pace again, deciding to text him.

Are you coming?
I'm waiting.

Do I send it? What's going on with me? I'm turning into this needy person I don't even like. My mind is scattered, frantic, and I have no idea what to do. Do I have real feelings for Brock? I mean, I must. I'm in a panic over here worrying he is out with someone else right now.

I hate this.

I hit send and I continue pacing.

Midnight arrives, and I lie in bed staring at the ceiling imagining somebody else in Brock's arms right now.

Is he looking at her the way he looked at me?

Are they having sex? Is he doing to her what he did to me?

Because if he is, she's going to be crazy about him too tomorrow.

My stomach rolls at the thought and I get a vision of some other woman laughing in his arms.

I have no one to blame but myself. I knew he was dangerous, and deep down I knew he would make me question my relationship with Simon, but like a fool, I jumped into the fire anyway.

This is why you don't fuck guys in the gym toilets, Tully, you fucking idiot.

I roll over in disgust and punch my pillow. *Stop thinking about Brock. It's a blessing that he doesn't want to see you.* If I spent any more time with him it would only make it harder to leave him when I had to.

I get a vision of myself living with Simon, but always secretly pining for Brock.

I close my eyes in sadness. I don't want to be that person who is married to one man and thinks about another. I've opened an ugly can of worms.

What the fuck have I done?

"I'll have the chicken salad and a Diet Coke, please?" I smile as I hand the menu back to the waitress.

"Hmm, I'll have the Beef Wrap," Rourke tells her.

"And I'll have the hot chips with gravy," Callie says flatly as she hands the menu back. "With a chocolate milkshake."

"Got it." The waitress smiles before she disappears.

I look at Callie. "What's wrong with you? Since when do you eat chips and gravy?"

"I feel like shit."

"Why?" Rourke frowns.

"Where do I start," she mutters. "I'm horny as fuck, I have PMT, and I have so much inner rage that I want to cut somebody up with a scalpel."

Rourke grimaces and holds his hands up. "Yikes."

"I'm just waiting for someone to piss me off so I can let them have it."

Two minutes later our drinks arrive. "Thank you."

I sip my Coke as I stare at my two friends. "So, I kind of messed things up with Brock," I say matter-of-factly.

"Why?" Rourke asks.

"I told him I was getting back with Simon."

Callie and Rourke exchange glances, and then look back to me.

"And I didn't think Brock would care." I shrug. "Until he stormed out of my apartment with the shits. I spent all night pacing and worrying that he was out with someone else."

Rourke widens his eyes and sips his drink, clearly holding back what he wants to say.

Callie rolls her eyes in disgust.

"What?" I ask.

"Nothing," Callie sighs. "Nothing you want to hear, anyway."

"If you've got something to say, just say it," I fire back.

"Okay, I will. You're a fucking idiot."

"What? Why?" I ask, taken aback.

"Because if you wanted fucking Simon, you would be with Simon," she growls.

"I would not. I just wanted a break." I pause for a moment. "To... travel and—"

"But you're *not* travelling, Tully," she interrupts.

"I've done four trips."

"That you could have done with Simon."

"I didn't want to lose my job." I frown.

"Bullshit. You didn't want to be with Simon. You're just too fucking gutless to admit it to yourself and break up with him."

My mouth falls open. "I am *not.*" I glance at Rourke. "Am I, Rourke?"

He winces again. "Having lunch with you two today was a bad idea." He gestures between Callie and I. "Too much progesterone or some shit going on here. It's like a fucking *Tampax* ad."

"I love Simon," I declare. "I've loved Simon since I was fifteen years old."

"I'm not saying you don't. But you're not *in* love with him anymore, are you?"

I narrow my eyes. "Don't take your PMT out on me."

"You know what?" Callie snaps. "You piss me off. Stop playing the victim here. What did you expect Brock to say when you told him you were going back to another man?"

"He said we were casual," I say defensively.

"Well, it's obviously not, is it? Because he would have stayed and had sex with you if he didn't have feelings with you. The fact that he left angry means that you hurt his feelings."

Shit.

I sit back in my chair, annoyed as our lunch arrives at the table.

"You know, Tully, as I see it, you have two choices. You can be with a man because you feel like it's expected of you, or you can be with another man because you want to actually be with him."

I stare at her flatly as her words roll around in my head.

"I know you always thought you were going to end up with Simon, Tully. Everybody did."

My eyes tear up. "Simon is perfect," I whisper.

"I know, but you need to listen to your gut when it comes to love. Everything is not black and white. Simon is perfect on paper but is he perfect for *you*?"

I drop my head. "I just don't know anymore."

Callie throws the first of her greasy chips in her mouth. "Well, you better work it out quick or you're going to fuck up any chance you ever had with Brock... or Simon, for that matter."

I shrug and look over to Rourke who has chosen to stay silent. Wise man.

Callie continues on her rant. "How do we even know that Simon is going to come back the same Simon? He's sleeping with other people, too. He's going to be different, Tully."

I stare at her. I hadn't even thought of that.

"You're different now, and whether you choose to believe it or not, sleeping with Brock has changed you. Simon might not like the new you, either."

God, this really is a mess.

"You and Simon together just has too many 'what ifs', if you ask me." She shrugs casually and pops another fry in her mouth.

I exhale heavily and pick up my knife and fork. "This lunch date is depressing." I sigh.

"I second that notion," Rourke mutters as he chews his food. "It's given me fucking PMT, too."

Brock

"Got a minute?" Ben asks with a knock on the door.

I look up from what I'm doing. "What's up?"

"We've done a complete search of all bank accounts of Chancellor."

"What did you find?"

"There is a lot more money missing than we first thought."

"How much?"

"Three million over the last eight months seems to have mysteriously gone walkabout."

"What do you mean? How does that much money go missing and nobody has picked it up before?" I scowl. That doesn't seem right.

"He's been selling stocks and shares that were in his company's name, and then he withdrew the funds but never deposited them anywhere."

I swing on my chair, my eyes hold Ben's. "The plot thickens."

"I know."

"Let's see what Jes comes up with today." I turn back to my computer. Ben remains in the chair, forcing me to glance up. "What?"

"Nothing."

I turn back to my computer and get to work, but I can feel him watching me still, so I lift my eyes to him again. "What?"

He shrugs.

My phone begins to dance across my desk, the name Tully Pocket lighting up the screen. I push reject and push the phone back across the desk.

"You're not taking her calls?" He frowns.

I keep my eyes on my monitor and type. "Yeah, that's done with."

"Why?"

"She's got a boyfriend."

Ben stares at me. I glance back up.

"So, she was fucking you behind her boyfriend's back?" he asks.

"No. She has an ex who she's already told me she is going back to," I tell him, sounding bored as I keep typing.

"And you're going to just let her go?" He frowns.

"Yeah, I am actually."

Ben raises his eyebrows.

"*What?*" I snap.

"You like this girl, Brock. Why don't you fight for her? You fight for fucking everything else. I've seen you want blood over a fucking parking space."

"Because I don't want to promise her something I can't deliver." I exhale heavily as I swivel on my chair. "I'm letting her go because I *do* like her."

"Why do you think you can't have a girlfriend?"

"I don't think I'm wired to be with just one person."

"I never used to, either. Not until I met Bridget, and then..." His voice trails off.

"Then what?"

"Sex wasn't the same for me anymore."

I clench my jaw as I watch him, the story sounding strangely familiar. "What do you mean?"

"I don't know. I would have sex with random women and just feel off." He shrugs again. "I can't explain it, but I didn't get the same buzz out of casual sex that I always had done before. It's like it just wasn't enough for me after Bridget. Unless it was with her, I just didn't want it."

I smirk. "Well, that's because you're a big sooky prick with a soft cock."

"Maybe." He chuckles and stands, making to leave before he turns back at me. "All I'm saying is that some things are worth fighting for."

My eyes hold his.

"Even if the person you are fighting with is yourself." Ben walks out, and I exhale heavily and run my hands through my hair.

I stare at the wall in front of me.

I hate this. I hate feeling like this. All fucking week, I've been thinking about her and trying to work out why I don't want to see anyone else.

What is it **about this one particular girl that is so different from the rest of them?**

If I were wired to be the boyfriend type of guy, I would know that already and I would fight for her.

I stand and stare out the window, looking down at the parking lot below.

Could I do it? Could I be a boyfriend kind of man?

A deep sense of dread fills me at the thought of letting her down. I remember the way I felt for those six weeks we were apart after the first time we met, and I can't stand the thought of ever feeling like that again. Most, if not all people are wired to be with one person, but maybe I'm just not.

It's best for everyone concerned if I let her go.

Tully

I stare at my reflection in the mirror. I don't even recognise the person staring back at me now. The girl I used to be was structured and focused on pleasing everyone else but herself—to sticking to a game plan. The girl I see now wants to follow her heart, and if her heart wants to drag her to Hell with a man named Brock Marx, then so be it.

I've been soul searching all week, imagining a future with a man I don't know versus a future with a man I know so well.

There's no comparison between the two. One life is the one I choose, while the other is the one I feel obligated to live.

I just can't live the lie anymore... and it hurts like hell to admit it even to myself.

I have to tell Brock. It's like a poison that is festering inside me now and I won't be able to relax until it's off my chest. I have no idea how he will react, but I do know that I will feel better once he knows everything I'm feeling.

Then it's up to him what happens with us, but I at least have to try.

I text Brock one last time, and I swear to God, my stalking is at an all-time high. This is my tenth call this week. I make him look sane.

Please come over.
I'm going out of my mind not seeing you.

I pace back and forth, this sick feeling invading my stomach.

I know what man I want, there isn't a doubt in my mind, and it isn't Simon.

I don't know if I'm doing the right thing. How can you, in all sensibility, throw away nearly ten years with someone after spending just two nights with another man?

Seventy-two hours.

Brock and I may not even be suited. He may not even want me?

I've hardly slept all week. I've called Simon twice hoping to feel that spark, praying that the stars will align and I will have this lightning bolt of electricity and clarity that will tell me exactly what to do.

But it's just not there, and I hate to say it but I feel like I'm speaking to my big brother. I just want to tell him about this amazing guy I met in the gym.

I keep walking back and forth for over an hour, and at 9:30 p.m. I decide to do what any self-respecting woman should do in this situation.

I'm going to drive past Brock's house to see if he's home, and I swear to God, if he's on a fucking date, I'm losing my shit.

I drive past the gym and scope out the parking lot. No car. I continue driving until I get to his house where I see his car in the driveway.

He's home.

What do I do now? I park across the road and turn off the car, sitting in the darkness, biting my thumbnail as I peer through the windshield.

I don't smoke but if I ever were to start, I think this stakeout would be the cause of it. I feel like I need something to do with my hands or some shit.

What the fuck do I do?

Do I march in there?

I drop my hands to my face and rest my elbows on the steering wheel. For half an hour, I sit in the car and go through my options.

I can either get over this craziness, go back to Simon and forever dream of Brock, or I can march in there and demand a second chance.

Out of all the options, the last one seems like the right thing to do.

My phone beeps with a text.

What are you doing?

I screw up face, is he going to come over to my house? I text back straight away.

I'm waiting for you to come over.

Another text bounces back.

**I mean, what are you doing sitting
outside my house?
I can see you.**

I wince and cringe. Damn it, I'm the worst spy in history. I text back.

**I'm stalking you
What does it look like?**

A reply bounces back.

Why?

I stare at my phone in my hands. Why *am* I here?

Because I need to see you.

I wait for his reply, but it doesn't come. For ten minutes, I wait. Damn it, Brock.

Why does he have to be so fucking difficult all the time? My life was so damn simple before I met him.

Damn gym junkie and his magic dick.

Screw it, I'm just going to go in. I get out of my car, cross the street, and knock on the big timber door. My heart is hammering in my chest. I have no idea how he is going to react to what I have to say.

He opens the door in a rush and looks at me flatly. "Yes."

I smile softly. "You're not on a date?"

He rolls his eyes. "No, I'm not on a fucking date."

I twist my fingers in front of me nervously, my eyes searching his. "Can I come in?"

He looks at me blankly. "Tully, I told you to go back to your boyfriend. We have nothing to say to each other."

My face falls. "Don't call me Tully."

He glares at me.

"You call me Pocket, remember?"

"What are you doing here? If you're here to fuck with my head, don't bother."

I grab his hand. "I'm fucking with my own head, Brock. I don't know what the hell I'm doing anymore," I whisper.

His jaw clenches as he watches me.

"I only know that I feel sick knowing that you don't want to see me."

His eyes drop to the floor. "Fuck's sake," he whispers, shaking his head. "You're turning into the crazy person now. I thought that was my position in the company."

I smile at his little joke. "We can take turns being the crazy person."

He scratches the back of his head. "I'm not your backup plan, Tully."

I nod. "I know."

"And I don't want to see you if you are going to go back to him."

"Okay, Brock." I pause as I try to get this right. "I've been thinking long and hard about this all week, you know?"

He crosses his arms and raises his brows.

"Don't give me that look," I plead. "Listen to what I'm saying, will you?"

He exhales heavily. "What are you saying, Tully? Do you even know?"

"I'm saying I want to see if we can be together."

He clenches his jaw as he stares at me, his internal struggle clear to see in his eyes.

"Well?" I ask.

Still, he doesn't answer me.

"What do you say, Brock? Can we try?"

"I don't want you seeing him again," he tells me coolly.

"Okay." I smile softly. "I won't see him again."

He presses his lips together, still looking down on me.

"You said you don't do relationships," I whisper.

He doesn't say anything.

I take his hand and press it to my cheek. "I've been frantic all week thinking you were going out with someone else."

"Is that why you're here? To see if I'm alone?" He sighs, annoyed.

I shake my head. "No." I pause as I brace myself to say the next sentence. "I'm here because I think I have real feelings for you."

He watches me.

I shrug. "And not the kind of feelings that you like receiving."

His eyes search mine, and suddenly, as if he feels what's between us too, he dusts his thumb over my bottom lip.

"Brock, I know you don't do relationships."

"How do you know that?"

"Because you told me yourself."

He tilts his chin to the sky but lifts his other hand to my face. "What do you want, Tully?" he asks.

I frown because I can't even believe I'm saying it. "Maybe we could see how we go together... without any kind of end date in mind. Just the two of us in, like, a real relationship."

He stares at me for a moment.

"You'll never know if you can have a girlfriend if you don't try it one time?" I smile hopefully.

"I'm not having him waiting in the wings for me to fuck up."

"What do you mean?" I frown.

"Just what I said. If you end it with him, we can see how it goes. If you are keeping him on ice then forget it."

"I know." I swallow the lump in my throat. "I'm going to end it with him regardless of what happens here with you and me. I know if I have these feelings about you, it's not right to stay with him."

He raises his eyebrow and I know his interest has piqued.

"You scare me." I whisper.

Tenderness crosses his face. "Why?"

"I'm just one girl. You'll probably be bored with me in a week."

He shakes his head as he wraps his arms around me, and in that moment, I know it's going to be all right. "You're an idiot." He bends and gently kisses my lips. "I'll probably be bored of you in two days."

I giggle. "Please work on some new romantic material," I mutter dryly.

He kisses me. "This is how I am."

"I like you how you are." I squeeze him in my arms. "But as the boss of us, I would like you to research the romantic material manual, please."

He chuckles. "I'll look into that."

"I've had the worst week, and I'm terrified this is going to fall apart and you're going to hurt me?" I whisper.

He brushes the hair back from my forehead and studies my face. "Maybe." He shrugs. "I don't know, Tully, I've never done this before." Our lips meet again.

"I'll make a deal with you," I whisper up at him.

He smiles against my lips. "What?"

"You teach me the physical things that you need me to know, and I'll teach you the emotional stuff that I need you to know."

His eyes search mine. "I don't know how good of a student I'll be."

I reach up and brush his hair back from his forehead. "I'm just asking you to try, Brock."

He nods and wraps his arms around me. "Okay." He kisses me softly. "We can try."

I smile into the darkness, my heart racing wildly in my chest. His body is still inside mine as he lies behind me.

I'm back in his arms and all is right in the world. He tenderly kisses the side of my face and I smile against him as he holds me close. He feels it, too, I know he does.

We just made love, and unlike all the other times, he was gentle and loving and everything feels so right. He slowly slides out of me and kisses my lips as he holds my jaw in his strong hands. "You want a glass of water?" he asks.

"Please." I doze back off in the darkness.

"Here you go." I open my eyes to see Brock in front of me holding my phone out.

I lean up onto my elbow. "Huh?"

"Call him."

"What?"

"Call him and tell him you're with me. You're not to speak to him again unless I'm in the room."

CHAPTER 13

Tully

I FROWN as I look up at him. "What?"

"You heard me." He sips the water from his glass casually. "Dial the number. Now."

"I'm not calling him with you listening."

He stands at the side of the bed completely naked. "Oh, yes, you are." He rearranges his dick with his hand. "You want to do this thing between us." He raises his chin defiantly. "Let's go."

"Let's go? What the fuck does *let's go* mean?"

"It means I don't do things by halves, and if you belong to me then I won't have you speaking to him when I'm not here."

"We're friends, Brock." What the hell?

"No. Your friends are Callie and that weird girl. This other guy is your ex and I don't do exes." He clenches his jaw and I can see his agitation building. "If you're with me, you don't fucking talk to him."

"Brock, this is going to be a drawn-out, painful conversation. It may take hours."

He sits on the bed. "I've got all night."

"I'm not doing it with you listening, Brock." I get out of bed in a rush and storm into the bathroom. "I can't believe that you even think that I would."

He storms into the bathroom behind me. "Oh, you better believe it. We can drive around to his house if you'd prefer." He nods as if processing that thought. "Yeah. Let's do that. Let's go and see him together. I want to meet this fucker, anyway."

I turn the shower. "Have you gone fucking crazy?"

"All week I've been going fucking going crazy, Tully, thinking you were with him."

I scowl and get under the hot water. "You're an idiot. Why would I be with him when I was calling you every minute of the day? He lives in Melbourne and he's going to London. I haven't been with him for eight months."

He crosses his arms and glares at me.

"What?" I snap. "Don't look at me like that. I don't do the jealousy thing, Brock."

"I do," he growls. "Get fucking used to it." He storms out of the bathroom and I hear him go downstairs.

I close my eyes as my heart beats hard in my chest. Simon was never jealous.

Not once. God, Brock's like another species of man entirely, one I'm not used to.

I take my time to shower, and then I put his robe on and head downstairs. I find him lying on the sofa pretending to watch television. I know that Simon is in the air flying to London, so I'm going to let him think that he won.

"Fine, I'll call him now," I say.

Brock snaps as his eyes stay glued to the television.

I bite my bottom lip to hide my smile and I dial the number. I hate to admit it but having a guy getting jealous over me feels kind of hot. The phone rings.

Oh shit, what if he actually answers?

You have reached Simon Austin.
Your call is important to me.
Leave a message after the beep.
Have a nice day.

I smile as I hear the message. His voice is such a contrast to the aggressive message on Brock's machine. I wait for the beep.

"Hi, Simon, it's Tully. I really need to talk to you. I'll call you back tomorrow night." I glance over at Brock, and he raises his chin in satisfaction, thinking he's won that argument.

Little does he know I'll be calling Simon tomorrow when he's not around.

There is no way I'm having this conversation in front of Brock.

I hang up. "Are you happy now?" I ask.

He pats his lap, and I smile and crawl over to him, curling up in a ball when he kisses my forehead. "Don't fuck me around with him, Tully. I won't stand for it."

I snuggle into his chest and I can feel him begin to relax. "I'm not going to, Brock. There is no need to be jealous. I'm a one-man kind of girl and I'm with you now." I kiss his chest.

He puts his pointer finger under my chin and lifts my face to meet his. "I don't do things in halves," he whispers. "If I'm in, I'm all in."

"I know." I smile softly, and I have to wonder if this is the reason he has never gone down the girlfriend path before. Maybe *all in* has always been too much for him to take. "How about you put that big dick all in?" I whisper as I widen my eyes to lighten the mood.

He smirks and then pulls me over his lap to straddle him. He looks up at me as I brush his dark hair back from his face. We fall silent and just stare at each other.

"I really like you." I smile softly.

"You'd better."

I wake to the feeling of a large erection in my back. Brock is nestled against me.

"Good morning, Tully Pocket." His lips drop to my neck.

I reach back and cup his face. "Good morning." I smile. "Is that thing always hard?"

"Only when it's around you."

"Hmm." I smile sleepily. "Smart dick."

He kisses my shoulder. "Genius, actually."

I giggle as I roll onto my back. "And what does your genius dick have to tell me this morning, Mr. Marx?"

He looks down at me with his big brown eyes, his face alight with mischief. He looks so playful. I run my fingers through his thick hair, and then down over the dark stubble on his face. "He just wanted to check on your girls."

"My girls?" I frown.

"Yeah. You know? Your party girls."

He cups my breast and then runs his hand from my knee up to my thigh where his fingers find that spot between my legs. He circles at just the right pressure. He pats my sex, as if I am supposed to know what that means.

My brows rise and I giggle. "My vagina is my party girl?"

He nods slowly with a naughty grin. "One of them."

"What's her name?" I smirk.

He narrows his eyes. "Princess Pussy Porridge."

"What the hell?" I burst out laughing. "Porridge? What the hell is porridge."

He chuckles as he bends and takes my nipple into his mouth before moving on to trail kisses down my stomach. "The breakfast of champions, that's what it is."

I smile goofily as he pulls my legs back to the mattress and sucks hard.

My breath catches instantly and I'm rendered speechless.

"Feed me, wench," he growls as he bites me, and I laugh, resting my hands on the back of his head.

God, this man is simply delicious.

I tap my pen on my desk and stare straight ahead. I've gone over the conversation I'm about to have at least a hundred times in my head this morning.

Simon, my beautiful Simon. The man I swore to love for all of eternity, only to develop feelings for another man just eight months later.

Am I doing the right thing? I am, I know I am, but how do I know that being with Brock is what's right? Is he just Mr. Right now? How do I know that my feelings for Brock are real and not just an infatuation with the way he makes me feel?

When I'm with him, I feel desired and excited, young and wild. What I know I should have been feeling all along.

Maybe I've just been hypnotised by Brock's magical dick, because I'm pretty sure it has supernatural powers. Huge, sweaty, spine tingling powers that make me forget my name or that any other man ever existed.

Callie's words from the other day come back to me.

You don't want to be with Simon, but you're too gutless to break it off with him. Unfortunately, I know she's right. I haven't travelled as much as I thought I was going to. I haven't done much of anything since Simon and I broke up. Not like I thought I was going to, anyway.

I'm supposed to be going to Hawaii next week, but the friend I was going with can't go anymore meaning I had to plan to go alone. But when all this shit went down with Brock and Simon, and my confusion over my feelings, it all just seemed too hard. The thought of going to another country on my own when I was in turmoil about Brock was too overwhelming, so I cancelled it. Another decision made on impulse. Is this an impulse decision too?

Rourke interrupts my thoughts. "Have you seen the sample from Lab A?" he asks.

I frown. "What was it?"

"I had a few strands of hair that was found in the hand of the body from the docklands this week. It wasn't hers. I checked it yesterday, but when I went back to run for DNA just now, it's not there anymore." He scratches his head as he looks around.

"No." I stand. "Where was it?"

"I left it in the file. It was there yesterday before we left, I know it was." His voice is rising as his panic begins to set in.

"It was bagged up?" I ask.

"Yeah, of course it was." He looks through the file. "Can you see if somebody has checked it out?"

I log onto the computer and type in the evidence file number.

Item 2778 Forensics Pending outcome

"Shit, no, it says it's still here."

Rourke begins to get agitated and flicks through the file case envelopes at double speed. "Where the hell is it?" he whispers angrily. "If I've lost it, I'm going to get fucking fired."

"It's okay, we'll find it." I begin to help him look. "Where were you yesterday when you were looking at it?"

"I was in Lab A. I checked her DNA against the hair and it wasn't a match."

"Okay." I shrug. "So, where did you go then?"

He frowns as he retraces his steps. "It was home time so I bagged it back up and put it into the filing system so I could work on it today."

"Under its case number?"

"Yes, of course under the fucking case number. Where else would I have put it?" he snaps.

"Okay. Don't get angry with me, it's not my fault," I say quietly. I begin to go through the filing system drawers while he turns the lab upside down.

Two and a half very stressful hours later there's no evidence to be found.

Rourke picks up the phone and dials down to forensic reception, putting the call on speaker.

"Michelle, did anyone sign out any evidence yesterday?" he asks in a rush.

"Hang on, I'll check." I can hear her typing before she comes back to the call. "No, there were five lots signed in, but nothing signed out."

"Fucking *great*."

"What's up?" she asks.

"Item 2778 is missing."

"Hmm. Call down to the officers handling the case. Maybe they forgot to sign it out."

"Yeah, okay." Rourke sighs. He flicks through the notes to

find out who the officer is. “Thanks.” He dials down to the station. “Hi, Charlie, can you put Andrew on, please?”

“Andrew is on leave until Friday next week.”

“Can I have his cell number? I have to speak to him urgently.”

“Sure, but I know he left to go to Bali on a surfing trip this morning. I’m not sure you’ll be able to reach him. Anything I can help you with?”

Rourke screws up his face, and I slap my forehead. What are the chances?

“Do you know if he signed out an item yesterday and forgot to log it?”

“I don’t know, man. I doubt it, but it could happen. I’ll check if anyone else signed it out. What’s the item number?” Charlie asks.

“2778.”

“Okay, I’ll track it down.”

“I’ll take the number anyway,” Rourke says. He listens and then scribbles the number down.

“I’ll find it, leave it with me.”

“Okay, thanks.” Rourke hangs up and nods as he tries to calm himself down. “He’s probably got it.”

“Let’s hope so.” I sigh.

My phone begins to vibrate across the table, the name Simon lighting up the screen. My heart sinks.

“I’m going to take this call outside,” I tell Rourke.

“Yeah, sure.”

“Hi, Simon.” I smile as I walk towards the elevator.

“Hello, Tully.” His calm voice soothes me. “Everything okay?”

I get in and push the button to the ground floor. “I just really needed to talk to you. How was your flight?”

"Yeah, it was long. Horrible, actually. Thank God for the minibar." He sighs.

I fake a smile as I walk through reception, out into the garden.

"Simon, we need to talk."

"Okay?" He pauses for a second. "You sound serious."

I sit on the park bench. "I am." I close my eyes as I try to remember how the conversation went in my head.

"What?"

"Si... you know when you met that girl and you started doing different things?"

"Yeah."

I swallow the lump in my throat. I really don't want to hurt him. "I met someone, too. Remember? I was telling you about him."

"Okay."

God, I hate this. "And the thing is, Si, I'm a bit confused about how I feel about us now."

"What do you mean?"

"Well, I know we love each other. We will always love each other, right?"

He stays silent.

"I just don't know if we are *in love* with each other anymore."

"Is it serious? Between you and this other guy?"

I close my eyes. "Not yet." I hesitate. "But I feel like I want it to be," I whisper.

He stays silent.

"I tried to stop seeing him this week and..." My voice trails off.

"You promised me this wouldn't happen, Tully."

"Si."

"You fucking promised me."

My eyes fill with tears as I hear the hurt in his voice. "I know, baby." I shake my head as I try to articulate my thoughts. "That girl you met, did you feel... close to her?"

"No. I feel close to you."

I close my eyes.

"I'm getting on a plane and coming home."

"No!" I snap, knowing I just have to say it out loud. "I don't want us to be back together, Simon. I don't want you to move in with me when you get back."

"What?" he cries.

"I don't think we're meant to be a couple anymore." I stand and begin to pace. "I saw you with that girl, Simon, and I saw how happy you were. Maybe you don't even realise it yet, but you will."

"You're just confused, Tully."

I shake my head as my tears fall. "No." I swipe my tears away angrily. "I've been confused for twelve months. I think I finally know what I want," I whisper.

"Him?" he snaps. "You want him? After everything we've been through, you think you want a complete stranger over me?"

"Just think about it. We don't miss each other. We're seeing other people. You're happy in bed with someone else and so am I. This is not normal behaviour for people who are supposed to be in love, Si."

He stays silent once more.

"If you were only meant to be with me, you'd be heartbroken that I was seeing someone else."

"Tully..." He sighs sadly, and I know I've hit a nerve with him. He knows that, deep down, I'm right.

"Simon, I know that we had our whole future planned out, but I think that you need to let yourself imagine a different future without me." I smile a sad smile for no one but myself. "A future where we can be friends and you can be madly in love with someone else. I can be happy knowing that you're happy."

"I love *you,* Tully."

"I love you, Si." I close my eyes, the lump in my throat no longer letting me speak.

"Do you love him?"

I frown. "No." But somewhere deep in my subconscious screams that I'm a liar.

He remains silent again.

"This isn't about him, this is about us." The tears roll down my face. "And the realisation that we don't make each other feel the same way we used to make each other feel," I say softly.

"And he does?"

Silence hangs between us.

I cringe, waiting for him to speak, but nothing comes.

"Say something," I whisper.

"What do you *want* me to say?"

"Tell me that you understand," I plead.

"What? Understand that you fell in love with someone else?"

I promised him this wouldn't happen. I promised myself that this wouldn't happen, so why the hell did it? How did I let it get to this?

The pain feels just like the day I left him and moved out.

Raw and deep.

"I'll never understand that, Tully," he whispers. "I love you."

All at once, the line cuts off and I know he's gone. I drop my head and sit for a few moments as I try to process what I've done. My heart is beating hard in my chest. This hurts so much. I get an image of Simon and what he could be doing now, and I feel sick. I really do care deeply for him and I can't stand the thought of hurting him. I stare out over the park in front of me, my tongue darting out to lick my lips and taste my salty tears as they roll down my face.

Maybe I'm just not a good person anymore?

Was I ever?

It's 8:00 p.m. and I pour my third glass of wine of the night.

I had the worst day in history. Searching all fucking day for evidence, breaking up with Simon, fighting my own thoughts about what kind of person I now am.

I know what happened between Simon and I couldn't be helped, and I also know that deep down Simon doesn't love me like he should, either, but it doesn't make it any easier. I know he will eventually see the truth for himself. One day, I hope we can look back at our time together with fond memories of each other. I have no idea where things are going with Brock, but I do know that when I'm with him, I feel safe. Which is just so weird because Brock is anything *but* safe. Strangely, though, when I was with Simon I always felt on edge. I was always petrified that I was going to fuck it up between us. He was so perfect that not even I could believe that he loved me.

Maybe that's why Brock feels so safe to me. I know that if anyone is going to fuck it up between us, it will be him.

I never thought I would see the day when it's a such a relief to be with someone who isn't a shining pillar of society. And I don't mean that in a derogatory way. Simon is amazing.

It's just that maybe I'm not.

The security buzzer sounds and I push the intercom. "Hello."

"Hey," Brocks deep voice says through the speaker, and a smile instantly crosses my face.

"I thought you were working tonight?"

"Got off early."

A thrill runs through me that he came over even though we hadn't planned it. "Come up." I push the button and open my front door for him. I take out another glass and pour him a wine. Only moments later does his broad smile come into view.

"Hey." He smiles sexily as he kisses my lips.

I smirk up at his gorgeous face. "Hey." I pass him his glass of wine and he clinks it with mine. "What are we celebrating?"

My brows rise. "We're commiserating, actually."

"What?" He takes a sip.

"The end of my nine-year relationship."

He frowns. "You spoke to him already?"

"I told you I was calling him today." I sigh.

"And I told you to wait for me to be here," he says, annoyed.

I roll my eyes. "Don't fucking piss me off tonight, okay? I'm not in the mood, Brock. I've had the worst day in history."

He sips his drink slowly, and I can tell he knows that I really am not in the mood. "Well, what did he say?"

I shrug. "He knows it, too. I can tell."

He watches me for a moment. "Did you tell him about me?"

I nod. "Uh-huh."

"What did you say?"

I exhale heavily. "I said I was seeing someone, and he asked me if I loved you."

The front door bursts open and Meredith comes waltzing in, her face falling when she sees Brock.

"Oh." She looks at him flatly and curls her lip in disgust. "What are you doing here?" she asks him.

Brock raises his eyebrows in surprise at her disdain. "I should ask you the same thing. Don't you knock?"

I roll my eyes and fill my glass to the brim. I'm not in the mood for this shit tonight.

"Well, it's wolf pack meeting night," she tells him matter-of-factly. "You should leave."

Brock scowls. "What?"

"This is a girls only zone." She gestures between her and I.

"Meredith," I sigh.

"I don't know what bitch-pack meeting night means, but it's you that should leave. We're busy," Brock hits back, unamused.

I frown and give him a subtle shake of my head. "Ten minutes," I mouth.

Brock rolls his eyes and walks into the bathroom.

Meredith crosses her arms in front of her, annoyed. "Where's Callie, anyway? We need to get the meeting started."

"There is no meeting tonight, Meredith. I've had a really bad day and I just want to relax with Brock."

She rolls her eyes. "Oh God."

The door opens again and my mother waltzes in. "Hello, Meredith. Hi, Tully," she says greets us both.

I frown. "Mum, what are you doing here?"

"I've come to talk some sense into you."

I give her a subtle shake of my head.

"What is this nonsense about breaking up with Simon for another man? Simon has been on the phone to me heartbroken on and off all night. I came over to see what on earth is going on with you."

Not now, Mum. I shake my head again, and right on cue, Brock walks out of the bathroom behind her. He purses his lips and assesses the situation.

"Hello," he says.

My mother turns in surprise, looking him up and down, her mouth falling open.

"Ha ha." I fake a smile as the blood drains from my face. "Mum, this is Brock."

She turns to me, and then back to him, repeating the process several times before she manages to actually speak.

"Wh—I mean. Wh—"

This is a first. She's been rendered speechless.

"Mum, Brock is my… friend," I add.

"Boyfriend," Brock corrects, looking very unimpressed.

My eyebrows rise by and I swallow the lump in my throat.

My mother frowns as he takes her hand in his and shakes it.

"And your name is?" he asks.

"Robyn." She twists her lips as she tries to hold her tongue.

"Would anyone like a beer?" Brock asks, making his way to the fridge.

I drain my wineglass in one gulp. Fucking hell, this is a disaster. This is not how I planned their first meeting to go.

"I can't drink beer," Meredith says. "It makes my vagina smell."

Brock's entire face curls up in disgust as he looks around at her, while I just carry on and pour myself another glass of wine. *God, help me*. I drain the glass quickly.

"I don't think you're her boyfriend, dear." My mother fakes a smile. "That's a bit premature, isn't it?"

Brock opens the beer and takes a sip, holding my mother's eyes. "Not at all."

The two of them enter some kind of stare-off. *Oh no.*

"Yes, because it's best if I drink wine, too," Meredith continues as she hints to be offered a glass of wine. "I don't want to smell tomorrow. I have a date in the storeroom."

"Meredith!" I snap. "We don't want to hear about your badly smelling vagina in the broom closet."

My mother winces at what I've just said, and then she turns

her attention back to Brock and fakes a smile. "Tully is just confused at the moment."

"Hmm." Brock glares at her. "Seems like a lot of people are."

I begin to perspire. Doesn't he know that my mother runs the Simon For Life fan club?

"Tully, I thought you said you were going to stick with your vibrator because it isn't an entitled ass that thinks it's God's gift to women like Brock does," Meredith says seriously.

My mother frowns in horror, and Brock smirks. How the heck does he find this amusing?

"Meredith!" I snap. "You need to go home now. That is *not* an appropriate thing to say."

"But you said it first. Remember? When you were fighting with Brock and he told you he was going to drag you to the car?"

My mother turns to Brock in outrage. "You threatened her with violence?"

Brock rolls his eyes. "No. But Meredith is in danger of some any second now."

"Tully is taking three weeks off to masturbate with all of her batteries," Meredith tells them both. "Aren't you, Tully?"

I widen my eyes and drain my glass of wine.

Help me!

"Good God, Meredith," my mother cries. "Stop talking about that. It's offensive."

"No, it's just natural," Meredith replies innocently. "You should really try it. It's very good for your stress levels. We can take you to the sex shop, if you like. We go there after the beach sometimes. They even have fake pussies with hair on them."

Brock glares at Meredith and points to the door.

She narrows her eyes. "You're not in the wolf pack, you know."

He points again but doesn't say a word, not needing to, and Meredith turns to walk through the door, turning back at the last moment. "This wolf pack meeting *sucked*."

Brock points to the door again and she finally disappears out into the hallway, the door closing behind her.

Brock turns to me and puts his arm around my shoulders. I know it's a power play to annoy my mother. "Would you like a glass of wine, Robyn?" he asks sweetly.

She glares at him. "I wouldn't get too comfortable around here if I were you."

He smiles calmly. "If you say so."

"Will you two stop it!" I snap. My head begins to spin from the litre of wine I have sunk in record speed. "Brock is my new friend, Mum, and we are having fun together. I can make my own decisions. I am not getting back with Simon. You need to get that into your head."

Brock rolls his lips as he listens.

"If I wanted to be with Simon, Mum, I would be with Simon." I throw my arms up in the air. "And quite frankly, I'm annoyed that he calls you like a baby to whine about me."

"He wasn't whining."

"He called you, didn't he?"

She exhales heavily and folds her arms over her chest. "You're just confused," she mutters under her breath.

"No. I'm. Not," I cry out.

"Tully." Brock tries to calm me, and I pull out of his arms.

"Now if you both don't mind, I've had a *really* shitty day. I'm going to bed. You two let yourselves out." I storm to my bedroom and slam the door shut behind me.

Fuckers.

CHAPTER 14

Tully

"So, then what happened?" Rourke frowns as he looks into the microscope, deep in concentration.

"I don't know. I went to sleep with the shits. When I woke up, they were both gone, so I'm assuming they left soon after I stormed off." I shrug. "They probably had a fight on the way out. Both of them are strong characters, and Brock was definitely not putting up with her interfering crap."

"Jesus." He picks up another slide and puts it under the microscope. "Why is Simon calling your mother now?"

"Because my parents love him, and his mother and father have become best friends with my mother and stepfather."

Rourke scowls. "It's just weird."

"I know." I blow out a deep breath. "And fucking annoying."

"Did you call Brock this morning?"

"No." I drop into my seat. "And I'm not going to. I'm not

getting railroaded by him, either." I turn on my computer and wait for it to boot up.

"Hey." I hear a familiar voice over my shoulder, and I smile. "How's my favourite sister?"

I smile as Peter walks into the lab. "Hello."

He turns his attention to Rourke. "Hey, Rourke." He smiles at everyone around us and waves.

"Got time for a coffee?" he asks.

"I can't. I just had a break." An idea comes to me and I narrow my eyes. "Has Mum sent you in here to talk to me?"

He smirks. "She may have called me at six in the morning to tell me you've lost your mind and that I need to speak to you urgently."

I groan out loud. "Oh, for God's sake." I slam the folder across to the other side of my desk. "She's a damn busybody, and she needs to mind her own business."

Pete chuckles.

"What did you say to her?" I snap.

He holds his hands up in front of him, sensing my frustration. "Just that I would check on you."

"Checked." I roll my eyes. "Now, I'm very busy and I have to get back to work. You should go."

He leans onto my desk with his behind. "Who's this guy that you're seeing?"

"Oh God, not you, too?" I begin to hit the keys on my computer with force. Why is everyone so fucking annoying?

"What?" He smiles innocently.

"I'd be careful if I were you," Rourke mutters as he studies his specimen. "She's in full bitch mode today."

I glare at Rourke and he withers, wisely choosing to go back to his microscope.

"I'm just seeing someone casually. It's nothing serious. It's just a guy I met at the gym."

"Okay." He stands and smirks at Rourke. "My job here is done. Information will be reported."

I roll my eyes. "You're as bad as Simon, running to Mum all the time."

He chuckles. "Nobody's as bad as Simon." He shakes his head as he walks out of the office. "He's got her on speed dial."

I walk to the bus stop, deep in thought. I haven't heard from Brock today and it makes me wonder what my mother said to him last night. The poor bastard. He didn't ask to be brought into all this shit with my ex and his little fan club. I'll call him when I get home. I lean on the side of the shelter, take my phone out and scroll through it. A message pops up from Brock. I smile and click it open.

You look gorgeous today.
Pink is your colour.

I smile and frown. How does he know I'm wearing pink? I glance up and there, across the road, he's standing, leaning against his parked car. He's wearing blue jeans, a white T-shirt, and his dark, messed up hair and sexy smile make my heart flutter in my chest. My phone beeps again.

Need a ride?

I smile and make my way over.

"Hi," I breathe.

"Hi." His playful eyes hold mine. He has that look about

him, the one that talks to my lady parts. No, actually, it doesn't talk. It conquers them and drags them back to his cave, Neanderthal style.

I smile as the energy swirls between us. It feels like I haven't seen him in forever. "You didn't call me today.

"You seemed like you needed some space."

"Not from you."

He takes my hand in his and pulls me close, wrapping his big arms around me. I close my eyes as he holds me tight. I don't think there is a better feeling than being in his arms.

"Do you want to go and get something to eat?"

I smile up at him. "Actually, I would like to fuck, but we can eat first, I suppose."

He chuckles and throws me a sexy wink. "Good plan." He opens the car door for me and I climb in, smiling to myself. I turn into a different person when I'm with him. I would never have said something that suggestive to Simon.

Brock starts the car, and ten minutes later we are sitting in a Mexican restaurant. Mariachi music is being piped throughout the garden courtyard, and there are beautiful fairy lights strung out overhead to create a magical feel.

It's a warm summer night, and for the first time in two days, I feel relaxed.

"What will it be?" the cute waiter asks us, armed with his notepad and pen.

Brock gestures to me and I frown as I peruse the menu. "Can I have a salted margarita in a martini glass, and the nachos, please?"

"Sure thing." He turns his attention to Brock.

"I'll have a Corona and the nachos." He folds his menu in half and passes it over before his eyes come up to mine. "Blow out."

I smirk. “What does that mean?’

“It means I don’t eat crap and drink on a week night. I’m usually at the gym right now. You’re a bad influence, Pocket.”

My mouth falls open. “Me?” I gasp. “You’re the only bad influence around here.”

He slides his hand up my leg under the table and licks his lips as his naughty eyes hold mine. There it is—that electricity I get from his every touch.

“Thank you.” I sigh.

A frown crosses his face. “For?”

“For not being demanding and obnoxious yesterday.”

Our drinks arrive. “Here you go. I have a salted margarita and a Corona.”

“Thank you.” We both smile as we take them from him.

Brock sips his beer and frowns. “Do you think I’m demanding and obnoxious all the time?”

“No.” I sip my drink. “God, this is good.” I gesture to my glass. “But sometimes you can be,” I add.

“Like when?”

“Like when you demanded I call Simon in front of you.”

His eyes hold mine for a moment.

“What?” I ask.

He shrugs. “It’s hard for me to deal with an ex on the scene when I’ve never—”

“When you’ve never had one?” I cut in.

“Yeah. I guess.” He drinks his beer and then places it back on the table. “I just don’t know if you’ll go back to him one day.”

I take the hand he is resting on my thigh. “Would it bother you if I did?”

He nods, and his face falls serious.

I smile softly. “I like this person.”

He frowns.

I cup his face and lean over to kiss him. "I like this person who is with me here tonight."

"What do you mean?" He frowns.

"Why aren't you like this all the time with me?"

"Like what?"

"Gentle and understanding." I smile.

"I don't know why I'm the way I am. I have this raging temper that... I don't know. I fly off the handle and can't control myself until it's too late."

"Too late?" I frown. "Is that why you've never had a girlfriend because of your temper?"

He smiles and then breaks into a chuckle. "Fuck, no, I never cared about a woman enough to lose my temper with them."

"So, why have you lost it with me numerous times?" I frown.

His eyes search mine, and I know he's trying to tell me that he cares.

I could push him to say it, but he doesn't probably even realise it himself yet.

"What do you mean by too late?" I ask. "When have you lost your temper and it's been too late?"

His face falls serious, with eyes glancing across the restaurant to avoid mine. Brock takes a swig of his beer. "I killed my father with my temper."

I freeze at once. "What?"

He stares at the floor in front of him for a moment and I can see he's right back there reliving it.

"My sister was dating someone I didn't approve of." He pauses, taking in a breath. "I lost my shit and attacked him at my parents' house."

My heart sinks.

"We had a fight, and my father tried to break us up." He looks into the distance and pauses again, the story obviously hard for him to speak of. "He had a massive heart attack on the spot."

I squeeze his hand in mine. "Brock," I whisper, pained for him.

"My cousin Cameron was there and was just out of med school. He tried to save him in the back of the ambulance with defibrillators."

Brock sips his beer again, his eyes void of emotion, and I feel sick as I imagine the horror of what it must have been like to be there on that day.

"He died anyway," he tells me sadly. "It fucked Cameron up for a long time, too. My father was the first patient he ever lost."

"I'm so sorry," I whisper. "And you still blame yourself?"

"Every day."

I drop my head and think for a moment. I don't know what to say.

"Every time I watch my sisters and my mother cry over my father's absence, I die a little inside."

I get a lump in my throat. "Brock."

His sad eyes come up to meet mine. I know that was a big deal for him to tell me that. I know it's probably something that he would usually guard closely. "Thank you."

"What for?"

"For showing me what's underneath your temper." I pick up his hand and gently kiss the back of it.

His eyes search mine.

"We can work with your temper, baby," I kiss his hand again, "if you give me this side of yourself more often. We can work with anything."

He looks so lost in this conversation and being open with me, I can tell that statement meant a lot to him. He just has no idea how to verbalise it yet. I get up and go around to his side of the table to sit on his lap. I wrap my arms around his neck and kiss him tenderly, our lips hovering over each other's. I wish we were alone right now. I need to change the subject and not make a big deal out of what he just told me.

"Did you know that I have next week off work?"

"You do?" He smiles, seeming grateful for my change of topic.

"Yep." I shake my head. "I was supposed to be going to Hawaii."

"You were going to Hawaii?" He frowns.

"Yeah, but I cancelled it last week."

"How come?"

"You're not the only idiot around here." I sigh, and he smiles, pressing a kiss to my shoulder. "The girl I was going with pulled out a few weeks ago, but then last week, when I was freaking out, I cancelled my trip, too."

"Why were you freaking out?"

"Over you." I push his hair back from his forehead and kiss him. "Told you I was an idiot."

He chuckles and bites my shoulder, making me jump. "How is this my fault? Why would you cancel a trip because of me?" He looks up at me, and he's so damn beautiful I could just bite him back.

The waiter arrives with our food, so I get up and go back to my side of the table. "Can you tell him to stop pulling me onto his lap, please? It's very distracting," I ask the waiter sweetly as I pull my chair in.

The two of them chuckle, and the waiter places our huge bowls of nachos in front of us. "Will that be all?"

"Two more drinks, please," Brock tells him.

"Of course, and please stay off his lap, miss," he jokes before he disappears again.

I dig into my nachos, pushing one loaded with salsa into my mouth, and then I smile mischievously over at Brock.

"You didn't answer me?" he reminds me.

"Oh." I stuff another nacho into my mouth. "Because I was feeling all clingy and attached to you." I roll my eyes. "And I knew I wanted to be with you, but I felt too guilty to end it with Simon." I shrug. "It just all seemed too hard."

He frowns, chewing on his food. "But why would you cancel a trip because of that?"

"I didn't want to leave you, dummy," I mutter dryly. "Clingy and attached means clingy and attached."

He smirks, and then his smirk turns into a grin, his grin soon turning into a huge beaming smile.

His smile is contagious, and I giggle as I continue to eat. "What?"

"Clingy and attached?"

"Don't." I smirk. "I know how pathetic it sounds, even to me."

His eyes twinkle in delight.

I roll mine. "You know how I changed the subject for you before?"

He smiles.

"You need to change the subject now for me. It's your turn to take the heat off me."

He rolls his lips and narrows his eyes at me as he pretends to think of something to say. "Hmm." He shakes his head. "Nope, I've got nothing that will distract us from the fact that you're being clingy and attached."

My mouth falls open as I fake shock. "Stop saying it out loud," I whisper.

"Nope." He throws another nacho into his mouth. The waiter walks past. "Excuse me," Brock calls to him.

The waiter turns back. “Yes, sir.”

Brock points to me. “She’s feeling clingy and attached to me.”

The waiter breaks into a broad smile, his eyes flicking between us. “Ah.” He nods. “That explains why she won’t stay off your lap then.” He turns and walks off.

“Exactly.” Brock smirks as he throws another chip into his mouth, his eyes dancing with mischief as he watches me.

I sip my drink. “Just hurry up and eat your dinner so you can take me home and do obscene things to my body. I’m just using you for sex, you know?”

Brock swigs his beer. “Your wish is my command. Tonight, your stage name shall be Miss Cock Pocket.”

I choke on my drink. “Well, at least it isn’t Princess Pussy Porridge,” I splutter.

He tries to swig his beer and then breaks out into a low chuckle.

“Where do you get this shit?” I giggle.

He shrugs. “It’s my hidden talent.”

Two hours later, the room is filled with steam when Brock bends and slowly slides my pants down to the floor. We’re in his bathroom, and the night has taken an unexpected turn.

I feel close to him. Whatever this is between us, it feels intimate.

He opened up a little, and while I know it’s far from everything I need from him, it’s definitely a start. He leans in and kisses my sex, and then rises and slowly pops open the buttons on my work shirt. My heart is beating fast in my chest and my breath quivers in anticipation. He takes my hardened nipple into his mouth, biting it as his two hands roam up and down my body. I know he's been looking forward to this as well. My hands run through his hair. I can feel my sex throbbing in anticipation. I can't take it, I need him naked. I slide his T-shirt up over his head, and my hands drift across his large chest and over his shoulders. His dark eyes hold mine before our lips collide. He sucks on my mouth with just the right amount of pressure and I feel my legs go weak beneath me.

I run my fingers down his rippled abdomen and slowly slide them down to undo his jeans. I pull them down and he kicks them off, leaving me free to slide my hand up his thick shaft and stroke a few times as we kiss. Pre-ejaculate beads, and I slide my hand over the end to smear it down his length.

He inhales sharply. "Shower," he says low and commanding. "I need you in bed." Our kiss turns desperate as his hand slides through my wet sex and slides three fingers into me. I wince from his aggression.

"I need this beautiful creamy cunt around my cock. Now."

He pulls me under the water and pins me against the wall. His hard cock slides back and forth up over my stomach as he takes the soap and carefully washes me.

Our lips stay locked, his hand roaming all over my body, through my sex, and then to my behind. My mind goes back to the first day he took me and how he said he was wired to do things that way. He hasn't touched me there since, and I hate to admit it, but I'm aching for it.

Aching for him to show me what he wants.

Aching to please him.

I take the soap from him and wash his large body, enjoying the way he's looking down at me. The hot water is running down over his head and knowing that I'm the only thing he sees or wants just might be enough to set me on fire. His eyes are dark, his big lips are a bruised shade of red, and his square jaw carries a two-day growth. I've never seen anyone so gorgeous in my life.

"You're so fucking hot," he whispers, almost to himself, as he cups my jaw in his hands, his dark eyes hold mine.

"Oh God," I pant. "Brock."

"Out," he commands. He steps out of the shower and holds a towel out to wrap me in. He dries me and leads me into the bedroom where we stand at the end of the bed and kiss for a moment.

The perfect kiss amongst all of the chaos. It's his kiss that brings me back to him.

"Show me," I mumble against his lips. "Show me how to please you."

His eyes flicker with a dangerous level of arousal, and my stomach flips with nervous excitement.

"You want me to show you?"

I nod.

He licks his lips and lifts his chin, bringing a soft smile to my face.

That's his satisfied look. His chin rises when he's pleased.

"Kneel," he whispers.

I swallow the lump in my throat and drop to my knees instantly. Brock walks around me slowly.

"Legs farther apart."

My eyes rise up to him.

"Do it," he growls.

I shuffle to widen my legs apart and, once again, his chin lifts in approval. He puts his thumb under my bottom lip and pulls my mouth open.

"I'm going to fuck your mouth, Pocket, and I'm going to blow my load down your throat."

I swallow quietly, trying to control my fear.

"Okay?" He raises a brow, and I know that wasn't a question; it was a dare.

I nod.

"Answer me."

"Yes, Brock," I whisper, overwhelmed by the power he's omitting. I haven't seen him like this before. Only snippets of his sexual aggression have ever come into play.

He puts his thumb just under my bottom lip and pulls my mouth wide open again, and he slowly slides his thick shaft across my lips, smearing the pre-ejaculate across my tongue. His dark eyes follow his cock, fascinated.

Christ almighty, this is off the hook.

He pulls my mouth open wider and slides his cock straight down my throat, forcing me to gag.

"Open your throat."

"I..." I hesitate.

"You what?"

"I don't think I can take all of you. You're too..."

Brock puts his hand on the back of my head and pushes me forward. "Learn."

Oh jeez, what have I gotten myself into here?

I close my eyes and try to calm myself down as he slowly slides out and then back in again. He moans softly and it spurs me on. He does it again, and this time his hand tenderly pushes my hair back from my forehead, his eyes finding mine. "That's it, Pock," he whispers.

I feel a rush of cream to my sex and I begin to throb. I rub my legs together to try and tame the fire down there.

"You want my cock, baby?" he asks.

I nod around him.

"You can have it soon." He pushes down my throat and I feel him swell in my mouth. He's close. He pushes harder, grabbing my head in his hands and slowly riding my open mouth. He tips his head back, looking up to the ceiling.

"Fuck," he moans. "You have no idea how fucking hot you look right now."

Oh God, I love this. I love bringing him undone like this.

He goes harder, and I gag again. He stills. "Stop thinking."

I hesitate.

"Take me."

I nod again, and he pulls out to kiss me. His lips suck on mine with just enough pressure to drive me wild, and he dusts my face with the backs of his fingers.

He slides his cock back in, and this time it's as if he has no control. He grabs my hair in his hands aggressively and begins to ride my mouth. "Fuck, yeah." He hisses.

I smile around him, spurred on by his arousal.

In, out, in, out. I bare my teeth and his head tips back. I feel a hard jerk and then I taste his salty arousal as it slides down my throat.

I drink it down.

His body convulses as he empties himself deep down in my throat, and I watch him slowly come back to Earth.

He has this glow. His body is covered in a perfect sheen of perspiration. I've never seen anything more perfect. I run my hand up his behind, kissing his lower stomach tenderly as he pulls out. Brock stills and holds my head close to his body for a moment. I look up at him in question. His haunted eyes search mine.

"What's wrong?" I whisper as he pulls me to my feet.

He runs his fingertips down my face. "Nothing, baby," he whispers before kissing me. His eyes close as he tastes his own arousal in my mouth, and then he slowly seems to regain his focus.

He walks to his bedside and takes out a box of condoms.

"I don't want that," I say.

"You don't want what?"

"Have you always used condoms?"

"Yes."

"I've only ever had one partner apart from you."

He frowns, as if confused.

"If we're only going to be with each other from now on, I don't want you to wear a condom."

He hesitates as he stares at me.

"I'm on the pill."

Fear flashes across his face. "I don't want a baby, Tully. I'm not ready for any accidents."

"I know." I walk over and kiss him as my hands drop to his behind. "Trust me."

He frowns as our lips meet.

"Trust me," I repeat.

I can see his internal struggle with this. God, he's never trusted a woman enough to do this.

"If I'm trusting you not to hurt me, you can trust me not to trap you," I tell him. I can't believe I'm begging for this. "I want all of you inside of me."

He drops his head and stills for a moment. What the hell? This is a really big deal for him.

"How do you want me?" I whisper.

His eyes hold mine, and I can tell he's still not sure if he wants to risk coming inside of me. "On your knees on the bed," he says devoid of emotion.

I kneel on the bed, bending over to rest on my elbows so that my behind is in the air, waiting for him. Brock inhales sharply and runs his fingers over my back entrance, remaining silent.

Oh fuck. I close my eyes and drop my head at the feel his tongue there.

I hold my breath. *Oh. Dear. God.* I try to move forward but he grabs my hip bones and yanks me back onto his face, his stubble burning my cheeks.

Fuck.

He licks me while his four fingers slide through the swollen lips of my sex.

I'm so wet it's ridiculous. The sounds of my wet arousal and my shallow breaths are the only things to be heard.

With his tongue lapping at my back entrance, he slides three fingers into my sex and I moan when he presses my back and pushes me down onto the mattress aggressively.

I can see his cock through my legs and its already hard again. Pre-ejaculate is beading once more, and it begins to drip. *God help me.*

He adds another finger, which makes me whimper from the burn. He begins to pump me hard, so hard that the bed begins to rock. I can see every muscle in his shoulders and arm contracting from his reflection in the mirror in front of me. *Holy fucking God.*

He slowly feeds his hard cock into my sex, forcing my mouth to fall open as the pleasure takes over. He rubs saliva into my back entrance and slides his thumb deep inside.

My body instantly convulses.

"Hold it," he growls.

My knees feel like they are going to give way beneath me. I've never felt anything like this. With my hip-bone firmly in his hand, he begins to rock me back onto his body. I'm being taken by his thumb and his cock, and to be honest, I don't know which feels better.

Brock hisses in approval. "That's so fucking good, Pocket."

I nod, unable to speak.

"Do you feel it? Feel how deep I am inside of you?"

I nod again. Oh God, this is *too* good.

He begins to really give it to me with deep, hard drives, until I can't even see anymore. His possession has completely blinded me. He raises a leg to rest on the mattress, his other taking his weight, and I cry out at the change of his position, convulsing as I'm thrown forward by a bone-shattering orgasm.

He pulls out of my ass and grabs both of my hip bones in his hands to slam me hard, so hard and fast. He pushes me into the mattress as he takes what he needs from my body.

I feel like I am having an out of body experience.

This is too good, too much, too fucking hard.

"*Ah.*"

He slams me one, two, three times, and holds himself deep, coming in a rush deep inside of me.

His body begins to quiver and he falls over me, dragging me to the mattress.

And then he kisses me, his touch soft, tender, and loving. The exact opposite of the beating his cock just gave me. He pulls out and rolls me over so I'm underneath him. I'm like a rag doll in his arms. He is completely in control of my body. If he wanted to take me again now, he could.

He kisses me again and again before he pulls back to look at me. "You want to know something, Tully Pocket?" he whispers as he pushes the hair back from my face.

"What?"

"I'm feeling pretty fucking clingy and attached myself."

I pull him close. "Glad to know I'm not in this alone."

. . .

I wake to the feel of Brock's lips on the back of my neck. "Hmm." I can feel his morning glory up against my behind.

He rolls me onto my back and kisses me. "I've got to go to work early, Pock."

"Okay," I mumble quietly.

"You don't have your car here."

I frown, realising he's right. "Ugh," I groan.

"Just stay here and I'll get you a cab for later."

I sit up slowly. "No. It's fine." I moan as I get out of bed. "I'll go now."

He disappears into the bathroom and I hear the shower turn on. "You getting in?"

"It's too early for showers."

"Grumpy," he calls back.

I sit on the edge of the bed as I try to get my bearings. God, what time is it? It must be, like, five or five thirty at the latest. The sun has only just started to rise.

Five seconds later I hear the shower turn off and Brock walks back into the room with a black towel wrapped around his waist.

"How's my little Come Pocket this morning?" he asks chirpily, walking over to his wardrobe area. "My boys swimming around well in there?"

I scrunch up my face in disgust. "For fuck's sake, Brock, what is with your nicknames? Don't call me that."

He chuckles, and when he comes out dressed, he kisses me and takes me in his arms. "I have drinks tonight with my work friends," he tells me.

"Okay."

"Do you want to come?"

I frown. "You want me to meet your work friends?"

"You'll meet them one day, anyway. May as well get on with it."

I watch him as he moves to walk around his room all chirpy and shit.

"Okay."

He looks through his drawer, taking out his gym clothes for after work. "I thought I might take next week off, too."

"Really?" I frown.

"Yeah." He walks over and kisses me again. "I kind of thought I might like to take my girl to Hawaii."

"What? Who are you, and what have you done with Brock?"

He shrugs casually. "Seems only fair. You *did* cancel your trip because of me."

I smirk at the progress we seemed to have made. "Are you serious?"

"Deadly. Now, get in the car or I'm going to be late."

"I don't have any clothes on."

"Find some," he calls back to me as he disappears down the stairs. "You have five seconds before I leave without you."

I smile to myself.

Brock Marx. The only man I know who can make me swoon with the most unromantic lines I've ever heard.

"Hurry, wench," he calls from downstairs.

I giggle as I throw my clothes on. "Shut up!" I call back.

"Don't make me come up there and get you. I am the boss of us, you know."

I giggle. "Like hell."

"Right, that's it." I hear him running up the stairs two at a time, and I try to run away into the bathroom, but he crash tackles me to the bed making me squeal with laughter.

"You're going in my car naked." He tries to pick me up and throw me over his shoulder. I fight him off, but he quickly drags me back beneath him, and the two of us fall serious. I can feel the erection in his pants. He flexes it against my stomach.

"I thought you were running late?" I smirk.

"With the way you feel, baby, I'll come in two minutes flat."

He unzips his jeans, holds my leg back, and he slides home.

"What am I going to do with you, Brock Marx?" I whisper up at him.

"Shut up and fuck me."

CHAPTER 15

Brock

DATE OF BIRTH?

I frown as I stare at the online booking form on my computer screen.

Hmm, I didn't think of that one. I don't even know her date of birth. I blow out a deep breath and dial her number. It rings a few times until I eventually hear her beautiful, husky voice. "Hi," she breathes.

I smirk. Just the sound of her makes my cock twitch. "Hello, my Tully Pocket."

"Ah, my handsome man is calling me at work now. I was right: you *are* getting clingy and attached to me."

"Or perhaps I just don't know your birth date to book the flights."

"Oh." She giggles. "You really are a bad private investigator. Don't you have that stuff on a computer somewhere?"

I smile as I swing from side to side in my chair. "But then I wouldn't get to hear your sexy voice."

"This is true. Are you really booking us tickets to Hawaii?" I can tell she's smiling.

"I told you I was, didn't I?"

"Well, how long are we going for?"

"Eight days." I frown to myself. "Or do you want to go for ten?"

"I'll be sick of you in eight days. I need to give you the money for the ticket."

I roll my pen across the desk with my fingertips. "I'll be sick of you in three, and you can pay me back by giving me good head."

She giggles, and I find myself smiling. She has the most intoxicating laugh. It does things to me that make me want to please her more.

"Okay, so I was born on eleven, oh five, ninety-three."

My eyebrows rise in surprise. "You're twenty-five?"

"How old did you think I was?"

"You look at least thirty-five," I tease.

"Watch it," she warns playfully. "How old are you?"

"I'm forty- six."

She bursts out laughing. "You are not."

I find myself chuckling along with her. "I could be forty-six."

"Not with that dick's stamina, you couldn't."

I smile. "I'm twenty-eight."

"See? We're perfectly matched." She laughs.

"If you say so."

"I know so."

We both fall silent for a moment. I wish I was with her now. "What are you doing?" I ask.

"I'm analysing mud from the sole of a boot. What are you doing?"

I'm booking a flight for a holiday. Quite frankly, I wish we were going today." I stand and walk over to the window to look out over the park next door.

"Me, too, but three days will come around quickly enough," she says.

"I know."

"What time are you picking me up tonight?"

"I'm going to try and squeeze in a session at the gym first. I'll be there around eight?"

"I can't wait to see you," she breathes.

I smile broadly. It feels weird having someone be so open with me. "Me, too."

"You hang up first."

I shake my head and chuckle. "I don't play hang up first games, Pocket. I'm not five."

"Good, hang up then."

I smirk and hold on the line.

"See, you do play them. You play them badly, too. I win." She hangs up on me, and I smile with a shake of my head.

"What the fuck, man?" Jes groans.

I turn suddenly to see Ben and Jes standing in the doorway.

"What are you two fucking doing here?" I snap.

"*You* hang up," Ben teases.

"No. *You* hang up," Jes mimics in a girl's voice.

I roll my eyes. "Fuck off, the both of you." I feel my face redden at them catching me being so soppy. "What?" I snap.

"We have new info." Ben smiles knowingly. He sits down and produces a large yellow envelope.

I sit back. "What is it?"

"We went through the footage from the hotel, covering the dates when Chancellor was there."

"And?"

"He was seeing three different girls. Sometimes he would see the same one twice in one week. Other times, he would see different ones." He slides over images of a woman and Mr. Chancellor entering a room. She has long dark hair and is wearing a short, tight white dress. There are five photograph stills taken from the footage. I flick through them.

"Always the same three women?" I frown.

Ben slides another two images over. There's one of a woman coming out of his room, and she is blonde, attractive, and wearing a tight black dress.

"Yes. Always the same three women."

"How many times in total?" I ask.

"It's gone on for over three years, so in excess of one hundred times."

I pick it up and study the image. "He knows them well, whoever they are?"

Jes slides another image across. "And this one."

This image is a close up and I can see her face clearly. "She looks familiar," I say. She has chocolate brown hair, a killer body, and I find myself leaning back on my chair as I study the image. "I know this woman." I frown as I try to recall where I know her from.

"Are they definitely escorts?" I ask.

"As far as we can see, that seems to be the case," Ben tells me.

"Who do they work for?"

"Not sure yet, we're working on it," Jes replies.

I swing on my chair as I study the image. "Is this...?" I frown and stare at the girl. "Shit, I think I know who she is."

"Who?"

"She's the prostitute who was found dead in the boot of a car down on the docklands."

Ben begins to type on the keyboard to bring up her records.

"Yes, this is her. Remember? She... she was hogtied in the trunk after being shot in the back of the head," I stammer, excited I made the connection.

Ben's eyes widen as he reads the report. "Fuck, look at the date of her death.

September twenty-second."

My eyes meet his. "That's the same day Chancellor died."

I take my keyboard back and begin to search for information on this woman. I wait for it to come up on my screen. "Her name was Talia Thompson." I read through the notes. "Twenty-three, high-end call girl." I hit images and a selection of pictures of her come up. Some of them are high quality modelling shots, too.

"She was fucking beautiful," Jes mutters to himself. "What a waste."

"I know." I sigh. "It says here that no known employer was found." I purse my lips as I think. "Bring up every image that the police ever had of her."

We go through image after image, and for over an hour we search through all the information we can find.

"Oh my God," I mutter as I concentrate on the image.

"What?" Jes frowns.

"Look in the right corner of that one." I point to people in the background of the image.

We all lean in and study the screen. It's a picture of her at a funeral, and there in the right-hand corner is a man we know. "Kissinger."

Ben shakes his head. "If she was one of Kissinger's girls she was always going to die."

"Who's Kissinger?" Jes asks.

"An ex-biker smart as a whip, who runs a high-end brothel service in Sydney. He gets his girls addicted to drugs, fucking them up so bad they'll end up doing whatever he asks of them."

Jes raises his eyebrows. "Looks like Tahlia didn't do what she was told."

I narrow my eyes as I stare at the screen. "Or did she?"

Ben frowns. "What do you mean?"

"What if he had Tahlia kill Chancellor?" I look up Chancellor's file. "What did he do for work again?"

"I.T."

I frown as I try to connect the dots. "Hmm, I'm not sure how this all ties together." I think for a moment. "Was he blackmailing him?" I turn to Ben. "Does this sound familiar to you?"

"I was just going to say the same thing."

"You think that Chancellor is somehow connected to these girls' deaths?" Jes asks.

"I think we need to talk to this Kissinger," Ben says.

"Bring him in." I reconsider that for a moment. "Actually, I'm taking next week off so wait until I get back."

"Why are you having a week off?" Ben frowns.

"I'm taking a trip."

"With who?" Jes asks. "You don't take trips."

I turn back to my computer and begin to type. "A friend."

They both watch me, and I look up. "What?" I snap.

"Tully?" Ben smiles.

I roll my eyes. "Don't get ahead of yourself. It's just a few days away."

"Where are you going?" He smirks.

I lick my lips, knowing full well how this is going to sound. "Hawaii."

Jes chuckles. "Aloha." He punches me in the arm. "You, like, honeymooning or some shit now? You romantic bastard?"

"Fuck off." I sigh.

Ben chuckles and massages my shoulders, as if he's my trainer. "This girl's got you by the balls. Your tiny, microscopic balls are in the palm of her hand."

I bat his hand off my shoulder. "She has not."

He slaps me hard on the back three times. "Happens to the best of us, man."

They disappear out of my office and I stare at my computer screen for a moment, smirking to myself

Maybe she has... a little bit.

Tully

I look at my reflection in the mirror as I reapply my lip gloss. I'm nervous. I'm meeting Brock's work friends tonight and my stomach is churning. I even went out during my lunch hour today and bought a new dress.

I turn to look at the back of it in the mirror. It's a cream mini with thin spaghetti straps that falls into an A-line skirt. It's cute without trying too hard. I don't like tight, trying-to-be-sexy clothes. Pants are usually my thing, but I wanted to try to impress tonight. I'm wearing high-heeled, tan strappy sandals with a matching clutch. My long hair is out and straight, and I have on Brock's favourite bronze lipstick. I'm assuming it's his favourite, anyway. Every time I wear it he comments on how fuckable my mouth looks. The security buzzer rings out, and I smile at myself in the mirror. Okay, let's do this.

"Hello?"

"I'm here to pick up my fuck pocket," his deep voice purrs.

I giggle. "You do have a way with words, Romeo. Come up." I push the button to open the front security door. Idiot. Where does he get this shit? Moments later, he appears and my heart sings.

"Hey," he says softly as he takes me in his arms and kisses my lips.

I cling to him and close my eyes. God, every time I see him I feel closer and closer. I missed him today, and not just his smartass mouth. I missed all of him. It was a soul-deep kind of longing. One I haven't felt for years.

He holds my face and kisses me again, and it's like he feels it, too.

"I missed you today," I whisper.

He smiles down at me and pushes my hair behind my shoulders. "You look fucking beautiful." He bites my neck and I close my eyes. He bites me harder and I get goose bumps.

God, what this man does to me.

He drops to his knees in front of me and kisses my thigh. "This dress," he purr's distracted.

I put my hands on his large shoulders. "Do you like it?"

He lifts it and kisses my sex through my white, lacy panties. "I love it," he breathes against me. He kisses me again, and then he lifts one of my legs over his shoulders and pulls my panties to the side.

"Just a taste to get me through the night," he whispers, and his thick tongue swipes through my flesh tenderly.

God, what a greeting. I look down at this beautiful specimen of a man on his knees in front of me, worshipping my body as if it's the most precious thing he's ever seen, and I feel my heart constrict.

I begin to feel my heart freefall into some kind of abyss. A place where I don't ever want to return from.

Could he be more perfect?

I tip my head back as the sensations overwhelm me.

He begins to eat me, suck and lick, and oh God… it's so good. My hands drop to the back of his head and he pulls me apart with his big hands.

He kisses my sex with an open mouth again and again, and I shudder, an orgasm close. That's when he carefully puts my panties back in place and stands up again. Our faces only millimetres apart. "I might have missed you too today, Pock," he whispers.

My eyes search his. Does he feel it, *whatever this is?*

"You know, with a greeting like that, I don't really want to go out anymore," I tell him.

His lips take mine and he sucks aggressively. My legs nearly fail me. "I'll be peeling those pretty little panties off with my teeth later." He bites my bottom lip and I yelp, looking up into his dark eyes. "Make sure I have something nice and creamy to suck on." He slaps me hard on the behind and I squeak in surprise.

My insides feel like they're beginning to melt into a puddle on the floor. God, he's fucking filthy.

"Promise," I whisper as my hand slides down over the large erection in his jeans. My lips drop to his neck and I bite him in return. I make to drop to my knees but he stops me.

"Pock, we're going out."

"But, I want a taste," I murmur against his lips. "It's my turn."

He grabs my cheeks of my behind and grinds my body hard

against his erection. "Baby, you're going to get more than just a taste. But you have to wait."

He kisses me again before he pulls me by the hand, leading me out of the apartment. Moments later, I find myself sitting in his car with a throbbing wet sex.

This man is off the fucking hook hot.

The old, timber staircase at the Angel Hotel in Sydney is steep. We are at a bar that I've never been to before. In fact, I never even knew it was here. It's four stories high and narrow. It feels like we've stepped back in time, although it's been decorated in a trendy way. The bars on each level are dark timber and fully stocked. The carpets are deep coloured, and the furnishings are vintage and antique looking. Music is playing throughout the bar, and it has a really cool vibe.

"What is this place?" I ask Brock as he leads me up another flight of stairs.

"This is where we drink."

I smirk. "Kooky."

He chuckles. "Like you."

We get to the top floor and my stomach twists in knots. I feel so nervous about meeting his work friends. I hope I get along with them. I can't think of anything worse than forcing conversation all night.

There is a bar that runs the length of the room, with three pool tables taking up space around it. Over in the far corner there's a small dance floor. It's quaint with a real small-town vibe. I can see why they like it here. Over in the far corner sits four bench tables pulled together with a large group of people around them. And when I say people, I mean men.

There are heaps of men, all huge, gorgeous, and the smell of their testosterone burns through the air.

I gulp. *Shit.*

Brock smiles, sensing my nerves, and he throws me a wink before he leads me over to the table. God, why did I agree to this?

"Hey," they all cry, turning to smile our way.

"Boys." Brock smiles proudly. "This is Tully." He puts his arm around my waist.

I give a small wave. "Hi." I can feel my face turning a deep shade of red as they all take their time to assess me.

Brock goes around the table and introduces me to them one by one, and I shake all of their hands, but I already know that I'll never remember their names. There is a blonde guy who is covered in badass tatts, and a holy hot African American who may just be God himself.

"Hey there." He smiles sexily, and I nearly swallow my tongue when I hear his American accent. Jesus, he could do some damage.

A European man, maybe Italian, smiles and picks up my hand, kissing the back of it smoothly. Brock slaps him over the back of the head and the boys all laugh. He continues to make his way around the table, introducing me to everyone until he gets to the last two. "And this is Jesten."

Jesten is tall, has sandy hair and a full sleeve of tatts. He has the bluest eyes I have ever seen, as well as a warm smile.

"Hi, Tully." He shakes my hand. "It's great to finally meet you."

"Hi." I smile nervously. Oh, I like him.

Brock rubs his hand up my back, as if sensing I need reassurance.

"And this is Ben, my brother-in-law."

Ben leans in and kisses my cheek. "Nice to meet you." He smiles, and I can't help but notice that he's allowed to touch me when the other boys weren't.

I swallow the lump in my throat. "Hi." Ben is hot. Damn, they're all hot.

Not just hot, but stupid hot.

The boys return to their conversations, leaving Brock to focus on me. "Do you want a drink, Pock?"

I nod. "Yes, please." I widen my eyes at him. "Maybe a jug?"

He chuckles as he walks towards the bar. "The girls will be here soon."

Don't leave me. I take off after him. "Girls?" I frown.

He takes my hand in his. "The boys' girls. They'll get here after they finish work."

"You do this often?" I frown.

"We come here one Friday night a month."

"Oh, okay." I nod and stand beside him at the bar like a little puppet.

"What do you want?"

"Erm." I frown as I look at the drinks menu. I don't want to drink cocktails, I'll look like a princess. "Sauv blanc?"

"Okay." Brock orders our drinks and I look back to his friends, noticing a girl is now standing with them. She's young and pretty. She glances over and looks me up and down, quickly snapping her eyes away as if she's agitated.

Hmm. Who's that?

I run my hand up Brock's back and whisper in his ear. "Who is the girl with the boys?"

Brock glances back over. "Oh, that's Cindy."

"Cindy?"

"My secretary."

I frown. "She's your secretary?"

"Yeah, why?"

I fake a smile. "Just wondering." I glance back over to see that she is openly glaring at me now. She has honey-blonde hair and a killer body. She's wearing a grey tight dress that leaves nothing to the imagination, and I'd say that she looks about twenty-one.

Hmm, okay. That's interesting.

Brock gets our drinks and carefully passes me my glass of wine. "Come on, I'll introduce you."

Really. Do you have to? "Great." I fake enthusiasm as he leads me over.

"Cindy."

Her face lights up. "Hi, Brock."

"This is Tully, my girlfriend."

Her face falls as she glances between Brock and me.

"G-girlfriend?" she stammers.

Brock smiles and puts his arm around me, pulling me close. "That's right."

She can't hide her horror, not that she's even trying to. "Well, when did this happen?" she asks.

"A few months ago," he replies casually.

Somehow, I don't think Cindy is too happy with me dating her boss. "You never told me you have a girlfriend."

He rolls his lips, and I can't tell he's annoyed at her tone. "Well, now you know."

She glares at me, and Brock glares at her.

Jeez, *awkward.*

"I'm getting a drink," she mutters before she disappears to the bar.

Brock's hand drops to my behind, and I turn to him. "Really?"

He smirks, knowing exactly what I'm about to say.

"Your secretary has the hots for you?"

"Is it obvious?"

I widen my eyes. "Slightly."

He runs his hand over my behind, bringing it up to rest on my hipbone. "She's always been into me."

I frown.

He bends and kisses me softly. "Jealous?"

"Pftt," I scoff. "No." I sip my drink and my eyes roam over to Cindy at the bar. She is gorgeous... and young.

"Have you slept with her?" I ask.

"Fuck, no." He winces.

I sip my drink, annoyed with myself for even asking.

"You have nothing to worry about there, Pocket."

"I shouldn't have anything to worry about anywhere, Brock."

He chuckles. "That, too."

I sip my drink slowly, but I really want to tip my head back and pour it down my throat.

Is he a player?

An attractive brunette walks up the stairs, and one of the boy's wolf whistles. She giggles and comes over to kiss him, and then she begins talking to everyone else in the group.

She sees Brock and me, and she smiles before she walks over to us. "Hi, I'm Emily."

"Hi." I smile, grateful to see a friendly female. "I'm Tully."

She bends and kisses me on the cheek. "Hello, Tully. It's so nice to finally meet you."

Hmm, she says that like she's heard of me before. Brock sits on a stool behind us, and two of his friends come over to sit with him.

"So, you are dating one of the guys?" I ask her to try and make conversation.

Brock's hand comes up around my thigh from behind, and he runs it up my leg, underneath my dress as he talks. His thumb brushes back and forth over the lips of my sex through my panties as he talks. I think he's unaware that he's even doing it.

"Yeah, I'm going out with big John." She points to a guy on the other side of the group who is sitting down.

"Big John?" I frown.

She giggles. "He's six-foot seven."

My eyes widen, and she then leans in and whispers, "He's big in all places."

I laugh softly. I like this girl already.

"What are you drinking?" she asks.

"Just a sauv blanc."

"Oh." She grimaces. "That stuff will kill a dog."

I nod, scowling at my drink. "I know, right?"

"Fuck that. Let's go and get some cocktails."

Six hours later

I have three new best friends, and their names are Emily, Freya, and Monika. They're going out with some of Brock's friends and have each gone out of their way to make me feel comfortable. We have been drinking anything and everything. It's amazing how much women can bond over alcohol. I could be best friends with anyone after a couple of rounds. To be honest, I've hardly seen Brock all night but I've watched him with the boys. He's definitely the leader of the group. He doesn't talk much, but when he does everyone hangs off of his every word. Ben left at nine. He had to get home to his pregnant wife. I think he's my favourite out of all the friends Brock has. He's so dry, and he has this *I don't give a fuck* attitude about him. The club is packed to the rafters because there is a band playing. It's getting loud, hot, and sweaty.

Cindy is on the dance floor, dancing for the group of boys as if she's some kind of stripper. They're all pretending not to look, but I can see them all casually glancing over and pretending not to see her. I stand and watch her for a moment.

"What's with her?" I ask the girls.

Emily turns to see who I'm talking about, and then turns back to us, rolling her eyes. "She's after your man, sweetie."

"Who, Brock?" I frown. I was hoping she wanted any man, not just mine.

"She's ridiculous," Freya whispers.

"She's obsessed with him."

"Brock?" I repeat.

"Yep. You should see what she wears to these nights out and how she puts on a show for the guys, hoping that, one night, Brock will take her home. It's actually a joke amongst the boys in the office. They all tease him about it."

We all look over to watch as Cindy swings her hips down until she's nearly at floor level before she snaps her whole body back up.

"Slut snaps?" I frown. Oh, please. What next? She's so fourth grade.

The girls all burst out laughing.

I lean into the group. "Has he ever... you know?"

I feel a large hand snake around my waist from behind, and Brock pulls my body back to his.

"Hey." He smiles as he kisses my cheek from behind.

The girls all begin talking.

"You having fun?" he asks, dropping his hand to my behind.

I smile and nod. "Now that you're here, I am."

He kisses me over my shoulder and then licks up my neck

to my ear. "You'll be coming on my face tonight, Pocket," he whispers.

Goose bumps scatter up my arms. I casually reach behind me to cup his cock, and he kisses my lips in return.

"Are you wet?" he asks so only I can hear.

Our eyes are locked when I give my answer in the form of a single nod.

"You want to go soon?" I can tell he's had as much to drink as I have.

"I want to come soon," I whisper back to him.

His eyes darken. "You want to come here?"

I frown. "What do you mean?"

He grabs my behind and grinds me onto his hipbone as his tongue trails down my throat. "You want me to fuck you in this club?"

My eyes widen. "What?" I glance around.

"Because I can," he whispers darkly, moving closer and kissing me aggressively. "I can fuck anywhere you want, baby. All you have to do is say the word."

He takes me in his arms and kisses me as if we are alone. I can feel his erection in his pants.

"Jesus, Brock. Down, boy," I whisper. "We'll go in half an hour."

His dark eyes hold mine, and then he licks his lips and disappears to the bar.

I turn back to the girls.

"Fucking hell," Freya gasps. "Are you for real?"

My eyes widen. I forgot they were even here. "What?"

"You should have just fucked him in the club." Emily laughs.

I cringe. "Oh, you heard that?" I put my hand over my face and laugh in embarrassment.

"Do you know how many women would kill to fuck him in a club?"

I crinkle my nose. "As long as it's not his fucking secretary, I don't care."

"He hasn't gone there," Monika says, and we all look back to the dance floor to see Cindy dancing sexily.

"But she would jump at the chance. Don't trust that little skank as far as you can throw her," Freya adds.

I feel big hands snake around my hips from behind, and I see Freya's face fall. I turn and get a fright. It's not Brock. It's another man.

"Oh." I pull out of his grip. "Don't do that," I say.

"Hey, baby," he slurs. "Come back here, I want a little fun." He grabs me again and pulls me towards him.

"Don't touch her!" Monika snaps, pushing against him.

"Fuck off," he growls. God, he's really drunk.

He leans in and tries to kiss me, but I push him back. "Don't!" I snap.

"Go away!" Freya yells at him.

He grabs me again and pulls me onto him. Oh, God, he's hard. I struggle to get out of his arms.

"What the fuck are you doing?" I hear Brock growl.

Oh no.

"Whatever I fucking want, cunt," the man answers roughly, and he pushes Brock back.

Brock glares at him. "Tully, go to the bathroom."

"B-Brock," I stammer. "Let's go."

"Move!" he yells and pushes me out of the way just in time to miss the man who takes a swing at Brock. *What the fuck?*

I'm grabbed from behind and pulled out of the way just in time to see Brock land a punch to this man's jaw.

"Stop it!" I cry.

I fight to break free from Jesten's grip. The man takes another swing at Brock and Brock punches him back. The next minute, it has turned into a full-on fist fight with men running in from everywhere. Both the man's friends and Brock's friends are involved in it. There are twelve men in this fight, and the noise forces the band to stop playing as the bar's security run in to try and break it up.

A table is tipped over and glasses smash everywhere. I see Brock on top of this man on the ground beating the hell out of him. He's completely lost control.

I put my hands over my face in horror. "Stop!" I scream. Brock punches him again and again. He's going to fucking kill him.

"Brock, stop it!" I cry.

But he doesn't, and a second later another of the man's friends runs over and kicks Brock as hard as he can in the stomach. Brock falls to the ground, and then Jesten goes crazy, finally letting me go. He dives on the man who just kicked Brock. It starts again.

I put my hands over my eyes.

What the fuck is going on?

When I look up again, I see Brock getting up. The look on his face is murderous, and I have to scrunch up my face as the tears begin to fall.

I can't watch this. I can't watch him be like this.

He's a fucking animal.

So I turn, and I run.

CHAPTER 16

Tully

I RUN down the stairs as quickly as I can, my heart racing in my chest. The brighter lights have all been turned on as the bouncers run up the stairs towards the fight.

I get a vision of how violent Brock was being, and I find myself wincing again. What the hell was that about? One minute he is whispering sweet nothings in my ear, and the next moment he turned into a total psychopath.

I can't deal with this shit... or him. I need to get out of here. I take the stairs two at a time until I get to the ground floor. I burst out through the front doors. A cab is just dropping someone off, and without asking, I dive right into the back seat.

"Can you take me to Darlinghurst, please?"

"Of course." The cab driver casually pulls out into the traffic. I turn in my seat to look at the Angel Hotel as it disappears into the distance before I turn back to face the road in front of us. My heart is beating so hard and fast in my chest. I see the look on Brock's face, and I wipe my tears away as swiftly as I can. He was like a different person.

The cab makes its way through the traffic and with every kilometre that we get farther away, I feel a little bit sicker about what I've just witnessed. Brock just kept hitting him, again and again. I mean, the idiot deserved the first punch, but why did he have to keep going with it?

I close my eyes. What if the man presses assault charges? But the guy did start it and was fighting back pretty bad. Maybe he wouldn't have a case.

Brock has no control over his anger. None. I saw it with my own eyes, and even though he had touched on it with me, it was a shock to my system to actually witness it.

I can't be with someone who can hurt someone like that with no regard for human mortality. I stare out the window through tear-filled eyes. I would have thought that after his father's death he wouldn't do this shit anymore. He's twenty-eight, not a young boy dealing with extra testosterone. When is he going to grow up? Things were going so well for us. I thought I was maybe starting to fall in...

Oh, God.

He's just too different to me.

I pay the driver and begin walking to the front door. My phone rings, the name Brock lighting up the screen.

"Hello," I answer.

"Where are you?" he barks.

"I left. I'm at my mother's."

"What the fuck? Why, Tully?" he growls.

I screw up my face in disgust. "If you don't know that, you're a fucking idiot," I snap and hang up, throwing my phone back into my bag as my blood boils.

The phone rings again immediately. I ignore it and walk

into my building, hitting the lift button when I hear a commotion coming from down the hall.

Peachy Sue's apartment door is open, and I can hear a man screaming.

Shit, it's probably her pimp. Fuck, I don't want him to see me. What do I do?

I hit the elevator button quickly, but it doesn't come. *Come on, come on*. I look up at the numbers and see it's still up on the tenth floor. Shit.

I hear something hit the wall down the hall, whatever it was being smashed to pieces.

"Get the fuck out!" she screams.

Oh my God, I don't want them to see me. I look to the front doors, and then back down the hall. The fire exit stairs are next to her door, so he would see me if I ran for those. I scurry down the hall, open the janitor's storage room, and I run in, pulling the door closed behind me. I stand in the darkness with my heart beating hard in my chest as I listen for more noise.

My phone rings again. Oh fuck. Brock, not now. I fumble to turn it to silent, and I concentrate, trying to listen again. Something else smashes and I hear a door open across the hall. Has someone else heard something?

I close my eyes as my heart hammers. I should call the police. What if he's bashing her up? But if he hears me, he'll probably hurt me, too. Oh God, why didn't the bloody elevator come? I think I need to seriously consider moving apartments.

Bang, bang, bang goes my heart. This is why you don't prostitute. Not only do you have to suck random dicks, you have to be owned by a fucking pimp who beats you up if you don't go to work.

My eyes widen as a different scenario comes to my mind. What if Brock turns up here in his raging state and he runs into them hurting Sue. He will go fucking crazy, and the pimp probably has a gun on him.

Oh my God.

Shit, shit, shit, shit.

What do I do? I put my ear up to the door and listen. It's all gone quiet. Fuck, do I just go out there how?

My phone vibrates in my bag again. For fuck's sake, Brock. *Go home, you idiot.*

Please don't be out the front of the building? No, he wouldn't be here yet. He only just called me a moment ago from the bar.

I wait for ten minutes before I open the door and peer out. The corridor is empty and Peachy Sue's door is now closed.

I swallow the fear in my throat. Okay… just act casual. Act casual. I'm just walking up the hall. I've seen nothing.

I walk up the hall, and I honestly feel like I'm about to have a heart attack. I hit the elevator button and, thankfully, the doors open straight away. I jump in quickly and hit the button. I hold my breath until I get to my floor, and then I run out and unlock my front door and dive inside my apartment.

I turn my phone off and storm to the bathroom for a shower.

What a disaster of a night.

Brock

I push the security button on Tully's front door. It's 3:00 p.m. and she is not taking my calls.

I fucked up last night. I fucked up bad.

She left and went to her mother's when I got into that fight. She didn't want to see me. I don't know what came over

me to lose my temper in front of her that way, and I hate that she saw me that angry.

I push the button again and I hear her pick up, but she doesn't answer me.

"Tully, it's me. Let me up." I sigh.

"No. I'm good," she snaps angrily.

"Can we at least talk about it?" I ask.

"I have nothing to say."

"I do, so fucking let me up."

The buzzer eventually grants me entry, and I push the door open angrily to make my way to the elevator. I inhale deeply as I try to calm myself down. *Don't lose your shit again, that's what got you in this fucking position in the first place,* I remind myself. I run my hands through my hair as I try my hardest to cool down. This is all new to me. I've never been in the dog house with a woman before. I don't fucking like it.

Tully opens her door, fury written all over her face. I try to kiss her hello but she turns head away from me coolly.

I put my arm around her, but she pushes me off her aggressively. "Don't touch me."

"Come on, Pock."

"You've got to be kidding me. Don't *Pock* me!"

Silence is all I can come up with in response.

"What the fuck was last night about, Brock?" she snaps.

"Pock," I whisper as is try to wrap my arms around her again.

"Don't *Pock me*!" she yells. "I'm so fucking angry at you, it's not even funny."

"Why?"

She puts her hands on her hips and narrows her eyes. "You can't be that stupid." Her hair is wild and her big lips are full. I can see her silhouette through her nightdress and I feel my cock harden. This woman could seriously turn me on at any given time, even when she's raging mad. The thought makes me smirk.

"You think this is funny?"

"No," I reply, but I kind of do for some reason. A stupid smile crosses my face again.

She picks up the cushion from the sofa and hurls it at my head. "You big fucking twat waffle," she yells in an outrage.

The cushion connects with my head, and I burst out laughing at the name twat waffle. That's a new one. Tully storms into the kitchen, furious.

I pinch the bridge of my nose. Any minute now, she's going to come back and lose her shit again. I already know it's coming.

Right on cue, she starts storming over to where I am again. "And another thing..."

"You didn't tell me the first thing yet," I tell her dryly.

She points her finger in my face. "Don't bait me, Brock. I hardly slept a wink and I am raging like a bull."

I exhale and look to the ceiling. "Obviously."

"That's it," she screams. "Get out!"

"What?"

"You think this is funny?" she yells.

"*What's* funny? Spit it out, woman."

"You!" she screams, and her eyes fill with tears.

My heart drops. Oh God, she's really upset.

"You didn't stop hitting him."

My face falls.

"I'm so traumatised from seeing you like that."

"Pock," I whisper softly. I hate that she witnessed me at my worst.

Why the fuck did I do that?

"Don't Pock me," she says through gritted teeth. "You have no idea how it feels."

I take her in my arms. "I'm sorry, okay?" I try to comfort her. "What are you talking about I hold her close.

"I can't be with someone who thinks that behaviour is okay, Brock. I-I won't do it."

"Tully, I have to do what's right sometimes. I can't just let things go. I won't have you disrespected, and that guy was asking for it."

"So, you beat him to a pulp?" she cries. "He could have died. What if he hit his head on the floor and died?"

I puff air into my cheeks as I try to calm her down. I pull her close to me and kiss her temple.

"H-here I am over here falling in love with you, and... and all you care about is being in control and winning," she stammers.

I still instantly. *What the fuck did she just say?*

My eyes find hers, and she screws her face up, making more tears fall, her disappointed and embarrassment clear from having just let that slip.

"You're falling in love with me?" I ask in a whisper with raised brows.

She stares at me but doesn't answer.

I begin to hear my heartbeat ringing in my ears as the panic sets in. I have this overwhelming urge to run.

"I can't be in love with someone who has that temper, Brock," she whispers.

My eyes search hers.

"You need to man up and be the man I need, or you need to step away."

"Step away? What does that mean?"

"I want a man to love, not a little boy who tantrums, lashes out, and hits people when he doesn't get his own way."

My heart sinks.

"You said you wanted to do this relationship thing, Brock."

I step back from her, a sense of fear sweeping over me like never before.

"Do you still want me?" she whispers.

"You know I do."

"So, at what age are you going to grow up?"

I frown.

"Are you going to stop this alpha-hole bullshit, man up and love me, or do you want to keep on fighting the world alone?"

"Alpha- hole isn't a word," I say, trying to change the subject.

"Yes, it is. It's code for Brock Marx."

I smirk.

"Brock." She puts her arms around me and looks up at tenderly. "I don't want the bad-tempered boy who fights the whole world for the rest of his life."

I swallow the lump in my throat as I stare down at her.

"I want the gentle man who I know can love me." She kisses me softly and her arms slide around my hips as she tries to convince me to change.

"I don't do gentle, Tully."

"Yes, you do, Brock." Her lips meet mine, and her tongue slides through my mouth. "I know you will because you care about me, too."

"Can we just stop talking about all of this love stuff, please?"

"No." She quickly pulls from my grip. "You want to be in a relationship with me, don't you?"

I hold my hands up in defeat, sensing that a complete meltdown is on the horizon.

"Then we *are* talking about it. Don't ask me to hold myself back from you because my feelings scare you," she snaps. "Don't you dare ever ask me to do that!"

Fuck. I drag my hand down my face. This is all a bit fucking dramatic, isn't it?

I stare at her and she slowly takes my hands in hers. "I care about you, Brock." She pauses for a moment. "In fact, I'm falling in love with you, and I'm not telling you that so you have to say it back or anything lame like that. I'm telling you this because you need to know that this is something special for me. This isn't just fucking around like I know you're used to. And I thought it was special for you, too."

I look at her blankly, but her hopeful face eventually makes me smirk.

"But you're just being a big jerk," she adds.

"Ease up, hey? I'm beginning to think you're the one with anger issues here, not me."

"Brock," she whispers, leaning up to kiss me. "I want us to work."

I stare down at her.

"Let go of the anger and jump... with *me*." She smiles hopefully.

My hands tighten on her behind. "I don't jump with twat waffles," I whisper against her lips.

She giggles and puts her hands in my hair. "You're doing it, even if I have to push you off the cliff."

I smile against her kiss. "I kind of thought that was what was happening here."

Tully

It's Sunday night, and Brock is taking me to meet his family. Apparently, his sister, Natasha, and her family are going home to L.A. tomorrow, and he wants me to meet them before they leave.

After our fight yesterday, and after I opened up to him and put my heart on a platter, I feel closer to him than ever. We spent the afternoon in bed making love. He was gentle and tender, and although he never once mentioned how he felt about me, he showed me in other ways. Last night we went walking and got Thai takeaway in our tracksuits. I don't feel like I have to dress up or wear makeup with him. I'm totally at ease. He makes me feel like the most beautiful woman in the world when I'm at my absolute worst. We stayed up late and watched movies at his house, and then this morning we even went for a run together.

There wasn't a trace of the violent man I saw at the club on Friday night, and with every hour that passes by, I feel the horror fading a little more.

Brock is a beautiful man, and if I want a future with him I know I have to be patient while he softens to my ways a little.

It's 6:00 p.m. now. He dropped me home a couple of hours ago so I could pack for our trip tomorrow.

Hawaii.

I'm excited to be getting him all to myself for a week—only the two of us, just how I like it.

I need to say goodbye to Meredith and give her a key to water my plants. I haven't seen her as much as I normally do this last week and I'm feeling a little guilty about it.

I knock on her door.

I wait but there's no answer.

I knock again. Still no answer. Hmm. She mustn't be home. I turn to walk back up the hallway when I hear her keychain unlock and her door open.

"Tully," she whispers as she peers through the crack in the door.

"Hi." I smile.

"Shh." She puts her finger to her mouth. "Shh."

I frown as she pulls me by the hand into her apartment and closes the door behind us, flicking all of the locks.

"What are you doing?" I frown.

She peers through the peephole. "He's coming back. You need to be quiet."

"Huh?" I whisper. "Who's coming back."

"Black jacket, black jacket."

I stare at her. "What are you talking about?"

"I didn't see anything." She begins to pace. "I didn't see anything." She shakes her head, puts her hands over her ears, and begins slapping herself on the head. "Know nothing, know nothing," she repeats over and over.

"I frown as I watch her. "Meredith, are you feeling all right?" Jeez, I think she's having some kind of psychotic episode. I don't know what to do. "Have you taken your medication today?" I ask.

She starts hitting herself on the head again. "Know nothing, know nothing." She is pacing back and forth and can't stand still.

"Meredith, how about I take you over to your mother's house?" I've gotten to know her mother and she's not as bad as I first thought. She handles Meredith a lot better than Callie and I do, anyway, especially in circumstances like this.

Her eyes widen. "Yes." She runs into her bedroom and

begins ripping her drawers open quickly. “Black jacket, black jacket,” she repeats over and over.

“Yes, bring your black jacket.” I say, jeez.... what’s going on with her?

I don’t think I should tell her I’m going away while she’s like this. I don’t want her to have a meltdown.

She runs to the bathroom and picks up her whole toiletries’ basket. She runs out and tips it upside down into her suitcase. Things go flying everywhere, and then she runs back into her bedroom.

“What did you eat today, babe?” I ask carefully. “Did you have any blue food colouring?”

She runs out and looks at me, her eyes wild and wide as if she’s having a sudden epiphany. “Yes. Blue Lemonade.”

I wince. “Blue Lemonade? That doesn’t sound good.” I walk to the fridge. “How much did you drink?” I ask.

“Four litres.”

“Four litres,” I repeat as I pull the two two-litre empty bottles out from the inside shelves of the fridge door. “What the heck?” I shake my head. “Don’t drink this crap, Meredith. It will make you feel bad.”

She nods. “Yes. I feel bad, very bad. I need to go to the hospital now.”

“What?” Oh hell. I need to get her to her mother’s as fast as I can. “It’s okay, sweetie, grab your things and we will go over to your mother’s.”

“Yes.” She runs from the room. “Mother’s, then the hospital.”

“Maybe you should stay with your mum for a little while,” I call.

She runs back out and stares at me through widened eyes. “Yes. Good idea.” She nods. “Know nothing, know nothing.”

She runs back into the bedroom, and I follow her, noticing how all of her furniture has been pushed to the door. "Why did you move the furniture, honey?" I ask.

She begins to shake her head as if really frantic about something.

"It's okay, it's okay." Shit, should I call an ambulance or something? "Give me your suitcase and we'll leave now," I say calmly.

"He's coming back," she whispers, clearly petrified.

"Who's coming back?"

"Black jacket."

What the fuck is she talking about? I lead her out into the corridor by the hand, down into the elevator, and she looks so scared that it breaks my heart.

"Baby, it's okay." I put my arm around her shoulders to try and comfort her. We get into my car and she looks around frantically. It's as if she's scared of something she can't see.

I pull the car up at her mother's soon after. Meredith gets out of the car and runs inside, as if she's being chased.

I hate that she has to go through this. Her mother comes out. "What's going on?" she asks, confused.

"I don't know, I just found her like this." I shrug. "I didn't know what to do."

"Has she missed her medication?" her mother asks.

"I'm not sure. She had a lot of food additives that may have made her nervous."

"Okay, thanks for taking care of her, dear." Her mother gives me a sad smile and goes back inside, leaving me to sit in my car for a moment.

I really hate that she has to go through this. Why was she so frightened?

It's one thing to have a friend like Meredith, but to see her like this is heartbreaking.

I slowly start my car and blow out a deflated breath. I turn the corner to head back to my house. Brock will be there at any moment to pick me up, and tonight, I get to meet his family.

I'm so nervous.

My phone alerts me to a text and the screen lights up. It's from Simon.

I'm at your house. Where are you?

My eyes widen. *What the fuck?*

CHAPTER 17

Tully

Oh my God, oh my God. They're both going to be turning up at my apartment at the same time. I put my foot down on the accelerator and begin to speed up. I can't have them meet like this, and what the heck is Simon doing back from London, anyway? He's supposed to be gone for another three weeks at least. I mean, I knew that he would come back to see me when he returned, and I always anticipated that he and Brock would one day meet, but I didn't expect it to happen now.

I turn into my street and see Brock's car parked with him sitting in it waiting for me. Simon is standing next to the front door.

Oh my frigging God!

Shit.

With Brock being Brock, this is not going to go down well. What the hell do I do?

I can't even avoid Simon. I'm not dressed to meet Brock's family yet.

What a fucking nightmare.

I park out on the street just down and opposite from Brock, and I call him. He answers on the first ring.

"Hey, Pock. Where are you?"

"Hi, babe." I sigh as I watch him in his car. He doesn't know I'm here. "Erm, so, here's the thing," I whisper.

"Here's what thing?"

"I just pulled up and I'm parked across the street."

He glances up, sees me and gives me a sexy smile. I wave feebly.

"Simon's here."

He frowns. "What?"

"See the guy near the door? The one on his phone?"

Brock looks over to the front doors of my building, and I see his jaw clench.

"Brock, please," I whisper. "If you care for me at all, you will let me handle this."

"Tully."

"Please, babe. I'm begging you. Despite what you think of him, he's done nothing wrong and is a dear friend."

He glares at me through his windshield, exhaling heavily.

"Don't say anything to him."

"Fuck off," Brock snaps.

"Brock, please," I beg. "I love you, I'm with you. Let me handle this."

He glares at me.

"Stay in the car and I'll be ten minutes."

"What does he want?" he barks.

I swallow the nervous lump in my throat. "He'll just want to talk to me, that's all."

"He'll want you to go back to him," he says as his angry eyes hold mine across the road.

"That's not happening because I'm with you. But I need to have this conversation with him, and I swear to God, if you say one thing to him I will never speak to you again."

He narrows his eyes. I can see his fury at my threat from here.

"Give me ten minutes and stay in the car," I whisper before hanging up.

I get out of my car and Simon sees me straight away. He flashes me a crooked smile, and then Brock gets out of his car.

Damn it, Brock!

My heart begins to hammer in my chest as I walk up to Simon.

"Hi." He smiles.

"Hello." I smile, twisting my fingers in front of me nervously. "What are you doing here?"

"I flew home from London. Your mother said..."

"Hi," Brock announces, moving to stand beside me. He puts his hands into the pockets of his jeans. His legs are wide, his chin tilted to the sky.

Arrogance. Pure arrogance.

I gulp and scratch my head awkwardly. "Simon, this is Brock. Brock, this is Simon."

Brock glares at Simon as they shake hands.

"Hey," Simon mutters. He frowns and looks between Brock and me. "Who's this?" he asks.

"Erm." I frown. Oh God, please let the earth swallow me up. "Brock is my..." I pause. "Boyfriend."

Simon's face falls, his eyes searching mine.

Instantly, my eyes fill with tears, I've hurt him. "Si," I whisper.

"It's true then?

Brocks jaw clenches but he stays silent.

I nod slowly.

"But you said..." Simon starts.

I nod again. "I know I did," I whisper. "I never meant for this to happen, and I care for you so much."

Brock's brow furrows as he watches me struggling.

"You know I love you, Simon, but I love Brock in a different way."

Simon presses his lips together and his eyes fill with tears. Brock drops his head. Simon's pain is palpable... even to Brock.

"I'll wait upstairs," Brock says quietly.

I smile through my tears and hand Brock my keys. "Thank you," I mouth.

He nods and turns to Simon, pausing for a moment, not knowing what to say. "Sorry, mate."

Simon's eyes stay glued to the ground.

Brock disappears inside, and I grab Simon's hands. "We're friends, Simon. We'll always be friends. But something was missing from our relationship."

"Not for me."

"Yes, for you. You were happy with that girl, I saw that you were."

"That was different to what we have, Tully."

"I know, but that doesn't mean it was a bad thing. What we have will never be replaced, Si." I squeeze his hands in mine. "We did all our firsts together."

His eyes search mine. "I'll come back now. I-I won't even go back to London," he stammers.

I shake my head. "It's too late."

"It's not," he blurts out.

"I never started anything with Brock until I saw you with that girl."

His face falls.

"You looked so happy… happier than you ever did with me."

"Tully," he whispers.

"I've made my decision. I'm with Brock now. You and I won't be getting back together."

"How can you say that?" he whispers, clearly panicked. "You don't even know him."

I shake my head. "I know, not like I know you. This decision isn't based on Brock. It's based on us, Simon, and what was missing between us."

Something snaps inside of Simon and he begins to get angry. "So, you're getting it from him! What's he got? A big fucking dick or something?"

My heart drops and I know I have to end this conversation now before it turns nasty.

"I don't want it to be like this between us. I want us to be friends."

"You want me to be friends with you and him, to play happy families together?" he snaps. "That won't fucking happen, Tully. You get in the car and come home with me now or it's over forever."

I stare at him through my tears. "I'm sorry." I take a step backwards.

"Tully, no," he whispers as he grabs me in an embrace. "Don't do this, I love you."

He screws up his face and we stand in each other's arms for an extended time. It occurs to me that this may be our last embrace, and the emotion of it all overwhelms me. I sob out loud.

"I hate hurting you." I wrap my arms around him.

"Well, you have."

My chest begins to ache. "Please forgive me." I kiss him softly. "Goodbye, Simon." I pull out of his grip, turn and walk into the building.

"Tully," he whispers.

Regret creases my face. God, I hate this.

"Tully, come back."

I close my eyes and walk through the foyer.

"Tully!" he cries, and I begin to run. I can't look back. I don't want to see him like this. The elevator doors open, and I dive in.

"Tullllllyyyy!" he calls out.

I tip my head back to the skies. Oh my God.

I run up the hall and open the door. Brock wraps me in his arms and holds me as I cry. "Hey," he whispers, my chest bouncing with distress.

"He was crying," I whisper. "I promised him I wouldn't meet anyone," I sob. "And I did."

"Shh," he calms me.

"But I don't love him. I love you, and now he's hurting because of me."

"Shh, baby." He leads me into the bathroom. "Have a shower and calm down."

Everything aches. "But we have to go to your mother's." I sniff.

"We can be late." He sighs. "I'll call her." He bends and kisses my lips softly. "Do you still want to go? We don't have to."

I look up at him being all sensible and caring, and I smile despite my tears. At a time when I thought he would go crazy, he actually acts like the man I need him to be.

"I love you," I whisper.

He kisses me tenderly, his lips lingering over mine. He holds my jaw in his hands, and then he pushes the hair behind my shoulders, looking like he wants to say something.

"I'm going to look after you, Tully. I know I'm not too good at this whole relationship thing, but I'm going to give it my best shot." His eyes search mine.

"Promise?" I whisper.

"I promise." He kisses me softly again, and I can almost hear my heart diving, free falling in my chest. This is the first time he has ever verbalised any emotion towards me.

And I needed it. I really needed it now.

"We go away tomorrow," he breathes against my lips. "And I'll take you dancing."

I smirk at his distraction tactics.

"And I'll buy you cocktails."

I smile.

"And you've got to pay off your trip by giving me lots of amazing head."

I giggle. "You're ruining it now."

He leans into the shower, turns it on, and then he carefully undresses me before I step in under the hot water.

"I'll make you some tea," he says, making to walk out of the room.

"Brock?" I call. He turns back to me. "Thank you. Thank you for being nice to Simon. It means a lot."

His eyes hold mine and he smiles softly. "I can't think of anything worse than losing you. I feel sorry for the poor bastard."

I smile sadly, and he walks back, leaning in to kiss me softly. "You ready to meet my crazy family?"

"If they're half as crazy as you, I already like them."

. . .

An hour later and we are on our way. "Okay, so let me get this straight," I say to Brock while he drives. "Natasha is your older sister and Bridget is your younger sister?"

He nods. "Uh-huh."

"And your mother is Victoria."

"Yes." He flashes his gorgeous smile at me.

"What?" I smirk.

"You *have* been listening."

"And Natasha is married to Jonathan?" I frown.

"Joshua. His name is Joshua Stanton."

"Right."

"And Bridget is married to your best friend Ben?"

"Yes. Well, he's one of my best friends."

I nod and blow out a nervous breath. "What are Natasha's kids' names again?"

"Jordana, Ellie, and Blake."

I nod and twist my hands in my lap. "Do you think they'll like me?"

"Maybe," he answers casually.

I frown as I watch him. "Maybe?" I gasp.

He chuckles. "Will you fucking relax? It doesn't even matter to me if they don't like you. I like you."

I stare at him, unable to stop the grin breaking free on my face.

He rolls his eyes. "Is that all you're going to talk about now?"

I smile goofily. "Uh-huh."

"Don't wear it out, Cock Pocket. That's a 'special occasions' kind of thing for me to say."

"Yeah, like every day." I lean over and kiss him as he drives. "We really do need to talk about the names you call me."

He reaches over and grabs my sex in his hand aggressively and I squirm in my seat to get away from him. "I'll talk about this hot fuck box all I want." He grabs my thigh, and I jump and squeal.

"Brock." I gasp as I try to get away from him. "You're such an animal."

His eyes dance with mischief and he grabs me again.

"You're going to crash the car, you know?" I laugh.

He turns into a street, pulls up outside a house and turns his engine off.

There's a black Audi SV and another Range Rover in the drive, as well as another black Audi Sedan out the front with four men sitting inside it.

"Who are they?" I ask.

"That's Stanton's security team."

"Why do they have security again?" I frown.

"Joshua is a mega rich app developer. He's well known. The security is more for Natasha and their kids. It's how I met Ben, remember? He was Joshua's private security guard for years before he married Didge."

I'm lost. "Who's Didge?"

"Didge is Bridget. That's her nickname."

"Oh." I shake my head. "God, I'm going to mess up these names tonight, I just know it."

Brock rolls his lips, pausing briefly before he gets out of the car. If I'm not mistaken, he seems nervous, too.

"When was the last time you brought a girl home?" I ask.

He inhales sharply. "That would be never."

My face falls. "Never?"

"Nope."

I frown. "Oh. Perfect. No pressure for them to like me then."

He smirks and gets out of the car. He takes my hand in his, and we walk up the driveway.

"They're here," I hear a little girl's voice call out from inside.

She's obviously been waiting for us at the window. "And she's pretty, too!" she yells. "She has red hair."

"Jordana!" I hear a man snap. "Come away from the window."

Brock smirks and squeezes my hand in his. I squeeze it right back. "I may vomit," I whisper as we walk up the front steps.

"I'm not cleaning it up. You're on your own," he whispers.

"Great."

The front door opens, and two dark-haired women come into view. They're smiling broadly, not hiding their excitement.

Brock rolls his eyes. "Will you two stop with that look." He sighs. "This is Natasha and Bridget," he says as he kisses them both on the cheek. "And this is..." He pauses and smiles at me with affection. "This is Tully."

Natasha bounces on the spot, her excitement bubbling over. Bridget grabs me and kisses my cheek. "Oh, it's so nice to meet you. Come in, come in."

Natasha kisses me, too, and grabs my hand before she leads me into the house like a prized pig. We walk into the living room, and I find myself gulping.

Fuck!

Double fuck!

The living room has four men in it.

Not four normal men—four stupidly hot men who are happen to be looking at me with bated breath.

I feel the blood drain from my face.

"Tully, this is Adrian. He's a dear friend of the family, and he's also the CEO of Joshua's company."

Adrian jumps up from his seat and wraps his arms around me. "We met before, at the bar, remember?"

I nod shyly, and I nervously look over at Brock just as he throws me a sexy wink.

"This is Joshua."

Joshua stands, smiles and shakes my hand. Oh jeez. "Joshua is my brother-in-law," Brock says calmly. "And this is Cameron. Joshua and he are brothers."

Cameron stands to greet me. He has dark hair with a slight curl to it, and his mischievous demeanour is clear to see.

"I'm the good-looking member of the family." Cameron smiles and shakes my hand. "I'll probably be your favourite."

"Oh, God," Adrian mutters, while Joshua rolls his eyes.

"Watch it." Brock smirks.

I giggle.

"And you know Ben and these are little Jordy, Ellie, and Blake," Brock announces proudly.

The children look about six, five, and four, or something like that.

"Hello." The eldest girl smiles as she takes my hand in hers. "I love your hair."

"Thank you." I smile nervously

She turns to Joshua. "Dad, can I dye my hair that colour?"

"Absolutely not," he replies flatly.

"Why not?"

"Because you're six."

Natasha and Bridget chuckle.

"Come over here and let me do your hair," Adrian says. She immediately runs over and sits on his lap.

Brock looks around. "Where's Mum?"

"In the kitchen." Natasha smiles. "She's a bit emotional today."

Brock nods and my heart drops. It's because of his dad not being here. Brock takes my hand and leads me out into the kitchen where his mother is stirring something on the stove.

The range hood is cooking up a storm, and I think she may not have heard us arrive.

"Mum?" Brock says softly.

She glances over her shoulder, and her face immediately lights up. "Brock!" She rushes over and kisses him on the cheek. "Hello, my darling."

"This is Tully, Mum," he tells her with reverence in his voice as he presents me to her.

She smiles and takes me in her arms. "Oh, hello, dear." She squeezes me tight. "I've been waiting all day for you to arrive."

And suddenly, I feel emotional, too. It's obvious how much she loves Brock as she hugs him. She gets teary, and Brock shakes his head. "Will you stop?" He smirks. She whips him with her tea towel, as if they are sharing an old but private joke.

I smile. He's never brought anyone home before.

"Can I help you with anything?" I ask.

She smiles warmly. "No, dear, I have everything under control."

"Please?" I whisper. "I'm really nervous."

She wraps her arms around me. "Well, in that case, come in here." She leads me farther into the kitchen. "I burn everything, anyway."

I giggle. "Me, too."

"We have that in common then." She smiles warmly. Oh, I like her already.

"I'll get you a glass of wine," Brock says, smiling softly before he disappears. Natasha and Bridget come in and sit at the kitchen counter. Bridget is clearly heavily pregnant.

"How far have you got to go?" I ask.

"Fourteen weeks." She smiles. "Twins."

My eyes widen. "Twins?"

"I know." She shakes her head. "I don't know how the hell I'm going to do it."

Natasha rubs Bridget's stomach. "It's going to be fine, stop worrying."

"Are you scared?" I ask.

"Petrified," she whispers. "But don't tell Ben. I'm totally faking this whole 'I have this shit in the bag' business."

Natasha has long dark hair and is wearing tight-fitting, faded blue jeans and a white T-shirt. Her hair is in a ponytail and she hasn't any makeup on. She's beautiful with the most perfect dimples I have ever seen. She has a friendly, down to earth vibe about her. Bridget's hair is a little lighter, and she's wearing an ice-blue summer dress. Her stomach *does* look huge. No wonder Brock said she's struggling.

Adrian comes out and sits at the bench with the girls. Brock reappears with a bottle of wine and pours me a glass, topping up Natasha's and Adrian's while he's here, and then he gently puts his hand on my hip and stands behind me. "You okay, Pock?" he asks softly.

"I'm good."

He leans in and kisses my temple. "I'll just be in the living room."

"Okay." I smile at him being so thoughtful. I look up to see the three of them grinning as they watched our interaction.

"God, you three are fucking busybodies," Brock grumbles before he disappears into the other room. We fall silent, and I nervously look at the three of them.

"So..." Bridget smiles. "We could probably act cool and casual, but that really isn't our style and we desperately need to know all the juicy details."

I grin bigger.

"How long have you been dating?" Adrian asks.

"A couple of weeks."

Adrian. "Oh, yes, that's right. It was around Natasha's birthday, wasn't it?"

Bridget says something in return, but my attention turns to Joshua as he walks in and puts his hands on Tash's shoulders from behind. She turns to him.

"Do you want a drink, Presh?" he asks softly.

She smiles lovingly at him and holds her glass up. "I'm full."

He licks his lips and bends to her ear. "You will be later." He looks down at her darkly and gives a subtle crack of his neck. Jeez, there is some serious sexual chemistry between the two of them. I wonder how they met? I feel myself getting quite hot under the collar watching them together. Natasha rolls her lips together and smiles cheekily up at him, raising her glass at his promise. I look down quickly, pretending not to notice their private interaction.

Victoria begins to put everything into the serving dishes to take to the table, and Ben comes in shortly after to wrap his arms around Bridget from behind. He puts his big hands lovingly around her stomach, and she turns her head and kisses his shoulder.

I smile softly as I watch their interaction. Oh, I like this family.

There is so much love between them all. I can feel it.

"Ouch," someone cries from the living room. If I'm right, it sounds like the eldest girl.

Joshua rolls his eyes. "Blake!" he calls, and I smile, how does he know it was Blake? Is this kid wild or something?

"I didn't touch her!" the little boy calls back.

"Come here, please," Joshua demands.

Blake comes in and puts his hands on his hips defiantly.

"Jordy started it, and I'm not sitting next to her at the table," he tells us all.

Joshua stares at him, deadpan. "You'll sit where we tell you to sit."

Cameron comes in and picks Blake up in a rush, throwing him over his shoulder. "Blake is sitting in the pot plant to eat his dinner."

He takes Blake over to the huge pot plant and pretends he's going to put him into it as Blake squeals in delight, kicking and screaming.

I smile as I watch them play while everyone goes back to their conversation.

Victoria rolls her eyes. "Damn Cameron. He can't be serious for one minute."

I giggle as I watch him play with the little boy.

Brock puts his hand at the small of my back, and I smile up at him.

"I like your crazy family," I whisper.

He smiles down at me. "Me, too."

I lie on my side in bed. Brock has just had a shower, and we are back at his house. It's late now, and he's walking towards me when he drops his towel and I smile up at him. God, I still get awestruck at his sexual confidence. No matter how many times he parades around in front of me naked without a care in the world, I find it intoxicating.

"My family loved you," he tells me as he steps into his boxer shorts.

"Do you think so?"

He lies down beside me. "I know so."

He watches me for a moment. "Are you okay? You were quiet on the ride home."

I smile sadly and roll onto my back. "I guess."

"What's wrong?"

I look over at him and shrug.

He raises his brow. "You can talk to me. I won't..." His voice trails off.

I pause for a moment. I really want to talk to him about this, but I don't want him to get angry with me. "Do you think I've treated Simon badly?" I ask softly.

He rests up onto his elbow. "Tell me why you broke up again."

I exhale and look up at the ceiling. "We met when we were fifteen."

He stays silent as he listens.

"And we were kids. Our love was puppy love." I look over at him to see how he's handling this, and he smiles over at me. His smile gives me courage to go on.

"But I always just thought we would break up one day, you know? And I was going to do all the things that I had always wanted to do."

He picks up my hand and kisses my fingertips.

"But we never did." I stare sadly at the air conditioning vent up in the ceiling.

"And then ten months ago he asked me to marry him."

Brock's smile fades, a frown taking over his face.

"But I didn't want to get married, and..." I shake my head as I go back to the dreadful day when I told him we were over.

"You don't want to get married?" He frowns.

My eyes meet his. "I do. Now, I do."

His face falls. "You want to get married now?"

I giggle. "Don't panic I don't mean now, now."

He smiles. "Go on."

I frown as I try to tell the story as accurately as I can. "I ended up asking Simon for a twelve-month break and he accepted. I promised him I would return to him and that I wouldn't meet anyone else."

Brock's eyes hold mine. He already knows how the rest of the story goes. "But you met me," he whispers.

I get a lump in my throat and I nod sadly. "Not only did I meet you, I fucked you in the worst way possible."

"Pock." He sighs as he cups my face. "Can you stop saying that? It wasn't like that. We were so attracted to each other that we couldn't help it."

That's not the real story and he knows it.

"The thing is, Brock... meeting you, being with you, it all made me realise that my feelings for him weren't real or true."

He frowns again, his eyes searching mine.

"I never..." I sigh heavily.

"You never what?"

"I never felt with him what I feel when I'm with you."

"What do you mean?"

My eyes search his. "Sometimes I feel like I will die if you don't touch me."

Tenderness crosses his face, and he leans in to kiss me softly.

"The thing is, I realised that I loved Simon, but I wasn't *in* love with him anymore." I run my hand through his hair. "And even if you and I hadn't have worked out, Simon wasn't the man for me."

He nods, not needing to tell me he understands. His face says it all.

"And it sucks, you know." My eyes fill with tears. "Because he never did anything wrong."

Brock cups my face in his hands.

"He loved me so much," I whisper.

He puts his arm around me, and I rest my head on his chest. I run my hand idly over his heart and his abs as I think.

"I hope he meets someone." Sadness overwhelms me as I imagine him sad and alone tonight.

Brock pulls me close and kisses my forehead. "It's not your fault, Tully."

I frown up at him. "You don't think?"

"People change."

"Have you changed?" I ask.

He nods. "Yeah, I've changed. A lot, actually."

"How?"

"Well, I had my first girlfriend when I was sixteen."

I smile up at him. "What was her name?"

"Rebecca."

I bite my bottom lip. "What happened with Rebecca?"

His eyes widen. "It was a complete disaster."

I giggle. "Why?"

"Rebecca fell in love with me and I fell in love with her mother."

I blink and stare. "Don't tell me you..."

He pinches the bridge of his nose, shaking his head, clearly amused. "God, no."

"You fell for her mum?"

He chuckles. "A bit. She was a total babe. Her name was Stephanie, and she was the focus of many a spank banking session."

I laugh out loud and slap his chest. "Brock. Who in the hell jerks off over their girlfriend's mother?"

He shakes his head. "Right? Anyway, I kind of realised that maybe girlfriends and I don't really mix."

I frown. "Wait, so...? You've never been in love? Like, ever?"

He shrugs. "I was away with the Navy, and I was never in the same place for a long time. I got a bit..."

"A bit what?

"Detached, I guess."

I smile as I lie in his arms. "We're a great couple, aren't we?"

He kisses my temple.

"I was too attached, and you were too unattached."

"Until I met you..." he admits quietly.

I smile goofily up at him. "Do you believe in fate, Brock?"

He purses his lips as he thinks.

"I think I was meant to meet you when I did," I whisper dreamily. "When the time was right."

"You think you were meant to dump me the next day like you did, too, huh?" He shakes his head. "I was fucking cut up."

"Exactly. If I hadn't dumped you, I would have been just like every other girl you met in the past and you'd be long gone by now."

He frowns as he listens.

"The only reason I got through to you was because I didn't fall at your feet."

He kisses me and pulls me close to his chest.

"You can fall at my feet now," he whispers seductively.

I close my eyes and smile. I feel so safe in his arms. "I always do."

CHAPTER 18

Tully

Brock is sitting on the floor with his back propped up against the wall while I lie with my head on his lap. We're waiting at the airport and our flight has been delayed by three hours—not enough time for us to go home but just enough time to drive you crazy. Brock is looking through the photos on my phone, and every now and then he smiles as he looks at an image of me. I keep catching him sending them to his phone.

"Where was this? He shows me a picture of me and Callie.

"Vietnam."

He nods and keeps scrolling.

"Why do you save all these motivational memes?" He smirks.

"To motivate myself." I giggle.

He shakes his head and chuckles as he keeps scrolling through. I smile as I watch him. He's learning about me from my photos, drinking in a little piece of me with every shot.

"Why do you take photos of menus in restaurants?" He frowns as he scrolls.

"So that I have all the menus handy and I can see what I want before I go there if I ever go back."

His eyes find mine. "Or could just wait until you get there and see it then."

"Don't make fun of my quirks."

He smirks and keeps scrolling, and then he frowns and looks up at me. "Why do you have this information on anger and anabolic steroids?"

Oh shit. "Erm." I frown, not knowing if I should I tell him why I saved that. "When I first met you in the gym I thought you were on steroids and that's why you had anger issues. I thought you were having a 'roid rage."

"What? Are you serious?"

I shrug. "Well, you are super buff, and you were slightly scary."

His face falls. "My anger scares you?"

I nod. "A bit."

"Why?"

"Because you aren't my Brock when you're like that. I don't like the person you become."

He swallows sadly, and his eyes go back to the images. He doesn't say anything, but I don't miss the way he starts to play with my hair as he processes my words and pretends to look at more photos.

"You said that we could deal with my anger as long as I gave you another side of me," he reminds me, his voice carrying a hint of hurt.

"I can, Brock, but you are no good to me in jail for murder, are you?"

He exhales heavily but doesn't reply, and I know I've hit a nerve with him.

I think I may have hurt his feelings, but it had to be said. I have no choice but to always be honest.

We walk onto the staircase of the plane and are immediately hit by a wall of heat. "My God, it's hot." I sigh. The air is humid and steamy.

We are in Hawaii. *Aloha!*

Brock raises an eyebrow and grabs my hand. "Careful," he says, gesturing to the stairs.

I look around and smile as we begin to walk down them. "Oh, look over there." I point to a building we can see in the distance.

He tightens his grip on my hand and gestures to the stairs again. "Tully, watch what you're doing, please."

"Oh my God, let me take a photo." I stop to get my phone out of my bag.

"You can't be serious!" he snaps. "You're going to break your fucking neck in a moment."

I smile mischievously. "Do you want to carry me down the steps, Dad?"

"It's a lot safer than you walking them alone, that's for sure. You're worse than a two-year-old."

"My two-year-old is going to be a lot naughtier than this," I huff.

He stares at me blankly for a moment, as if the thought that he may one day have naughty children has never crossed his mind before now.

"What?" I smirk as we get to the bottom of the steps and walk across the tarmac.

"You think your children will be naughty? Doesn't everyone usually start out with belief that their children will be perfect?" He frowns.

I smile goofily at the ridiculous notion. "Well, I was a nightmare as a child, and I'm pretty sure *you* were a nightmare, too. Together, that's a whole lot of nightmares."

His eyes flick over to me as he does the math. "Whatever. We'll be too busy having wild sex to parent any kids, properly," he mutters under his breath.

"Brock, we can't have sex if I have children," I tell him seriously.

He frowns over at me. "Why not?"

"Because my vagina will be too stretched out," I whisper, glancing around to make sure no one else can hear us.

He smirks as he hands his passport over to the customs officer on the desk. "Lucky we have option B then, isn't it?"

The custom officer's eyes roam over Brock as he approaches the desk, and she smiles as she reads his name

Ugh, I'm right here, you know!

She goes through all of the official checks with us both, and then she looks up and smiles sexily at him. "Have a nice trip, Mr. Marx."

His eyes hold hers. "Thank you. I will."

She twirls her hair and her smile turns into a flirtatious grin. Brock looks over at me and smirks as we walk off. He loves the fact that every woman who sees him goes weak at the knees.

"I wouldn't get excited," I whisper. "She probably fucks anything that moves."

He chuckles as he takes my hand in his. "I'm sure she does."

. . .

Our driver pulls into the large circular driveway. I peer out of the car like a little child. "This is where we're staying?" I frown.

"Uh-huh. Out you get, Pock." He kisses my fingertips and climbs out of the car.

I read the hotel sign:

The Halekulani

"Wow," I whisper in awe. This is the most beautiful resort I have ever seen. There's a large, marble open foyer filled with fancy looking bellboys. It has huge archways that lead out onto beautiful manicured lawns. Beyond that there's a huge pool with white deck chairs and umbrellas lining the edges. At the back of the pool you can see the ocean. This place has restaurants, cocktail bars, and beautiful people scattered everywhere. I look around, lost in the magic of it all.

Brock comes around, opens my door, and pulls me out of the car by my hands. "Brock, this is amazing."

"Only the best for my girl." He smirks down at me.

"My blow job skills aren't *this* good." I giggle.

He smiles broadly and raises an eyebrow. "I'll be the judge of that."

We make our way through the building, and a private attendant gives us a tour of the resort before she takes us up to our room. She opens the huge double doors and my breath instantly catches in the back of my throat. The whole back wall is glass windows that overlook the pool and ocean. The king bed and all the furnishings are luxurious. I gasp out loud.

"My God, it's beautiful," I whisper to myself.

The kind looking attendant smiles. "It's the Halekulani way."

"Wow," I mouth. Halekulani Heaven, more like it.

"This is your air conditioning temperature control." She shows us. "This is your in-house service." She flicks through and shows us everything. "Your rooms will be serviced three times a day."

"Three times?" I gasp.

She smiles warmly. "You have your morning clean, and then we top up your ice bucket and deliver your fresh fruit platter every afternoon. We also offer a full turn down service every night."

I look over to see a silver ice bucket is filled with ice, and there are thick crystal glass tumblers sitting beside it. There's also a large tray of exotic fruit all cut up into fancy shapes. There are beautiful orchids in vases in the bathroom and the bedroom.

Holy shit, this place is on another level.

"Would there be anything else?" She smiles.

I shake my head. "No, thank you."

"All of the concierge staff members here are bilingual, so if you need anything at anytime from anywhere, we're at your service. We also have an in-house doctor and physiotherapist in case you have an injury during your stay."

Oh. The tipping thing. "Brock, the tip," I whisper.

Brock retrieves his wallet.

The attendant holds up her hands. "We don't accept tips here." She smiles. "It's the Halekulani way." With a bow of her head, she disappears out of the door.

I turn to Brock. "Oh my God." I gasp. "This place!"

He smiles darkly and throws me on the bed. "Now it's Hale-fucktully time at the Halekulani."

I burst out laughing as he crawls over me. "Room service!"

. . .

The sun is setting over the water, the sound of the ukulele filling the air.

Every afternoon at the Halekulani there's a traditional trio of music played with a hula dancer out on the back lawn overlooking the water's edge. There are fire lanterns throughout the garden, and the sound of the waves gently lapping on the shore is beyond peaceful. The staff are all wearing flowers in their hair, and the entire place has a relaxed party atmosphere about it. Brock and I are relaxing on our deckchairs near the pool as we take in our surroundings. We are drinking Mai Tai cocktails, and we've been in the same position all afternoon. We've talked about everything, from schools to jobs, to hopes and dreams, and with every minute that passes I feel myself falling just that little bit deeper in love with him.

Brock is intelligent, witty, and so *un*romantic that I somehow actually find it romantic. He says what he thinks with no filter, and it's a very endearing quality to have. It's rare.

I know how lucky I am to have met a man who makes me feel this way.

We connected before, sure but this trip has cemented what I already suspected about us.

This is it.

This is the feeling that I've been searching my whole life for.

Everything I never knew existed is right here with him.

"You want to get some dinner, Tully Pocket?"

We look up and see that everyone else has gone. The staff are packing up for the night. I think we've been in the same position, deep in conversation, for twelve hours straight.

"Where is everyone?

He shrugs and laughs. "Fuck knows?"

I didn't hear the music stop, see the people leaving or even eating dinner.

I was too focused on him.

Brock. My beautiful Brock.

He stands and pulls me from my chair. "It's okay, I'll eat you instead." He smirks.

I lie back and inhale the sun's rays.

We are lounging around the pool again with a cocktail each. We've been swimming and beaching all day. This is the life. It feels so good to be this relaxed. "I can't believe this place. It's so beautiful. Thank you for booking this holiday."

Brock smiles, his eyes remaining closed as he puts his hands behind his head. "I know. You should probably pay off your debt tonight."

I giggle.

"You want to come for a swim?" he asks.

"Hmm. No."

He looks over at me. "Let me rephrase that: we're going swimming."

"I'm not."

He bends, picks me up, and throws me over his shoulder.

"Put me down," I whisper-cry.

I glance up to see everyone around the pool is watching us. "Everyone's watching us." I giggle and slap his behind.

"All the men are wishing they could throw you over their shoulder and steal you away from me."

All the women are wishing he was throwing them over his shoulder and taking them back to his room, more like.

He walks straight into the pool, sending me under the water, and when I come up gasping for air he dunks me again.

"Brock," I croak, trying to breathe and laugh at the same time.

He splashes me and swims off. I swim after him, laughing as I go.

We really do need to talk about him working on his romantic side.

Brock

I lie on the bed with my hands behind my head as I watch Tully walking around the room, tidying up in her little black crochet bikini.

"I swear that bikini was put on this earth to drive me insane," I say quietly, my eyes flickering over to the television. "Today, at the pool, I had to bite the inside of my cheek to try and control my dick."

She giggles and turns to me, placing her hands on her hips and giving them a quick wiggle. "You like my bikini?

I nod, my eyes drinking her in. The week has been really cool—the best vacation I've had in a long time. There's been sun, shopping, and then dinner and dancing every night.

Laughter, too. Lots of laughter.

Tully hasn't stopped laughing for the entire week, and damn, it's a sound I've gotten used to. It's addictive... ***she's addictive.*** **She's fucking beautiful. I've never been with a woman like her. I don't want to have sex with her just to come. I want to be close to her. And even when I'm deep inside of her, it never seems close enough.**

She carries on chatting to me as she walks around the room, oblivious to my thoughts. Her strawberry blonde hair is in a high ponytail and the skin on her body is shimmering from her tanning oil.

"What do you want to do tonight?" she asks.

I smile and raise an eyebrow.

She widens her eyes. "Let me guess: me?"

I nod, and she leans over to kiss me. "Why put off 'til later what you can do now."

I slide my hand up the back of her thighs, feeling every muscle in her legs. Her lips take mine and I pull her over me. She falls onto my body with a sexy giggle.

We kiss, and damn if she's not the best kisser in the world.

All these emotions she brings out in me are beginning to take over. When she kisses me the hairs on the back of my neck stand to attention. It's as if every cell in my body feels how special this thing is between the two of us.

I don't know how long I can hold myself back from her. It's getting harder every day—every hour. She's opened up a part of me I didn't even know existed and now I can't turn it off.

I wouldn't even if I could.

My hands slide up her back to slowly untie her bikini top. I throw it to the side and enjoy the feel of her large breasts pushing against my chest.

She smiles down at me, and I have this overwhelming urge to tell her...

"What are you thinking?" she whispers, as if reading my mind.

My eyes search hers, and in that moment, I know it's time.

"I'm thinking I love you," I whisper.

Her face falls. "Brock." Her eyes search mine.

Suddenly, it's urgent. I have to be inside her now. I lift her body and tear down my shorts, undo the strings on her bikini bottoms, and tear them off, too. She sits up and looks down at me.

"I love you too," she says with a shy smile.

My eyes follow my hands as I run them up over her shoulders, and then down over her breasts to cup them tenderly in my hands. They move down over her stomach to her tiny patch of well-groomed strawberry blonde pubic hair before they drift to her hipbones.

"Lift up, Pocket," I whisper.

She moves up onto her knees, and I lift my cock to her entrance then slowly pull her down.

She stills, winces, and then she moves from side to side to try and loosen herself up. No matter how many times I watch her struggle to take me, I'll never get enough of it. She needs me to talk her through it every single time. It's as if my voice calms her.

"Take your time, baby," I whisper, my eyes holding hers.

She bends and kisses me with affection. I reach around and pull her lips apart around my cock, and I slowly slide home as deep as I can. Her soft moans as she struggles to accept me start a fire inside my body. She's so fucking tight. That fire starts in my balls, and I have to close my eyes and clench my teeth to try and stop myself from coming.

Every time.

Every fucking time I'm inside of her, I'm trying to rein myself in from blowing in five seconds.

It's the weirdest thing for me. With other women, all I wanted to do was come, and I could fuck them all night. With Tully, all I want to do is be close to her and I blow in a minute flat without any control. She's the only woman I do actually want to fuck all night.

The irony.

"Brock," she whimpers as she sits back up.

Our eyes are locked, and I can feel every muscle as her

tight body ripples around me. “So... fucking... good,” I push out.

Kneeling, she begins to rock back and forth, and I clench my teeth as I watch her.

Feminine, confident, sexy as fuck... and she’s all mine.

I’ve been waiting to feel like this my whole life.

I give her a dark smile. “You ready?” I ask.

She smiles and nods, knowing what’s coming.

“Legs up.”

She slowly brings her legs up into a squatting position and I test the waters before I bring her down harder onto my body.

Her head tips back and she moans. She loves my cock and what it gives her.

Her moan is my green light. I pick her up and slam her down.

“Deeper,” she moans. “Fuck me deeper. Oh God, Brock, don’t ever stop doing this.”

I grab a handful of her hair and drag her face down to mine, my tongue taking control of her mouth. “I won’t, Pock,” I promise against her lips, and I pump her hard. “You’re stuck with me now.”

The sun is setting on the horizon. I inhale the sea breeze as I sit on the balcony, watching as a boat pulls out on the water and disappears into the distance. Tully is in the shower getting ready to go out tonight. I dial Ben’s number and he answers on the first ring.

“Hey, man,” he greets me.

I smile at the sound of his voice. “Hey, what’s happening? How’s Didge?”

"Yeah, she's good. No problems over here. How's the trip?"

"Good." I smile. "Like... really good."

"You getting on well?" he asks.

"Yep." I sip my beer and smile to myself. 'Well' is the understatement of the year. "Anything new at work?

"Oh, we got a lead on the Chancellor case. And another working girl was murdered."

"Damn. Have they identified her yet?" I frown.

"Her name was Felicity Thompson."

I frown. "I don't know that name."

"Her street name was Peachy Sue."

"What happened to her?"

"She was shot in her apartment over the weekend. Her body wasn't found until Tuesday. She'd been dead a few days already when they got to her."

"Any witnesses or prints?"

"Not that we know of. We're looking into it now. I'm going to go door knocking at the apartment block this afternoon."

"What are the police doing?" I ask.

"Nothing, as usual. In their eyes a working girl is a working girl and she'll get no special treatment from them. They literally don't give a fuck." He sighs, his irritation clear to hear.

"We need to find who's doing this." I sigh with him. "Is that the tenth girl?'

"Over the last seven years, it's the eleventh."

"Hmm."

"How's Tully, anyway?" he asks.

"Fucking perfect."

"You're not sick of each other yet?"

"Just the opposite. We're home in two days and I could happily stay for another month."

He chuckles just as Tully walks out of the bathroom wrapped in a towel. I smile as I drink her in. "I'll see you later, hey?" I say to Ben.

"Okay, I'll keep you posted if we get anything new in."

"Thanks, mate." I hang up as Tully slides onto my lap and kisses my lips.

"Where are you taking me for dinner?" she purrs.

I smile down at her. "Anywhere you want."

Tully

I lie on my side and stare at Brock. It's early afternoon now, and we have spent the morning swimming at the beach. We came back to the hotel, had lunch on the water, and now we're back in the room relaxing. The television is on in the background but my attention is on my love.

Beautiful Brock.

I've never felt so close to anyone before. It's as if he's a part of me; an extension of my heart. Since he told me he loved me he's stopped holding himself back, and even though I thought he was perfect before, it hadn't even touched the surface on how amazing he actually is. I've laughed, swooned, and sighed my way through this vacation. I don't want this feeling to ever end.

I am irrevocably and completely in love with Brock Marx. Every cell in my body wants to please him. His hands are constantly somewhere on me, making sure I'm close and checking I'm all right.

Who would have thought that the aggressive man I met in the gym could turn out to be the tender man who is now obsessed with my safety? I smile over at him, reach up and push my fingers through his dark hair.

"Brock." I frown as I try to get the wording right in my head before I say it out loud. "You know the first time we had sex... in the gym bathroom?"

His eyes hold mine. "Yeah?"

"Why did you take me anally?"

He frowns, surprised by my random question.

"At the time, you said it was the way you were wired," I remind him. "Why haven't we done it like that again since?"

He inhales, his eyes searching mine. "I don't want to scare you away." He runs his fingertip over my bottom lip. Our faces are only centimetres apart.

"Why do you like anal sex?" I whisper. "Help me understand."

He pauses for a moment. "It's just... different."

"It feels different?" I ask.

"Yes, but it's more than that."

I listen as my eyes stay locked on his.

"I guess it's a control thing. I have my strongest orgasms that way."

"Because you completely control the woman?" I ask.

"Not necessarily the woman."

My eyes widen. "You've had sex with men?"

He chuckles. "Fuck, no. I only like women. I mean I get to control the situation as well as the woman."

"Hmm." I think for a while longer. "Why do you think it would scare me away?" I whisper.

His eyes hold mine. "It did last time, and I would rather live without it than risk frightening you again."

I smile softly and I cup his face. "But it's a part of who you are."

"So are you," he whispers.

"Have you always done it that way?" I don't know why but I really want to know this part of him.

He frowns. "Do you really want to talk about this, Pock?"

"Yes. I want to understand you."

"You don't need to understand my former sex life. It's irrelevant now." He sighs.

"Do you have anal sex with every woman you sleep with?"

He frowns, clearly uncomfortable with this conversation. "I only sleep with you, Tully, so no."

"I mean casual women," I correct myself. "Women you would meet casually in the past."

His eyes hold mine for a moment and I can see him to an internal risk assessment on how this conversation is going to go. "I like rough sex."

"And?" I frown as I watch him.

"Anal sex gives me an extra thrill. It's tighter and takes more skill on my behalf to make the woman enjoy it," he answers honestly.

"Is that why you have always gone for wilder girls? Because they know what they're doing there?"

"Yes," he replies without hesitation.

"Oh." I twist the blanket between my fingers. "And you would give that up to be with me?"

"I already have. I've no interest in it anymore if I can't have it with you. I've made peace with it." He already sounds bored of this conversation.

I smile softly.

"Another woman just won't do for me anymore, Tully. This is it for me." He smirks as he kisses my lips.

"I love that this is it for you," I tease.

We kiss, and I want to do this. I want to give him everything that he desires from a woman.

"We need to go the drugstore," I whisper.

"What for?" He frowns.

"We need to buy some lubricant."

His eyes search mine and he swallows the lump in his throat.

"I need you to teach me how you like to fuck. I want my man to be satisfied."

"I am already."

"You only think you are," I counter.

"You don't need to do this to please me. I'm happy, satisfied, and completely in love with you."

I lean in and kiss his big, soft lips. "Please," I whisper. "I want to give this to you." We kiss, and he pulls me close. "I want to give everything to you," I breathe against his lips.

"I don't want to lose you again," he tells me quietly, and I can feel his hesitation.

"You can't. I promise."

Half an hour later, I close my eyes and blow out a deep breath. Brock went to the drugstore alone while I took a shower. My heart is beating fast as I stand under the hot water and let it run over my head.

I'm just about to give myself over to him completely.

I hear the door open and I blow out a deep breath. I feel so nervous—more nervous than when I lost my virginity, I think.

I don't know why. We all know I've done this before. Brock walks into the bathroom and slowly peels his shirt off over his head, and then slides his shorts off and kicks them to the side. I smile when I see his erection. He's aroused just by thinking about what's to come. He steps under the water and takes me into his arms, kissing me softly.

"Did you get it?" I ask.

"Yes."

His eyes are dark, and the water is beading over his face from the shower. My eyes roam down his body, his broad shoulders, rippled abdomen, and his dick is hanging heavily between his legs. It's engorged, and I can see every vein that runs down to the thick head.

He's hungry for this. I can see it in his eyes, too.

Seeing him naked always has the same effect on me. I never knew that you could love someone and be so physically attracted to them so that nothing else matters. He takes the soap and tenderly washes my breasts, my back, down both of my legs and my sex, and then my behind.

Our eyes are locked as he washes me there. *Fucking hell*, this is already intense.

I return the favour and wash every inch of him in between kisses, and then he turns the shower off and my heart begins to flutter. He gets out and dries himself, and then dries me before he leads me to the bedroom.

He's quiet, and I know he's preparing himself to hurt me. Or perhaps he's just excited and doesn't want me to know how much.

He leads me into the bedroom and turns to face me. "You sure about this?"

I nod. "Yes."

I drop to my knees and kiss his penis. He flexes it against my mouth. I lick up the length of him and then take him into my mouth.

He inhales sharply, and I taste his pre-ejaculate as it leaks out. He places his hand on the back of my head, watching on in awe.

Fucking hell, he looks so damn hot with his cock in my mouth. I rest both of my hands on his thighs and really begin to take him deeper. His soft moans only add to my pleasure, and I feel a rush of cream to my sex.

He pulls me up by the arms and kisses me as he holds me tight. His hands roam up and down my skin in reverence.

"Get on your knees on the bed."

I slowly do as I'm told, my stomach fluttering wildly.

Oh my frigging God.

"Now drop to your elbows," he commands.

I drop to my elbows and look through my legs. His cock is dripping with excitement and I close my eyes as I wait for his touch.

He pours some lube onto his hand and then slides it up his shaft. He slowly strokes himself as I watch on. His stomach muscles contract on the upstroke, and my sex clenches in appreciation. "Do you know how fucking turned on I am seeing you like this?" he whispers as he jerks his cock hard.

My stomach dances with nerves. He has that tone about him. He had it the first night we slept together at the gym, and he's only had it a few times since.

It's like he's on the edge of control and at any moment he's going to lose his mind.

The sound of the lubricant slaps against his hand, and I close my eyes. Even hearing himself wank is a fucking major turn on for him. He gives himself a beating before he walks over behind me and pushes me hard into the mattress. I land head first into the blankets. I know this is it.

He's lost the last of his control.

It's on.

He slides his lubricated fingers through my sex, his eyes lingering on his fingers as they disappear into my body.

I close my eyes, moaning softly, and he strokes his cock with the other hand, unable to wait. Then his tongue... it laps at me, his whiskers on my cheeks. His fingers are in my sex, and God...

I hold my breath as I begin to lose all composure.

For fifteen minutes, he brings me to the edge with his tongue, only to let me down again and deny me. My body is writhing on the bed, rippling as I try to get the traction that I need. His cock in his hand the whole time, taunting me as he strokes it.

Fuck's sake. Brock Marx is the hottest man in the history of men.

Watching him jerk himself off is driving me wild with need. My body is quivering, and I have to fight to keep myself on my knees. Then I hear him flip the cap on the bottle of lube, and I close my eyes.

Here we go.

He warms it in his hand and then rubs it into my behind, sinking his finger into the knuckle. I hear his sharp intake of breath.

"Oh," I moan.

It's such a weird sensation. I hate the thought of it... *but fuck, does it feel good.*

He massages me some more, adding another finger inside. My eyes roll back in my head as he begins to work me.

Oh dear God.

He grabs my hip in his hand and gently begins to rock me back onto his fingers to get me used to the sensations.

I want to moan in pleasure, but it feels so damn naughty, like I shouldn't be enjoying this.

He applies more lube, and then I feel the tip of his cock at my back entrance.

"Pock," he whispers.

"Yes."

"You okay, baby?"

"Uh-huh." I nod, although I'm not quite sure I really am.

He pushes forward, and I close my eyes and try and block out the burn.

Fuck...!

The pressure and weight of his body forces me into the mattress, and I screw up my face in pain. He pushes in again, and this time the air is knocked out of my lungs. "Argh," I whimper.

"Nearly there," he whispers. "That's it." He reaches around and with his four fingertips massages my wet clitoris. I instantly feel the pain begin to disappear.

Fuck, my eyes are rolling back again.

He adds two more fingers to my sex, and he begins to pump me until the last of my body's resistance disappears and he slides deep inside my body.

We both cry out, the pleasure taking over us, and he leans down to kiss me gently on my shoulder.

"You okay?"

I nod, and he grabs a handful of my hair, dragging my face to his. His mouth takes mine and he kisses me deeply. He slowly pulls out and then slides back in. Then again... slowly... now faster.

Oh God, he has complete possession of my body.

He turns my head straight ahead. "Watch us," he whispers darkly.

I turn to the mirror to see myself naked on my knees on the bed with my legs spread wide. Brock is behind me and he has my ponytail wrapped around his hand while he's fucking my ass.

I can see every ripple in his abdomen clench as he thrusts. His body has a perfect sheen of perspiration over it, and I swear to God, I have never seen or felt anything so damn good in my life.

With one hand on my hip and one hand full of my hair, he rides me. He works harder and harder until our skin is slapping and his head is tipped back in ecstasy. "Oh, fuck," he cries. "This is too fucking good." His eyes drop to the spot where our bodies meet. "Fuck, fuck, fuck." He pumps me, and then he growls, and I scream out as a freight train of an orgasm tears me to shreds and he holds himself deep inside of me. His whole body begins to quiver as he slowly empties himself into me, and eventually whispers, "I'm going to pull out, Pock."

I wince as he does, and he falls to the mattress with a thud, pulling me over him. He gifts me with the perfect kiss so soft and tender.

"I love you," he whispers.

My heart is hammering in my chest. The feeling I have inside of me this time is far from shame. It's love.

Bright, shining love.

I giggle against his lips. "You'd better."

CHAPTER 19

Tully

I BEND and peer inside the fridge.

"There's nothing to eat at all. We should've got milk on the way home from the airport last night." I frown.

Brock puts his hands around my waist and kisses my neck from behind. "We'll stop on the way to work and get something, plus a coffee."

I slam the fridge shut in disgust. "I'm going to have to go grocery shopping for us tonight." I sigh. "Great. Just like that, reality bites."

He turns me in his arms and smiles down at me. "I like that you have to go grocery shopping for us tonight." His hands snake down to my behind and he squeezes me firmly.

I put my arms around his neck and kiss his big lips. "You're easily pleased, Mr. Marx."

He kisses me again. "What? Isn't a man allowed to like his woman barefoot in his kitchen?"

I giggle. "The phrase is barefoot and pregnant, and I can assure you, that is not happening at any time soon."

He smiles down at me, as if knowing a secret.

"What?" I ask.

"Move in with me."

My face falls. "*What?*"

"Move in with me, here. We've slept in the same house every night since we've been together anyway. What's the difference?" He shrugs. "It just means your things will be kept here."

"Brock, we've been together for, like, a month." I frown.

"So?"

"You don't even know everything about me." I gasp.

He grabs my behind and grinds me against his pelvis. "I know all I need to know."

"Brock." I shake my head and pull out of his arms. "You don't just move in with someone because you have declared your love to them."

"I do," he snaps, obviously annoyed that I'm not jumping at the chance.

"You don't even know my family," I say as I put my hands on my hips.

"Then organise for me to get to know your family." He begins to slam around the kitchen cupboards looking for something. I watch him, knowing he's annoyed that I'm not jumping at the chance.

"You seriously want me to move in here?" I frown.

He rolls his eyes. "Do you listen to anything I fucking say at all, woman? Yes, I want you to move in with me."

"Why? What's the rush?"

He takes me in his arms. "Why wait? I love you, you love me, and we're going to end up living together anyway. So why would you pay rent for your apartment when you are staying here every night, anyway?"

I smile up at him. He looks so hopeful and in love as he waits for my answer.

"You told me you wouldn't hold yourself back from me, Tully," he says softly. "Isn't that what you're doing by not moving in with me?"

I walk back to him and take his lips with mine. He's right, I did say that. Maybe I am holding back. And maybe this is the most stupid fucking thing I have ever done.

"Okay," I whisper.

"Okay?" he asks, surprised I've given in so easily.

"Okay, but I'm not cancelling my lease just yet. I'm keeping my apartment for a while so we can get used to each other. We can just move my stuff over gradually. Each time we go back to my house I'll bring a few things over," I say. "But..." I add. "You're cooking and cleaning."

He smiles mischievously. "I'm the operations manager, Pocket. I can only take care of physical activity. Anything other than that is out of my jurisdiction."

I raise my brows. "Oh, is that right?" I smile. "And what do I do in this house?"

He squeezes my behind and pulls me onto his hard, waiting dick. "Well, you're the boss."

I drop my mouth open, feigning shock. "Are you finally admitting that I'm the boss of us?"

"You're the boss of the house," he corrects me calmly.

"And as the boss of the house, what exactly do I need to do?"

"Just wear your uniform."

"My uniform?" I smile.

"Your uniform is. Naked."

I giggle as he walks me backwards and pins me to the fridge.

"Cook naked, clean naked, watch television naked, molest the operations manager while naked."

I laugh again, and then fall serious. "Brock?" I whisper.

"Yeah, Pock," he replies, distracted as he begins to grind himself against me.

"You need to put your dick away and get me some breakfast before I hurt you."

He chuckles. "Yes, boss."

Brock

I sit back in my chair and stare at the girl across the table from us. I exhale heavily, wishing I was back in Hawaii with *my* girl.

The woman we're interviewing has long, naturally blonde hair, and she has a definite confident air about her. Her legs are long and athletic, and she's wearing a next-to-nothing floral summer dress. She's definitely sexy as fuck, and someone that would probably have peaked my interest in the past. Why the fuck she would suck cock for money is beyond me.

Ben is taking notes, and Jesten is back at the office. It was too much having three of us here with her.

"So, when was the last time you saw Peachy Sue?" I ask.

We are in a café and this girl was one of Peachy Sue's known friends.

She lights up a cigarette and blows it out, trying to be sexy. Her dark eyes hold mine. I know that look. I roll my lips and stare at her. Why do women do this? Why do they purposely try to turn you on so that they can gain control of a conversation?

"You going to keep looking at me like you want to fuck me, or are you going to answer my fucking questions?" I breathe.

She smiles, licks her lips then takes another drag from her cigarette. "Do you get that often?" she asks, exhaling a thin stream of smoke above our heads. "Do you have girls begging to suck your cock? Is it big?"

I stay silent as I watch her. I'm not playing her fucking games.

Ben licks his bottom lip as he watches her, also unrattled.

She begins to look at her long red nails, feigning boredom.

I lean into the table. "Here's the thing," I say firmly. "Somebody is killing girls just like you, and you..." I pause, "could be next. I'm here to help you. So. Start. Fucking. Talking."

She glances between the two of us. "What will it take for you to protect me?"

I stare at her.

"I can satisfy the two of you more any other woman ever could."

Ben and I look at one another, and then I turn my attention back to her.

"You can do me together. We could meet up a few times a week. No payment, all you need to do is protect me. I love double penetration," she admits darkly.

I exhale heavily. She's scared, and the fact that she offered what she offered means she already does it.

"Who do you already satisfy to protect you, Mia?" I ask.

She swallows the lump in her throat.

"You're a high-end working girl. You don't need this shit.

Two-thousand dollars for two hours? You don't give away that kind of service for nothing," Ben says.

"Don't judge me," she whispers. "I do what I have to do."

"Exactly, and society needs women like you," I tell her calmly. "We appreciate what you do."

She smiles to herself, thinking I'm going to try and make a deal with her.

"But here's the thing: I really don't want to fuck you," I add.

She tilts her chin in annoyance.

"I want to protect you." I lean into the table. "You don't have to suck my cock."

Her eyes darken, and she licks her lips. "Maybe I want to."

Ben bites his bottom lip and I know he's trying not to smirk.

"Tell me what you know and you'll be protected," I tell her, ignoring her last comment.

"You can't protect me from them. They'll kill all twenty of us eventually"

"Who?"

She leans into the table. "You're so fucking stupid," she whispers angrily. "You don't get it. This is coming from the inside."

I watch her.

"Someone in prison?" Ben asks.

"Who are the twenty?" I ask.

She shakes her head in disgust and begins to stand.

"Give me a name. What does he have on you, or what do you have on him?"

"They use us as if we're their personal sex slaves."

"Who?" I ask.

"They promise us protection if we do what they want," she whispers angrily. "But our girls are still dying."

"Who?" I whisper.

She takes a drag of her cigarette and rubs her fingers together as she looks at us.

"We aren't the cops, Mia. We're ex-military. We've been hired by Henrietta Jones' mother to bring her killer to justice, whoever the fuck that may be. Give me a place or a name and we can help you."

She looks around the café, guilt and fear crippling her facade.

Ben passes her his pen and notepad. "Write it down."

She licks her lips, takes the pen and paper, and she jots down a single word.

Cops

I read it. "More than one?"

She nods once.

"Organised?" I frown.

She nods again.

"I need a name."

She shakes her head and stands.

"Mia," I say. "Come on."

"Your answers are at The Roundhouse," she says, and with one last look between us, she leaves.

Ben hits the end of recording button on his phone, and the two of us sit for a moment. I Google The Roundhouse and frown when I read what comes up.

"The Roundhouse is a gentlemen's club. Entry is by membership only."

Ben pinches the bridge of his nose. "Fucking great." He sighs. "That's going to go down like a lead balloon."

"You going to have trouble explaining that one to the missus, mate?" I smirk.

Bridget hates undercover work. She especially hates anything to do with women. Her being pregnant with twins while Ben is at this club is going to make her go batshit crazy.

"Don't you fucking talk. I'm sure Tully will be thrilled with you going there, too."

"Hmm." I run my hands through my two-day stubble. It's weird having to think about undercover jobs now.

"We'll go tonight, see what we can find." I sigh.

"Hey, did you see the address of where Peachy Sue got murdered?" Ben asks.

"No. Why?"

"I think it's in Tully's neighbourhood." He frowns as he looks it up on his phone. "The street name was familiar." He brings it up on his screen and passes it over to me. I instantly frown.

"What the fuck? That isn't just Tully's neighbourhood. That's her fucking building!" I snap.

I take out my phone and dial her number. She answers on the first ring.

"Hey, boss," she teases, and I find myself smiling at the sound of her voice.

Ben shakes his head and rolls his eyes.

"Hey, Pock. What time are you having lunch today?" I ask.

"In about an hour, why?"

"Ben and I have to talk to you. Can we come meet you?"

"Yeah, sure." She hesitates. "Is everything all right?"

"Of course. Some shit's gone down and I just wanted to run it past you."

"What kind of shit?"

"Nothing to worry about. See you in an hour."

An hour later, we are sitting in a crowded restaurant. Ben is at the counter ordering. Tully is with me.

She takes my hand over the table. "Is everything okay?"

"Yeah." I frown as I sip my drink. "Nothing serious."

Ben comes back and sits down.

"How's Bridget feeling?" I ask.

"She's good." He smiles. "Until I speak to her and then she becomes feral."

I laugh roughly.

Ben rolls his eyes.

I turn to Tully. "So, we have to go undercover tonight at a gentlemen's club." I sigh.

Her face falls. "Oh. What does that mean?"

"We have a tip off, which means we have to go to this place to see if we can dig deeper," I reply.

"Well, what happens at this gentlemen's club?" she asks.

I shrug. "I don't know." I scratch the back of my head, feeling uncomfortable. "It's probably full of strippers and shit, I imagine."

"How deep undercover are you going?"

I pick up her hand and kiss the back of it. "Not that deep, babe. Don't worry." I sip my drink again. "But you'll have to stay at my house tonight."

"If you're not going to be home, I'd rather be at my house."

"Not happening. Someone connected to all of this was murdered at your apartment building while we were away."

Her eyes widen. "What?"

"A prostitute," Ben adds.

"Not Peachy Sue?" She gasps.

My face falls. "You know her?"

"Oh my God." She puts her hand over her mouth. "Someone was bashing her up the weekend before we left."

"What? Who?" Ben snaps. "That was when she was murdered."

She puts her head into her hands. "I should have called the police. I thought it was her pimp," she whispers in distress.

"Why didn't you tell me about this?" I ask her coldly.

"It was the night we went out with your work friends, and I..." She pauses as she remembers. "I came home early because you were being a psycho, as usual. I was waiting for the lift and I heard something smash against the wall, followed by her scream."

Ben and I exchange glances.

"And I didn't want them to see me, but the lift was taking forever so I hid in the janitor's closet."

I scowl, furious. "You didn't think to fucking tell me this shit?"

"Oh my God. I was so outraged with you, and I thought it was just another bit of apartment drama."

I roll my eyes.

"Tell us exactly what you heard, Tully," Ben urges her.

She slides her hands over her eyes as she thinks. "I heard Sue scream *get the fuck out* before something smashed up against the wall. I thought that was her throwing something at him—her pimp. That's what it sounded like, anyway."

She frowns as she thinks. "And then it was really quiet, and I heard another door open."

She stills, remembering as much as she can.

"What?" I ask.

"Meredith," she whispers.

"What about Meredith?" I frown.

"On the Sunday, remember before Simon came over? I went to say goodbye to Meredith and she was freaking out. Talking about a black jacket and..." She pauses. "Oh my God."

"What?" Ben snaps.

"It was her. It was her door that opened." She turns to me. "I think Meredith saw it. She was friends with Peachy Sue."

"Friends?" I frown.

"She hangs out with all those girls. Wendy Woo. All of them."

"Who is Wendy Woo?" Ben asks.

"She's a lady boy who fucks men for money."

Ben and I exchange looks. "What does she look like?" Ben asks as he scrolls though his phone.

"Dark hair and gorgeous," she says quietly.

Ben brings up a photo of the woman who was seen leaving Chancellor's room. "Is this her?"

Tully stares at the image on the phone and her face falls. "That's her."

Fuck. Another piece of the puzzle.

"Where is Meredith now?" I ask as my heart rate rises.

"I took her to her mother's." Tully is wide-eyed and on the verge of a major freak out, I can tell.

Ben dials a number on his phone. "Miller, it's me. I need you to get over to... wait." He turns the phone down. "What is Meredith's mother's address?"

Tully scrolls through her phone and brings up the address, passing it to Ben. He reads it out to Miller.

"What's going on?" Tully whispers. "Brock, this is scaring me."

I take her hand in mine. "I don't know, babe, but you can't go home. Why don't you stay at your mother's tonight? I have to do this work thing, and I don't want you being anywhere alone."

She nods. "Can you come over and meet my family before you go?" she asks hopefully.

I smile and lift her hand to kiss her fingertips. "Sure."

"Brock," she whispers. "Is Meredith in danger?"

I dust a thumb over her bottom lip. "We have some men on their way around there now. It will be okay."

"Do you promise?"

I shake my head. "I can't promise that."

Ben hangs up the call. "We got two cars on their way there now. Let's hope she's there."

I pull into the driveway and exhale heavily. Tully smiles from her place beside me.

"I met your family and now it's time for you."

"Yep." God, I hate this shit. I don't want to meet her family. I already know they don't like me.

Suck it up... *for her.*

I get out of the car, and Tully comes around to the driver's side, draping her arms around me. "Don't say anything about me moving in with you just yet, okay?"

I clench my jaw. Here we go. "Why not?"

"Brock." She widens her eyes at me. "We need to give them time to warm up to the idea of us first."

"How about we just get married and really piss them off?" I reply deadpan.

She smirks. "The weird thing is that you're so crazy, I actually have no idea if you're joking right now or not, so I'm just pretending I didn't hear that."

I raise my eyebrow as she leads me up the front path.

"Hello?" she calls out when we get to the front door.

"Tully." A man smiles and comes to greet us. He's middle-aged and overweight, but he smiles my way, anyway. "I'm Michael," he says to me.

"Michael, this is Brock. Brock, Michael is my stepfather."

"Hi." I smile and shake his hand.

"Come in." He holds his arm out and we walk through the house. It's small and quaint with dated furnishings. It's also impeccably clean. We walk out into a large area at the back of the house that looks like an extension, and there I see Tully's mother.

"Hello," she says, faking a smile.

I fake smile back right back. "Hello."

No love lost here. She still hates me.

"Where's my little sis?" I hear a male voice call down the hall, and I turn just in time to see a blond man swooping in to tackle Tully in his arms. He's good looking, tall, and probably around my age.

I glance over to see another man come in from the backyard. He rolls his eyes at the man's interaction with Tully. Hmm.

"Put me down." Tully laughs as she slaps him.

"Brock, this is Peter, my stepbrother."

"Hi." I smile and shake his hand.

Peter looks me up and down, sizing me up, but I just look at him blankly. Does he have a problem with me, too?

"And this is Brad, my brother." Tully smiles affectionately.

I turn and shake the other man's hand. He seems to be around the same age as Peter, but with the strawberry blond hair and similar features that make him look like Tully. This must be her biological brother.

"Hi, mate." He smiles warmly, and we shake hands.

"Would you like a drink or something?" her mother asks.

I smile politely. "Just a soda, thanks."

The two parents disappear into the kitchen and my eyes roam over to the mantle where there's a huge photograph of Simon and Tully in each other's arms on display. They're at their prom or something, all dressed up. I hate that she has a past with him.

I clench my jaw. *Calm, calm... keep fucking calm.*

A Labrador comes running in from the backyard and Tully bends to pat him. I glance up to see Peter's eyes drop to her ass. The edge of her G-string is showing slightly as her jeans ride down.

He stands there and stares as if nobody else is in the room.

What the fuck?

"So, what do you do, Peter?" I ask. I've seen him before but I'm not sure where from.

He glances up from his ogling of Tully's ass, and he stands and folds his arms in front of him, spreading his legs. "I'm a detective."

My eyes hold his. Yeah, I thought so. "Ah." I nod. "Interesting line of work."

"What do you do?" He raises a brow.

"I work for a security company." I'm not telling him my shit. I already know this guy is a fuckwit.

Tully drops to the floor and rolls around with the dog. Peter's eyes drop to her again, and his tongue comes out to slide across his bottom lip as he watches her lie on her back.

Okay, what the fuck is going on here? He's checking her out.

"So, you're Tully's stepbrother?" I ask.

He smiles slyly. "Yeah, we're joined at the hip. Aren't we, Tull?"

I glare at him. *Not any more, fucker.*

I turn to Brad. "What do you do, mate?"

"I'm in I.T—"

"He's unemployed," Peter interrupts.

"He got retrenched—" Tully cuts in. "Your dream job is coming any day, Brad." She smiles enthusiastically. "I just know it is."

Tully stands, and the dog jumps up on her again. She bends with her back to Peter, and he puts his hand on her hip.

The hairs on the back of my neck stand to attention and I can't help but glare at him.

He glares back.

What the actual fuck is going on here?

Stepbrother?

"Tully, take the dog outside, please," her mother calls from the kitchen.

"Okay." Tully makes her way to take him outside. "Come on, Mitchy. Come on."

I step forward and get in Peter's face once Tully is out of earshot. "Let's get one thing straight, cunt," I whisper angrily. "You look at Tully's fucking ass again and I will break you like a fucking twig."

Peter's face falls, clearly in shock that I called him on it.

Brad hisses and breaks into a chuckle. "Fucking finally," he whispers.

Peter lifts his chin. "What are you talking about?" He sneers. "And I wouldn't get too cocky if I were you. She's going to dump you any minute now."

We stand face to face glaring at each other. "This is your first and final warning. You keep your filthy fucking mind out of Tully's panties."

"Fuck off," Peter scoffs.

"I'm not trying to win a popularity contest with the oldies, so you should know that I basically don't give a fuck if you die," I whisper, and I know I've got to get out of here before I start swinging.

Brad chuckles again.

Tully comes in from the backyard, wraps her arm around my waist and smiles up at me lovingly.

"I got to go to work, babe," I say through gritted teeth as calmly as I can.

Her face falls. "You're not staying?"

"I can't, I'm sorry." I walk into the kitchen to her mother and father. "I'm sorry, an emergency has just come up at work. I have to go."

The stepfather actually looks disappointed, but Tully's mother's face lights up. "Oh, dear," she fakes disappointment.

"Next time?" I smile. "Maybe you can come around to our house?"

Tully's mothers eyes widen. "Your house?" She frowns.

"Oh, didn't Tully tell you?" I act surprised. "She's moving in with me." I smile broadly, watching as the blood drains from their faces. "Have a nice night, everyone."

I turn and grab Tully by the hand. "Walk me out, babe." I

glare at Peter and wink at Brad before we disappear out of the front door.

"Brock," Tully whispers on the way out to the car. "I thought I told you not to say anything!"

"Yeah, well." I pause for a moment. "I changed my mind."

"You're impossible," she whispers angrily.

I smile, lean down, and I kiss her. "But completely loveable, too, right?"

She smirks and kisses me, and after a sweet goodbye, I start my car and drive down the street, shaking my head.

Well, that's got to go down as the worst meet-the-parents moment in history.

Her fucking stepbrother is into her.

Ben frowns at me from across the table. "Are you sure?"

"Positive."

"Her stepbrother was looking at her ass?"

"Yes." I sip my beer, anger pouring out of me.

We are at The Roundhouse, sitting in the back corner, and I want to be anywhere but here. Gorgeous women are parading around, dressed to the nines in designer clothes, each of them available for a hefty price.

It's a different crowd to the normal strip joint. This place is for the wealthy—a gentlemen's club that cost thirty-thousand to join. "I better get my fucking money back when we solve this case," I whisper as I look around.

"So, what did you do?" Ben asks. "To the stepbrother?"

"I told him I was going to snap him or some shit." I shake my head in disgust. "I don't even know, and then I had to leave before I belted the crap out of him."

"Jesus," Ben mutters. "This shit could only happen to you."

"Right?"

We look over the crowd again. It's men in suits, mostly.

"We're looking for a cop then?" Ben sighs. "I have Tane in the office waiting to look up the IDs of any suspects we send him an image of."

I nod. "Or a group." I shrug. "It's hard to tell. The witness said it was a cop, but she said *they*... which means there are more than one of them."

He narrows his eyes as he thinks. "Meredith and her mother are missing, but the neighbour seems to think they've gone on vacation. What do you make of all this?"

The boys went around to Meredith's today and nothing seemed amiss. There were no signs of anything being wrong. The neighbour said that they went away unexpectedly because their grandmother was ill.

"I think the girls are being made to film themselves with these rich men, and then sometime soon after, they're forced to find them and bribe them with the footage."

"Like the other case?" He frowns.

"Just like the other case, but somehow the girls have started to fight back. Or something is going wrong somewhere."

"You think the girls are double crossing whoever the boss is?" He sips his beer.

"Why else would he be killing them?" I frown.

"Maybe he kills them after their job is done?"

"No, because then the girls wouldn't do it anymore. He's doing it to keep them in line, which means they're doing something wrong or getting close to turning him in."

"Hmm."

I sip my beer again and look over to the door. That's when my mouth literally falls open.

"Peter's here," I whisper.

"Who's that?' Ben frowns.

"The stepbrother."

Bens eyes widen. "You don't think…?"

"He's a cop. He's here." My eyes hold his. "What are the fucking chances of this shit happening?" I exhale heavily. "Fuck," I whisper. "I got to get out of here before he sees me."

We watch him walk through the club and take a seat at a table with three other men.

Ben zooms in on his camera, pretending to read something on his phone as he takes the shot. "You go, I'll stay. I'll send these to Tane and get an ID."

Tully

I wake up with a start to my phone dancing across the bedside table. I glance at the clock and see that it's 3:00 a.m.

"Meredith." I scramble for my phone. I've been frantic all week trying to track her down. Brock won't even let me go back to my apartment until she's found in case they're watching over there for her. He went out and bought me new clothes, toiletry supplies and everything.

I frown when I see the name light up. Deborah…that's weird.

Brock sits up, half asleep. "Who is it?"

"Simon's mother," I whisper. "Hello, Deborah."

"Hi, Tully."

"Is everything okay?" I ask.

"No, darling, it's not."

I listen, and my eyes flicker to Brock in bed as he begins to sit up, still half asleep.

"We're in London," she says.

"What's wrong?" Panic starts to make my body go cold.

"Simon's collapsed."

"Is he okay?" I whisper as my heart begins to hammer in my chest.

"No, Tully. He's not. He has... he has Leukaemia."

My whole world stops.

"W-what?" I whisper.

"They're not sure if he's going to make it."

My eyes fill with tears. "What?" I whisper. "No. Are you sure?"

"He's asking for you."

I nod, barely able to speak through the lump in my throat. "I'm on my way."

CHAPTER 20

Tully

I STARE AT BROCK, dumbfounded.

"What's wrong?" he asks.

"It's Simon. He's collapsed in London."

Brock takes my hands in his as I sit onto the bed. "Is he okay?"

I shake my head, the horror too real. "He has Leukaemia," I whisper. "They don't know if he's going to make it."

"Fucking hell," Brock mutters under his breath as he runs his hands though his hair.

I stand with renewed purpose. "I have to go to him."

"What?" He frowns.

I put my hands in my hair as panic begins to set in. "I have to get a ticket." I begin to pick up my things from the room and start throwing them on the bed quickly.

"You can't go to London, Tully. His parents are with him, they can take care of him," he says softly, trying to comfort me.

"I *have* to go!" I snap, and then my crazy eyes turn to him. "Come with me."

I nod frantically. "Yes, yes. You need to come, and we'll go now. You can wait in the hotel while I visit him. Please..."

"Tully, I can't do that. I just had a week off, and we have to find Meredith."

"Brock, please," I whisper as tears fill my eyes. "I need you to come with me."

He wraps his arms around me. "I want to, but you know I need to find Meredith. She's in real danger."

I drop to the bed.

"I don't want you flying over there on your own. I'll call your mother," he says, concerned. "Or do you want to take Callie?"

"No," I snap. "I don't want Mum there." I think for a moment. "Callie has to work. I'll go alone, I'll be fine."

His eyes hold mine. "I'll buy you a ticket and get you on the first plane," he says.

Fear begins to fill me. "What if he dies, Brock?" I whisper.

He takes me into his arms and holds me tight. "He won't. Medicine has come so far. He'll be fine," he whispers into my hair as he holds me.

I drop my head to his shoulder, but deep down I know that medicine hasn't come that far. Let's hope I'm wrong.

I sit and stare out the window of the plane, completely numb.

This is all my fault.

This is God punishing me for doing the wrong thing.

I get a vision of Simon outside my apartment that night, and the tears in his eyes as I told him I was in love with Brock.

I didn't even have the decency to ask him in.

I was too wrapped up in myself—in my own selfish needs to think about his feelings.

He didn't fight. He was too hurt. He never thought he would hear those words coming out of my mouth. Neither did I.

And then I went over and met Brock's family without a second thought for Simon or what he was going through. What kind of person does that?

When did I get so cold?

I put my head into my hands in despair.

Dear God, if you're out there, if you exist...

Please don't let this be happening.

Not Simon. Not my beautiful Simon.

Take me instead.

You can have me, just don't take him.

The tears roll down my face. "Are you okay, dear?" the stewardess asks, interrupting my thoughts.

I turn to her, startled. I nod, devoid of emotion. "Yes, sorry," I murmur to her as I wipe my tears away. The man sitting next to me gives me a sympathetic smile. I know he's concerned about me too.

She passes me a blanket. "Why don't you try and have another sleep?"

I nod and spread the blanket over myself. I recline my seat. The last thing I can do is sleep, but I don't want them fussing over me. They've been watching me do this for eighteen hours now, and I'm sure they think I'm on the edge of a breakdown.

Maybe I am.

The man puts his hand over mine on the table between us. "It will be all right."

I nod, and my eyes fill with tears again. Please don't be nice to me. I just can't deal with someone being nice to me. I deserve to be treated with disdain.

My mind goes to Brock, my king. He bought me a first-class ticket and took me to the airport. Not an argument or a derogatory comment to be heard. He was worried about Simon, too. *He's a good guy.*

God, I love him.

The kind man next to me takes my hand in his. "I'll hold your hand while you sleep," he whispers.

I smile softly, my faith in the human race restored. "Thank you."

I pull up my blanket, close my eyes, and with the warmth of a stranger's hand against mine, I drift towards my nightmares.

"He's in room two-one-six." The kind nurse smiles.

I walk up and peer through the window in the door.

Simon is in bed, his father is by the window, and his mother is sitting beside him in a chair. They look so sombre.

I close my eyes as I try to prepare myself. *You can do this.*

I slowly walk into the room. Simon's face lights up and I smile. "Hi, Si."

His mother and father stand and rush to me, holding me tight. I can feel their fear through their embrace.

"Hi." I smile, despite my tears.

I walk over to Simon, bend, and take him into my arms. He looks so sick and feels so weak, and all the pep talks I gave myself about being strong are thrown out of the window. I sob out loud. "I'm so sorry, baby," I whisper.

We cling to each other for an extended time. The horror before us way too real.

"What's going on?" I ask as I turn to them.

"He's having blood transfusions as we try to get his blood count up," his mother says softly. "He's very tired."

I nod. "Okay." I take his hand in mine and stare down at him.

"Lie with me, Tull," he whispers.

The lump in my throat is so big, I don't think I can stop myself from sobbing out loud again. I nod, scared to speak. I kick off my shoes and I climb onto the bed beside him, holding him tight.

"We'll give you some time alone," his mother says.

"I'll stay with him tonight," I tell them.

They glance at each other.

"Mum, go to the hotel and get some sleep," Simon says. "Tully's here now, it's okay. It's all going to be okay," he whispers, his eyes stay fixed on my face.

His parents eventually leave, and we lie in the dimly lit room, face to face, just like we have so many times before. I run my fingers through his hair as I try to will him to sleep. He's too weak to talk for too long.

"I love you, Tully," he whispers so softly that I can barely hear him.

"I love you, Si." I cup his face, and in this moment, I do love Simon. For everything that we've been through together and everything that we taught each other. "You're my best friend." I smile softly.

"Kiss me," he whispers through tears, and I know his time with me may be coming to an end.

The tears break free from my eyes, and I lean forward and tenderly kiss him as I hold his face in my hands. Our wet faces scrunch up against each other's in pain.

He smiles, closes his eyes, and the two of us lie still for a few moments...

Until he seems *too* still.

"Si," I whisper in a panic. "Simon," I hiss as I try desperately to wake him up.

"Simon," I say louder. "No. Don't you leave me," I sob. "Simon. No. Don't you leave me," I cry. "Please, no, Si... please?"

I jump up and press the buzzer. The nurses come running in and take over at once. I stand back with my hands over my mouth, frozen with fear.

The nurse turns to me. "Call his parents."

I take out my phone with frantic shaky hands, and I dial the number.

"What's wrong?" she answers.

"You have to come quickly. Something is happening," I whisper in a panic. "Hurry."

Two days later, I lie next to Simon on his bed. It's late at night, and a thin stream of light is drifting through the crack in the bathroom door.

I smile. "Remember the time we wanted McDonald's so we took your mother's car when your parents were out, and when we got back we left the hand brake off and the car rolled into a telegraph pole?"

He smiles. "How old were we?"

"Like, fifteen."

"Mac attack." He chuckles. "Remember Dad's face when he found out?"

I giggle. “What about the time we tried weed?”

“We were hardcore,” he whispers.

I smile. “We smoked joints in the park and fell asleep on a rug. Our parents called the police frantic because we didn’t come home all night.”

Simon looks over at me. “Remember how many mosquito bites we had?”

I laugh. We were covered head to toe. “That was hell, and we were grounded for forever.” We fall silent again. “Remember when you kissed me?” I whisper.

He smiles and nods. “I paid my friend to dare me to kiss you in that game of spin the bottle, just so you would go along with it.”

I run my hand down his face and cup his jaw. “I would have kissed you without the dare.”

His eyes search mine and we fall silent again. “I’m sorry.”

I frown in question. “What for?”

“I’m sorry I let you go,” he whispers. “That I didn’t try harder to make you happy.”

My eyes fill with tears. How could he possibly think that this is his fault.

“You did make me happy, Si. Every day you made me happy.”

He stares at me, and I know he wants to know why I left when there was so much good between us.

“I don’t know why,” I whisper. “If I knew the answer as to why I had to leave, I would never have left. I would have stayed and fixed it.” I put my head on his shoulder and we lie in silence for a while. I feel him smile above me, as if remembering something.

“Remember the time you made me put spray tan on you and I got it in your eye.” He smiles.

"I had to go to the emergency room over that." I giggle.

"And only one side of your face was brown." He chuckles. "And your mother was screaming at me for rubbing it on your face."

I burst out laughing as I remember the commotion in the hospital that day.

We lie sleepily for a long time, and then his regulated breathing tells me he's drifted off to sleep.

So many good times together. Too many to remember them all.

The hospital room is silent, and I sit on the chair next to Simon's bed. I haven't left his side in six days.

The silence is suffocating, as if our sadness has stolen all of the sound. The birds have stopped chirping and the children have stopped playing. He's declining, and I feel like the world is about to end.

Simon is asleep, too weak to stay awake now.

Three days ago, the chaplain came in to bless him into the afterlife, and we've been told to make peace with his illness. They can't get his blood count back up no matter how hard they try. The care he has been receiving has been remarkable, but it's just not enough.

How is peace possible?

How can I make peace with an insidious disease that is threatening to take him from me forever?

Brock's been calling me non-stop, but it doesn't feel right speaking to him when things are so dark over here. I've been giving him short texts as replies. I want to speak to him today, though. My phone lights up, and the name Brock lights up the screen. I know I need to take this.

I slowly walk down the corridor and answer. "Brock?" I whisper.

"Oh, thank God." He sighs. "I've been going out of my mind with worry. Are you okay?" he asks in a rush.

I shake my head and feel the tears begin to build again. "No," I whisper. "They don't think he's going to make it."

He stays silent.

"I can't help him, Brock."

"I'm at the hotel."

I frown. "What?"

"When I couldn't get you on the phone, I was frantic, so I came to London."

"You're here." I smile sadly, but somehow feeling full of hope at once.

"Yeah, baby, I should have come with you in the first place. I'm sorry I didn't."

The tears fall free. "Where are you?"

"I'm at the Intercontinental. Where are you staying?"

"I haven't been back to my hotel since I got here."

"Where have you been sleeping?" he asks.

"On the chair."

"Babe." He sighs.

"I'll come soon, okay?"

"Okay, I love you." He hangs up.

I walk back into the room. Simon's mother is sitting on the chair, and his father is at his usual place by the window. "I'm going to go back to my hotel for the night if that's all right."

"Of course, dear." His mother smiles, standing to take me into her arms. "Thank you so much for coming over," she whispers into my hair. "Having you here is going to give Simon the will to come back to us. He loves you so much, Tully."

I smile.

She pulls back, and her eyes search mine. "He needs you, Tully, now more than ever."

I nod. "I know."

She leans in and kisses my cheek. I bend over Simon and push the hair back from his forehead. "I'm going home, Si. I'll see you tomorrow?" I whisper as I gently kiss his forehead.

He's so lifeless now. He needs me… and *I'm leaving him to go see another man.*

The horrible taste of guilt fills my mouth, but I desperately try to block it out.

I turn and walk out of the hospital room, and I don't look back.

I can't have my last image of Simon lying in that bed as I leave him for Brock again.

What's happening to me? *Who have I turned into?*

Knock, knock.

The door opens in a rush and Brock's beautiful face comes into view. "Hey, Pock." He smiles warmly and wraps me in his arms.

I cling to him, the lump in my throat hurting so much. He's so big, so strong, and he feels so… healthy. He pulls back and looks down at me as he holds me by my arms. "My God, you look exhausted. How much weight have you lost?" he asks as he pulls me into the room.

I wrap my arms around him and hold him tight. It feels like he can make everything better. As if knowing just how fragile I am, he stays still and lets me just be. He brushes the hair back from my forehead and looks down at me. "Are you okay?" he whispers.

I shake my head. "No." I kiss him softly. "But I'm better now that you're here."

"I should have come in the beginning, babe. I'm sorry." He leads me into the bathroom. "Shower and sleep for you. I'll get some room service."

"Any news on Meredith?" I ask.

He shakes his head. "No, her debit cards haven't been used at all."

My heart drops. "What does that mean?"

He takes my shirt off over my head. "I don't know, babe." He sighs sadly.

He slides my pants down my legs, and then my panties and bra, and I stand before him naked. He holds my face in his hands and kisses me softly.

"I've missed you," I whisper. "It's been so long since I've been in your arms."

"I've missed you, too," he breathes against my lips, hesitating as he waits for an invitation.

"You getting in with me?" I ask.

He smiles softly and slides his shirt over his shoulders, and then he drops his jeans.

My eyes roam down over his beautiful body. Suntanned skin with a dusting of black body hair. Every muscle is on display, and his dick is dying for my attention. We kiss and, unable to help it, I slide my hand down and cup his balls, stroking his thick penis.

It feels like a lifetime since he's touched me.

"Let me wash you," he whispers as he pulls me under the hot water. A shower with Brock is the best kind of therapy. With the steam and his hands massaging the soap into me, I feel myself relax for the first time in a week.

I need to be close to him, closer than I am. I turn to him,

take his hand, and place it between my legs. "I need you," I whisper.

His eyes darken, and he kisses me, slowly circling his fingers through my wet flesh before he slides two of his fingers into my body.

The hot water and the feel of him... oh, how badly I've missed him. I feel like I'm going to come already. My body shudders and I lean forward. He picks me up and wraps my legs around his body, pinning me against the tiles as he slowly slides in.

Our eyes are locked, our bodies connected, and this is one of those perfect moments of clarity where everything just feels so right.

"I love you so much," I whisper as the water falls down over us.

"I haven't been able to breathe all week without you," he mumbles against my lips. My eyes fill with tears as he kisses me. The emotion between us too much. He slowly pumps me, and I smile up at him in wonder.

"Don't look at me like that or I'll come." He smirks.

"What? Like I love you?" I tease.

He shakes his head, as if disgusted in himself.

"Did you ever think a day would arrive when you could come just by knowing how loved you are?"

He closes his eyes to try and block me out, grimacing as he tries to hold it.

"I love you so much," I breathe against his lips. He pumps me harder.

"Fuck it." He growls and his cock jerks deep inside of me. I giggle, and he slowly rides me until my fingers are digging into his back and my head is tipped back.

He's thick and deep and so fucking perfect.

It's taking me longer today. "Deeper," I whisper.

He pumps me harder, lifting my legs higher, and he finds that perfect spot that makes my head roll back and my moan roam free.

He hits me again, and I shudder as I am shook with a violent orgasm.

I drop my head to Brock's shoulder, my exhaustion taking over, and we stay still for a long time. It's as if he knows I need him inside of me. I want to sleep like this.

"Bed, Pock," he whispers softly.

He pulls out and washes me again, and then he carries me to bed.

I wake to gentle kisses dusting my neck.

My love is here.

"Morning," I whisper as I reach behind me to push my fingers through his hair.

Brock's hands slide down over my hip and I can feel his erection behind me. I smile sleepily. "God, I don't even remember going to bed."

"You were zonked. How long is it since you've slept?" he asks.

"Honestly, not since I was in your arms."

He exhales heavily. "What's in the plans today?" He kisses my shoulder again and I smile peacefully... just for a moment.

"Shit." I gasp as I sit up in a rush. "What time is it?" I jump out of bed to retrieve my phone. There are ten missed calls from Simon's mother. "Fuck."

"What?" He frowns.

"The specialist is coming to see Simon this morning. I have to be there."

He stares at me as if I've lost my mind. "His parents are there with him." He crawls out of bed and walks into the bathroom.

"I know, but I need to be there, too," I say as I rush past him and turn on the shower.

"Why?" he asks. "Why do you have to be there?"

I scowl at him. "What do you mean?"

"I mean..." He narrows his eyes for a moment. "I mean, what exactly is your role here with Simon?"

"What's that supposed to mean?" I snap angrily as I step into the shower.

"Well, are you here as a friend or are you here as his girlfriend?"

"Don't be ridiculous." I sneer. "I'm your girlfriend."

"How long do you plan on staying here?"

I look at him, deadpan. "As long as it takes."

He tilts his jaw to the ceiling and puts his hands on his hips. "Is that so?"

"What do you mean, is that so?"

"I thought you would be coming home with me, Tully," he growls. "I thought I would be bringing you home." He rushes out of the bathroom.

"What?" I call after him. He doesn't answer, so I turn the shower off and follow him. "What do you mean you came here to bring me home?"

"Just what I said. You needed to see him. You've done it. Now it's time to come home."

"Are you fucking crazy?" I yell. "I can't leave him."

"You're not his girlfriend!" he yells back.

"He needs me."

"I need you. What about me, Tully. Where the fuck do I fit

into all of this? Put yourself in my shoes. Would you like me on the other side of the world comforting my ex-girlfriend?"

I point at him, my fury escalating to a dangerous level. "Don't you fucking dare."

"Don't what? Demand that you treat me with respect?"

I pull the hair brush through my hair as I begin to rage.

"You came, you saw him. You've done all you can. Now it's time to come home with me. Your boyfriend."

"Don't make me choose, Brock."

He stills. "What's that supposed to fucking mean?" His voice has taken a nasty tone… one I don't like.

I glare at him. "Exactly what I said."

"So, if I made you choose, you would choose him, is that what you are saying?"

I glare at him.

"Say the fucking word, Tully, and I'll leave so you can be with him." He jaw is set, his eyes burning as he stares at me and waits for an answer.

My eyes fill with tears.

And in that moment, he knows.

He steps back from me, flinching like I've just stabbed him. "I handed you my fucking heart on a platter in Hawaii," he whispers.

"Brock…"

"So." He frowns. "I was the pitstop all along. You were always going back to him?"

"Brock," I whisper, and I try to grab his arm and he hits me away.

"Is this what you did to Simon? Promise him your undying love and then throw it in his face?"

"That is not fair!" I cry. "He is *sick*."

"I know!" he yells. "But you need to work out what the fuck you're doing and what your fucking role here is."

I stare at him through my tears.

"Do you want to be his girlfriend... or mine?"

"I love you," I whisper as the tears roll down my face.

"That's not what I asked, Tully."

I drop my head and stare at the carpet. I can't leave Simon. I just can't do this. "I need to do what's right," I murmur sadly.

"And staying with him is what's right?"

"Yes."

I look up, and his eyes search mine, the room falling deathly silent.

He screws up his face as he loses control, turns to the wall and punches it hard, making a hole in the plaster. I jump back in a complete fright.

"Brock!" I gasp.

He turns and storms out, not saying a word, just slamming the door behind him.

I stare at it, my vision blurred. The lump in my throat constricts and I sob loudly.

"Brock," I whisper into the silence. "Don't go."

CHAPTER 21

Tully

"So, the results are good?" Simon asks the doctor.

The doctor smiles with pride. "Yes, the results are great. The levels are on their way back up."

I let out a sigh of relief and squeeze Simon's hand in mine.

"You have a long fight ahead of you, young man. But I'm confident we can get you over this crisis," the doctor tells him.

I smile and Simon's parents hug each other in relief.

I look between the doctor and Simon. "When do you think he will be able to transfer back to Australia?" I ask. I'm so grateful for the medical treatment he's had here in London, but Australia has cutting edge medical technology and we really want to get him home.

"I'd say he'll be fit to travel in around three or four weeks."

My heart drops. Four more weeks. That's a long time. My mind instantly goes to Brock and the fight we had this morning.

I exhale heavily. I want to be here with Simon. I couldn't go home at this point.

God, this is a fucking mess.

The doctor fills out the charts and talks to the nurses. I hug Simon's parents, and then him. "This is great news, Si," I whisper as I hold his forehead to mine. "You're going to be okay."

He smiles and lies back, his eyes never leaving mine. My phone rings, and I scramble to pick it up. It might be Brock. I frown when I see the name Meredith lighting up the screen. I answer immediately.

"Meredith?"

"Oh, hi, Tull," she says without a care in the world. "What's up? Why did you call me so many times?"

I roll my eyes. Damn Meredith. I cover the phone with my hand. "I've just got to take this," I whisper before I dart out into the hall. "What the hell, Meredith?" I whisper angrily. "Where the hell have you been?"

"My gran got sick, so we took a road trip to Queensland."

"Oh." My face falls. "Is she okay?"

"No, she's not. She's dead now. Buried in the ground," she replies flatly. "Worms in her head. Wolf pack meeting tonight?" she asks, as if this is the only thing that matters.

I close my eyes as I try to get my head around the worms in the head comment. "I'm in London, Meredith." I pause. "Simon is really sick, so I came to see him."

"Oh, okay. Fly home now so we can have our meeting tonight."

I sigh. "I can't."

"Yes, you can. Tell him you're busy."

I smile to myself. If only things were as black and white as Meredith sees them, life would be a lot easier.

"Meredith, Brock has been looking for you. He was worried that everything wasn't okay."

"No. I'm fine."

I stay silent. I'm not sure if I should mention anything about Peachy Sue until the boys are physically with her. I bite my bottom lip as I listen. She's seems fine. Maybe this *is* all a crazy mix up?

"So, when are you coming home?" she asks.

I glance up the hall towards the room. "I'm not sure," I sigh sadly. "Simon needs me."

"Oh." She thinks for a moment. "I thought you broke up with him?"

"I did." I pause. "It's complicated."

"Are you having a threesome with him and Brock now?"

"No, Meredith, for God's sake, I'm not," I snap angrily. For fuck's sake, she's annoying sometimes.

"Is Callie going out with Brock now?" she asks.

"No!" Damn it, I'm not in the mood for this crap today. "I'll call you later."

"Bye, Tully." She hangs up, completely unaware that she's just ruffled my feathers. I exhale heavily, knowing I need to call Brock.

I've felt sick since our fight this morning. Hopefully he isn't already halfway back to Australia by now. I dial his number and he answers on the first ring.

"Hey, Pock," he says sadly, and I instantly know he isn't angry anymore.

"Brock, I'm sorry," I whisper.

"Yeah. Me, too, hey?"

"Where are you?" I ask.

"I'm in the hotel room."

I smile and stare at the wall in front of me, letting the silence hang between us. "I'll come back there now, okay?"

"Yeah, okay."

"Oh." My eyes widen. "Meredith called me."

"What?"

"She called me just now. She said her grandma died and she had to take a road trip with her mother."

"Thank fuck." He sighs. "Where is she now?"

"At her apartment."

"I'll get straight on it. See you soon."

I hang up and walk back into the hospital room to Simon's face light up when he sees me. My heart drops, and I fill with sadness.

He deserves better than this.

Brock deserves better than this.

The term torn between two lovers has never rung as true as it does right now.

I love both men; one for what we were, and one for what we are. A future with either of them seems impossible.

I need to decide.

Brock

I hang up and stare at the phone in my hand for a moment.

She called.

I'm glad I didn't get on the first plane home like I wanted to. I even called the airline to try and change my flight, but I knew that if I got on that plane it would have been it for Tully and me. I get that she wants to be here. I get that she cares about Simon's welfare, but when she said the words *don't make me choose*, I lost my shit. It never occurred to me

that choosing between us was even an option for her. Maybe I'm wrong.

Maybe I'm here in London making a fucking idiot of myself. Maybe I've given over a part of myself to her that was safer buried deep inside.

Stop it. She wouldn't. I know she doesn't love him, she loves me. I'm sure of it.

I call Ben's number.

"Hey."

"Hi. It's me. Meredith is alive."

"You're kidding?"

"Nope, she just called Tully. Seems her grandma was sick, and she went on a road trip. Get a car around there and check on her, can you?"

"Okay, I'm on it."

"Oh, and Ben..." I say.

"Yeah?" He listens.

"She's got..." I pause as I try to articulate what I need to say. "She's a bit out there. Not the norm kind of chick."

"What do you mean?"

"She's smart as a whip but is socially awkward. She says random things at random times. Tully says she's somewhere on the spectrum."

He exhales heavily. "Fuck's sake." He thinks for a moment. "Well, how do I handle this? Can I question her?"

"I'd probably spend some time with her first and see if you can draw the information out slowly. I think if you go in with all guns blazing she's just going to shut up shop."

"Okay got it. I'll get Jes onto it. He's a softy. Everyone loves him."

"Good idea," I reply.

"When are you home?" he asks.

"Soonish."

"Is Tully coming with you?"

"Who knows?" I sigh. "That's a whole different fucking nightmare."

"Just be patient, mate. She didn't ask for this to happen."

I exhale heavily. "Yeah, I know, I'm trying."

"Okay, I'll be in touch after I speak to Meredith," he says. "Catch you." He hangs up.

Half an hour later and there's a knock at the door.

I smile, knowing she's here. I open the door in a rush and Tully stands before me. She's been crying, and my heart drops when I see her sad face.

"What's wrong?" I frown.

Shit, did he die?

"Can we talk?" she mutters weakly.

I stare at her and the hairs on the back of my neck stand to attention. "Sure."

She walks past me into the room and I frown. What's going on here?

"I'm sorry about this morning," I say as my eyes hold hers. "I had no right to order you home. I don't know what came over me."

She smiles up at me. "Yes, you did. I'm your girlfriend. You had every right to order me home. I'm sorry I said you shouldn't make me choose." She runs her hands through her hair, as if uncomfortable. "That was wrong, and it most definitely wasn't fair."

I smile and go to take her into my arms but she pulls away.

"What's going on?" I whisper.

Her eyes fill with tears. "I love you, you know I love you."

Time stands still.

Don't say it. Please don't say it.

"But, I need to be fair to everyone concerned," she adds.

"What's that supposed to mean?" I begin to hear my heartbeat thudding in my ears.

"Simon has a long road to recovery in front of him."

"I know."

"I'm going to be here for him for as long as it takes," she says calmly, as if all this is some kind of pre-rehearsed speech.

"I don't expect you to walk away from him, Tully," I tell her.

"I know, baby." Her haunted eyes hold mine. "I'm walking away from you."

"What?" The ground moves beneath me. "What do you mean?"

"Simon needs all of me," she whispers.

"What are you fucking saying?" I growl.

"I'm saying that it's not fair to you to be constantly waiting for me at home while I sit at the hospital with my ex-boyfriend."

"But you don't love him."

She scrunches her face in pain. "I know. I love you."

"What the fuck are you doing, Tully?" I shout, losing the last of my control.

"What's right, Brock. I'm doing what's right. What anyone with a heart would do for their ex."

My face falls. "You're going back to him?" I whisper.

She shakes her head.

"Tell me. Tell me out loud that you are not going back to him." I feel my chest beginning to close up.

A slow-moving tear rolls down her face, her eyes holding mine with a resolved strength. "I can't," she breathes.

I step back from her as pain tears through me.

She's going back to him.

I grab the wall as I suck in air to try and stop myself from freaking out and completely losing my shit.

"This could go on for years with Simon. I won't have you end up hating me for it," she whispers as her tears continue to fall. "I care about you too much to leave you waiting at home for me."

She doesn't love me.

I drop my head so that she doesn't see my blurry eyes. "Get out," I whisper.

"Brock. Can't we at least be friends?" he pleads.

I lose control. "I have enough fucking friends, Tully," I yell, my own tears breaking free. "Get the fuck out."

I drop my head, and my chest shakes as I try to regain control, but there's no chance of that.

"I love you," she whispers.

I turn on her like she's the Devil himself. "You fucking liar! Get the fuck out of my life. Right now!"

She steps back from me, wincing and aching with emotion. "I'm sorry," she whispers.

Our eyes are locked, and then she slowly turns and walks out the door, leaving it to click closed quietly.

I close my eyes. The room is silent apart from my thudding heart.

I drop my head and inhale deeply as I try to block out my emotions.

I need to get out of here.

Now.

I walk to the phone and dial reception.

"Hello, reception."

"Organise a car to the airport, please," I say calmly.

"Of course, sir. When for?"

"Now."

The cab pulls up at my house. It's 1:00 a.m. The street is dark and quiet now. I pay the driver and walk up to my door to let myself in. I flick the light on and look around the living room, exhaling heavily.

Same street, same house... only she's not here anymore.

It's been a long trip home—the worst. A five-hour delay on my stopover brought it up to thirty hours of travel.

Thirty hours alone, unable to get out of my own head.

I'm cut.

Deep.

I can usually fight my way out of any situation but this time it's different.

And I keep going over and over that last conversation in my head, wondering if there was anything I could have said to have changed the outcome.

Tell me you're not going back to him.

I can't.

Two words have never hurt so much.

I walk into the kitchen and turn on the light, immediately spotting the two keys I had cut for Tully sitting on the counter.

Her keys to my house.

The keys she doesn't want anymore.

A deep sadness fills me, and I run my hands through my hair as emotion overtakes me. I turn and run to take the stairs two at a time. I need to sleep. I need to get back to work. And I need to forget that I ever met Tully fucking Scott.

"Hi," I call out when I walk into work. Everyone looks up from their computers in surprise.

"Hey." Ben frowns as he follows me into my office. "What are you doing here?"

I dump my bag on the desk. "I work here."

"I mean what are you doing back from London?"

"Just decided to come home."

"Why?"

"Ben, shut the fuck up and stop hassling me," I snap.

He raises his eyebrows. "Fine." He turns and walks out of the office, and I close my eyes for a moment. *Stop it.*

I turn on my computer and begin to read the notes on all of our cases. Then I go to the notes on the interview with Meredith.

Verdict - Was not a witness.

What? I stand and walk out into the office. "Ben and Jes. Can I see you both for a moment, please?" I ask.

They both stand and come into my office. "What's up?" Jes asks.

"What's with the notes on Meredith?" I ask. "What happened?"

They both fall into the seats at my desk. "She seemed calm, reckons she didn't see a thing. Said she wasn't home the night that Peachy Sue died," Ben replies.

I frown. "Are you sure? Do we have confirmation on that?"

"No proof that she was home," Jes says. "But, she was as

cool as a cucumber." He raises his eyebrows. "Weird as fuck, but nothing seemed astray."

"Hmm." I think for a moment. "Okay, I'm going to go around and see her myself, see what I can dig up." I flick through the files on my desk. "What about Chancellor?" I ask.

"Nothing new on Chancellor. We're searching through his company files at the moment. There's a large file that has been deleted, but we're trying to get someone to go back and find it." Ben shrugs. "We really need to find ourselves an I.T. person. We can't keep outsourcing this stuff."

I roll my lips as I think for a moment. "Actually, I might know someone," I say. "Let me follow that up."

"Oh, and the job vacancy went up this week for our new person. What are we looking for again?" he asks.

I exhale and swing on my chair for a moment. "We need a woman with past armed forces or police experience. We're cutting our undercover work in half because we don't have a female." I sigh as I think. "We may have a job coming up. One where she will need to go undercover and develop a relationship with a drug lord. We need information that can only come from the inside, so she needs to be made aware of that before she starts. She needs to be mentally tough and physically strong. A detective or from special forces... something of that calibre."

Jes nods as he jots down the information. "Got it, boss."

"Do you want me to come and see Meredith with you?" Ben asks.

"No, I'm good." I turn back to my computer and Jes leaves the office. Ben stays behind, and I keep typing.

"What?" I eventually snap.

"Want to talk about it?" he asks.

"Nope." I keep my eyes on my computer screen.

"You okay?"

"Yep."

His eyes linger on me for a while and I shake my head. "Fuck off, man. Just leave me alone, hey?"

He nods, sensing how close I am to losing my shit, so he wisely chooses to leave me alone and exits the office.

I pick up a folder of photos and exhale heavily.

Okay, Meredith, let's see what you've got.

I knock and wait. "Who is it?" Meredith calls from behind the safety of her locked apartment door.

"Meredith, it's me, Brock."

"Is Tully there?" she asks hopefully.

"No, but she's coming back soon."

She opens the door but leaves the keychain on to peer through the crack.

I force a smile. "Hi."

"What do you want?" she asks.

"I was hoping you could come and have a coffee with me at the café. Tully is away, and I thought you might like some company."

She frowns as she considers my proposal. "I don't drink coffee."

"An ice-cream?" I ask.

"I do like ice-cream," she murmurs to herself.

"We'll be quick."

Meredith frowns harder. "Tully said I'm not allowed to go out with people's boyfriends."

Tully's not fucking here. "That's okay, we're just friends. It's different for friends," I say.

"Oh." She thinks for a moment. "Okay. Is Callie coming?"

"No, she's at work."

She bites her bottom lip. "Yes, because she wants to sleep with her boss."

I try to hide my smile. "Yeah, I know," I say. I didn't know that, but I do now.

She closes the door, and then I hear her keychain unlock before she opens the door. I smile and glance down at her. She's wearing pink pyjamas.

"Are you ready?" I frown.

"Erm." She thinks really hard and then looks down at herself. "No pyjamas outside of home," she mutters to herself in singsong.

"That's right." I smile.

"Just a minute." She looks to her bedroom and then back to me, pointing to a stool at her bench. "Sit there."

"Okay." I take a seat where I'm told to.

She goes into the bedroom and closes the door. I look around her apartment. It's immaculate. Everything has a place. Small rugs lead a trail to the bedroom and bathroom. Why? Ah, so she doesn't get the carpet dirty.

I smirk as I look around. It's not at all what I expected. This apartment is actually very nice.

She reappears and smiles nervously. "I'm wearing Tully's top."

I frown. "Oh." I'm not sure what to say.

"Tully gave me her clothes because she didn't think mine suited me."

"I see."

My stomach rolls at the thought of Tully. *What's she doing right now?*

I stand. "Let's go."

. . .

We sit at the ice-cream bar and I watch Meredith intently.

How do I handle this?

Meredith is licking her ice-cream like her life depends on it.

"How was your trip?" I ask.

Meredith shrugs. "My gran's dead. Buried in the ground, worms in her head."

I frown. Gross, for fuck's sake.

"It's all natural," she assures me. "Everything dies."

"Oh, I see," I murmur as I lick my own ice-cream.

Hmm.

"Have you seen your friends lately?" I ask.

She frowns. "Tully is away with Simon." She licks her ice-cream again. "But she doesn't want to have a threesome with you and Simon."

My head just about explodes. "Why the fuck would you say that?"

She rolls her eyes. "Duh. I asked Tully."

I bite into my ice-cream cone, and it crunches between my furious teeth. "Whatever," I snap angrily. "What about Wendy Woo?"

Meredith's face falls. "You know Wendy?" she asks, as if surprised.

"Yes, I know Wendy. She's my friend," I reply casually.

"She came to Queensland with my mother and me."

What?

"Oh, yeah, I know." I act as if I already know. "She had to get out of here before they found her," I tell Meredith.

Meredith nods as she licks her ice-cream. "Because they killed her friend. Now they want to kill her."

I watch her sharply. Fuck, don't blow this now, Brock.

"Because she did that thing, didn't she?" I say as I try to act as casual as casual.

"Yeah, she hid it now but..."

"That's right," I reply. "How many were there?" Fuck, I have no idea what I'm asking about here but hopefully she's falling for this act I'm putting on.

"Memory sticks are easy to hide."

I stare at her as my mind races. Memory stick. Memory stick. What the fuck is on a memory stick? Hmm. I'm just going to throw something random out there.

"Her friend who knows computers did that for her, didn't he?"

She nods. "But he's dead now. In the ground, worms in his head."

Fuck, did Chancellor make the memory stick? Was he trying to help Wendy Woo?

"What happened to Peachy Sue, Meredith?" I ask.

Her eyes snap to mine. "I didn't see anything," she blurts out in a rush.

"I know you didn't," I reply calmly.

She begins to shake her head. "Act calm and nothing happens to you," she says.

I frown as I watch her. "Who told you to act calm?"

She stands suddenly. "We need to go home now."

"Why?"

"I'm tired, very tired. I need to go to bed." She begins to get agitated.

"It's okay," I tell her as I stand, too. "We can go home now."

She puts her head down and rushes to my car. She's fidgeting with her hands in front of her, clearly rattled as soon as I mentioned Peachy Sue. Fuck, I need to get more information from her. She knows what happened to Sue, I'll bet my life on it.

We drive back to her apartment as I try to think of a plan. I can't ask her outright or she freaks out. The only way I am going to get more information from her is if I spend more time with her.

Fuck's sake.

We pull up outside her apartment. "Do you want to have ice-cream tomorrow?" I ask.

She thinks for a moment. "Can't we go dancing instead?"

I wince. "Sure." I fake a smile. "I might get the guys to come, too. Is that all right?"

She smiles broadly. "Can Callie come, too?"

Fuck, it gets worse. I don't want to hang out with Tully's friends like a fucking loser.

"No, Callie can't come."

Her face falls. "Oh, okay then."

"I'll call you?"

"Do you have my phone number?" She frowns.

"Actually, no. What is it?" I already have all of her details, but I can't tell her that.

Tully

I lie on the small sofa in Simon's hospital room. It's been three weeks since I lost my love. Twenty-one days since Brock left, and I haven't heard from his since. I know I won't. He's too proud to ever contact me or take me back.

Every night I cry myself to sleep. Every day I just about make it through without falling apart. Why did this happen?

Why did it have to be Simon? Why do bad things happen to good people? Simon didn't deserve this sickness.

Brock didn't deserve this.

I'm a bad person. No matter what I was going to do, someone was going to be hurt. It couldn't be the man who is already sick.

I just want to know if Brock's okay. I can't bear the thought that I've hurt him. I called Callie and Meredith, as they've both seen him when he interviewed them over Peachy Sue's death. They said he's normal, that he seems fine.

I, however, am not.

I feel like I'm being punished for leaving Simon. It's as if God wants me to know how much a broken heart hurts.

A punishment for my crime.

I'm carrying on as normal on the outside, but inside I'm dying a little every day without Brock in my life. I'm suffocating in grief. I don't feel like a whole person anymore. It's like the shell of me is here with Simon... but my heart left with Brock. Now it's smashed into pieces and buried in the depths of Hell.

I swipe the tear away quickly before it leaves my eye. I'm trying so hard to put a brave face on for Simon but it's getting harder, not easier.

I've sacrificed my own happiness for someone else's, someone who is fighting just to stay alive.

I did what I had to do.

Simon is a good man. The best. I'm the one who's fucked in the head.

"It looks like we can transfer you back to Sydney early next week." The doctor smiles as he closes his folder.

I sit up quickly. "That's great."

"I'll make the arrangements and we can get the ball rolling."

I walk over and sit on the bed next to Si, taking his hand in mine. “See, it’s all working out.” I smile. “Australia, here we come.”

The nurse takes Simon’s vitals and writes in her chart. “Everything looks great.” She smiles.

The last three weeks have been a blur.

Hope for Simon has been followed by sadness for Brock.

I honestly don’t know whether I’m coming or going anymore.

Simon was transported back to Sydney last night. The flight was long and filled with worry. But we made it and, hopefully, some sense of normality will return to our lives soon.

I go back to work on Monday. I drove past the gym last night on my way home from the hospital, and when I saw Brock’s car parked there I burst into tears and cried for two hours.

I’m so sad, working on autopilot.

When Brock left me in London, he took a piece of me with him.

Simon and I had the talk last week. He asked me if we could get back together and I had to be honest and tell him the truth.

It’s not like that for us anymore, even though I love him so much. It’s just a different love now. A family kind of love, not a romantic kind of love. He was down for a few days, but I think it would have been much worse if I had lied to him about my feelings.

I care about him way too much to ever lie to him. Simon’s parents have gone home for some much-needed respite. I’m going to stay another hour or so, and then I will head home, too. I haven’t seen my friends or anything yet. Last night I was too tired and emotional to be good company.

There's a knock at the door, and I look over to see an attractive blonde girl.

"Hi." She smiles nervously from the doorway.

"Hi." I smile back.

Simons face falls. "Penny?" he gasps.

Her face lights up. "Hi, Simon." She looks nervously between us. "I... I.' She pauses for a moment. "I hope I'm not interrupting."

"Not at all, please come in," I say.

Her eyes meet Simon's, and they both smile softly. I glance between them. The chemistry is palpable.

Oh my God, is this...?

"Tully, this is Penny," Simon says with reverence.

Simon told me that the girl he was seeing while we were apart was called Penny.

"Penny," I gasp. Unable to help it, I grab her in an embrace. "Simon told me all about you."

Her face falls and her eyes flicker to Simon. "He did?"

I smile and take her hand in mine, and she swallows nervously.

"I was wondering if I could talk to the both of you?" she asks.

"Of course." I smile.

Simon frowns and looks uncomfortable with Penny and I being here together.

"I know you two are back together and everything—" she whispers.

"We're not back together," I interrupt.

She looks at Simon, pausing, as if nervous. "I'm pregnant."

Simon and I stare at her.

"The baby's yours, Simon."

CHAPTER 22

Tully

MY EYES ARE WIDE as I stare at her in total shock.

Simon's face falls. "What?" He glances at me nervously. "But we didn't..." His voice trails off.

"I know, but I haven't had sex with anyone else in two years. The condom must have broken or something," she says quietly. "I didn't come here to stress you out or bother you. I came because I feel you should know."

Simon stares at her, unable to speak. He is so shocked.

A smile crosses my face. "Of course." I look between the two of them. "I'll leave you both alone."

Simon becomes panicked. "T-Tully, where... where are you going?" he stammers.

I smile. "Home, Si. I'll be back tomorrow." I take Penny's hand in mine. "You stay here." Unable to help it I wrap my arms around her. "Congratulations, this is wonderful news," I whisper into her hair. I turn to Simon and kiss his forehead. "A baby, Simon," I whisper with glee. "This is so amazing. Congratulations." I take both of their hands in mine. "You are going to be a wonderful father, Si." I smile through tears, and I turn, leaving them alone to talk about their future together. I walk out into the corridor and I swipe my tears away as carefully as I can.

I don't know why I'm crying.

I'm happy. I... I... I just don't know how I feel about this.

I'm so shocked.

This is the absolute last thing I ever expected to hear. It doesn't mean it's a bad thing, though, does it?

God, wait until Simon's parents find out. A baby out of wedlock. I wish I could be there when he tells them.

I make the trip to my car, and with every step I get closer to it, a little bit more excitement fills me.

Simon has something to live for, something that isn't me, and I could feel that he and Penny have a connection.

I close my eyes as I wait for the elevator.

Please let them fall in love.

Please let him have the happy ever after that he deserves.

A baby... it's so much motivation to give him the will to live.

I stare at the ceiling above me as I hear the clock tick over again.

I don't remember driving home. I don't remember walking up to my apartment, getting in the shower, or going to bed.

All I remember is the sound of a huge chapter of my life closing.

I'm happy that this has happened, but strangely enough, I'm a little sad.

It's bittersweet.

I sacrificed Brock... for what?

Where does this leave me?

"Hello, hello." I laugh as I grab Rourke in an embrace.

He laughs out loud and spins me around. "Thank fuck you're back," he teases.

I nod as I pull out of his arms. "I am so back, and I am not going anywhere ever again." I smile.

It's my first day back at work in a month. Who knew I would miss the place so much?

"What's been happening?" I smile. "What do you want me to do today?"

"We have lots to do." Rourke sits down at his desk and puts his finger to his lips, looking around to make sure no one can hear us.

I frown. "Huh?"

He writes down on a piece of paper.

We need to talk.

I scowl and look back up at him.

"Let's go and get a coffee," he says.

Rourke doesn't even like coffee. "Okay." He links his arm with mine before he practically runs me out of the building.

We break out through the front doors. "What the heck is going on?" I ask.

"F-fuck, fuck, fuck," he stammers. "Something is going on in the lab."

"What do you mean?" I frown as we walk towards the coffee shop.

"Evidence is being moved at night."

"*What*?"

"You know that hair sample I thought I lost? The one we thought had been signed out a couple of weeks ago?"

"Yeah."

"It turned up."

"What do you mean it turned up?"

"Just that. It was just there one day, but I know I checked that very spot. Somebody had put it there overnight."

I frown. "You think it was tampered with?"

"I know it was."

My eyes widen. "By who?"

"Fuck knows, but it got me thinking, so I've been testing a few things, and I think the lab is bugged."

"Bugged?" I shriek. "By who?"

"Shh." He looks around nervously. "Keep your voice down."

"Who would bug the lab?" I whisper.

"Somebody who is up to no fucking good is my guess," he whispers.

"Why would they do that?" I shake my head as I try to think clearly. "I'm so confused."

"I don't know, but the other night I told Angela where I was putting another DNA sample that had just came in from another murder victim. I told her I hadn't tested it and I was going to work on it in the morning, so I was leaving it in the drawer. Not the drawer it was supposed to be in, but another drawer."

I listen.

"Then I booby trapped the sample."

I frown. "Booby trapped it, how?"

"I put a piece of my own hair into the bag and hid the real sample."

My eyes widen in horror. "Fuck, Rourke. You could lose

your job for tampering with evidence. What the heck are you thinking?" I whisper angrily.

"Get this. In the morning, the hair in the bag... it *wasn't* mine."

"What?" I gasp. "Are you sure?"

"Positive. The only way this could have happened is if the lab is bugged. They knew where the evidence was, and then it was switched overnight."

I put my hand over my mouth. "Oh my God." I think for a moment. "So... who? Who do we think is responsible?"

He shrugs. "I don't know. It could be a cleaner or someone from downstairs."

"Did you tell anyone?" I ask.

"No. The only people who can come up here undetected is management."

"You think this is someone in management?" I frown.

"Fuck knows. I've been waiting for you to get back so we can come up with a plan. If they are tampering with evidence, it means they are the ones who killed these girls. It also means that they have the means to kill *me*."

I put my head into my hands. "Fucking hell. What do we do?" I whisper.

"Just don't say anything out loud until we work something out, and be vigilant. Be aware of everyone who comes into the lab. We have to work out who we can trust."

I nod as I drag my hands down my face. "Shit, what a fucking nightmare. It's like a crime show or something."

Rourke links his arm with mine. "Welcome back, bitch."

I bubble up a giggle. "I swear, the universe is trying to give me an ulcer."

Rourke winks. "I've got two."

Brock

I sit at the restaurant and wait for my meal. I couldn't be bothered to cook tonight. In fact, I can't be bothered to do anything lately.

I glance up and see a guy and his girlfriend laughing at the bar, and my stomach twists with jealousy.

She's reading out the menu and laughing while he is standing there holding one of her hands, his other hand on her behind.

They look happy… in love.

I frown as I watch them, and a million memories of Tully wash over me.

I wish I'd never met her, because then I wouldn't know what I was missing by not having her by my side.

It's as if the whole world has been tainted, all because now I know how the other half live.

A life that never interested me before happens to be the only one I want now.

To feel settled and calm with love and laughter.

To feel what I had with Tully. But it will never be the same now because the girl will never be Tully.

Our ship has sailed.

Fuck this, I'm going home. I stand just as the waitress arrives at my table with my dinner.

"Oh." She frowns as she sees me standing to leave. "Your dinner is here."

"Yeah." I shrug. "I'm not just feeling it anymore. You eat it." I turn, making my way of the door and out to my car.

I don't even know who I am anymore.

Tully

The rain is falling heavily as I sit inside my car. I'm parked outside Brock's house, peering across the street. It's dusk now. I need to talk to him, if for no other reason than to apologise for how I treated him.

I frown as I think back to the day when I ended it between us in London. I was so sure I was doing the right thing at the time.

But hindsight is the worst form of torture.

If only, the worst words you can whisper to yourself.

I've been back in Australia for a week and I have wanted to call him every day, but I didn't know what to say.

What can I possibly say now that will make what I did okay and take away the pain from us?

I never thought I would make huge, life changing mistakes at this age. I thought I would have my shit well and truly together by now. Know exactly what I'm doing and with who.

What a joke. I had the love of my life and I threw him away with no regard for anything but Simon. And I don't regret being there for Simon, I just wish I thought things through a lot more clearly before I followed through with it.

The rain is really coming down when his black Range Rover pulls into the driveway. I close my eyes.

Here we go...

I've been sick with nerves all day worrying about how tonight will go.

Brock gets out of the car, soon seeing me sitting in mine. He turns towards me and stares, not looking away, despite the rain.

I stare back and smile softly. Then, without showing any emotion, he turns and walks inside without acknowledging me at all, the door slamming shut behind him.

My eyes fill with tears. There's my answer.

My chest shakes, rising high as I try to hold back my impending sobs of despair. Brock hates me.... the sound of the rain is loud in my car and the windshield is fogging up as I sit alone in the darkness.

What have I done?

For fifteen minutes, I sit in my car trying to work out a plan of action, trying to work out what the hell I can do to make this better. But, I've got nothing... nothing except this overwhelming sense of dread. I need to talk to him. I need to try and explain everything. I need to make him see my point of view.

I get out of my car and run across the road in the rain. It's pouring down now and I'm saturated. I bang the big brass knocker on his door.

Bang, bang, bang.

I wait.

Please answer, please answer.

Bang, bang, bang.

"Brock!" I call. "I know you're in there," I cry, trying to make myself heard over the sound of the loud rain.

I pound on the door with my fist.

"Brock!" I cry. "Open the door. Please," I beg. "I need to talk to you."

But the door stays shut, and I hear the lock click from the other side. He's locked it.

My heart drops.

I screw up my face and I begin to cry uncontrollably. He doesn't even want to speak to me.

I'm standing here in a storm from hell and he doesn't even want to talk to me.

I bang again and again, and I start to plead with him. "Please, Brock. I'm sorry!" I cry. "Please, open the door."

The door stays shut, and eventually, I slip down it to sit on his front step in the rain.

My chest is throbbing, my head, too.

I've hit an all-time low.

After an hour of sitting in the cold rain and dark night, I eventually pick myself up and drag myself back to my car. For a long time I stare through the fogged up windshield, doing nothing but looking at his house.

I start the car and pull out into the street completely numb.

My life is a complete disaster.

I sit and stare at the computer screen in front of me. My mind is a million miles away. I get a vision of myself begging Brock while standing in the rain outside his house last night, and shame fills me.

Who am I?

I completely lost my shit last night, along with any dignity I ever had. I think back to all the things that have happened between us, including the gym where we met. Then him seeing me here when he was asking about that police car.

Hang on a minute. I frown. Shit, I had completely forgotten about that. I wrote that number plate he was asking about down somewhere that day. Where did I write it?

What did I have with me that day? The case notes, my diary. *My diary*.

I take my diary out from my drawer and begin to go through it, looking for a number plate number.

I look on every page, but I can't see it. Shit, where did I write that down? I know I did somewhere.

I go over the meeting I was having that day, and I type the

job into the computer to find out the date of that meeting. Got it.

I flick through the diary at double speed and open it on that date.

With my finger, I trace through all the notes. At the very bottom of the page I see it.

NGH 167

Okay, it was the night before, so that makes it...

I check the dates, go downstairs and make my way out to the backroom. The car rosters go up for two months at a time, so it may be still up on the wall.

I go through the dates. Here it is. I trace my finger across

NGH 167 Peter Mulgrave.

What the fuck?

Peter?

I put the key into my apartment door at exactly 6:00 p.m. It's been a long day at work and I just don't know what to make of all this Peter business. Maybe it's just a bad coincidence. I didn't say anything to Rourke. I can't until I know for certain what the hell is going on.

Peter is not a crook, I know that. A sleaze? Maybe. But not a hardened criminal... *is he?*

I open the door and freeze.

The energy is different and my spine tingles. I look around to see if someone is here.

"Hello?" I call into the silence. I look around the apartment, but everything seems the same. There's no trace of anything missing. But something is definitely off. "Hello..." I call again, and I hear a noise come from the bedroom.

A sense of fear grips me. I calmly walk back out and close the door, and then I run down the hall and jump into the elevator. I get out on the ground floor and I run across to Meredith's apartment, banging on the door furiously.

"Who is it?" she calls.

"Meredith, it's me!" I cry. "Let me in."

The door opens in a rush and Ben is standing before me. Huh? What's he doing here? I step back in surprise. My eyes look past him into Meredith's apartment, and I see that it's completely trashed. Meredith is sitting on the couch with Jesten.

"What's going on?" I whisper, officially terrified.

"Come in," Ben says. I walk past him and step into the apartment. I stop still in my tracks.

Brock is standing by the window. He glares at me for just a second before he snaps his eyes away angrily.

Fuck.

My heart begins to beat hard and fast at the sight of him.

"W-what happened here?" I stammer.

"Meredith has been robbed. It seems they were looking for something."

"I think they're in my apartment right now. That's... that's why I ran down here," I tell them, out of breath and nervous.

"What?" Brock frowns.

"I heard a noise come from the bedroom as soon as I walked in," I whisper.

Brock and Ben take off out the door and run up the hall. "Be careful!" I call after them.

I look around Meredith's apartment. The entire place is

destroyed. Everything is upturned and ripped apart. I drop to the couch beside her.

She's rattled and physically shaking. I put my arm around her. "It's okay, baby," I whisper as I pull her close. "It's okay."

But it's not okay, I can tell by the look on Jesten's face. This is as far from okay as it gets.

"Wendy Woo is dead," she whispers.

My eyes widen. "What?" I look over to Jes, and he gives me a subtle nod of his head to confirm what she's saying is true.

"What the hell is going on?" I whisper.

"A *lot* of shit," he answers quietly. "I'll let Brock explain."

I drop my head into my hands. This is a fucking nightmare. Poor Meredith. Two of her friends have been murdered and now this has happened to her apartment.

"Who did this?" I turn to Meredith.

"I don't know anything," she replies calmly—too calmly. I frown at her. That's a practiced speech, I can tell. She does know who did this.

"Meredith?" I whisper.

Jes gives me a subtle shake of his head. "Wait for the boys."

Oh, okay.

I take Meredith's hand in mine and we sit in silence.

We wait, and we wait. Jes seems to be getting worried too because he goes to the door and peers down the corridor.

He waits for a moment and then he dials a number. "You okay?" he asks.

"Good. See you soon." He hangs up. "They're coming back up now."

"Oh, thank God," I whisper.

Brock and Ben walk through the door and I hold my breath. "What's happening?" I ask.

"Your apartment is clear. Meredith is going into a safe house," Brock tells me matter-of-factly.

"What?" She frowns.

"Don't argue with me, Meredith. This is serious. Tell me what you know!" Brock snaps.

"N-nothing," she stammers nervously. "Don't know anything and you can't get hurt. Don't know anything and you can't get hurt," she begins to chant.

"Did Wendy Woo tell you that?" I ask.

Meredith's eyes come to me, as if she's surprised that I knew who told her that.

"I want to go home, I want to go home." She starts to get agitated and begins to pace back and forth. I look up to Brock, but he snaps his eyes away from mine in disgust. He can't even look at me.

"I'm going to take Meredith now," Brock says.

I stand. "I'm coming, too."

"No! You don't go anywhere near Meredith until we say so," he tells me firmly, leaving no room for argument.

My eyes flicker between the three men. He thinks I'll be in danger if I spend time with her. *Shit.*

"You'll have protection in your own apartment," he says as he pulls Meredith from her chair.

Oh good. "Are you coming back?" I ask hopefully. Maybe I'll get to talk to him then.

"No." He looks to Ben. "Organise someone to come and stay with Tully, will you?"

"I-I don't... No, I don't want a stranger in my apartment."

Brock's cold eyes rise to meet mine. "Tough shit."

CHAPTER 23

Tully

I SIT on the sofa in my apartment. Ben is in the kitchen and Jesten is out in the hall.

Brock is nowhere to be seen. He left hours ago with Meredith and hasn't returned since. Ben is being polite, but it's obvious he doesn't particularly want to talk to me, either.

My mind is racing.

Am I really in danger? Is Meredith in danger, or have these guys just been watching too much cable?

What the heck happened to Wendy Woo? And Peter… is he really capable of all of this? I wouldn't have thought he was intelligent enough to pull this shit off and I know for sure he's not violent. If people are dying and he's responsible, then he must be getting someone else to do it for him because he can't even kill a fly. It just doesn't add up, not at all. None of it.

Screw this, I want some answers. I march out into the kitchen. "I would like to know what's going on," I say to Ben.

Ben looks up from his phone, unimpressed with my demand or the tone of my voice.

I wither a little under his gaze. He's so much like Brock, it's insane. *Alpha-holes.*

Anyone would think they are biological brothers and not just brothers-in-law.

"Somebody is killing escorts who are being forced to blackmail any wealthy business men they do business with," he replies flatly.

I frown.

"Your friend Meredith was friends with two of the murdered women. She probably has more information than she is letting on."

I stare at him as my brain struggles to take it all in.

"We believe that a memory stick with evidence proving who is responsible for these crimes is in circulation. That's what they were looking for in Meredith's apartment."

My face falls, I don't know what to say. "Why do you think *I'm* in danger?" I ask.

"We don't know that for sure. We watched the security footage of your apartment back and nobody was in here earlier. You were probably just a bit freaked out."

I stare at him, lost for words. "Oh..." I think for a moment. "What did Meredith say about it all?"

"She's saying that she doesn't know anything."

"But you don't believe her?"

"Not really." He hesitates for a moment. "There's a lot of bullshit being slung around here at the moment." His eyes hold mine, and I know he means by me.

I stare at him for moment, feeling like I need to explain myself.

"I did what I thought was right at the time, Ben." I pause.

"I'm not saying it was, but I thought I was doing the right thing for everyone."

He purses his lips. "You see, I have no idea what you're talking about right now."

I frown. "Brock didn't tell you what happened between us?" I ask,

"Nope." He stares at me but doesn't say anything further. I feel myself wither again.

Do I tell him?

No, this *is* none of his business.

But he's Brocks best friend. "He won't even talk to me," I say quietly.

Ben looks at me flatly.

"I went around to his house last night and cried in the rain for over an hour. He wouldn't let me in."

Still, he remains emotionless.

"Has Brock ever forgiven anyone who hurt him?" I ask softly.

He shrugs, as if uninterested.

"You're not going to talk to me about this, are you?"

He shakes his head. "Nope."

I cross my arms over my chest. I don't like the way he is making me feel. "You don't have to be so rude about it," I say, agitated.

"I'm not being rude. I'm being polite. This is none of my business, and trust me, you'll know it when I'm being rude," he replies coldly.

Frustration fills me. I shouldn't have said anything. These men are a different breed. I feel uncomfortable now. "Well then, you can leave. I'm not having a stranger in my house overnight."

"You'll have to clear that with the boss," he says dryly.

"The boss isn't here." I sneer as my anger begins to bubble.

Fuck this, who do these guys think they are? "I'll call the police if you like and they can ask you to leave."

He smiles sarcastically. "Go right ahead... if you want to get yourself killed." His eyes hold mine. "You call the police and let them handle this."

"You think the police are responsible for this?" I ask.

"Certain of it."

I stare at Ben for a moment and think. I'm going to tell them about the evidence going missing at work. I have to. Something is definitely going on here. There are just too many coincidences.

"I have some information in regard to the lab and evidence," I announce.

Ben narrows his eyes. "Such as?"

"I'll only talk to Brock." I tilt my chin in defiance. "Alone."

Ben smirks, showing the first bit of emotion he's shown all day. "You're going to blackmail some time with him?"

"Yep." My eyes hold his and I tilt my hip like a petulant teenager. "That's exactly what I'm going to do."

I pace around in my bedroom. It's just turned 10:00 p.m. and I've negotiated a deal.

Brock is coming to talk to me.

What a joke. I really am at rock bottom with not a shred of self- respect left at all.

He thinks he's coming here for information regarding evidence but I'm having my say first, and he *will* listen if it's the last thing I make him do. He's going to be furious that I'm forcing his hand, but he's left me with no choice.

Desperate times call for desperate measures.

Ben is here, and I think Jes is still out in the hall. I don't know where Brock was but he's taking his sweet time getting here.

I've been on tenterhooks and have been pacing for two hours now.

I hear a knock at the door and close my eyes. *This is it.*

The next fifteen minutes will determine my future with him.

Good or bad, I'll know where I stand.

I go to the door and open it. Brock's cold eyes hold mine, his jaw clenching in anger. He's clearly furious that I have pushed him into a corner like this.

"You have new information?" he asks, raising his eyebrow sarcastically.

Nerves dance around in my stomach. I nod and move back from the door.

"Come in."

He walks past me, and I get a waft of his aftershave. It nearly makes me burst into tears.

I miss him.

Ben nods as he sees him, and then he walks out of my apartment without saying a word.

God, he's a rude prick.

I sit down, watching as Brock takes a seat on the couch opposite me.

"What is this *new* information?" he asks flatly.

I swallow the lump in my throat. "I do have information for you, Brock. It's vital information."

He raises his brow again, not believing me at all.

"But... I want to talk about us before we talk about that," I add.

His cold eyes hold mine. "I'm not interested in anything other than the case."

My eyes instantly fill with tears. He's so cold, and his tone is filled with hatred. "Brock," I whisper. "I miss you. I want you back."

I try to take his hand in mine but he stands and turns his back. It's as if he can't stand the sight of me anymore.

"Don't!" he snaps.

"Brock, please, just listen to me. I thought I was doing the right thing." I stare at his back. "I thought..." My voice trails off.

He remains silent and still.

"I felt guilty, Brock. I felt guilty for falling out of love with him and falling in love with you."

He stays silent.

"I kept going over and over the night that I told him I loved you. I kept seeing his hurt." I pause for a moment. "And then I just went upstairs with you and went to your mother's house without any regard for his feelings at all."

Still, he doesn't look at me.

"I didn't want you waiting at home for me while I sat in the hospital." I screw up my face. "I didn't want you to hate me," I whisper.

Silence.

"I love you, Brock, and more than anything, I was hoping..." I inhale sharply. "I was hoping that we could try and work this out."

He doesn't acknowledge a single word I'm saying.

"Can you at least look at me!" I shriek in frustration. "You let me cry in the rain for an hour last night outside your house and you didn't even care."

He turns, and his eyes meet mine.

"Can we?" I whisper hopefully. "Can we try and work this out... please?"

He stares at me.

"Say something," I whisper. "What are you thinking?"

"What's the information you have on the case?" he asks calmly.

My face falls. "I asked you a question."

"And I asked you a question." He rolls his lips. "Answer mine first, and then I'll answer yours."

I nod. Okay. He's going to talk to me. "Fine," I murmur. "Evidence is going missing from the lab."

He narrows his eyes, his interest piqued. "What do you mean? What evidence?"

"Only evidence on the prostitute murders, too. Nothing else seems to be out of place."

He frowns as he listens to me.

"Rourke set up a trap and hid some fake evidence one night. The next day, when he came in to check it, it had been switched..." I continue.

He frowns. "How does he know it was switched?"

"Because he put his own hair in it as a test. When he checked it the next day, it wasn't his. Rourke thinks the lab is bugged somehow and that maybe someone is listening in on our conversations."

He clenches his jaw and thinks for a moment. "I need to get a camera in the lab. How do I get in there?"

"You can't, its completely blocked to the public."

He puts his hands on his hips, lost in thought.

I think for a moment. "I could do it," I offer.

"No."

"Why not?"

"I don't want you involved in this."

"I already am, though. It's where I work. It's one of my good friends. It's in my apartment block. I couldn't be more involved if I tried."

"I'll think about it," he says calmly, and then he walks towards the door.

"Brock?" I call.

He turns back.

"You didn't tell me what you were thinking?"

His eyes hold mine. "I was thinking that I wish I'd never met you," he says flatly.

I swallow the lump in my throat, and my vision blurs. His words cut like a knife.

He turns and walks out, and I stare at the closed door feeling numb all over again.

He's never going to forgive me. I've fucked it.

I place the slide into the microscope and peer through the lens. I can barely see through my bloodshot eyes. I've hardly slept a wink. Rourke is downstairs in a meeting with the other technicians. I pretended I had to do something urgent so that I didn't have to go. I didn't really. I just couldn't stand the thought of sitting in a meeting for two hours talking about accreditation standards.

The door opens and then clicks shut, and I turn suddenly.

Peter has let himself into the lab. Oh no. Does he think I'm in the meeting downstairs too? I don't want to startle him or see something that I shouldn't.

"Hello?" I call.

His face lights up when he comes around the corner and sees me. He's genuinely surprised. "Hello, my beautiful Tully." He smiles and pecks me on the cheek. His hand grabs my hipbone and he pulls me snug to his body.

Erm...

"How are you?" He smiles as he tucks a piece of my hair behind my ear.

My skin crawls. He's very touchy today.

"Fine." I force a smile. "How are you?"

"Lonely." His hand lingers on my hipbone and he squeezes it tightly.

My nerves begin to rise. "You should get a girlfriend." I look around the lab.

Fuck...

As if reading my mind, he glances around the lab, too. "It's just me and you up here today?" he asks.

I nod. "Uh-huh."

"Mum told me about Simon and the baby," he says.

I smile, relieved for a change in the topic. "I'm happy for him. She seems really nice. I was at the hospital with her the other night."

His eyes glance down to my lips, looking like he's going to kiss me.

What the fuck?

"And you left the other guy, too?" He smirks.

"Brock." Get his name right you dipshit.

"I didn't think much of him, anyway. Good riddance." He gently squeezes my hip again. That's it.

"What are you doing?" I snap, flicking his hand off me.

"Come on, Tull," he whispers. "You're lonely, I'm lonely." His eyes drop to my lips again. "We can help each other out."

"What... by fucking?" I snap, outraged.

He inhales sharply and grabs my hand, placing it on his hard dick. "You know I've always wanted you."

My eyes widen in horror. "What the hell, Peter?" I whisper angrily as I snatch my hand away. "The feeling is *not* mutual. I'm offended. You need to leave."

"Bullshit! I've seen the way you look at me. You want it." He grabs my hand and puts it back on his hard cock again.

I pull my hand away and shove him in the chest. "Get the fuck out!" I snap.

"Come on, Tull," he whispers, pushing me backwards and pinning me to the bench. "We would be so good together," he breathes on my neck.

"What the actual fuck?" I knee him as hard as I can in the balls, and he doubles over in pain. I run to the stairs and take them two at a time.

I get to the bottom of the stairs and push the double doors open, panting and gasping for breath.

That's it. Fuck him! I'm telling them what I know.

Peter is a fucking asshole.

"Are you kidding me?" Rourke whispers from across the table.

"I wish I was," I whisper as I lean forward in my chair. "So, Brock and his team think it's a policeman who is forcing these girls to blackmail wealthy businessmen, and then he's murdering the women once they've done it."

He frowns as he sips his Coke. We are at lunch in the middle of a crisis meeting, and I'm telling Rourke everything.

"And now you are suspicious that someone is switching evidence," I whisper.

"Not suspicious. I'm sure of it," he says with conviction.

"Remember when I saw Brock downstairs at reception, way back when I hardly knew him, and he was wanting to know who was driving a certain police car?" I ask.

"Yes."

"I just checked it." I glance around and lean in. "Peter was driving it."

His eyes widen. "Peter… your stepbrother?"

I nod. "Yep."

He puts his hand over his mouth. "Fucking hell," he whispers and runs his hands through his hair. "Maybe it was a coincidence?"

"Maybe. Brock said he wants to put a hidden camera in the lab."

His face falls. "We can't do that. If we get caught we'll lose our jobs."

"But we can't tell anyone," I whisper. "We have no idea who we can trust. If we tell the wrong person, they'll kill us, too."

Rourke puts both of his hands on his head. "Fucking hell, Tully, what do we do?"

"I don't know. But we had better start thinking of something fast."

"And they really think this is so serious that Meredith is now in protective custody?" He frowns.

I nod. "Uh-huh."

"Where is she?" He frowns.

"I don't know," I whisper angrily. "I have no damn idea what the heck is going on anymore." I throw up my hands in exasperation. "The whole world has turned to shit."

"Did you speak to Brock?"

I roll my eyes. "He told me he wishes he'd never met me."

Rourke winces. "Ouch."

Now it's my turn to put my head in my hands. "I went to his house the other night during that big storm. He wouldn't answer the door, so I sat on his front step and cried in the rain for an hour."

Rourke curls his lip in disgust. "Playing hard to get, hey?"

I pinch the bridge of my nose. "I can't believe what a fucking idiot I've been."

Rourke widens his eyes. "I wouldn't say a fucking idiot. A martyr, yes."

My face falls. "You think I was being a martyr?"

He shrugs casually. "I think that you never dealt with your guilt over leaving Simon and you channelled it very badly by dumping Brock."

I stare at him sadly.

"I can't believe Simon got someone pregnant," he sighs.

"Do you know how fucked up I am?" I ask. "I'm thrilled that he got someone pregnant because it means that I'm not the bad guy in our relationship anymore."

"You were never the bad guy, Tully. Breaking up with someone is not being a bad guy. It's just being honest. You did the right thing... right up until you threw away what you had with Brock." He points at me. "*That* was fucking stupid."

"I know."

"And he will probably never get over it," he adds.

"I know that, too." I sigh as I put my hand over my forehead.

"I wouldn't be surprised if he hates your guts now."

"Shut the hell up, Rourke," I snap. "You're pissing me off with all your honestly."

"Listen, back to business before we go back to work. I think we need to seriously consider what Brock is saying. He won't let anything happen to you."

I shrug. "Can you come and talk to him tonight with me, please?" I ask. "I'm so lost in all of this."

He takes my hand over the table. "Yeah, sure."

Brock

I sit in the car across the road from Tully's mother's house. This is the last place I want to be but it's a necessary evil. I

blow out a breath as I wait. According to their usual schedules, her mother and stepfather should be leaving for work any minute now. The garage door goes up, and I drop my head. Her stepfather pulls out and I watch his car disappear down the road. I wait another twenty minutes. Is her mother ever leaving?

I tap on the steering wheel as I wait, and I think back to the last time I was here. I frown as I remember how happy I felt. Tully had just agreed to move in with me.

We could have been so good together if only she hadn't fucked it up.

Her words from last night come back to me.

I love you, I made a mistake.

I clench my jaw as my anger begins to resurface. I've never been so angry with anything or anyone in my entire life as I am with her. She thinks that she can just waltz back in here, click her fingers, and I'll run to her like a puppy dog?

I don't think so.

I'll never trust her again.

That horrific thirty-hour flight home from London is ingrained into my soul.

I will never, ever put myself in a position to be hurt like that again.

She can go to Hell... or marry Simon. Either way, I don't give a fuck.

Finally, the front door opens and her mother walks out. She gets into her car and I watch it slowly pull out and drive down the road.

Okay, let's go.

. . .

I knock on the door. Come on, answer. He's unemployed. Fuck knows what time he drags himself out of bed.

I knock again, harder this time.

No answer.

Shit, he may not even be home.

I bang on the door. "Brad?" I call. "It's me, Brock."

Silence...

I shake my head in disgust. Come on, man. I don't have the fucking time to be waiting here all day for you.

I bang hard again, and I hear a creak from inside. I put my ear to the door and listen. Footsteps.

Yes.

I step back, and the door opens. Brad is wearing only his boxer shorts, and he looks dishevelled as he frowns and scratches his head.

"What the fuck, man? What time is it?" he moans.

"Seven-thirty." I smile.

He frowns at me.

"Can you hack?" I ask.

"Huh?"

"I need an I.T. person to hack computers for me."

He scratches his head again. "Yeah, I can hack."

"Do you want a job?" I ask.

His brows rise in surprise. "What?"

"I've been looking for a person I can trust for a while."

Brad's face falls. "Is this some fucked up way to get back with Tully?"

I look at him flatly. "No, Tully and I are done with."

He stares at me.

"I'm serious, I don't want anything to do with your sister. No offence."

He frowns.

"I do, however, want some information on your stepbrother Peter."

A smile crosses his face. "What kind of information?"

"I think he's up to something," I say.

"He would be. He's a seedy prick."

I smile. "You and me are going to get along just great. Get dressed. You start your new job now."

I knock on Tully's door at 8:00 p.m. Jes picked her up from work and has been here with her until I arrived. I've been with Meredith all day and I'm about to go out of my mind. That woman is annoying as fuck. Rourke, Tully's partner in the lab, is coming to talk to me. Apparently, there is more news that could help us with the case.

Tully opens the door and smiles warmly at me. "Hi." Her hopeful eyes search mine and I clench my stomach. She's freshly showered and smells… like home.

Stop it.

I walk past her into the apartment. "Please, take a seat," she says in her husky voice.

I feel my cock harden, and I bite my bottom lip. *Not now.*

What is it with her? Every time, every single time I'm near her, my body is aroused whether I like it or not.

I need to learn how to shut it down, and I need to learn quickly. I drop to her couch, watching her as she sits opposite me. I get a vision of her laughing above me in Hawaii when I told her I loved her, and I frown. The memory hurts.

She begins to talk about her day, but I can't hear a word she's saying because her scent is making so many memories wash over me.

The beach, time out… *love.*

I have no control with her. I couldn't even open the door when she was outside my apartment because I knew if I did…

This is stupid. Get the information and get the hell out of here.

She says something and crosses her legs, tucking up underneath her bottom. I can see the muscles in her thighs. I get a vision of her muscular thighs up over my shoulders, and I remember how good she felt around me, how her arms felt around me...

Jesus Christ.

This is the worst form of torture.

Perspiration beads on my forehead as I try to concentrate on what she saying.

What if...? No.

I watch her talk for a moment, but I can't concentrate on a word she's saying. My eyes are focused on her big, pouty lips.

One more time...

No.

Rourke knocks on the door and Tully jumps up to answer it. "Oh, hi," she says as she lets him in.

I wince. For fuck's sake. The last time I saw this guy, I dragged him out of his chair at the restaurant.

"Brock, this is Rourke," she introduces us, her nervous eyes flickering between us.

I shake his hand. "Hello."

He forces a scared smile. "Hi."

I need to apologise before I say anything. "Ah, listen. I'm sorry about the first time we met."

"You scared the crap out of me. I ran all the way back to the office."

I smirk. "Sorry." Who fucking admits that? Even if it's true, this guy is a dork. A chickenshit dork. "Take a seat," I say, and they both fall onto the couch. "Tell me about this new information you have."

Rourke and Tully exchange glances, and I know they have talked about what they are going to say to me.

"Well, this makes me uncomfortable to say out loud, but I feel that in order for you to understand my theory, I have to tell you everything," Tully says.

I frown.

"Remember when you were wanting to know who was driving a police car with the number plate that you had?"

"Yeah." I look between her and Rourke. Rourke nods at Tully, urging her to go on.

"Peter was driving that car."

My eyes narrow. I fucking knew it.

"B-but," she stammers. "I don't think he did this. At least, if he is involved, I know he didn't kill the girls himself. He must have a partner."

"Why?"

She swallows nervously and looks between us.

"Peter is gentle. He's a dick, but he couldn't kill a fly when we were kids. He can't even watch boxing on television because he thinks it's too violent. He's just not capable of physically killing these women."

"I don't think—"

She cuts me off. "There's more." She pauses and blows out a big breath. "You know how Rourke thinks the lab is bugged?"

"Yes," both Rourke and I answer.

"Yesterday, when you were all in the meeting downstairs, Rourke, Peter came to the lab." She swallows and pulls her hand through her hair.

I frown as I listen. She seems nervous. What's going on?

"He hit on me," she whispers.

"*What*?" I snap.

"He hit on me, pinned me up against the counter, and he was really quite aggressive."

My fury bubbles over, and I stand immediately, as the whole sky turns red.

"But, it proves he didn't do it."

I turn to her. "How?" I snap. Wait until I get my hands on that fucker. He's going to die.

"He's not killing these girls himself. He's just not capable, and if the lab is being bugged, he wouldn't have hit on me for whoever is involved to hear about it. If he knew someone else was listening, there is no way he would have done it." Her eyes are wide as she tries to prove her point. "Think about it, Brock. He would lose his job immediately and give someone else extra ammunition against him. If he knew the lab was bugged, he wouldn't have done what he did. No way in hell. It doesn't make sense."

I frown as I think. She may have a point. My blood runs cold as a new scenario enters my brain.

"But if he's not killing the girls, what would he be doing?" Rourke frowns. "How would he be involved if he's not involved?"

"He's offering them protection in exchange for sex," I tell them as all the pieces of the puzzle fall into place.

"What do you mean?" Tully asks, shocked.

"I was told that someone within the police force is offering the women at risk protection in exchange for sex whenever they want or need it. Gang bangs, threesomes, all kinds of shit. But he can't protect them, because he nor the others involved have any fucking idea who's behind all this."

Tully's eyes widen. Rourke's, too.

"That makes more sense to me," Tully whispers. "Peter's a

sleazebag, but he's not violent. I know that for certain. I grew up with him."

"So, you want us to put a camera in the lab?" Rourke asks.

I stare at the two of them for a moment as I think. Rourke's a wimp, and Tully's safety is non-negotiable. If they get caught, there is no way that either of them could defend themselves. "No," I say. "I'm not putting you two in the firing line." I exhale heavily. "At this point, all we know for certain is that Meredith is in danger and knows something she's not letting slip." I shake my head. "I need her to tell us what she knows so we can get to them. More girls are going to die unless we do." I begin to pace. "How do I get Meredith to open up and relax?" I ask. "I'm at a loss with her. She's the most difficult person to read."

Tully thinks for a moment, her eyes flickering to Rourke and then me. "We take her dancing."

CHAPTER 24

Tully

I SIT on the couch and pretend to watch television. Brock is outside my apartment with Ben. Rourke left about an hour ago. They are making plans for us to go out tomorrow night. I'll call Callie now and let her know.

I dial her number. "Hi," she answers happily.

"Hey," I say.

"What's wrong with you?" she asks.

I can't tell her anything about the evidence crap from work. Or the case, other than what she has seen on television, and I can't even tell her about Peter yet.

What can I actually talk to her about?

"All this crap with Meredith is stressful. They want us to take her clubbing tomorrow night and try and loosen her up a bit. Can you come?" I ask hopefully.

"Sure." She hesitates for a moment. "Are you okay?"

"Yeah," I sigh sadly. "It's official, though. Brock hates me."

"What do you expect?" she huffs.

I roll my eyes. "Yeah, I know. Like you tell me every fucking day: it's my own stupid fault." I throw the cushion off my lap and onto the floor. "It pisses me off, okay?"

"Whatever," she sighs. "Text me the details for tomorrow night."

"Yeah, okay." I exhale heavily, feeling bad for snapping at her. "Do you want to have lunch tomorrow?"

"That depends."

"On what?"

"On whether you're going to sit there like a sad sack of shit feeling sorry for yourself the whole time or not."

My mouth falls open. "I'm going through a hard time right now, okay?"

"See, here we go again."

"You're fucking pissing me off, Callie."

"Good, I'm trying to. It might snap you out of this Brock bullshit."

I roll my eyes again. Trust Callie to say it how it is.

"I want my best friend back," she says.

She's right. I haven't been myself since Simon got sick five weeks ago.

"I'm trying," I whisper.

"Try harder. Because the Tully I know wouldn't be begging any guy to take her back. She would be using her brain to actually fix the problem."

I frown.

"The Tully I know wouldn't be blaming the universe for her break up. She would handle it."

"I just don't know how to."

She exhales heavily. "I'll see you tomorrow."

"Yeah, okay," I say softly. "Bye."

I close my eyes and a tear rolls down my face just as my front door opens and Brock walks in. I quickly wipe it away.

He stills when he sees I'm crying. "What's wrong?"

I shake my head, unable to speak through the lump in my throat.

"Has something happened?" he asks, falling serious.

I shake my head as I stare straight ahead at the television.

"What is it?"

I turn to him. "I've made such a mess of everything between us."

He clenches his jaw.

"I don't know how to fix us, Brock," I whisper. "And I want to so badly."

He rolls his lips.

"You look at me like you hate me." My eyes search his.

He pulls his eyes from mine, and they drop to the floor. He doesn't answer me.

"You don't have to stay here tonight. I know you hate my couch."

He blows out a defeated breath and drops to sit beside me. "I have to stay here, nobody else can do an overnight shift tonight."

The lump gets so big in my throat. He's only staying because nobody else can.

"I'm fine," I whisper as I wipe more tears away. "I don't need protection."

"I'm staying."

"We can go and stay at your house if you want." I shrug. "That way you will be able to sleep better, and you won't be tired tomorrow?"

"No."

"Why not?"

"Because I don't want you in my personal space." He stares at the floor, unable to make eye contact with me.

Oh God. *He's so hurt.*

I nod, the tears rising again.

He doesn't want me in his personal space and that cuts me to the bone.

I stand, needing to get away from him before I completely lose my shit. "Okay, I'm going to bed. Do you want my bed and I can sleep out here?" I ask.

He shakes his head.

"You know where the blankets are."

Silence.

I walk to my bedroom door, turning back to look at him. "I love you," I whisper.

His eyes rise to meet mine. "Don't." He stands in an outrage. "Don't you dare use those three words as a fucking weapon!"

I step back.

"Who the fuck do you think you are to come back here and act as if nothing has happened?" he yells at the top of his voice. He picks up a coaster from my coffee table and hurls it at the wall.

I flinch, blinking through my tears. I've been looking for a trace of emotion from him, but now that it's anger I've unleashed, I don't want any of it.

"Don't tell me that you love me, Tully. Don't you ever fucking tell me that you love me again," he growls. His eyes fill with tears as they hold mine. "If this is what love feels like, I want nothing to do with it," he whispers angrily.

I sob out loud, seeing how hurt he is.

He drops his head.

Silence hangs between us.

Eventually, he turns towards the door. "I'll be outside." He walks out, and it quietly clicks shut behind him.

I look around my silent apartment, my vision blurry. My quivering breath is the only sound I can hear.

Every time I try to fix it I only seem to make it worse.

I look over at the clock. Its 2:21 a.m. Brock is on my sofa, but I can't sleep.

Callie's words are playing over and over in my mind.

Fix it.

The only way I can fix this is if I get him to let down his guard and talk to me. Tonight, when he got angry, was the first time he has shown any type of emotion. And all because I told him I loved him. I can't believe that telling him I love him would make him so furious.

Well, I'm not apologising anymore. Callie has a point.

I did what I thought was right at the time, and if he can't even speak to me about it, then what am I supposed to do?

I roll over and punch my pillow in disgust.

Fucking men.

I sit at lunch with Callie and sip my Diet Coke.

"Where are we going tonight?" she asks.

"The Ivy, I think." I shrug. "Meredith knows that place so it will make it easier for us all."

Callie smiles as she cuts into her salad.

"Thanks for the pep talk last night, by the way," I say. "You're right, I have been feeling sorry for myself since I got back, and I needed a good kick up the ass."

"You have every right to wallow a little." She shrugs. "I

didn't mean to sound cold, but a boyfriend leaving you..." She widens her eyes. "Or *you* leaving *him* in this instance, is not the worst thing that can happen."

"I know." I bite the food from my fork. "This is true."

We eat in silence for a moment. "Did anything happen last night when you saw him?" she asks.

"I told him I loved him, and he lost his shit and screamed at me. He told me not to use those three words as a weapon against him ever again."

Callie's eyes hold mine.

"He seems to only show me any emotion when he gets angry," I sigh.

Callie bites the food off her fork. "So... piss him off some more then."

I frown as I chew, my eyes holding hers.

"He only loses control when he's angry, right?"

"Yeah."

She smiles like a Cheshire cat. "Then piss the bastard off so bad that he has a complete meltdown on you. Break him down."

I put my knife and fork down, and they hit my plate with a clang. "Callie, you are diabolical," I whisper with a sly smile.

Her eyes dance in delight. "How are you going to piss him off?"

I tap my chin with my fingertips as I think. "Where will I begin?"

Knock, knock.

I take one last look at my reflection in the mirror, and I smile broadly. I'm wearing my black leather pants with a white, low-cut top. My girls are boosted to the sky. I have sky-high stilettos on, and I'm wearing Brock's favourite lipstick. I know he loves me in white. I also know he loves me in these pants. He can't keep his hands off me whenever I wear them. I'm also wearing the fragrance he bought me in Hawaii. At the time, he told me it had a hotwire to his dick, which is convenient for me seeing how I plan on starting a few fires tonight.

We are going clubbing, and Brock has just come to pick me up. They have been and collected Meredith and Callie already. I'm last on the pick-up list.

I open the door in a rush and he stands before me.

His broad shoulders are covered in a black T-shirt, and he's wearing dark blue jeans that fit snugly in all the right places.

I grin in greeting and purposely bend to pick up my bag. I might even try some of those slut snaps his secretary does tonight. It couldn't hurt. I need all the ammunition I can get.

I put my hand on my waist and wiggle my hips. "Do I look okay?" I ask innocently.

He tilts his jaw, and his annoyed eyes drop down my body and back up to my face. "You'll do," he replies flatly.

I smirk, and Brock narrows his eyes at me, as if sensing I'm up to something.

"Are you ready?" he asks.

I grab my clutch and smile sexily. "Sure am."

He opens the door and we walk down to the elevator in silence. I make sure I walk in front of him so he can see my behind. I walk with an over exaggerated sashay.

He stays silent as he lingers behind.

What the hell is he thinking back there?

We make it to the car, and Callie and Meredith are in the backseat. "Hello, my friends." I laugh as I climb in and kiss them both on the cheek. Ben is driving, leaving Brock to climb into the passenger side. "What's been happening?" I ask.

"Brock and I have been watching House Flippers all day," Meredith says.

My eyes widen. "Really?"

"Yes, we watched six episodes today, didn't we, Brock?"

"We did," he sighs.

Ben smirks over at him and I see Brock mouth the words, "Fuck off."

For the rest of the trip, Meredith continues to explain to us all in great detail why she loves House Flippers. So much so that Ben is continually looking over and smirking at Brock who is just staring through the front windshield.

We arrive at the Ivy and climb out of the car. The boys briefed us earlier today. We are to act natural, as if we're on a regular night out, and then we should casually throw questions to Meredith and see what information she lets slip. We need to find out if she knows about this memory stick they think that Wendy Woo had in her possession, or if she actually did see who killed Peachy Sue. Any answers are good answers.

We walk into the club and one of the doormen smiles at me, looking me up and down with hungry eyes. Brock glares at him and I feel a flutter deep in my stomach. It's working.

Game on.

Brock, Jes, and two other men from his work are with us, standing just to the side. Ben is downstairs parking the car.

"Let's go to the bar and gets some shots." I smile mischievously.

"What are you going to do?" Callie whispers.

"Whatever it takes."

We buy Meredith three shots, getting only one for ourselves

as well as a round of margaritas, and then we head back to the spot where the men are standing around.

There's a smoky glass mirror on a nearby column and it's perfect. I can see Brock with my back to him without him even knowing it. I stand, talking to the girls, moving my hips to the beat. Every now and then, I see Brock's eyes flick down to my behind as he watches me.

A guy walks past us and stops to say something cheeky. I laugh and put my hand on his bicep as I speak to him. I'm being way touchier than I normally would be. I mean, I have to make it believable.

I glance up to the mirror to see that Brock is glaring at me. There's practically a red glow around him.

"Do you want to dance?" the guy asks me.

Oh, it's a little bit early yet. Brock will be onto me. "Can we dance in an hour?" I ask. "I just got here, and I want to talk to my friends first."

"Sure." He smiles. "It's a date. I'll be back in an hour."

Three hours later, and the three of us are on our way to being very drunk indeed. We have been talking and talking to Meredith, but I honestly don't know if she does know anything more that can help us.

Would the call girls have told her if they knew something? I know that she hinted about a memory stick but she's so cool and relaxed now. I don't know if it was ever really a thing? The more that I think about it, the more I'm confused. She can't keep a secret at all. If she had a secret, she would have blurted it out by now.

The guy from before comes back. "Do you want to dance yet?" he asks.

My eyes flicker over to Brock, and he glares at me as he sips his drink. He's openly angry now. I've danced with just about everyone in the club.

I smile up at the poor, unsuspecting fool in front of me, and he puts his hand on my behind.

Eek, I don't know about that. I don't want to start World War Three here.

I frown when I feel a hand grab the top of my arm.

"A word?" Brock growls in my ear.

Before I know it, he's dragging me up the corridor towards the bathroom.

I try to remove my arm from his grip. "What are you doing?"

"What the fuck are *you* doing?" he snaps.

"Dancing," I answer innocently.

"I'm not fucking stupid, Tully." He sneers.

"It's okay, Brock, I know. We're done with. Never going to happen. You told me. I get it."

He lifts his chin defiantly.

"Hence why I'm going to go out there and I'm going to dance with that man, and if he wants to, I'm going to let him kiss me."

His eyes widen. "Don't you fucking dare!" he growls.

I step closer to him. "The thing is, Brock, I want to kiss somebody tonight."

My eyes drop to his lips, and then back up to his eyes.

Contempt drips from his every pore, but he grabs a handful of my hair, jerking my head backwards with force, our faces nearly touching.

I moan softly at our close proximity and stare up at him.

"Don't fucking threaten me, Tully."

"Or what?" I whisper.

The air crackles between us and he inhales sharply. I can

feel his erection up against my stomach. His eyes drop to my lips.

Kiss me.

He stares at me, and I slowly put my hand up and cup his erection through his jeans. "Show me how angry you are with me," I whisper.

His eyes flicker with arousal and he jerks my hair again. I whimper, my head pulled back and now only millimetres from his face.

He blinks and regains control, his composure sliding back into place. He suddenly let's go of my hair and walks back out into the club without saying a word.

I close my eyes. Fuck. My heart is thumping hard. I stand for a moment as I try to work out what the hell to do. I've come too far to back down now.

Desperate times call for desperate measures.

I walk back out into the club and grab the guy from before, leading him out onto the dancefloor. I glance over and see Brock and Ben glaring at me from the side.

Oh shit, now Ben is going to hate me, too.

Ah, what the hell am I doing?

I slowly put my arms around the guy's neck and smile up at him.

Just do it, just fucking do it.

My heart is beating so fast, I feel like I'm running a marathon. This could be the worst mistake I'll ever make, but I have no idea what else to try. I lean up and kiss the guy on the lips. He smiles against me and slips his tongue in, his hands dropping to my behind.

We kiss again.

Shit, Brock where are you? Don't tell me this is for nothing.

We kiss again, and his tongue is really working my mouth.

Suddenly, I'm pushed from the side and thrown off balance.

"You have got to be fucking kidding me!" Brock yells at the top of his voice.

"Who are you?" The man frowns, his face falling while mine lights up.

I don't have chance to respond. I'm being dragged by the arm out of the front doors of the club, then marched through the parking lot. Brock has completely lost his shit, and, oh God, I may be found in the trunk of a car tomorrow, too.

Have I gone too far?

We get to the car and he opens the door, shoving me in and slamming the door shut.

He goes around to the driver's side, gets in, and he starts the car like a maniac.

"You are fucking infuriating." He punches the steering wheel and I jump in fright. He tears down the street, and I hold on for dear life.

"What the fucking hell do you think you're doing, Tully?" he screams as he pulls to the side of the road to try and calm himself down. "You don't kiss anybody else." He punches the steering wheel again. "Do you hear me? You belong to me. Is that fucking clear?" He's yelling so loud and so angry that veins are popping in his forehead and neck.

I've never seen him like this.

His chest is rising and falling as he fights the adrenaline. Then he turns to me and he grabs a handful of my hair, dragging my face closer to his. "You belong to me," he whispers again.

I nod. "I know, baby."

The electricity crackles between us.

Then he is on me, his lips taking mine and his hand painful in my hair. He jumps out of the car and comes around to my side, opening the door and dragging me out. I'm thrown into the backseat, and all I can do is watch as he climbs over me.

We kiss like animals. Brock undoes his jeans frantically and slides them down. He wastes no time in taking off my trousers, pulling my panties to the side, spreading my legs, and impaling me in one hard slam.

"Ah!" I cry out. "Careful, Brock," I whimper.

"I will not be fucking careful," he growls as he slams into me. "You'll take it how I give it. Tonight, it's fucking hard."

He pulls out and tears my panties all the way off, lifting my legs so they are around his chest, and then he pushes himself back in.

My body instantly contracts around him, and I cling to his shoulders.

He's furious, like an animal that needs a release.

And I'm in Heaven.

His smell, the weight of his body over mine, the burn of his large cock stretching me wide open—it's perfect. My hands roam up and down his back and I kiss his neck, but he isn't kissing me.

"Kiss me," I whisper.

"No." He slams into me again.

"Brock," I whimper. "Kiss... me."

He stills, and in a perfect moment of clarity, his lips take mine softly. Emotion creases my face.

Oh, I've missed him.

His eyes close as he holds me tight and we kiss tenderly for a moment. Then, as if remembering that he's still angry, he slams me hard again, and I know that the short window of intimacy he gave me has now gone.

He lifts my legs higher so that they are over his shoulders, and he buries himself deep inside, coming in a rush. That sets me off, and I shudder as I cling to him.

He pulls out and rises onto his knees. His haunted eyes hold mine and he drops his head. Without a word, he gets up, fastens his jeans back in place, and he gets out of the of the car, slamming the door.

I lie alone in his backseat in the dark.

What the fuck just happened?

CHAPTER 25

Tully

THE DRIVE HOME is spent in complete silence. My sex is still throbbing from the beating he has just given it. I stare out the window as the night races by.

No foreplay.

No lube.

No emotion.

It all leads to me feeling like one sore and sorry girl.

He takes the turn off towards his suburb, and I close my eyes in relief. He's taking me back to his place. Maybe this isn't so bad, after all.

He parks the car in his driveway, getting out before he walks around to open my door in complete silence.

My eyes search his, but he just looks back at me flatly. Eventually, he turns and opens his front door. I tentatively follow him inside and so many happy memories immediately flood back. I feel like I'm at home here.

"I'm going to take a shower," I tell him quietly.

"Okay."

I watch him for a moment, not knowing whether to push for a conversation or just leave it.

I don't want to fight with him. I'm here. I'll just see what happens.

I climb the three flights of stairs to his bedroom and bathroom, and I take a long hot shower. He doesn't come in at all. I have no idea where he is or what's going through his mind.

Just get into bed and go to sleep. Don't push him tonight, I tell myself.

I dry myself and hop into his bed, knowing it's late. Half an hour later, he walks through to the bathroom and showers. Then he comes out of his bathroom in boxer shorts and climbs into bed beside me, turns his back to mine.

I stare at the ceiling, my heart dangerously close to breaking.

"Are you not talking to me?" I whisper into the darkness.

He stays silent for a moment. "Just go to sleep, Tull," he sighs sadly.

I cuddle his back and kiss his shoulder blade. I feel him exhale heavily as if he has the weight of the world on his shoulders.

Maybe he does.

Brock

"Want to get some lunch?" Ben asks as he pokes his head around the corner of my office.

I glance up at him. "Yeah, okay."

We go to our favourite pub and I order two beers—something I never do on a weekday during working hours. Ben

watches me for a moment as he sips his. "What's going on, man?" he asks.

I shrug. I haven't told him anything that's been going on. I haven't wanted to talk about it at all.

"You came back here from London a month ago and you've been in a filthy mood ever since. Then you and Tully act like you don't know each other, and she kissed someone else last night before you dragged her out of there. What the fuck is going on?"

I shrug. "We're not together anymore."

"Why not?"

"She went back to her boyfriend."

He frowns as he watches me. "When?"

"When he was in hospital."

He narrows his eyes. "Is she still with him?"

I shake my head. "I don't think so."

"What do you mean, you don't think so? What did she say?"

"I don't know. I don't want to talk about it with her."

"Why not?"

I shrug. "What's the point? I went to London, she dumped me and told me she was too busy caring for him to be with me. She cut me to the bone, and then I came home alone."

He watches me for a moment. "And you fucked her last night?"

I sip my drink and clench my jaw. "I didn't mean to."

"Did you talk to her this morning about it?" He frowns.

"Nope."

"What the fuck are you doing?" he snaps angrily. "You're in love with this girl, and whether you like it or not, she did the right thing by staying with him while he was sick."

"Don't," I warn him.

"What kind of a person would she have been if she didn't give a fuck about him? Nine years is a long time, man. They're friends."

"So, it's okay that she just dumps me on a whim?" I snap. "I'm nobody's fucking back up plan."

"No. It's not okay. But did she get back with him?"

"I don't think so. She said..." My voice trails off.

"She said what?'

"She said she still loved me but didn't want me to wait for her while she was at the hospital."

He stares at me for a moment as he processes her words. "And then she came back and said she wanted you back."

I bite my bottom lip. I'm not even answering that fucking question.

"Did she?"

I nod. "She sat out the front of my house the other night in the rain for an hour crying. She keeps crying and shit, telling me she loves me."

"Why didn't you just ask her in and talk about it like a fucking man?"

"What am I going to say, Ben?" I throw my hands up in the air. "What the fuck could I possibly say that will make me feel any better?"

"Why don't you just listen?" He frowns. "You don't need to say anything. Just listen, you hot-headed prick."

"You know, Brock, Bridget forgave me when I left. She made a decision to try and work it out because she knew I loved her, and she loved me."

My eyes rise up to his.

"Being stubborn will only hurt you." He sips his beer. "Nobody else gives a fuck if you go back to her or not. But you'll be the one who loses a life with her if you don't at least try to work things out."

I sip my beer and stare off into the distance.

"I'll tell you one thing," he says. "It doesn't go away. Once you've met her, nobody else will do. Trust me, five years I pined for Bridget. Five fucking long years."

I sip my beer again.

"And it won't go away, so you can listen to her now, or you can wait five years and then have the conversation." He raises his brow sarcastically. "But you will have it, because if you don't, you'll go insane," he adds.

I shake my head in disgust. "Just shut the fuck up, will you?" I sigh. "What are you, a fucking marriage councillor now?"

He smirks as he sips his beer. "Yeah. That'll be two-hundred and fifty dollars, thanks."

I roll my eyes. "I'm not paying for your shitty advice."

"Suit yourself. Stubbornness will get you nowhere, my friend."

Tully

"See you." I wave to my co-workers as I head for the bus stop.

I've been flat today. Brock and I hardly spoke this morning when he dropped me off at work. He wasn't screaming at me, but it was an icy wakeup. Especially since I woke up in his arms, lying on his chest, our legs tangled together and his erection up against my hip. I thought I may have pushed a few of his buttons last night, but obviously not. I'm going to have to find another way of reaching him. I make my way to the bus stop and take a seat on the bench. My phone beeps.

Need a lift?

I glance up and see Brock parked on the other side of the road. He gives me a crooked smile in return, and my heart swells. I stand and run across the road to him. A car horn blares to life when I nearly run out in front of it in excitement.

I bounce into Brock's car. "Oh my God, did you see that?"

"Be fucking careful."

Hope blooms in my chest. "Hi."

"Hello, Tully Pocket," he says casually as he starts the car.

I smile goofily. He called me Tully Pocket. He hasn't called me Tully Pocket for a month.

"How was your day?" I ask.

He shrugs. "Okay, I guess." His eyes drift to mine. "Yours?"

"Better now."

He rolls his eyes and turns his attention back to the road. Something is different about him this afternoon. I'm not going to push it. I'll just try and let the conversation flow naturally. "Any news on the case?" I ask.

He shakes his head. "Are you sure Meredith didn't say anything last night?"

I shrug. "Nothing." I think for a moment. "And we were pumping her full of questions. I honestly don't think she knows anything. The girl can't keep a secret at all." I look over to him. "Remember when she told you about my vibrator?"

He rolls his eyes in disgust. "Where is that fucking vibrator, anyway?"

I smile. "In my top drawer."

He smirks but keeps his lips firmly clenched closed. "Meredith has been moved into a different house today. We're going to go and see her tonight, if that's okay. Just grab your things and we'll head off soon," he says as he watches the road.

I smile and widen my eyes. "Am I sensing that you're beginning to like Meredith?" I tease.

He smiles this time. "She's okay… I guess."

I point at him. "Ha. See, I told you. Once you get past her weirdness she has a heart of gold."

We pull up at my apartment and I climb out. "Are you coming in?" I ask.

"No, I'll wait here," he says, then he frowns. "No, actually I'll come up." He climbs out of the car. The two of us walk up into my building and into the lift.

He's silent, keeping his hands to himself while I stand patiently beside him.

We make our way into my apartment, and I walk into the kitchen, turning to him. "Would you like a drink?"

He shakes his head, and his eyes hold mine. He looks like he has something on his mind. "Start talking."

"Start talking?" I frown. Does he mean…?

"You heard me." He waits for a moment. "Tell me why?"

"Why?" God, what is he talking about?

"Why you fucking left me, Tully. I did everything right. Everything that you wanted, I handed it to you on a silver fucking platter. Now I want to know why you left me."

My heart sinks in my chest. He has a point; he did do everything right. "Brock, I didn't want you to hate me. I know it sounds lame."

He watches me intently.

"When you came to London and we had that first fight, you said you were there to take me home." I throw my hands up in the air. "I knew that giving Simon my attention was going to be an issue for you. And I know you came around and said it wasn't an issue at that time." I take his hands in mine. "But if it had gone on for three, four, or even six months, you'd have become bitter. Anybody would have, Brock. Even me."

He rolls his lips as he looks down at our entwined hands.

"I'm sorry that I left you, but I don't regret it," I say.

He frowns.

"I needed to be there for Simon, Brock. He's very sick... still is very sick. I've already visited him three times this week." I smile. "Did you know he's having a baby?"

"What?"

"With Penny, that girl he was seeing."

His face falls. "And you're happy about it?"

"I'm thrilled about it. She's really nice, and hopefully they're going to try and make a go of it. He's going to be a dad. I'm so darn happy for him. It couldn't have come at a better time."

He frowns, confused.

"When I tell you that my feelings for Simon are platonic now, I honestly mean it. I care about him but only as a friend."

He drops his head.

"I love you, you big twatwaffle."

His eyes rise to mine and he stares at me for a moment. "You need to come up with better nickname material than that, Princess Pussy Porridge."

Tears instantly fill my eyes. In that moment, I know it's going to be okay. I rise onto my tippy toes and kiss him softly. "Take me to bed," I whisper.

He wraps his arms around me. "No. You're in time out."

I giggle up at him. "For how long?"

"Life."

I smile, and we kiss. I hold him tight.

"We need to get going. Grab your things," he sighs in defeat.

"Okay." I run into my room and grab my overnight things,

smiling at my reflection in the mirror as my heart bursts with hope. Please let us get through this.

We make our way downstairs.

"Oh, I'll just check my mail." I get the key and open the mailbox.

The janitor, Meredith's friend, walks past. "Oh, Tully, hi. Can you take Meredith's mail to her at her mother's, please?" He hands me a big wad of mail of hers that he's collected.

"Sure." I stuff it into my bag. "Thank you."

Brock's phone rings. He digs it out and answers it. "Hey."

He frowns as he listens for a moment. "Fuck's sake," he sighs. "Fine, tell her she's a pain in my ass." He hangs up.

"What's wrong?" I ask as we walk out of the building.

"Meredith left her phone on charge in the safehouse. We have to swing by and pick it up."

"Okay."

"It's not okay because it's out of the fucking way," he snaps. "She's so annoying. How do you forget your phone?"

There he is, my impatient man. I smile goofily.

"What?" He frowns.

"I missed your cranky ass."

He rolls his eyes, unimpressed, and we make our way out to the car, and then over to the safehouse. He wasn't joking, it is out of the way. It's on a private piece of land that sits on the edge of the national park. We haven't spoken much but he held my hand on his lap the whole way here while I smiled like a two-year-old.

We pull up to the side of the house and I peer in. It's an old house made of sandstone.

"God, this house is creepy." I shudder.

"Wait here, I won't be a minute. I'll grab it and be right back."

As he gets out of the car, his phone rings. "Stan." He smiles. "What are you up to?" He chuckles as he disappears into the house.

I smile and put my head back to the seat, closing my eyes. I finally feel like I can relax. I think everything is going to be all right. At least he is open to working on it.

Something hard and cold buts up against my neck, and I look up and find myself staring straight into the evil eyes of Cole, my boss.

And the cold, hard thing pressed against my neck happens to be a gun.

Holy fuck.

CHAPTER 26

Tully

"C-COLE," I stutter. "What... what are you doing?"

My boss?

He jams the barrel of the gun up under my jaw. "Hand it over," he growls.

"Please, what do you want?" I whimper.

"You know what I fucking want. Hand it over."

"Cole, please..."

He opens the car door, grabs a handful of my hair, and he drags me from the car. The gun is still firmly in place. My eyes flicker to the house. Oh no... Brock.

"Ouch!" I cry. "You're hurting me."

"I'm going to fucking kill you in a minute. Give me the memory stick."

"I don't have it," I whisper. "I swear, I don't."

He hits me hard across the face with the barrel of the gun. Pain sears through my head and I become dizzy before I fall to the ground. He kicks me hard in the stomach, and then he pulls me down the driveway and into the forest.

Oh my God, *help me*.

Brock

I answer my phone and hear Joshua's deep voice. "Hey, fuck knuckle."

I chuckle. "Oh, it's you, you ugly prick."

"What are you doing?" he asks.

"Picking up a phone for a pain in the ass client. What are you doing?"

"I'm still at work. I was calling to see if you wanted to come to Kamala with us. Bring your new girl if you want."

I walk around the back and struggle with the key. It's sticking and won't open the door properly. I stand and jiggle it for a few moments as I try to loosen it. Finally, it clicks and turns.

"When are you going?" I ask.

"June, I think. We're waiting for the twins to arrive, and then we'll head over for a month. I'll be working from there."

I narrow my eyes as I consider his offer. I'm not even with my new girl anymore. "I'm not sure. Thanks for the offer, but I'll have to think about it," I reply. "Hey, how did you get on at the weekend?" I ask. Joshua played in a major polo tournament over the last few days.

"We kicked some ass," he tells me. "Hey, Ben told me you are having some issues with your chick."

I roll my eyes. Now we get to the real reason he's calling. "Nothing for you to worry about, Nana." I sigh.

"You know why I'm calling?" He laughs.

"Tell Natasha to butt the fuck out." I sigh again. Obvi-

ously, Tash has made him call and check up on me. "Listen, I got to go. I'm working."

"Yeah, okay. Think about Kamala. Ben and Didge can't come this year because of the babies."

I smile. "Sounds fucking weird, doesn't it? Babies, as in plural."

"Fuck, I know. They're going to know their alive real soon. Catch you later." He hangs up the call, and I hear the car door slam shut.

Tully must have got sick of waiting and is coming to see where I am. I go to retrieve the phone but it's not in the kitchen like they said it should be. I go into the living area and check there. I can't find it. I wander into the bedroom where she was sleeping. Ben said it was on charge.

I dial his number.

"Yeah, what's up?" he answers.

"Where's this fucking phone, man?" I ask. "It's not where you said it was."

"Oh, it's in the bathroom."

"Why the fuck is it in the bathroom charging?" I snap. "Who charges a phone in the bathroom?"

Ben chuckles. "Apparently, if it explodes, it's less likely to start a fire."

I roll my eyes, grab the phone and charger, and then I leave, locking the door behind me.

"How far away are you?" Ben asks as I walk down the driveway to the car.

I see the door open, and I stop dead in my tracks. I look up and down the driveway, noticing blood on the ground.

"Fuck, Tully!" I cry.

"What's happening?" Ben asks suddenly.

"He's got fucking, Tully. Shit, there's blood, get over here now!"

I hang up and run down the embankment. I can see drag marks where he has pulled her. There are large drops of blood on the ground, so he's obviously hurt her. My heart begins to hammer hard, and I run back to my car to grab my hand pistol from under the seat. I run back and slide down a muddy hill under a thick canopy of trees.

I look left and then right, trying to get my bearings. It's just getting dark and the shadows of the trees aren't helping. It's eerily quiet.

What the fuck?

I pant as I try to catch my breath. I don't want to call out and alert him to where I am, but I need to find them before they see me. I bend to the ground and put my finger through a droplet of blood. My adrenaline surges.

Not Tully. You're not getting Tully.

"It's time to give up!" I call out, and then I wait.

Silence.

Fuck, what do I do? My chest is rising and falling as I suck in some much-needed air. I run back to my car and flick open the glovebox, searching through it manically.

Bingo! The memory stick with photos of Hawaii on it.

I run back down the embankment. "I have the memory stick!" I call out.

"Hand her over and you can have it." I look out into the trees as it gets darker and darker.

More silence.

Fuck.

I hold the memory stick up in the air and grip the gun tightly in my hand.

Where are you, motherfucker?

"Tully?" I call.

"Brock," I hear her cry from somewhere farther down the hill.

I take chase and sprint down the hill, sliding and slipping on rocks as I go. All at once, I see her being rammed into a car, and my heart stops.

Cole, her boss, has her by the hair with a gun nuzzled deep against her neck. He's pushing her into a parked car.

She has blood all over her face, clearly terrified.

"No!" I yell as I run towards the car.

He hits her hard again and knocks her unconscious. I run faster, slipping down the embankment as I go.

He shoves her in the car and takes off at an unreachable speed. I turn back and sprint back up the hill as fast as I can.

I slip and scramble as I make my way to the top. I'm out of breath, gasping for air as adrenaline beings to take over my body.

I jump in my car and tear down the driveway. A truck is passing, and I punch the steering wheel.

"Get out of my fucking way!" I scream.

I pull out around the truck and veer onto the wrong side of the road. A car screeches, twisting and turning to avoid hitting me. I dial Ben's phone number as I tear down the road.

"What's happening?" he shouts. I can tell he's driving as frantically as I am.

"He's taken her in a car. White commodore, number plate DRT745.

"I'm nearly on the road coming in now," he says.

"There's only one way in here, Ben. You're going to come across him." I'm shouting, and I don't care. There's no way I can keep calm through this.

"What do you want me to do?"

"Whatever it takes. He can't get away."

"Roger that," he says, and then he hangs up. My foot slams down on the accelerator.

"Tully, hang on, baby," I whisper through gritted teeth.

The road is winding around a mountain. Dusts seems to be moving in the air as if a car has just sped through here. He's not far in front, I can feel it.

I speed up and lose it on a corner, the wheels skidding out beneath me. I nearly roll the car. I correct myself as quickly as I can, and I drive around the next bend, immediately spotting two cars.

Ben has crashed into the car to stop it. It's literally just happened. He hit the commodore in the driver's side, causing the car to flip. Ben's airbags have gone off, and he appears to be okay.

A gunshot fires from the car and I duck down.

I think Cole's trapped inside. Did he just shoot her?

Tully?

I sprint for the car and a shot fires out at me, but I don't stop. I hold up my weapon and shoot him through the window.

He slumps, bleeding from a gunshot wound straight to the head.

Tully is still unconscious in the passenger side, trapped by her legs.

"Tully, are you okay?" I whisper frantically. "Tully!" I cry. I can't get to her.

She moves and puts her hand to her head, squeezing her eyes shut tighter. Relief washes over me, turning my skin cold at the thought of having lost her.

But she's okay.

A police siren creeps in from the distance, and I know Ben has called for backup.

I drop to my knees as the lactic acid in my body takes over. "You okay?" I call to Ben.

"Yeah, man," he calls back.

Fuck... that was close.

Tully

I lie in the hospital bed as they take my vitals. "I'm fine," I sigh.

"You're not fine," Brock grunts. "You have a fractured cheekbone."

"Which is going to be fixed after surgery tomorrow."

Brock kisses my hand. He hasn't left my side for two days. His family have all been to visit me, and Ben even brought Meredith in. It seems the boys all have a soft spot for her now. Callie has been here at night, too. Simon can't come as he is in another hospital, but he's called me every few hours. I'm blessed to have so many people care about me.

My mother smiles nervously from her chair across the room. I know she's impressed with the way Brock is looking after me. I think she may finally be beginning to accept that Simon and I are just friends now. Watching her and Brock play nice to each other is really quite entertaining. They're both being so polite, I fear I may be sick any moment. I know it's completely for my benefit only, but I'll enjoy the peace between them while it lasts... which I already know won't be for long. Peter and my stepfather arrive, and I see anger flare to life in Brock's eyes. He steps back and folds his arms over his chest, raising his chin as he glares at Peter. Arrogance personified.

"Hi," I say.

"Hello." Peter smiles, glancing nervously between Brock

and me. It's obvious that he's trying to work out if I told Brock about the little incident in the lab this week. Well, yes, I did. Peter stands at the back of the room next to my mother, scared to come too close to me.

"You gave us a fright, Tully," Peter says.

I smile sleepily. "It's all okay now, though."

Peter nods as he watches me. "I thought it was Cole all along. I thought it was Cole, but I just couldn't prove it," he says.

Brock rolls his eyes in disgust. In the investigation with the police, and with the evidence Brock had on Peter socialising with the girls after hours, Peter has had to come clean about sleeping with the working girls. He's saying it was for fun and that no deal was ever negotiated, but Brock doesn't believe it for a moment.

Brock thinks that Peter falsely promised the girls protection in lieu of sex.

A crime that may never be proven. There is no proof. All the girls involved are dead now.

They weren't protected at all.

"I just can't believe that Cole was responsible for everything," I say quietly.

"He's blackmailed millions of dollars from wealthy businessmen and murdered thirteen innocent people," Brock says. "Wendy Woo had secretly taped Cole threatening her if she didn't blackmail another client, and he confessed to the other murders by telling her she would be next. Scared for her life she went to Chancellor, a man she trusted, and he had converted the file and put it onto a memory stick for her to hand into the police. But it never got there because she didn't know who she could trust in the police department." Brock side-eyes Peter again. Peter drops his head in shame. "So many innocent people died for no reason other than money," Brock adds.

I frown as I listen. "At least Chancellor's children know that he didn't commit suicide," I whisper. "And his wife knows everything now?" I ask Brock.

"Yeah, but she isn't telling anyone the gory details, only that he was murdered. She doesn't want his name dragged through the mud or his children to know that he had anything to do with those types of women," Brock says. "How people can carry through with such atrocities for money is beyond me." He stares down at me. I pick up his hand to kiss the back of it and he brushes the hair back from my forehead.

I smile up at him, and he bends and kisses me softly. "But you're safe and that's all I care about.

Brock

"I'm going to get going, Tull," Peter eventually says.

"Okay." She smiles softly. "Thanks for coming."

He nods and smiles my way. I clench my jaw and watch him leave. Tully and her mother begin to talk among themselves.

"I'm just going to the bathroom, babe," I tell her.

"Okay." Tully smiles and turns her attention back to her mother.

I walk out into the corridor and follow Peter down to the parking lot.

I'm furious.

For how he treated Tully.

For how he treated the girls who were murdered.

For his blatant lack of respect for women and their rights.

It's about time someone taught him a lesson. That person will be me.

He walks down through the main doors and out into the parking lot. It's dark and there aren't many people around. Peter weaves in and out the cars until he gets to his. He opens the door, and I walk up to him and get in his face.

"W-what are you doing?" he stutters.

"So, you think it's fair game to force yourself on Tully, do you?" I growl.

His face falls. "What are you talking about?"

"Don't act dumb," I snap before I punch him hard in the stomach. He doubles over in pain, coughing and winded by my hit. He stands slowly, and I hit him square in the jaw. He staggers back, his body slamming into the car. "That's for Tully," I snap. He falls forward and I hit him again. "And that's for the way you treat women, you piece of fucking shit," I growl.

"Stop it!" he wails. "Don't hit me again. Please." He holds his hands up over his face like a coward.

I roll my eyes and grab him by the throat. He coughs as I cut off his air supply. "You step one foot out of line again, and I will fucking break your neck, just like I promised."

He whimpers. "I won't, I promise."

I throw him back and he hits his car with a thud, his body sliding down it onto the ground. I glare at him, watching as he cowers in fear, and then I walk back inside the hospital before I really hurt him. I would love to, believe me.

Yellow-bellied fucking sleazebag.

TWELVE MONTHS LATER

Tully

I lie on the deckchair between the ocean and the pool and feel the sun's warmth on my skin. Brock and I are at our favourite destination. The place we fell in love. The Halekulani in Waikiki. I bought this trip for him as a surprise for his birthday a few months ago.

It's been a hard twelve months.

Brock has had major trust issues with me, and has been waiting for the other shoe to drop.

I moved in after a month at my insistence. Even though I knew he loved me, he just couldn't say it out loud for some reason.

I hurt him a lot more than I realised. I hate that I did.

Brock is lying on his back on his deckchair. His eyes are closed, and he's wearing a black pair of board shorts.

I smile as I watch him. He's tanned now, his big body

rippled with those muscles I love so much. How I ever got a man this delicious, I'll never know.

"I was thinking, Pock," he mutters with his eyes closed.

I smirk. "Did it hurt?"

He smiles up at the sun. "A bit."

I reach out and take his hand in mine, but he pulls his away. "I'm not lying here holding hands like a schoolboy." He frowns.

Such a Brock thing to say. "What were you thinking?" I sigh happily.

"I was thinking we should maybe get married."

My eyes snap open. "What?" I lean up to rest on my elbow and face him. "What did you just say?"

He opens his eyes just a little bit, and he smirks over at me. "I was wondering if you wanted to be Queen Pussy Porridge instead of just a Princess."

My mouth falls open in shock. "Brock Marx! Are you... proposing?"

He gives me a breathtaking smile, full of hope and love and so much promise. "I was simply offering you a promotion."

I giggle. "You really need to work on your romantic material. That proposal was appalling."

He smiles and reaches over to take my hand in his. He kisses the back of it.

"But then you wouldn't like me," he says quietly.

I'll never admit it out loud, but Brock being Brock is the most romantic thing in the world to me. I love that he doesn't try to be something he's not.

I move to lie down on the deckchair beside him. He wraps his arms around me and kisses my forehead.

"So, what do you say?" He smiles down at me.

I kiss his lips and smile goofily. "Position accepted, what's the rate of pay?"

Twelve months later

Read open for an excerpt of the next book in the Stanton series; Dr Stanton.

DR STANTON EXCERPT

Las Vegas, 1 OAK Nightclub

Ashley

I frown as the man covered in perspiration tries to cling to me. *Oh, for Heaven's sake.* "Do you mind?" I rip my arm from his grip. The music is pumping and I'm waiting at the bar.

"Not at all," he slurs.

Oh God. My eyes flicker over to my group of friends and I watch as they all smile and raise their glasses to me in jest. Damn them. This bachelorette weekend away is reminding me why I am eternally single. I fake a smile. *Bitches.*

"I mean it, baby. Let's dance."

I roll my eyes. "I can't, I'm waiting for someone so you should probably run along."

"Who?" he asks. Give up, you pushy bastard.

A tall and dark haired, handsome guy walks past, and I

quickly grab him by the arm. He frowns as he turns back toward us.

"Erm... This guy. "I smirk.

The creepy guy frowns and curls his lip to check out his competition.

My eyes scan up and down the man I've just grabbed.

Oh, he's gorgeous. I timed that well.

The guy raises an eyebrow as his eyes flick between the other guy and me.

"This is my husband." I smile as I link my arm through his. He looks like he could be nice. I'm sure he'll save me.

The tall guy raises an eyebrow in surprise and smiles. "And you are my... wife?" he questions.

I nod. "Uh-huh." Oh boy, don't blow my cover.

Mr. Tall dark and handsome turns his gaze onto the man before us as he snakes his arm around my waist. "I see you've met my gorgeous wife then?"

I narrow my eyes as I listen to his voice. I think he's Australian.

The creepy guy narrows his eyes. "You don't know him." He sneers. "I don't believe you."

Mr. Tall dark and handsome smirks and leans over, grabbing the back of my head before he pulls me towards him. His tongue rims my lips and he sucks on my mouth. His tongue takes no prisoners as it swirls deeper into my mouth.

What the frigging hell?

His hand drops to my behind and he squeezes the cheek in his hand. Oh my God, this was not in the brochure.

He pulls away and licks his lips as his eyes drop to my breasts then back up to my face.

I fake a smile as my mind goes totally blank. "Huh." My eyes glance back at the other guy as I lick my lips. Holy crap. What kind of kiss was that? "Umm."

Mr. Tall dark and handsome takes my hand in his. "Fuck off, mate. She's with me." He then pulls me by the hand through the crowd. What, wait! Where are we going? I look over at my friends who are all high fiving each other over my random kiss with Mr. Holy Hot. Should I just pull out of his grip? What the hell for? This guy is freaking delicious. Oh shit. We arrive at his group of friends and he puts his arm around my waist to pull my body close to his.

"Boys," he calls to his large group of friends. "You will be pleased to know I just got married on my way back from the bar. Please meet my new wife."

Their eyes meet and they all shake their heads and laugh.

"Hello." They all smile.

"Nice to meet you," one man replies as he shakes my hand.

I smirk as my fake husband's fingers tighten around my waist."

"About time," another guy says as he shakes his hand. "Congratulations, mate. What's your wife's name?"

His eyes flick to me as he thinks before he smiles sexily again. "Blossom."

I laugh out loud. "Blossom?"

His friends all look me up and down, smiling before then going back to their conversation as if this exchange is a common occurrence.

His eyes drop to my breasts again.

"My eyes are up here," I tell him. He can't even pretend not to stare.

He picks up his beer and drinks it. "So?"

I frown, of all the nerve. "So... you keep looking at my boobs."

"You noticed?"

My mouth drops open. "Well, yeah. I'm not imagining it."

He smirks as he sips his beer. "That's exactly what I'm doing."

His friend returns with a tray of drinks. "Murph," he calls. "Come meet Bloss."

His friend raises his eyebrows. "Hello." He smiles as he shakes my hand and passes me a drink.

"Thank you." I smile gratefully. I look between the six men he is with. These guys are all gorgeous... and cultured. Expensive suits and clothes. I glance back at my friends on the other side of the bar and I bite my bottom lip. I'll just have this drink and then go back over to them. It can't possibly hurt to have one drink.

His friend turns back to the other men, while tall dark and handsome's eyes drop to my breasts again.

"What are you doing?" I shake my head.

"Imagining."

I raise a brow. "Imagining what?"

"How those tits are going to look around my cock tonight while I fuck them."

My mouth drops open in shock.

He smiles a slow and sexy smile. "You were safer with the other guy."

My eyes hold his. I have no words.

"Because, unlike him, I will get you to do what I want to do. And tonight I want to fuck those big juicy tits of yours."

My brain misfires as I get a visual of him naked above me, sliding his cock between my...

Woah. It's been too long.

"T-that's not happening," I stammer.

He shuffles around in his suit jacket pocket and pulls out a fifty-dollar note. "Do you want to place a bet on that?"

"What an over confident prick you are." I shake my head. Never have I had such a cheap pick up line used on me. "And yes..." I snatch the fifty dollars from his hand.

"I will bet fifty dollars on you *not* getting your cock between my boobs tonight."

He winks and clinks his glass with mine as he raises a sexy brow. "Thank you. I will take that as a personal challenge."

I shake my head as I sip my drink. "Does that ridiculous pick up line work on many women?"

He smiles and winks cheekily. "You would be surprised."

I smirk. There is something extremely honest about this guy. He isn't pretending to be someone he's not.

It's disarming.

His hand drops to my behind again, and he rubs it as he smiles to himself, looking me up and down.

I raise a brow. "You can stop looking at me like I'm your next fuck. There will be no physical activity between us tonight. I'm not that kind of girl."

He leans over and kisses me again. "Stop talking." He smiles against my lips. "You are only making the challenge so much sweeter for me. I am a goal orientated man, you know."

"Happy wife, happy life," I reply sarcastically.

"Blossom, do you really think I couldn't make you happy as my wife if that were my intention?" He raises his brow.

I laugh out loud. "Shut up, you freak. Who says this shit and gets away with it?"

He laughs out loud as his hands drop to my behind again.

Two hours and six cocktails later...

The sight of his huge cock sliding between my breasts is driving me crazy. We're back in his room, unable to control our mutual attraction, acting like animals. This is casual sex at its absolute finest. This guy is gorgeous, intelligent, funny, and sexy as fuck. Not to mention he's hung like a bloody horse. I've died and gone to Vegas Heaven. His knees are on either side of my body as he kneels over me. Large, dark brown eyes stare down at me, and I arch my back, unable to hold the urge to fuck. How did he get me here, doing this?

I'm not this kind of girl, but holy hell, he makes being bad so much damn fun.

He bends and kisses me, his tongue seductively dancing with mine. "You owe me fifty bucks." He smiles against my lips.

I laugh out loud. "Bastard."

"Time to work off your debt," he whispers as he drives his body forward through my breasts. His eyes close in pleasure as his hands encase my breasts around his cock. "You have the best fucking tits I have ever seen." He growls.

My eyes roll back in my head. God, this is payment enough. What could be better than this visual sensation?

He begins to really pound my chest until the bed starts to rock and my sex clenches in pleasure. Holy fuck, I need this dick inside me *now*.

I laugh out loud. This is unbelievable. How the hell did this guy get me back to his room, having me owe him fifty dollars for the privilege?

He smiles sexily as his mouth hangs slack with arousal. "Arrête de rire ou je vais te remplir la bouche avec ma queue," he whispers as he looks down at me.

Translation: Stop laughing or I will fill your mouth with my cock.

An unexpected thrill runs through me as I reply, "Je pourrais facilement tout prendre"

Translation: I could take it all.

His eyebrow rises in surprise. " Tu parles français?" he asks as he rolls a condom on.

Translation: You speak French?

I grab the back of his head bring it to mine. "Je baise aussi en français," I whisper against his lips.

Translation: I fuck in French, too.

His mouth ravages mine and I feel his hard cock slide between my wet lips. Back and forth he glides his length. I smile. Let's up the anti.

"Obwohl ich jedoch am besten bin, wenn ich auf Deutsch ficke," I whisper as my arousal hits a fever pitch.

Translation: Although, when I fuck in German is when I'm at my best.

He laughs into my mouth and lifts my legs over his shoulder as he impales me in one hard slam. We stay still and our eyes close in pleasure.

Holy fuck.

This guy is good... and *huge.*

"Du solltest aufpassen, was du sagst, Deutsch ist meine Schwachstelle," he whispers as he pulls out and slides home again.

Translation: You should watch what you say, German is my breaking point.

My back arches off the bed. Oh God, this is too good. His brain is as sharp as his body. I don't know anyone else bilingual, and these exchanges are blowing my freaking mind. "Ich wollte deinen Schwanz in meinem Mund," I breathe.

Translation: I wanted your cock in my mouth.

He pulls out and immediately hovers above me as he feeds his cock into my open mouth. I taste my own salty arousal. Shit. This guy is off the fucking hook.

"Tes désirs sont des ordres, ma chère femme."

Translation: Your wish is my command, my dear wife.

I smile around the large penis as he slides it down my throat and I feel my sex start to pulse. “J'aimerais que tu exploses dans ma bouche. Si j'étais vraiment ta femme, j'avalerai tout.”

Translation: I wish you could blow in my mouth. If I was really your wife, I would drink it down.

He shakes his head and smiles sexily down at me as he pushes the hair back from my forehead. ““Putain, moi aussi. Tu me fais halluciner putain.” he whispers through his blanket-thick arousal.

Translation: Fuck, so do I. You are blowing my fucking mind here.

I smile as I flick my tongue over the end of him. His knees are on either side of my head, and his body is moving fluently so he slides in and out of my mouth. His dark eyes watch me struggle to take him fully.

This man has the body of a god and the mind of an angel.

I am in Heaven.

"J'ai envie de te goûter."

Translation: I need to taste you.

He growls as he pulls out of my mouth and drops between my legs, his tongue swiping through my swollen flesh.

Fuck. My knees try to close as I struggle to gain control of the sensory overload. He pushes them back to the mattress aggressively as his tongue really takes charge, licking and tasting all that I am.

“How do I taste?” I whisper as my hands drop to the back of his head.

He groans into me as his eyes close in pleasure. His tongue circles and swipes, and I feel myself start to quiver. Oh God, it’s been too long. I’m going to come already.

"Come," he breathes into me. "I want you to come on my tongue. Give me some cream, Bloss Bomb."

Holy fuck, this guy is frying my brain. He bites my clitoris and I shudder into him and he groans in pleasure. I grab the back of his head to try and still him.

"Stop," I pant, this is too much. I am too sensitive. He sucks deeper and his eyes roll back in his head. "You are one hot fuck." He growls as he laps it all up. He climbs up and over me and slides home in one swift movement.

I frown at the ceiling as my hand runs through his messy curls. I can hardly breathe. He's so *big*.

He leans back on his knees and holds my legs in the air as his eyes drop to my sex and he watches my body struggle to take his large muscle. His thumb gently circles over my clitoris, knowing full well that will release me and allow his entry.

He's experienced and he knows how to loosen a woman straight up

I watch him as I pant, somewhere in between disbelief, denial, and utter ecstasy. I didn't know that sex could be like this. I haven't had this before. I thought I'd had good sex... but now I've had this...

I realize not.

He gently kisses my ankle next to his ear, and he smiles sexily down at me. My eyes hold his for an extended moment and a frown crosses his face as I hold my breath. His hand gently brushes my hair from my face, his thumb running over my bottom lip

God. I close my eyes to block him out. This fucking guy is ridiculous.

"Regarde-moi," he whispers.

Translation: Look at me.

I force my eyes to open and drag them up to meet his.

"Tu es la plus belle femme avec laquelle j'ai jamais été, putain," he whispers softly.

Translation: You are the most beautiful fucking woman I have ever been with.

He drops his body to mine, and his lips dust mine with reverence. We kiss for an extended time, as if forgetting that he's still inside mine. An intimacy that is as beautiful as it is petrifying. Slow, gentle, and tender.

Stop it. You don't even know him and this is a one- night stand.

"Cesse d'être sentimental et baise-moi," I whisper.

Translation: Stop being mushy and fuck me.

He smiles against my lips. "That's a first." He smirks as he starts to slowly pump me.

"W-what do you... mean?" I pant.

"Nobody has ever said that to me before."

I laugh as he pulls out and slams back into me, knocking the air from my lungs. He pumps me hard again. "And if I want to be mushy with my wife I have every fucking right to be."

I laugh again as he lifts my legs over his shoulders once more and really lets me have it. His knees are wide to give him traction, and I can see every muscle in his stomach ripple as he moves. Strong, punishing hits as the bed smacks the wall with force.

Oh, he won't be easy to forget.

My body starts to quiver again, and he smiles darkly, sensing my orgasm's arrival. He knows his way around a woman's body.

Damn.

Of course he does.

Our bodies are covered in a sheen of perspiration and I close my eyes to try and stop the orgasm. I want this to last.

I need this to last.

"I… don't want… to come," he pants.

"Me neither," I breathe as I pull him back to my lips. "Promise me we will do this again in a minute."

He laughs against me. "We can do this all night, Bloss."

I smile as he lifts my behind with his hand to really hit the end of me, and I cry out as my body contracts around his large muscle.

"Fuck, yeah!" he calls as his head rolls forward and he comes in a rush.

We stay still, both gasping for air. Both wet with perspiration.

Jesus Christ…

What the hell was that?

His mouth meets mine and he kisses me softly as he cups my jaw. I smile against his lips and he kisses me tenderly again. "What an excellent wife you are."

I laugh and he rolls us so that I am now on top of his large body. I rest my head against his chest as I try to catch my breath.

His lips dust my forehead. "Don't bother going to sleep." His hand drops between my legs and he spreads them so they hang over each side of his body. He starts to work me again; his three large fingers slide into my wet, swollen flesh. "That was the entrée and this is a ten-course meal."

* * *

Four hours and four showers later, I lie in the semi-darkened room with my fake husband. The light is just peeking through the crack in the drapes. My head is on his chest and his large, muscular arms are around me. The night has been unbelievable to say the least.

We have devoured each other, and if he wasn't out of

condoms we probably still would be. I think we must have used a whole box.

"Where do you live?" he asks.

"New York," I breathe. I cringe when I hear my husky voice —a symptomatic problem from lasts night's Tequila and giving head activities, no doubt. "Where do you live?" I ask.

"Texas. Originally from Australia."

I gently kiss his chest and smile in contentment. "I had a good wedding night."

He kisses my forehead. "Me, too." I feel his lips smile against my skin. "You probably won't be walking for a while."

I giggle into his chest. "Actually, can you organize a wheel chair to get me back to my room, please?"

"I would, but I think I will be using it myself."

We lie in comfortable silence for a while longer. His hand runs back and forth over my behind, as if he's memorizing every inch.

"Are you using the theorem of calculus to measure my ass?"

He laughs out loud and rolls me onto my back, holding my hands above my head. "Your mind is a fucking turn on," he breathes before his tongue gently explores my mouth.

I just can't get my fill of this guy. "I could say the same thing. I've never had bilingual sex before." I smile. Hell, most guys I've slept with can't even speak English to me when we have sex, let alone drop in and out of three languages.

He smiles as he bites my bottom lip and pulls it toward him. "Moi non plus. Je crois que je suis accro."

Translation: Me neither. I may be addicted.

I have always had a love of languages. They were my stress reliever when I was in high school and my parents were divorcing. I would lock myself in my bedroom and listen to language tapes through headphones so I couldn't hear them fighting. Looking back, all those hours alone in my room spent teaching myself was worth it just to experience the night I had with him.

He challenged me, but I challenged him right back, and I know I surprised him. Hell, I surprised myself.

It was empowering to be able to keep up with such an obviously intelligent man. Our eyes lock and something clicks into place as I feel a flutter deep in my stomach.

"What do you do for work?" I ask to change the subject.

He lies naked on his side and rubs his hand over my breast, squeezing it hard. "I'm a mechanic."

I bite my lip to stifle my smile. He has softer hands than me. No way is he a mechanic.

So, we're playing that game, are we?

"What do you do?" he asks.

"I work in an ice cream shop."

He can't hide his smile. "You are a dreadful liar. There is no way in Hell you serve ice cream."

I laugh. "You lied first."

He laughs as his lips drop to my nipple and he takes it in his mouth. "Touché." He smirks.

"What do you think I do?" I ask.

He narrows his eyes as he thinks. "Your body tells me you are a gym instructor, but your mind tells me you're a scientist."

I smile as I bring his lips to meet mine. "I have to go." I sit up.

He frowns and leans up onto his elbow. "What? Where are you going?"

I stand up, and his eyes drop down my body. "New York," I answer.

He frowns, "You're going home? Today?"

I nod as I walk around his room picking up my clothes.

"Uh-huh." I pick up my phone and check the time. "I fly out in three hours. I've got to get a move on."

His face drops. "But..."

I pick up my bra and put it on. "But what?"

"I wanted to see you again," he says as he watches me dress.

I smile and lean over the bed to kiss his gorgeous lips. "Hmm." I smile against them. "Sorry. Bachelorette weekend is over."

He leans up and grabs me, pulling me back on top of him. "Stay another night."

God, I wish. He kisses me again.

"I already have my plane ticket for today," I breathe.

"I'll buy you another ticket for tomorrow," he offers.

For a brief moment, I consider it.

"*I'm* here until tomorrow," he tells me. "We could spend another night together." He smiles sexily.

Could I?

Who am I kidding? We don't even know each other's names and he just lied straight out and told me he was a mechanic. Besides, I'm totally out of money. I wouldn't even be able to pay for my dinner tonight. Damn it. "Sorry, hubby." I stand and put my black lacy panties on as he watches me. "This is where our marriage ends."

He puts both hands behind his head as he lies back down and smiles broadly.

My face mirrors his. "What?"

"I kind of like being married to you."

I widen my eyes at him in jest.

"I know. Shocking, isn't it?" He smirks.

I pull my dress over my shoulders and slip into it.

"Come back to bed. I'm not finished with you."

I sit on the bed and kiss him once more. "I'm not finished with you, either, but I have to go."

He frowns and begrudgingly gets out of bed. My eyes drop down his naked body. He is one hell of a fine specimen— tall, athletic, muscular broad chest with a scattering of dark hair. His hair is chocolate brown with a little bit of length on the top allowing it to have a *just fucked* messy look. His eyes are dark brown and he has a two-day growth going on. My eyes drop lower to the short, dark, well-kept pubic hair that encases his grand jewels. The man is well endowed and hell... he knows it. I imagine that every woman he sleeps with falls madly in love with him. He has money. He smells of it. Plus the clothes he had on last night. The *Rolex* watch. The well dressed large group of men he was with. I think his shoes alone would have cost a couple of grand. This room is luxury, it's not even a room, it's a suite... incomparable to my shitty, shared room with two single beds next to each other that my two girlfriends and me are sharing because we have no money. He pulls on a pair of shorts and a T-shirt. "Can I take you out for breakfast?"

I glance down at myself. Ugh, I look abysmal, but I fake a smile. "No. But thank you."

He frowns as he pulls me against him again. "Are you trying to get away from me?"

I smile. "No, I just got to go."

His lips linger on mine. *Oh to hell with my budget. Stay and fuck this guy stupid.* I pull out of his grip and pick up my handbag.

"Hold on a sec until I get some shoes on and I will walk you to your room." He disappears into the bathroom. I quickly take out fifty dollars and put it on his bedside table, scribbling on the hotel notepad sitting next to his phone.

Whoever said gambling never pays;

has never lost to you

I needed this money, but a bet is a bet.

He won it fair and square.

He fucked my tits until they were chafe, just like he said he would.

He exits the bathroom. "You ready?"

I nod and smile as I follow him out of the door.

"Morning," he greets the man standing next to his door in a suit.

"Morning," the man replies.

I glance around. All of the doors in the surrounding hallway have men in suits outside them. He takes my hand in his and we start walking down the corridor. "Who are they?" I whisper.

"Security," he answers casually as he strides along.

I nearly have to run to keep up with him. "What for?" I whisper.

"Oh. My brother is here..." He hesitates for a moment. "He has money." He rolls his eyes. "I forget they are even with us; I'm so used to it."

"Oh." I frown. That's random. I turn back and see one of the men following us down the corridor. "He's following us," I whisper.

He smirks as he kisses my hand and keeps walking. "Relax. Ignore him."

I frown as my eyes flash to the man behind us. "Oh, okay."

We get to the elevator and I have to take out my key card to see where my room is again.

"We'll be fine," he tells the security guy before we enter the elevator. The guy nods and stays where he is.

We get into the crowded elevator and stand at the front. I smirk up at him as he holds my hand.

"I can't believe you are ditching me on our first day of marriage," he says loudly so everyone can hear.

My eyes widen in shock. What is he doing?

"So you just used me and abused me all night, is that it?" he asks in an exaggerated voice. I hear a lady behind us gasp in shock while the other people pretend not to listen.

I smirk. Bastard! Two can play this game. "Yeah, well, what happens in Vegas stays in Vegas. And you were totally shit in bed, by the way," I reply dryly.

"What about our kids?" he asks, acting offended.

I drop my head to hide my smile. Oh, this guy is something else.

"Your kids are bastards. One of your other wives can bring them up. I've had enough. I'm going back to prostitution."

"Just don't give anyone anal. You know that asshole is mine." He scowls, acting serious.

I widen my eyes at him. He did *not* just say that out loud.

"Oh my God," the lady behind us whispers.

"Shh," her husband hisses.

He drops his head to stop himself from laughing, and he squeezes my hand in his. I squeeze it back as I bite my bottom lip.

The elevator doors open and he walks out, striding down the hall toward my room. "What number?"

"Three Two Two." I smirk.

We continue walking until we get to my room and I turn toward him.

"This is your room?"

"Yep." I smile. Oh, I don't want to go in. I want to stay with him another night.

He takes out his phone. "Can I have your number?"

I raise a brow. "Why?"

"So I can sell it to the highest bidder. Why do you think?" he replies dryly.

"I live in New York, you know..."

"Yes. I'm coming to New York next weekend."

"Since when?" I frown.

"Since now." He smiles as he kisses me. His tongue rims my lips. "Donne-moi ton numéro avant que je te rembarque dans ma chambre."

Translation: Give me your number before I drag you back to my room.

Could this guy be any more fun?

He takes out his phone and types *Wife* into the contact list.

I laugh. "You can't save me as wife?"

"Who says?"

"Me."

He grabs my behind and pushes me up against the door. "While you're in Vegas, you're my wife, and if I want to fuck you up against the door here, I can." He growls against my neck.

I laugh into his shoulder as I push him away. I take his phone and type in my number, and he smiles, his lips lingering on mine.

"I'm coming to New York next weekend and getting a hotel for us. Where do you want to stay?"

I laugh. "You're crazy."

"And you are fucking addictive." He smiles on my cheek as he grips me tight.

We laugh our way into one final lingering kiss before his lips drop softly to my neck.

"Goodbye, my beautiful wife," he whispers as his eyes search mine.

I feel my heart somersault in my chest. "Goodbye." I smile softly.

He starts walking backwards up the hallway as he points at me. "I will see *you* next weekend?"

I smirk as I cross my arms in front of me and watch him go.

"Don't bother packing clothes because you won't be needing any," he calls.

I smirk again and shake my head. God, he's a bona fide sex maniac.

A porter walks past and he calls out to him. "Excuse me, do you have any wheelchairs available?"

I cover my mouth to hide my giggle. He wouldn't?

The porter looks down at his legs, wondering what is wrong with him that requires a wheelchair.

"Oh, its not my legs. I have a very sore dick." He points to his groin. "Hard night."

The porter frowns as he looks at his crotch.

I burst out laughing, and they both turn to look at me. With an embarrassed wave I walk into my room and close the door. I shake my head in disbelief at the crazy events that have panned out over the last twenty-four hours. I lean against the back of the closed door with a broad smile on my face.

Wow.

What an unexpected night.

What an unexpected man.

To continue reading this story it is available now on Amazon.

AFTERWORD

Thank you so much for reading and
for your ongoing support
I have the most beautiful readers in the whole world!

Keep up to date with all the latest news
and online discussions by joining the Swan Squad VIP
Facebook group and discuss your favourite
books with other readers.
@tlswanauthor

Visit my website for updates and new release information.
www.tlswanauthor.com

ABOUT THE AUTHOR

T L Swan is a Wall Street Journal, USA Today, and #1 Amazon Best Selling author. With millions of books sold, her titles are currently translated in twenty languages and have hit #1 on Amazon in the USA, UK, Canada, Australia and Germany. She is currently writing the screenplays for a number of her titles. Tee resides on the South Coast of NSW, Australia with her husband and their three children where she is living her own happy ever after with her first true love.